MW00803033

The Primeval Maze

by

Seth Overton

Seth Overton

__Books by Seth Overton__

The Mortal Gate

Upcoming Epic Fantasy Series:

Age of Reckoning:

Forged in Flames

Seth Overton

Copyright © 2024 Seth Overton

ISBN: 979-8-218-39315-1

The Primeval Maze

To everyone that said, "When's the next one coming out?!"

Seth Overton

Table of Contents

The Primeval Maze

Seth Overton

The Primeval Maze

Prologue

"What happens when we die?"

Flashes of hazy visions, dull and gray. A battlefield with bodies littering the ground.

"Is it just darkness? Nothing?"

A single warrior is cut down by a large blade. Their blood soaking into the ground as the attacker moves on. The lights in the warrior's eyes fade.

"Or does the soul embark on another journey?"

The same eyes reignite. A shell of the warrior scanning their surroundings. Countless whisps and spectral forms cowering, wandering, or fighting.

"In this fabled realm, souls awaken in a dark and dangerous landscape to either return to the land of the Living or ascend to the Awakened Fields."

The fallen warrior takes up arms, deciding between a blade, a bow, or a wand.

"To do this, they must find and cross the Abyssal Bridge that will determine their path."

A great vision of a colossal bridge, humming with power that lead to a waving curtain of magic, guarded by great beasts at either end of it.

"But evil forces aim to capture and control souls in order to expand their influence and overtake the Awakened Gods."

Two armored figures are seen cutting down or capturing souls within artifacts they hold.

"Enter the Soulscape and emerge reborn."

The warrior faces the two evil entities, poses and readies for battle. The three of them run into a final clash.

"Coming Summer of 2026."

Chapter 1

The video presentation is cut, and I wait. Standing next to the promo art of my two-year long project in front of my employers. A long oak table in the center of the room, three executives on either side with the CEO sitting at the head of it. I can feel my heart thumping in my throat.

"Is this all the progress you've made, Connor?"

This isn't enough progress for you, he thought to himself. "N-no, sir. We've finalized the environmental programming and character diagnostics. The difficulty has been coding the initial program for alpha testing."

The executives murmur to themselves in a way that makes me nervous. Diagnostics class with Professor Torres was less intimidating than this. I gaze up to Matt Bauer, sitting in his chair with his chin resting on his fist peering back at me through his glasses. I can't read him any more than I could when I first met him before he took this position.

With a small sigh, he sits back in his chair with a stern look. "Connor, *Soulscape* has been consistently running into these coding issues. It's been pushed back once already, and our resources are getting limited on this project. If we don't see any progress or alpha testing results soon, it could mean shelfing it altogether."

My heart sinks. I've been trying to get this project off the ground for almost four years now. If it wasn't for the God damn coding bugs that keep popping up during trial runs, this wouldn't be happening. "I understand… I'll keep trying."

One of the other executives stands up, buttoning her blazer like a typical business power move. "We expect to have your results by the end of the month. This meeting is adjourned." With that, the other five stand and leave the room. Only Matt and I are left here.

"God dammit."

Matt comes and sits on the table while I hang my head in defeat. "Connor, what happened? I thought it was getting resolved."

"The damn bugs are the problem, Matt. I scrub them up at the end of one day, they spring up like a fucking plague the next." I pull one of the seats to me and flop down. "I thought I had this. I never ran into these problems back at the U."

"So, it's our programming and equipment you're blaming, now?" He replies, clearly annoyed.

I retort defensively, "No!"

"Sure, sounds like it." He crossed his arms with disappointment.

I can't believe this!

"I thought you were on my side, here!"

Matt unfolded his arms and pointed a finger at me, "I am. But I'm also the CEO of SnoWire now. I have to do what's expected of me, just like you do." Matt sighs and stands up, adjusting his blazer, "Connor, we've been through a lot. I brought you on so we could keep Dominic's legacy alive while fixing his mistakes. I don't want to do that without your help."

It comes flooding back. Dominic's pleading eyes looking at me as he holds his crazed daughter, Lorena, back for us to leave *The Mortal Gate*. Two years of recovering from that virtual prison has not been easy. I thought I would be able to move past the nightmares and focus on my career. Matt thinks that pouring himself into the company's success will help him overcome his guilt. Are we both wrong?

I sigh with defeat, "You're right. I'm sorry. I'll try harder to work on giving you a beta product."

"Good." He looks at me sympathetically and pats me on the shoulder, "We'll circle back to this later. In the meantime, go check in on Mr. Woods and see how his draft boards look. He was supposed to join this meeting and has been radio silent."

Dammit, Riley. I nod and leave the boardroom. If this isn't the definition of a clusterfuck, I don't know what is. First the presentation is a bust and the board is already giving up on my project, now Riley is skipping out on meetings that we were both supposed to tackle. Every time I think he's forgiven me for pulling him back from the game, he turns around and gives me the cold shoulder instead. He wanted to stay in a world where he felt strong and powerful rather than be some "struggling paraplegic store owner"—his words, not mine. I thought giving him a chance to create this game with me would be enough to keep him occupied to the point he'd forget about it.

I take the elevator to the floor he and I share in the building. The same floor where our entire testing team has been busting their asses trying to help me get this game off the ground. I approach Riley's door and knock, "Riles? You in there?"

No response. I knock again and go inside. Riley's hunched over his desk in front of his laptop, typing quickly and sharply not tearing his eyes away from the screen.

"Riley?"

He doesn't look at me. Just keeps staring at the computer, "What is it?"

"You missed the meeting."

He looks up at me from his computer with a stoic face, "Sorry. Been busy with this whole scripting mess for the level progression. How bad was it?"

"Gee, thanks for the vote of confidence," I reply dryly.

He sighs and rolls his wheelchair around his desk to get closer to me. "Look, I knew it was gonna be bad. I've been trying my best to help with progressing the work, so it doesn't look like we haven't been getting shafted for the past five months."

"And I appreciate you doing that, but it's getting worse. Matt is barely keeping the board interested in *Soulscape* and he's breathing down my neck to get this going."

"Fuck him." Riley turns his chair back around and returns to his desk. He pulls a drawer open and grabs a stack of papers before throwing them on the desk. "He's been shoving these notices down my throat and I'm sick of it. If he wants the development to work, I need to work. So do you. Rather than bitch about the coding, find a way around it and get the team to bust down on production."

I feel a vein pulsating in my head. He has been like this for the past year since we've gotten past the initial programming and the story was approved. Before that, he was getting chummy with me again. I thought we were past all of our issues when he agreed to help me with this. I've started losing my best friend and he keeps shutting me out.

"Riley, you've gotta stop stalling me here. You seriously need to move past what happened."

He goes quiet and returns to his computer. "I *am* moving past it. There are… bigger things coming. So, let's make it happen."

With a sigh, I nod and leave his office. Walking through the halls back to my office, his last words ring in my head. I want to believe he really is moving past what happened. I have. Krissy has. Mark and Danica, maybe not so much. But still, it's been two years. Long enough for us to return to reality. But I'm afraid Riley is still living in *The Mortal Gate*, even now.

Chapter 2

The workday drags on after that. Everyone on the development team bombarded me with questions and issues of the same kind that we've been running into for almost a year. The coding has been spawning spontaneous bugs and errors that we can't find the source of. With that going on for several hours, I give everyone a break and let them go home for the day. Once I finish answering my emails and find decent points to pick back up on for the next day, I gather my belongings and leave the office, taking the elevator down. Alone with my thoughts in the elevator, the day makes me think back on Riley and the others.

The last two years have been a real mess for everyone involved. While Riley and I joined Matt at SnoWire, the others have been dealing with their own problems and finding ways to move forward. Mark and Danica fought for a whole year over what happened until the point they broke up. They tried hard to make it work, but the game drove them apart more than we all thought. Mark went on to try and pursue his music production, but from what I know it hasn't taken off like he thought it would. Since then, he's shut me out harder than Riley. I have no clue what happened with Danica or where she is now, but I hope she's doing well. Krissy is probably the one doing better than the rest of us with her owning and running her own self-defense studio and being quite successful with it.

The elevator arrives at the lobby, and I walk out while giving a wave to the receptionist. The company building is in the business district of Salt Lake City, one of the tallest around. The downside is the constant foot and vehicle traffic around here. Because of where I work and live, I don't have the luxury of using my bike as much as I did before. Now it's all transits and cabs; disgusting. But thankfully, my destination is a few short blocks from here and gives me time to ponder to myself. The coding bugs in *Soulscape* didn't spring up in the initial trial run of programming. We had weeks to do tweaks and upgrades to the original software before advancing to the alpha testing schedule. One full year with no issues and getting our brand of gaming out there on the market. It was all downhill after that. Suddenly whole lines of code were being deleted, NPC builds started falling apart, and compatibility bugs kept popping up. All leading up to today's crappy conclusion.

Three blocks later I arrive at a little strip mall with various shops in it. I approach one with the name "Valkyrie Muay Thai" on the door and peer through the window. Inside, a dozen or so people are all in clinches and fighting positions, throwing attacks, and tossing each other around. I walk inside and stick close to the nearby wall, watching the mayhem unfold.

"Class! Attention!"

Everyone suddenly stops their activities and stands at attention. At the front of the class, the instructor takes center point in front of them. She's got her hair pulled back in a tight ponytail with beads of sweat rolling down her face with her hands behind her back standing tall. She's wearing the gym's gear with the symbol of a Norse Valkyrie stamped on it all. Her eyes scan her students intently, "Our focus today is on breathing through our strikes, pacing each attack with focused breaths. Too many of you are breathing like winded hippos. Without control and focus, you'll be flat on your backs before throwing your first strike. Myers! Macias! Front and center!"

The gym floor is cleared until the two students, roughly in their late teens, are in front of the rest of them. They stand facing each other awaiting instruction.

Crossing her arms, she looks them over before instructing, "Touch gloves and demonstrate circuit five."

They touch gloves before getting into a fighting stance. The one called Macias begins bouncing back and forth on the balls of his feet, while Myers calmly waits for an opening. After a couple of moments, Macias kicks out with a heavy breath and a heavy right kick. The kick misses as Myers leans back and spins around with a reverse roundhouse, connecting with his padded helmet and knocking him down. She stands over him in a ready position before the instructor holds her hand out.

"Macias, you breathe like my neighbor's bulldog. Control your breathing and don't give away your attack." She holds her hand out for Macias to take, hoisting him back up onto his feet. Turning and addressing the whole class, she adds, "Practice your breathing techniques through toe-taps and minute-long jump rope before next week's practice. Dismissed."

The whole gym bows before dismissing and grabbing their gear. The instructor starts removing her gloves and elbow pads, diverting her attention from the rest of the class. I walk up to her past all the students, "Got time for a private lesson?"

Krissy turns around to me and smirks, "You wouldn't last a round." She punches me in the shoulder before pecking my lips.

Rubbing my shoulder, I laugh, "You're an aggressive teacher."

She shrugs, "They wouldn't still be here if they weren't learning anything."

She's very proud of being able to pull this off. The year we escaped the game, Krissy wanted to take up self-defense. That same year, she received her black belt in Tae Kwan Do and her certification as a Muay Thai instructor. She found this small workspace and took a chance to teach her own class. She denies that it's because of her experience as Nevine in *The Mortal Gate*, but I think it had something to do with it.

She continues to carry conversation while I'm admiring her, "How was work? Make any progress?"

I must have given it away in my face because she gave me the furrowed brow. "It… could've gone better. Things are just getting tougher. More than I expected."

She puts a reassuring hand on my shoulder, "It'll get better. Can't get better without hitting some rough spots, right?"

I give her a smile and a nod, "Thanks, babe. I'll meet you outside."

Fifteen minutes goes by as Krissy's students all leave after paying dues or asking questions before she meets me outside and locks up the studio while the Uber I booked approaches. We decompress on the car ride back to our apartment, mostly talking about her class for the day and the little interactions of my day. I'm leaving out the part about Riley and I getting into it, not feeling up to hashing out the same concerns over and over. When we get to the apartment, she and I throw our bags on the ground, flop on the couch and sigh as loud as we can. Daily routine.

Dramatically, she stretches and pouts, "Ah, my legs are killing me."

I laugh a little, "You did decide to focus on kicks today. You did that to yourself."

"I said it so you would rub my legs, dick." She throws both up into my lap and arches her eyebrow expectantly.

I chuckle in defeat and start massaging. Krissy and I have been living together since we escaped the game. Between the two of us, she's the one who stayed in college by switching to online courses while I focus on the job at SnoWire. With the way our schedules work, we're able to see each other in the evenings while having a couple of days a week to have completely to ourselves. Those days would normally be spent with Mark and Danica before they split, now it's just days at home relaxing from work.

Which reminds me, "So I spoke to Riley today. He missed our update meeting with the board. Again."

"Why? Why is he still lashing out like that?"

I shake my head with a shrug, "He says he's getting tired of Matt's shit. I can only imagine that it's because of… what happened. He's still sour about it."

She pulls her legs away, scoffing loudly. "Seriously, send his ass to therapy! If he was still in that place, he'd be in the same state as Dominic and Lorena. You did the right thing, and he needs to get over it."

Running a hand through my hair, I lean back defeated. "I want to be upset with him more… but it's hard. He got his legs back, he was a wizard and a warrior, everything he would pretend to be when he games. To have all of that taken away is something we can't really understand."

"But it was all fake," she points. "His magic, his horse legs, all of it was made up. The only thing that wasn't made up was his crush on a video game character."

"But some real things came out of it as well, Kris. Look at you? You felt strong in the game and wanted to feel that same strength on the Outside." The real world, as we called it in the game," I took all my experience and used it to build my career."

"And what about Mark and Danica? They took that hellscape and let it drive them apart."

Silence falls between us before her phone rings. "Speak of the devil…" She accepts the video call on the couch. "Hey, Dani."

Danica's face lights up in a smile, "Sup, girl? You and Connor at home?"

13

I pop my head into frame, giving a smile. "Hey, Dani. How's it goin?"

"Goin good! Got my internship at the real estate agency I've been looking for!"

Krissy and I say at the same time, "Congrats!"

Danica smiles victoriously, "How about you two? Things going well?"

"Can't complain here. Got my studio running smoothly," Krissy replies. "Connor's job is going steady." I give a thumbs up to confirm.

"Awesome! So, when we havin' another girl's night? I need one."

Krissy giggles before standing up from the couch to take the call in the bedroom, "Soon. You're lucky we're only a couple hours from each other."

When she closes the door, I can barely make out anything they're saying. I take this chance to go to the closet and pull out a box from behind some junk. I open it and gaze at the ring sitting inside, feeling my heart thump a little harder. It took me a year to find the right one that I wanted to give her, now it's just all about the time and place to ask. I've had a lot of time to think about how I want to do this, even convincing my folks that I'm ready for this step.

I hear the doorknob turn, making me throw the box back up in panic. She comes walking out in her pajamas before pocketing her phone, "She says bye. What are you doing?"

"Just… killing time. Waiting for you."

She chuckles at me before getting serious. "Mark called her. He's trying to get more stuff back from the breakup."

Yikes. "What did she do?"

"What do you think? Told him to shove it. She misses him, but they didn't end on good terms, so she won't admit it."

According to what Krissy gathered, Danica was having nightmares for weeks after we escaped. Something I'm familiar with. Mark, on the other hand, dumped himself into trying to get his music production career off the ground, eventually losing the connection they had before. From what Mark has told me, he tried consoling her during the nightmares, but she claimed that he was being passive with it and not doing a great job of being sympathetic. Either way, they both couldn't stop fighting.

Krissy tilts her head at me and asks, "When's the last time you talked to him?"

"Um… last month, I think. He was putting out feelers and cards trying to advertise his work," I reply scratching my head.

She breathes a familiar annoyed sigh, "Connor, you've gotta talk to him. He needs you."

Does he? He blamed me for most of the issues the first few months we were out. "I'll try reaching out this week. Just give me time."

Krissy nods, taking my hand in hers. "We've been through hell. It all has to get better soon. Come on, let's go to bed."

"I'll meet you in there shortly." I kiss her nose before she walks back to the bedroom. In the moment with my thoughts, I start to reflect on what Riley had said and how it's reflecting everyone's situation. Whether we all have had a chance to move on or not, that game seems like it will always be at our backs to haunt us

Chapter 3

The next morning runs about as normally as any other day; coffee and pastries for breakfast, dress and get ready for work, Krissy drinking coffee at the table getting started with her online courses, hug, and kiss goodbye on my way out the door. Once aboard the transit bus I start swiping through my phone for the emails from my development team. Aside from a few invites to parties or some common complaint emails, it's pretty normal for a workday. That's before Matt's name pops up on my screen calling me.

I instantly pick up, "Hey, Matt, I'm on my way to the office. Something you need?"

"Have you heard from Riley this morning?" He sounds worried or upset. If Riley's involved, that's not a good sign.

"No. I normally see him on my way in. Why what's going on?"

"I've been trying to reach him all morning. He's not answering me, and no one has seen him."

I feel everything in my body seize up, "Wait, what?"

"Call him. Meet me in my office when you get here." He hangs up.

Immediately, I call Riley's number. Straight to voicemail. Two more times, same result. I text him to call me. Once. Twice. Three times. By the time it's my stop, still no answer. *Dammit, Riley, where are you?* I race in the building, completely passing the receptionist and into the elevator. Sharing the ride with a few others, I anxiously keep checking my phone to get any kind of response from him. The door opens to my floor, and I mutter an apology as I push past the others. My testers are all at their stations going through their work, but I blow right past them to find Riley. As I turn the corner to where his office is, I see two executives walking out of it. They notice me but turn to leave.

"Wait!" I run to catch up with them, prompting them to turn around. "Is Riley in there? Were you meeting with him?"

The short one looks to me with a stink eye, "None of your concern, Mr. Wright."

"None of my concern? That's my partner you're talking about."

The tall one with him steps in front, "Forgive him. He's a little uptight today. As for Mr. Woods, I must apologize for not forwarding this notice. He has been asked to take his process in the project to another location for the time-being. Due to some complications between him and the board, we want him to work in a less stressful and complicated environment."

They *what*? My palms are starting to sweat, "What? Why wasn't I notified? What about Matt?"

"Mr. Bauer is being notified as we speak. Due to some reports of tension between you and Mr. Woods, we figured it would be best to tell you on separate terms. Rest assured, you will be getting the agreed updates and progress from him accordingly." With that, both execs turn away and start walking off, leaving me with more questions than answers. I approach Riley's door to go inside, but it's locked.

"What the hell is going on?" My phone chimes with a text.

Matt: *'My office.'*

I dart back to the elevator to take it up to Matt's floor. I call Riley again, still nothing. Either he's pissed off and won't talk or there's something weird going on. As soon as the elevator doors open, I race to Matt's office and knock on the door. He opens the door and waves me in with a hushed word, "Hurry."

Once the door closes, I start in. "Matt, what the hell is going on? Two execs locked Riley's office and told me they sent him off campus? That they told you this beforehand?"

He holds his hands up, "Easy. Look, they just sprung this on me too. I demanded that they explain further, but they kept stonewalling me. Did you have any luck getting him on the phone?"

I hold it up and check it again, "Nothing. If he's really that pissed off, he may be at home or at the Cache. Those are his havens."

Matt nods, "Okay. Well… you said they locked his office, right? Let me try to get it opened myself. Maybe it'll have something we can use to find him. If he's really been suspended, I want to clear this up. Call the Cache and see if he's in."

Matt walks out of his office and towards the elevator and I follow, matching his pace while typing the shop's number into my phone. "Thanks for hailing the Cache. This is J.D., how can I help you?"

"J.D., this is Connor. Is Riley working today?"

A brief pause. "Uh… no? Riley gave up ownership of the store last year. I haven't seen him since."

My heart drops. The Cache was Riley's entire life, his home away from home, his friggin' empire. There's no way he would give up the Cache for anything. *What the fuck is he doing?!* "Oh…uh… thanks J.D." I hang up and look at Matt, shaking my head. We're both now in a state of panic at this point before the elevator opens. We walk together to Riley's office as Matt pulls his keys out to try and open the door. We both take a breath of relief when it unlocks, but it's short lived as we walk into an empty office. Bare walls, nothing on his desk, absolutely nothing in the office.

My heart thunders so loud against my chest, I'm surprised Matt can't hear it. I look over at him as he murmurs, "This… this can't be right."

I squat down, leaning my elbows on my knees and lace my fingers behind my neck. "What the fuck, Riley?"

"They… they would've stored his items somewhere. His work is crucial to the development of the product. They either passed it off to someone else or put it all in storage," Matt tries to deduce.

"Then where the hell is he?" My anger and anxiety are a Molotov cocktail at this point.

"I don't know. Listen, I'll see what I can find here, you go see if he's at home. Call me with any details, and I'll do the same. Okay?"

Taking a moment to myself, I nod and get back up to my feet. Without another word, I leave the office and go straight to the elevator, determined to find him. I get strange glances and looks from the beta testers, but I ignore them completely to get into the elevator. The ride down is eerie as I'm blankly staring at my phone, rereading all the unanswered texts I've sent to him. My mind then begins to race about the possibilities of what is happening. First the board grills me, then Riley grills me, board executives secretly locking up his now empty office and no clue as to where he is or what they've done with his work. Now I need to hunt this asshole down and demand some answers, including why he has completely abandoned his treasured store and didn't tell me. Once I'm out of the building, I flag down a cab to take me to Riley's apartment in East Bench. In a last-ditch effort on the trip, I call his phone one more time for good measure. It sends me to voicemail, to which I leave one: "Riley, you need to answer me. I know you're pissed at me, at Matt, at everyone right now, but you need to answer me. I'm worried, man, and I don't want you to be doing something stupid. Please, call me back." I keep tapping my foot in the back of the cab until it comes to a stop in front of his apartment complex. I race up and pound on his door. "Riley! Riley, you home?!" I look down at the foot of the door and see pieces of mail sticking out from under it on the other side. *That makes no sense... when was the last time he was here?*

"Hey, can you keep it down?"

I whip around to see a woman scowling at me from the adjacent apartment. "Uh... yeah. Hey, do you know the guy that lives here? Have you seen him?"

"You mean when he's not blasting loud T.V. noises? No. Now go away." She slams her door.

Wrought with more confusion, my phone starts buzzing. Thinking it's Riley, I quickly look at the screen. My face falls a bit as I rein in my disappointment and swipe to answer Matt's call. "Hey, tell me you've got something."

"They took his materials to the administrative wing. I've gotta get some paperwork signed because of the God damn bureaucracy. Is he home?"

"No. There's a bunch of mail stashed under his door and his pissy neighbor hasn't seen him either."

I hear him sighing through the phone. "So, he's not at home and not at the Cache. Where the hell else would he be?"

Takin an exasperated breath and run my hand through my hair, I glance down at the floor outside of his door when one of his pieces of mail sticks out to me. "Is it still illegal to read people's mail?"

He pauses before cautioning me, "Connor, don't do anything stupid that'll get you arrested."

"It'll be quick. Hold on." I lean down and grab the envelope, scanning the contents when the sender information grabs my attention. Downtown Self-Storage.

I scan the letter quickly and my breath catches in my throat, "Oh shit... Matt, I know where he is."

"Send me your location, I'll pick you up."

~~~~~~

Twenty minutes later, Matt picks me up from the apartment and I get the directions from the envelope put into my phone's GPS.

After giving him my theory, I could see a vein in Matt's temple pulsing as he rambles, "Why the hell is he doing this? The program is dead, and the software was deleted! There's no way he—"

"Just focus on getting us there!" Boss or not, I can't think straight with him yapping like this, "On the chance he's there, he's probably just rented it out to work on while he's suspended from the company."

Matt shakes his head angrily, "None of this is right! The board doesn't meddle in level workers like this! What are they thinking?"

"Matt! Just drive!"

The rest of it is filled with silence. I don't want to think about anything else other than what Riley is doing back at the storage facility where it all began. Traffic is flowing slowly, giving me more anxiety and negative thoughts the

23

longer it takes us to get there. In that silent space, Matt's points keep echoing in my head. *Riley... please don't be doing anything else other than either reflecting or stockpiling.* The turnoff comes up and we fight through some more traffic. The moment the storage facility's sign is within viewing distance, my heart leaps into my throat. Everything from two years ago comes rushing back like a bad flood. Everything I've been trying to forget.

Matt pulls his car into the lot, "Which one?"

"Go to G-Block."

He nods and starts traveling through the blocks of the facility. My chest aches with every block we pass through until we finally hit G. At first glance, it's just another block of storage units. To me, the memory of him meeting us all here and scolding us for being late. I slowly get out of the car with Matt trailing me. He follows as I saunter towards the door of the unit where it all began. I open it, losing my breath knowing it's unlocked, even more so when I see lights on inside. The only things inside are a crate with a laptop set up and a person in a wheelchair sitting in front of it.

With a running start, I scream, "Riley!"

Just like my phone and his apartment, no response. I run up to him before skidding in my tracks when I spot something shining on top of his head. *No...nonononono!*

I slowly pan around him. Sitting on top of his head is a Crest, his face is void of expression, and his eyes are glassed over.

Matt's eyes are glued on him in shock. "Is that… a Crest?" There is clear panic in his eyes and sweat beginning to build on his forehead, "Where did he get that?"

I don't answer. Instead, I turn to his computer. In bright, neon yellow letters, the screen reads the scariest words I've read in two years:

"SnoWire Presents: The Primeval Maze"

Chapter 4

I fix my angry stare at Matt and demand, "What the fuck is *The Primeval Maze*?!"

Matt is looking at the screen with me now, yet even he is dumbfounded. "I... I don't know."

I shove him out of instinct, "Don't bullshit me! What is it?!"

"I don't know, Connor! We haven't put out any major projects since the start of yours!"

Angry tears are burning my eyes as I look at Riley in his catatonic state. Now with even more questions than before, I can't begin to understand what led him to this or even from where it comes. I take the time to study the setup; unlike *The Mortal Gate*, it doesn't have a placemat to interact with. Riley's hands are free of interfacing gloves that were required for synchronization for the first system we were part of before. It looks like that whatever system this is using only requires a synchronized Crest and a CDROM program to operate. "This is the same design as *TMG*. Matt, you're sure that you have no idea what this is about?"

He hesitates for a moment while inspecting the Crest closer. "Connor... these are designs for the new base set of VR projects we haven't even completed yet. Dominic said he had plans for new systems that would revolutionize RPG platforms, but I thought these plans died with him..."

"Clearly not!" I can't contain the amount of rage I'm feeling, "What are you talking about!?"

"Look, let's not do this right now. We need to get him to a safe and stable environment. Whatever we do, we shouldn't eject the program or shut it down until we know more," he urges me.

I look back at Riley's blank eyes. He's done it again. Trapped himself inside of a virtual prison. And for what? To escape his real life? *I swear I'm gonna kill him after I get him out of this.* I stow my feelings on the matter and nod, grab the handles of Riley's chair and pull him away while Matt grabs the laptop and stays close. It takes some effort to get both him and the equipment loaded into Matt's car safely. His body is limp and deadweight without his conscious mind awake. This is the first time I've really seen what these Crests do to a person without having one on myself. It's like his entire being was sucked out of his body with glassy blank eyes, no muscle reaction or spatial awareness at all.

"Where are we going?"

Matt keeps his eyes fixed on the road as he drives, "We're going to the performance lab. Where Dominic and Lorena operated from while playing *TMG*."

My heart skips like a kick in the chest. "No, absolutely not! Let's take him back to my place and keep an eye on him there."

"We can't. We don't know his state of awareness or his vitals with that equipment. We need a controlled environment where we can monitor his brain activity while working on how to get him out safely."

Fuck! It's like being stuck in a hell loop in the show Lucifer!

Matt speeds through the city trying to avoid all the red lights along the way until we reach the company campus. Instead of going straight to the main building, he veers off towards a smaller facility detached from it. I've never been to it before because I was only told that it was a maintenance and admin building, nothing to be concerned with.

"*That's* the performance lab?" I ask pointing it out.

He nods, "We have very little staff assigned to it as it's meant for Research and Development purposes. We'll have everything we need to keep him stable while we investigate the software."

Matt pulls up to the front of the building and parks, prompting me to get out while he joins to help lift Riley out of the car. The deadweight of his body causes us to drop him. Matt groans and runs inside only to return with a rolling office chair. We heave his body into the chair and push him through the doors, passing a very confused security guard. I follow Matt through the halls until we reach a door with a card scanner titled "Performance Lab", to which he scans his ID for entrance. It declines.

"What?" He tries it again. Same result.

Oh, this can't be good.

"Matt?"

"My card isn't working. It shouldn't be doing this." Two more tries, he's still locked out. "Dammit! Wait here." He runs back from where we came from. I lean down to eye level with Riley's glassy, blank ones. It takes everything I have to not reach back and smack him back into consciousness. With any luck, we can remove him from the game he's playing without frying his brain. Two sets of footsteps grab my attention as I watch Matt return with the security guard in tow.

"Get me in there, Curtis."

The guard huffs loudly, "Mr. Bauer, I can't. The security chief was given orders not to let anyone into the labs until further notice."

Matt's face drops, "What? By whom?"

Curtis shrugs, "I don't know."

"Unless you wanna lose your job, you'll clear us through right now," he threatened coolly.

Curtis looks at me then at Riley before looking back at the CEO of the company. "Goddammit. Fine." He takes his ID and scans the reader, getting greenlit.

"Not a word about this to anyone else. Understood?" Matt snarls with a finger pointed in the guard's face. Curtis signs and nods, walking back to his desk at the front.

I follow Matt inside while pushing Riley after him. The inside of the performance lab is dark with the lights of computers and monitors blinking rapidly. Matt flips a couple of switches and lights up the room. The middle of the room is made up of operating and monitoring stations with about a dozen screens and processing towers all booting up with the power being turned on. Along the walls are various whiteboards with multicolored scribbles and projector screens slowly turning on. At the far end of the room is a tinted glass window, spreading across the wall and peering into an adjacent room. While Matt starts flipping switches at one of the stations, I approach the window and look in. On the other side is a bigger room with about ten different stations, all equipped with human-shaped chamber beds hooked up to EKG machines and processing monitors that all look suspiciously familiar.

That's when it dawns on me, "Matt… is this where your beta testing team hooked into the game?"

Without missing a beat, "Yes. This is where we all participated in *The Mortal Gate*. Now help me with him."

It takes me a moment to shake out of my stun before I help him wheel Riley into the room. Once inside, we take him to the nearest station and hoist him up onto the chamber bed. Matt starts applying wires and attachments to his body while sifting through programs on the attached monitor. "Okay… his vitals are all running normal… showing signs of REM and brainwave activity… we can keep him stable here until we figure out how to remove him."

"This tech… how did you get all this?" I run my hands along the equipment and mentally study it.

"We're not the highest grossing game developers for charity and kicks, Connor. This is all through years of development and study," he says with a hint of pride in his voice. He then goes back to the main room and grabs the laptop with the game running, quickly hooking up the laptop charger and the external connection cable to a nearby monitor. "I need to break this programming down bit by bit to find out how it operates."

"Matt," I pause. "What is *The Primeval Maze*? I know you know more than what you're telling me." The time for bullshit is over. I need answers.

He sighs heavily and pinches the bridge of his nose. "*The Primeval Maze* was a prematurely drawn expansion to *The Mortal Gate*. Dominic was so sure of himself when developing the game that he was ready to build on it more. This expansion was to act as a follow-up where players explore the opposite of the original game's world and endure a new kind of adventure. The *Maze* would serve as the primary encounter point for the players; they would be challenged to enter the maze, encounter monsters and level up, find the endgame boss, and destroy the source of the maze's power to win."

If I wasn't so concerned or freaked out by what was currently happening, I'd think this concept is pretty cool and would want to help build it up. "But how did it get to the operating stage if it was just a concept?"

Matt shook his head, "I don't know... Dominic must have been developing it along with *TMG* on the side... or maybe Lorena was tasked with building it. I don't claim to know how the Dawsons work."

I look back through the window and to Riley's unconscious body. How the hell did he get hold of this project? What was he thinking?

"I'm going to keep him overnight for observation. Go home and get some sleep. Come straight here tomorrow; I'll

31

close off all other access," he instructs. "We're gonna figure this out. But I need you at a hundred."

I'm thinking of every reason to tell him no, stay here with Riley and make sure he doesn't go braindead. With a loud groan, I nod in agreement and leave the building. My mind is screaming, my heart is pounding, sweat is building up in my hands. I feel my phone buzzing. Four missed calls from Krissy. *Shit! Do I tell her? What if she doesn't want me involved? What if* she *wants to get involved?* Too many things happening at once, I can hardly keep up with it. I take a seat at the nearby bus stop and call her back.

"Connor? Where the hell have you been?" She sounds more worried than annoyed.

"Hey, sorry. It's… it's okay. It was just a rough day. You okay?"

I hear her sigh loudly on the other end, "I'm fine. I've been calling you. What's going on?"

It's itching in the back of my mind. Do I say something or not? She's been through enough from that game. Does she really need to be involved in this shit show too?

"Uh… it's Riley… he got canned…."

"Oh shit! What happened?"

You're an idiot. "He… fell behind on a lot of projects. The board kept throwing deadlines at him and he didn't meet. He's pretty upset about it."

She groans, "Poor guy. He went out on a limb trying to help you and move on. I'm sorry, babe."

You cannot be okay with lying like this. "It's… it's fine. He wanted to be left alone to cope with it. I've been trying to help, but he kept pushing me away," I explain with defeat. *Not far from the truth, but still.*

"He'll be okay. It's not the first time he's been sour about something. Give him time. Come back home soon, I've got dinner ready."

"Sure. I'll see you soon," I say before hanging up. What's worse about all of this? Leaving Riley in a tech-induced coma, lying to Krissy, or having to postpone the proposal *again*? Any way I cut it, there's no easy way out of this situation. This didn't end with the game, or with Dominic's sacrifice. It just started a new level.

Chapter 5

They came back. The nightmares. Giant spiders, toothless raiders, zombified monsters, and Terrorghasts. Tons of them, everywhere, surrounding us like a plague. I wake up in a cold sweat and raspy breath, but thankfully I don't wake Krissy up. I ease myself out of bed and head to the bathroom, closing the door behind me. Cold water running out of the tap, I cup it in my hands and splash my face. In the mirror, I stare at my reflection with my hair draped over my eyes. I stand and stare at it. I find myself thinking back to those moments in Albistair where my back was against the wall against all those nightmares, scared and full of adrenaline. Just when I thought it could be it for me and everyone else, we pulled through. Because we had each other's backs. Even Riley. Sure, he treated it like his personal fantasy playground, but he had my back at every turn. Not once did he question a decision I made; not even the ones that almost got us killed. I glance down at the sink before looking back up at the mirror. I see *him*. Zarimm, the Orc Warpriest. The warrior that has always been there and has never wavered from helping his friends, or anyone else in need.

Knock, knock, knock. "Baby? You okay?"

"Y-yeah… sorry."

I turn the faucet off and open the door. She's standing in the doorway with her arms crossed. "Connor, talk to me. You've been off for the last few days. And don't try to bullshit me."

With a groan, I take her by the arm and lead her back to the bed where we both sit down. "It's… the nightmares. They came back. I see everything that happened in the game. Everything we faced, everything that almost killed us. Something in me is telling me it's not over."

Her eyebrows furrow while she listens. "What do you mean?"

"I mean, there's something off at the company. Something left behind by Dominic and Lorena that is causing problems, and I think it's what got Riley into the mess he's in now," I explain.

She swallows hard. I can see her shoulders drop from thinking back to the game. "What are you thinking?"

"I'm thinking I need to find out what Dominic was planning with the game and how it's still affecting the company and us. Matt's not in the same control as we thought before. He needs my help. But I don't want you involved," I say plainly.

"What do you mean? What are you planning? You're not in the game anymore, Connor. You don't have magic or weapons or anything."

"No, I don't." I take a deep breath, "But I've got to do something. I want this to be over so we can move on. We need to move on."

A long pause settles between us, just sitting on the bed with only the bathroom light on for us to see each other's faces. I don't want her involved with whatever dumbass stunt Matt and I are gonna pull. The less she knows, the better it is. At least, I hope.

She grabs my hand and gently squeezes it. "Fine, as long as you check in with me periodically. If I have to come and find you because you did something stupid, I'll kick your ass from here to Houston. Got it?"

I nod before I lean in and kiss her. With that agreement, we crawl back into bed and sleep until morning.

I leave a note on my pillow and kiss her temple as she sleeps before walking out the door. I text Matt that I'm heading to the office while I sit in silence on the transit gripping the strap of my bag. Inside are notebooks filled with things I think will be useful in understanding the setup: All my notes from my classes at college, the productive and progression notes of my startup, and everything I remember from being in the game. Whatever I can use to be prepared for what's coming. Matt messages me back an updated keycode to get into the labs. For his sake, I hope this doesn't come back to bite him in the ass. He's taking a huge risk going behind the company's back to infiltrate secret projects. Especially if those monkey suits find out about unauthorized use of the lab equipment. The transit finally pulls up to my stop, prompting me to close my bag and walk off.

Approaching the building, some are looking at me strangely; especially the ones that know who I am. I'm not in my usual business casual look, but just my standard clothes with a hoodie on like I'm eighteen again. I avert my gaze as much as possible to avoid contact with them as I walk around the main building towards the back. It's starting to feel like a "secret agent" movie trope as I'm walking with my head down towards the labs. The door comes up quickly and I move straight in, avoiding eye contact with the guard on duty while flashing my badge at him to go past the second door. The halls are empty and quiet. I push my hair out of my eyes as I approach the coded door, punch in the new passcode, and walk in. I hear the clacking of keys being pressed when Matt comes into view, looking like a stressed-out mess. Hair disheveled, bags under his eyes behind his glasses, the top two buttons undone under his loosened tie, and sleeves rolled up to his forearms.

His eyes dart back and forth between two monitors before he sees me. "You're late."

"Yeah? Well blame the transit," I retort. I look past him and into the room Riley's resting in, "How is he?"

Matt looks at the room before back at his monitor, "Stable. No change. His REM spiked a couple of times, possibly from some in-game encounters."

I nod before pulling my notebooks out of my bag and lay them out on a nearby empty table. "This is everything I have on the basics of coding and interactive software, field notes of *TMG* and its equipment, and anything else I thought might be useful. I took extensive notes during our alpha testing sessions and bugging issues."

He nods without looking at me, "Good. We'll need those. Here, come check this out."

I walk over to peer over his shoulder while he points at the monitor to the left, "These binaries and code streams are erratic. There shouldn't be any way for the human brain to try and process this much chaos in waves. But that Crest has been rigged and retrofitted in some way I've never seen before. Whoever redesigned this... they knew what they were doing."

I glance back at Riley in his station with the Crest attached to his head, his body making slight little jerks and twitches. It's so strange to see him without the interface gloves and game mat attached to him. Someone rigged the system to be where players don't have to require extra equipment, but just the headset and game disc. "What else did you find?"

"The framework is complicated. Whatever programming it's connected to, it's safeguarded with a lot of firewalls. I won't be able to get through it easily, but I'm going to try while you're busy."

I blink rapidly, "Come again?"

Matt takes a deep breath, pulls his glasses off and looks me in the eyes before reaching under the desk to pull out a box. He hands it to me silently and nods, prompting me to open it. Under the lid sits a duplicate Crest.

"What? No, absolutely-the-fuck-not."

"Connor, you *have* to. This is *The Mortal Gate* all over again, and we need someone to go in and get him."

"Then *you* go! It's your crazy idea, so you do it!"

He slaps his hand on the desk, "I can't! Connor, I've got this company to handle, and I need to be on this end to get past the safeguards and trace the IP address back. Until then, Riley needs help. If it's anything like the last time, one of two things will happen: Either he's going to get killed or he's going to do everything he can to stay in there."

Shit! He wants me to go in this thing. No, no, no! We can figure this out from the outside! "Matt, you can't ask me to do this. Not with everything I've done to escape what happened. Not with all I've done to try and do things differently."

He sighs deeply and pinches the bridge of his nose. "Look, you're not the only one who's suffered from all of this. I thought we were done too. I wanted to forget about losing my friends… losing Robert… even losing Dominic. I have wanted to make sure his legacy and genius didn't die with him. But something… some*one*… is trying to stop that from happening. I need to find out what's happening. We have our parts to play, Connor. Please don't make me do this alone."

He really pulled out all the stops on this argument. There's no denying at this point that something bigger is happening and it all has to do with Dominic and his games. You see this kind of thing in movies or comic books where big corporations pull the wool over the eyes of their employees while they hash out dastardly plans against everyone under them. As cliché as it sounds, it really seems like that's where this is going. What if they are trying to do something bigger? What if the others get caught in the crossfire? Mark and Danica? Krissy?

"What do we know about the game itself? The plot, the objectives, character creation, classes, and such?"

Matt nods and moves to the screen on the right, pulling up the game manual. "*The Primeval Maze* takes place years after the events of *The Mortal Gate*, but not in Albistair. It's another continent in the game's world called Preydor, untouched by the events of the Violet Moon or the Chasm. The continent itself is split into two regions: the coastal region of Braveshire, and a jungle-terrain called Kerogema. The game's main conflict involves a vast, magical labyrinth that opens at random to release monsters on unsuspecting colonies and villages. You play the role of a monster hunter for hire, choosing between three archetypes before starting your journey. I don't know if you'll keep the race you choose, but I'd go 'human' just in case things happen in your favor."

I take a deep breath before nodding, taking his place in front of the screen. I select the most basic of character details in order to start quickly by choosing evenly distributed skill traits. While I do this, Matt is preparing a station for me next to Riley. I quickly enter in all the information I feel that I need to and head into the room.

Sounding much braver than I actually feel, I say, "Okay, I'm ready."

Matt nods intently, "Take your hoodie off and empty your pockets. Anything that could possibly interfere with the equipment."

I nod back and do what he says, dropping my hoodie, wallet, and keys. The last thing to go is my phone, but I hold it for a moment thinking about Krissy. I type a message; "Going dark. Check in soon. I love you." With that, I climb up onto the station in a sitting position. Matt approaches with the Crest and holds it out to me. Reluctantly, I take it and look at him, "This is some scary shit, Matt. You sure you'll be okay out here? I can get people to help."

"It has to be us, Connor. When it comes down to it, I know what to do. You focus on getting him out, okay?"

Damn, he's stubborn. Just like the old days. "Okay. It's your show out here. Just… check in on Krissy for me, okay?"

With a silent nod of agreement, he taps on the keyboard to set up the system. I place the Crest on my head and lie back, waiting for lights-out. I take one last look at Riley before I feel the soft tingling in my head.

"Game on." The lights go out.

Chapter 6

The last time I woke up in a SnoWire game, I was in a semi-comfy bed made of straw surrounded by four walls and the smell of cooking meat before starting my "adventure". This time, I wake up in aching pain. My body is aching, and I feel intense weight holding me down. My eyes flutter open to get a bearing on my surroundings, and it's a mess. Broken, splintered wood all around me, rafters and beams busted down everywhere, broken glass from something, all scattered on the floors of my starting point. I reach out in front of me to grab anything that can help get me out of this state, but I'm struggling hard. I manage to grip onto a heavy post and pull, grunting loudly with a strangely high voice. I feel the pressure on my legs and feet slip away as I free myself from the trap. I shuffle up to my feet and dust off before looking down at myself. I'm wearing a dirty and torn white shirt that has a leather vest over it, baggy gray pants torn at the ankles tied by a rope belt, and ratty shoes with holes at the toes.

"Not bad so far…" The pitch of my voice puts me off again with how high it is than my normal one. My gaze goes up and I see what else is higher than normal… *everything*. With some of the posts of this destroyed building still intact and standing, I can see they're tall. Like "you must be this tall to ride" tall. "So… either I'm in a world of giants… or I'm *really* friggin short…"

A rattling comes from nearby, but I can't see what made the noise. I walk out of the rubble where I woke up and into the open to get a bearing on my surroundings. Like the one I was just in, there are destroyed and burning buildings all around me. The moon is shining down dimly over me, obscured by layers of smoke rising in the air. It looks like a war zone that left no survivors. It's eerie and empty.

The rattling returns, making me spin around rapidly to try and find the source. "Hello? Anyone there?" No answer.

I slowly walk further into the destroyed settlement to look for the noise. I'm in unfamiliar territory here with no friends, companions, or weapons. I don't know how to defend myself or if I have spells like I did with my former character, Zarimm. Anything is possible in here... even a quick and early death.

"Hello?!"

The rattling comes back louder, along with the sounds of whimpering. A large shadow of a humanoid figure projects on the wall of a nearby building. I have got no protection, so I run and hide behind a nearby post. Thanks to my short stature, it's easy for me to hide, but I feel like a coward. The shadow begins to shrink in the firelight and the whimpering gets louder as it does. From around the corner of the partially standing structure, a human female comes limping with her long black hair covering her face. She's wearing tattered commoner clothes that look dirty from soot and soil.

I slowly step out from behind cover and start to approach, "Lady? You okay? What happened here?"

She doesn't say anything, just keeps whimpering and limping towards me. The dust and smoke keep me from making out any other details about her. One of her arms lurches over her chest and the other is hanging loosely by her side. Her shambling legs crawl forward, giving me a very uneasy feeling.

"Lady?"

The moon comes out from its cover behind clouds and smoke, illuminating the area. The moonlight lends its shine to the strange woman and reveals that she has numerous stitches at her joints and in patches all over her exposed arms and calves. Her skin is multicolored in different shades and complexions. Her head tilts up just enough for the moonlight to reveal her dead white eyes, stitched face, and decayed teeth. She stares at me and snarls slightly, letting out a raspy breath that almost chitters.

"Oh shit."

She lets out a horrid screech and charges at me full sprint. I quickly whip around and run as hard and fast as my little legs can take me. I hear her chittering gaining on me quickly. *Dammit, run!* Ahead of me, another figure pops out and makes me skid to a stop. This one is male but has the same stitch patterns and undead look as the other one. Then another one comes to their side. Then two more. Including the one behind me trying to box me in, there are about ten of these creepers surrounding me.

"So… any chance we can talk this out? I'm kind of new around here…" They just stare at me with their whitened eyes and jagged snarls. *Something tells me they're not conversationalists.* The one behind me screeches again, and they all pounce quickly. One manages to knock me down on the ground and pin me there while the others claw and scratch at me with their broken fingernails. It feels like they're trying to pull me apart and I can't escape it.

Suddenly, a loud, hulking roar tears through the chitters and screeches before one of the monsters is cleaved in half, spraying black ooze all over me. The ones that are still attacking me suddenly break away and run after their attacker. I'm bleeding from numerous scratches all over me and grunting from the stinging pain. I manage to lean up from the ground and look back to watch what is happening. Towering over the monsters is a stone-gray skinned, hulking humanoid gripping a large great axe dripping with black ooze. He swings it wildly in front of him, decapitating one of his attackers but leaving his back exposed for one to jump onto and attempt to bite into his shoulder. The teeth don't puncture anything in the hulk's skin as he reaches back, grips it by the neck, and hurls it away from him.

"Don't just sit there, half-pint! Either help or get the hells out of my way!" He roars at me with a deep voice. "There's some gear in that hut over there!" The creepers continue to pounce and swipe at him, but it hardly fazes him. In that instant, I look at the hut he pointed to and notice it's still intact. I scurry to my feet and limp quickly to it, pushing the door open and find an almost empty room with a large table against the far wall. On the table is a splintered wooden club, a leather whip accompanied by a whistle, and a weighted net with some curved barbs tethered on the end. Each one is matched with a leather satchel that reminds me of what we were given in *The Mortal Gate*. Considering how short I am, I don't think I can lift the club and use it effectively. I am indecisive between the other two options until the door slams open behind me, revealing one of the stitched monsters. It screeches loudly as it charges, so I instinctively grab at the table and take the net in my hands, throwing it blindly at the monster. The barbed ends of the net hook into its skin as the net wraps around it, causing it to flail and entangle itself until it drops to the ground. I quickly sift through the satchel that the net came with and find a small rusty hunting knife. I grab it quickly and run over to the trapped creature, still writhing and growling, waiting for an opening before I plunge it into its head. Instantly, the monster stops flailing and lays limp on the ground. I huff and puff looking at the creature in the net while trying to catch my breath. It doesn't dissolve or dissipate like the monsters I've faced before, but instead it sort of melts away into a puddle of black.

"That's fucking disgusting," I mutter. I pick up the net and inspect it before I hear another loud roar coming from outside the hut. I look back at the table to see if I can grab anything else, but it's left empty aside from the satchel I got the knife from. *Single selection options. Annoying.* I sling the satchel's strap around my shoulder and run out of the hut. The warrior is now surrounded by more of those things, but it doesn't seem to faze him in the slightest. He's just laughing like a psycho with every swing of his axe. I run up to the fight with the net in my hands, taking a couple of steps before spinning around and hurling it at the pile of monsters. It manages to hook into a couple of them, making them pull and tug to get free while tearing away at their skin.

The hulking humanoid roars with a psychotic laugh, "Nice work, Half-Pint! Now let us dispose of the rest of them!"

Slight aside, I nod and look at the monsters caught in my net, writhing and lashing at each other to try and get free. I hold the dagger in my hand and run to the one with its back to me and slash at its leg with a wild swing, causing it to screech out and kick back at me, connecting with my chest and sending me back onto the ground. I grunt loudly, gripping my chest before looking back up at the monsters. One of them manages to tear itself away from the net and shambles towards me. I look around me for anything to help, only finding splintered boards of destroyed houses. One is pointed down into the ground and leaning on top of a mound like a seesaw, making something in my brain click. I shuffle up to my feet and stand on the edge in the ground, whistling at it to grab its attention.

"Come on, ugly! Come here!" I jump up and down to get its attention. The creature screeches out once more and charges, scratching and clawing at the air. *Wait. Wait. Wait.* I slowly shuffle backwards as it charges me, then quickly turn around and jump on the elevated end. The moment it shoots up, the monster runs straight into the splintered end of the board, piercing its heart through its back. A loud squelch sounds from it, followed by hollow screams and cries. The creature stops twitching seconds after and then melts away.

Another loud roar rips through the air. I look back to see the giant lodge his weapon into the last one that was caught in the net I threw. He untangles the remains from the net and walks it over to me. This guy is enormous; bulging muscles like legs growing out of his shoulders with light scarring all the way down to his wrists. He's wearing a leather vest clearly too small for his frame as it's opened in the front, exposing more scarring on his body almost like a pattern. His lower half is covered with some form of cloth pants and leather boots held up by a small chain around his waist. He has some kind of darkened or aged bandaging around both of his hands except for around his fingers. The giant stalks up to me with a grin of a couple of missing teeth, but otherwise in good health. His eyes are dark, almost black, but shining with a crazy satisfaction that gives me the creeps. One of the most prominent things on his head was his mohawked hair that barely hides more scarring along his face and scalp. *Holy shit, this guy is tall. Or am I just that short?*

"Ha, ha, ha!" he bellows out loudly. "Great fight, Half-Pint! You're a credit to your people. This is yours." He hands the net back to me rolled up. I look at the satchel around my shoulder and open it, stuffing the net in. Thankfully, it's like the ones in the last game and swallows up the net with no issues.

"Thanks. And thanks for the help back there. What's your name?"

Suddenly, the giant looks offended. "My name? Surely, you jest! Everyone has heard of Doxo the Stonesplitter! Fabled monster hunter of Braveshire!"

I don't want to offend the guy that saved me, so I just rub the back of my neck with a sheepish smile. "I... I'm not from around here. Sorry."

Doxo groans and shoulders his giant axe, "Ugh, such a task receiving a reputation these days. Anyway, what do you call yourself, luthien?"

I tilted my head at "luthien", promptly pulling my new logbook out of my satchel and flipping the pages. Like before, it gives me a character sheet with a name, race, and stat blocks. Apparently a "luthien" is a race of gnome-like people, explaining my height situation. I look up at Doxo, whose eyebrow is cocked up in confusion.

"I'm Bimbik. Bimbik Steamspanner," I introduce myself. He looks more confused than I felt giving him that name. "What were those things?"

"Stitchlings," he explains. "Possessed creatures that stitch the parts of their victims to their bodies to make themselves more menacing. Easy to hit, hard to kill. So far, they are the worst things to be vomited out of the Primeval Maze."

I freeze. The name of the game. "The Primeval Maze? What do you mean?"

"Gods, boy, you really are not from around here. Come, I will explain on the way to my next destination." He begins walking away from the battlefield, taking giant strides away from me. Looking around at the scene, it gives me terrible flashbacks to the attacks in Albistair by the terrorghasts. They were a single swarm of monsters that overtook the land. If these stitchlings were only a small portion of what's to come, it won't be as easy as the first time.

Chapter 7

Doxo doesn't have a horse or any kind of mount, so we proceed on foot. Every one of his steps requires me to power walk just to try and keep up with him. During our walk, I'm able to take in the landscape of this place called Preydor; it reminds me of coastal California because it is lush, green, and open with the smell of salt water in the air and warm atmosphere.

Reading further into the logbook, I learn that Preydor is a single continent separated into two regions: the coastal Braveshire and the jungle-like Kerogema, just as Matt described. As an "expansion", it's located in the same worldly plane as Albistair on the eastern hemisphere. The moon is casting a bright light down on us along our walk to wherever Doxo is taking me, giving me a chance to observe the stark differences between this world and the one from before. There are less trees and mountains here than Albistair, but more open fields and the scent of the ocean in the air. The ground is soft, and the air is breezy, taking away some of the warmth. The sky is just as clear as it was in the last game with breathtaking stars and constellations and intermittent clouds every so often.

"Doxo?"

The giant looks down, "Hmm?"

"Do you know anything about Albistair?"

"That place? Never been there myself, but I know they had a bloody history about a century ago. Something about stones and gates that almost killed everyone there. Nothing like that happened here until the Maze opened," he explains.

A century? So, everything that happened with the Archon and Mortal Gate happened 100 years ago in Preydor's history.

Nervously I respond with, "Oh… yeah. Well, that's where I came from originally. I didn't expect to see all of this… this chaos."

Doxo just laughs, "Half-Pint, there is chaos everywhere. If there is not, then it is best to just find somewhere else to be."

Surprisingly insightful. I struggle to catch up, "So what is the Primeval Maze? Why is it so important?"

He keeps pressing forward and points ahead, "We will stop at that ravine up ahead, and I will tell you all you need to know."

I look ahead to where Doxo points and see a small stream of water babbling from west to southwest. He takes the lead as he presses forward and buries his axe head into the ground before kneeling over the water. He starts scooping handfuls of water to either drink from or to wash off the bile from his body. Walking up to the ravine, I place myself a few feet to his left to gaze into the water in order to get a good first look at myself in this new form. I look at my hands, tanned reddish skin tone, no clawed fingernails, only dusty from the ground. Looking at my face in the water's reflection, my jawline looks less pronounced than when I was an Orc, and my nose is a little more of a button-nose. It's not until I really look at eyes; and they are *huge*! They look the size of half-dollar coins! Giant eyes! My hands slide to the sides of my face and meet two oversized, pointing ears. My hair is the next thing I notice, which is short, spiky, and deep blue. I run my stubby hands through my hair and take a deep breath, softly trying to accept this new face and body. I dip my hands into the water and wash it over my face, letting the cool rush wake me up a little bit. *Seems the sensations are still there.* This brings me back to *TMG* when we all rested at an oasis to drink and relax, which transitioned to the memory of Lorena being with us. There's hardly a time that I don't wonder what happened to her and Dominic when the game was decommissioned.

"Oi! Steamspanner!" Doxo calls over to me, pulling me out of my line of thought. He waves me over to join him as he dips his feet into the ravine. I hobble over the best that my feet can carry me before sitting down next to him. My feet barely skim the surface of the water.

"So, the Primeval Maze. It is a phenomenon of magic that is unlike anything that anyone in Preydor has ever seen. Most believe that it is a bridge between our plane and the Abyss, or as my people refer to it, the Depths. The Maze randomly opens a mouth or some form of a door before spitting out all manner of monsters and horrors. This has been going on for the past several moon cycles. There have been military bands and platoons that have attempted to breach the Maze and stop whatever is causing it, but none have returned before the mouths close again. Those beasts ravenously attack the settlements and then move on to the next one. Those stitchlings back at Elmsfield came through from attacking another smaller settlement, which I followed and ran into you."

I listen intently, hearing the kind of chaotic events that sound very SnoWire of the developers, whoever they are. "So, how do you know it's a maze and not some direct portal or cavern system?"

"That is exactly what we are going to find out when we arrive in Spearhead," he explains as he stands back up and starts putting his boots back on his giant feet. "Supposedly, there is someone there that has entered the Maze and managed to escape. I am going to find them, see what they know, then go into the Maze myself."

My eyes go wide, "What? You're going into the place full of monsters?"

He laughs loudly, "Yes, I am, Half-Pint. Glory awaits to the one who can destroy those beasts and saves Preydor!" He shoulders his axe and starts walking upriver alongside the bank.

I shuffle to my feet and rush to try and keep up with him. "That sounds suicidal, Doxo. Why put your life in danger like that?"

He lets out another bellowing laugh, "For glory! What else? I aim to become the most fabled monster slayer in all Preydor!"

His enthusiasm is almost contagious, but I can't shake the uneasy feeling I have on the whole monster maze thing. Whoever created this game wanted there to be danger right out of the gate, so to speak, thrusting the player directly into the fire without any tutorial, preamble, or settings selections. At least in the last one we had a chance to get to know our characters and surroundings. And those things. The stitchlings. What twisted mind comes up with creatures like that? That thought sends me into another line of thought: What if I had died in that encounter? Would I be stitched into a monster and made to suffer for the entirety of the game's existence? I did not want to start asking these same questions again, but Riley is in trouble somewhere in here and I can't leave him. No matter how badly he wants to stay.

The walk is mostly spent with Doxo boasting about his previous kills and bragging of his strength. Admittedly, he reminds me a lot of Mark any time he had something to brag and boast about because he always got excited and loud about it. *I wonder what Mark would make of this place. What would any of them make of it?* While I fully understand why they don't want to have anything to do with this stuff anymore, I really wish they were all here. My train of thought gets pulled away as we start to walk towards a collection of exotic trees, vibrant greens and blues with trunks of wood ranging from deep reds to ashy grays. As we pass, some of the branches start to shake and make noises I've never heard before. Suddenly, out from the trees come flying creatures like I've never seen. Large blue birds that look like hawks or eagles at first glance with chromatic feathers in their wings, frayed crown heads that spread every time they call out, red-tipped tail feathers and black feet with red talons.

"What are those?" I ask in a trance.

Doxo looks up and tenses his jaw, "Vulsprites… something spooked them. Prepare yourself."

I am visibly confused at first, but I dig into my satchel to grab my net. Once it's out, I stand ready. I suddenly hear something that sounds like hoofprints coming quickly in our direction. Doxo grips his great axe, ready for whatever is coming.

"Ah! Ow! Damn you! Come back!" A loud female voice rings out from behind the tree line along with the stomping of hoofprints and a strange cracking sound heading right in our direction. A tall shape started to form coming from the woods. I panic and hurl my net directly at the shape. It doesn't drape over it, but it does cause the shape to suddenly jerk forward to the ground with a loud "Oof!" Doxo raises his axe but stops himself as he looks down at the figure. I peek from behind his giant leg and look at what I caught; a young woman looking creature with pale green hair in a pixie cut with two small brown horns curling out from the sides of her head. She is wearing a set of robes that are colored like a Girl Scout's uniform and holding a black whip in her hands. Below her robes are a set of furry legs with cloven hooves for feet. When she leans up to look at us, her face is soft and pale with a few freckles on each cheek. Her nose is a little upturned and her grimaced face reveals a couple of sharpened fangs on the top and bottom rows of teeth.

"What in the blazes are you doing?" She yells at us from the ground.

Doxo lowers his axe and looks at the girl suspiciously, "We could ask you the same thing, *varlese*."

I tilt my head up at Doxo, "Varlese?"

"Aye, inhabitants of Kerogema's forests. Stubborn and tricky folk, they are," he mutters.

"My name is Veyanna! And you disrupted my studies! Get me out of this net," she demands.

I gulp a bit and approach her legs, fiddling with the net around her ankles, "Sorry… it's been a bit of a day for me. I'm a bit jumpy."

"More than most Pucks I've met," Veyanna comments as she maneuvers her hooves out of the net. Luckily none of the barbs cut into her skin.

"You still have to explain yourself," Doxo growls down, leaning on his axe handle.

Veyanna stands up from the ground. She's about a foot shorter than Doxo, but still rather tall compared to my size. "I'm studying the vulsprites and their behaviors. I'm hoping to tame one and study it further for my academics."

Doxo tilts his head to the side, "A Handler? You?"

"A Handler in training, but yes," she hisses back.

"Okay, could you two relax for a moment?" They both look at me with cocked eyebrows. "Well… I mean, this doesn't exactly seem like the kind of place to hash out issues. We still need to get to Spearhead."

Veyanna's curious expression changes to one of confusion. "Why are you going to Spearhead? That place is being evacuated by the Crownshields. They believe that some magical door is going to open in their settlement and bring forth doom."

Doxo and I look at each other, mentally connecting with each other on what she meant. "Would they be able to know if the Maze is opening there?"

"Not that I am aware of," he thinks aloud. "It is hard to say how anyone would know if it would appear within their settlements. But I am now interested in getting there quicker before everyone abandons it."

Our conversation causes Veyanna to tilt her head to the side. "What? You two believe in this so-called 'Primeval Maze'? Certainly, you must be joking. I'd expect it to be believed by the likes of a gnolid, but not a luthien."

Before Doxo has the chance to spit off whatever insult is dangling in his head, I interject. "We just came from Elmsfield, or what was left of it. There were beasts called stitchlings that attacked and destroyed the whole village. They were spat out from the Maze, and it is going to happen again."

She looks unamused and rolls her eyes. "Idiotic superstitions of people who fear the unknown. Because these creatures are unfamiliar, and unknown does not mean that they are conjured beasts from the Abyss sent to destroy us. We need to merely study them and understand their mannerisms before assuming they are monstrous."

"You are absolutely cracked," Doxo blurts out.

There is too much tension between these two and I have no clue where it's leading. "Look, let's go to Spearhead and see what we can find out. This should be enough to either let Doxo be satisfied that there are more monsters to kill or prove Veyanna's suspicions about the creatures. Okay?"

They look at each other carefully before looking at me, giving me a nod of understanding. "No idea why I am taking advice from a puck, but the world itself has gone straight out of its wit. Shall we then?" Veyanna gathers her things and heads back into the forest where she came from, prompting Doxo and I to follow her.

"So, what is it about the vulsprites that makes you want to tame one?" I ask in a quickened step to keep up with them both. *Damn these little legs!*

Veyanna keeps her gaze forward, trying to keep ahead of us both I assume. "They are a powerful breed of avians in Preydor. We have nothing like them in Kerogema and it is fascinating to the Tamer's Guild. I wish to study their kind and see what benefits they bring to the ecosystems and overall wildlife populations."

A virtual fantasy environmentalist. Interesting.

Doxo snorts, "You waste your time with studying beasts. If they do not attack you, let them be. If they attack you, kill them. Simple as that."

And then there's the textbook barbarian.

The amount of tension between these two is unsettling. I can't tell if it's distrust between species, difference of philosophy, or some sort of sexual tension, but I'm not here for it. I'm here to find Riley. With any luck, he'll be in one of the settlements around Preydor. On the other hand, what if he's inside the Maze? I hope I find out soon.

Chapter 8

What is nice about these kinds of systems is the amount of detail spent on the graphics, environmental presence, and overall showmanship of the general landscape. My time working for SnoWire introduced me to a new world of creativity and innovation through various trials, alpha and beta tests, bug detection, and story writing. It makes me wonder what the worlds that Dominic and Lorena had made would have looked like if things were different. Maybe they would still be alive and working together to bring awesome video games to life for us to play. Maybe they would have worked things out between each other so that they stayed a family. On the other hand, if things hadn't gone the way they did, I may not have ended up with Krissy knowing my cowardly ways before all of this. But what about Danica and Mark? That experience caused them to break up. And Riley? He went rogue because he lost his fantasy world. There's really no point in asking these questions, but it's all I can do while the three of us walk to Spearhead because Doxo and Veyanna are silent the whole time while I try to keep up with them.

"How much farther?" I complain.

"Not much. Just past the next clearing," Veyanna answers. "As I said before, you may not find much there by the time we arrive. The Crownshields take their orders rather seriously."

Not exactly comforting to me. "These Crownshields. Are they a body of soldiers? Guards? Hired mercenaries?"

"More of a militia of men and women in service of the queen of Braveshire," Doxo answers. "She believes that those willing to protect its borders deserve the chance to."

His burn on the queen made me chuckle, "Heh, sounds a lot better than the last big ruler I ran into."

Veyanna looks back at me with a tilt in her head, "You are well traveled, luthien?"

Me and my big mouth. I rub the back of my neck, "Eh… kind of. I come from Albistair."

"Really?" She stops and turns, crossing her arms. "What is it like there?"

I stop as she does, much to Doxo's annoyance. "Well… it's a big place with constant change. If you know its history, it used to be a lot worse with the Mortal Gate, Crimson Order, terrorghasts, Archon and such."

She looks like she's studying me. There's nothing I said that wasn't true, just probably not up to their history. She puts her hands on her hips, "What about their wildlife? Have you ever come across a ferodon?"

"Gods, can these questions wait until we are in a tavern with ale?" Doxo groans out before he turns back around and starts walking.

While Veyanna and I are left to try and catch up with him, I half-whisper up to her, "Yes I have and they're awesome." I'm not sure if she can understand my words, but my excitement gets a smile of approval from her. The three of us press on past the tree line ahead and come upon a beautiful clearing lit up by the moonlight and decorated with a field of flowers colored with reds and yellows and whites. Flowers that I haven't seen on the Outside before appear to have a sort of glittering aura around them. I reach down and pick a white one from the ground, observing it carefully. The stem is dark green like damp grass, the petals are sparkling white like marble, and the center has a scent that reminds me of springtime and vanilla. I get so lost in thought that I don't notice an animal approaching from out of the right side of the clearing. I glance up at it and see that it is about the height of a small deer, but the huskiness of a pig. Its face has two bulbous brown eyes perpendicular to each other atop a short trunk hanging over its mouth. The large body is supported by four thick legs with what look like oversized rabbit's feet as it gingerly steps forward to eat from the field. Its fur is a strange swirl of black, white and brown from front to back, except for a stark black tail with a yellow tip. Its big eyes look up and meet mine, tilting its head at me as if it's studying me. A small tingling comes from my side; my satchel is glowing. I reach in and pull out my logbook, flipping to one of the empty pages, and watch as a page begins to fill itself out with small notes and an illustration of an animal. The same animal in front of me. The page reads:

'Elephuin, indigenous herbivore of Braveshire forests. Common among the natural habitats and known for their large, plump size. Elephuins are often herded for their milk production or as domesticated pets.'

"Whoa! I can catalog animals." I stare at the page in amazement as there are more notes about the animal that appear until it is filled. I smile and flip around to see if there were any more of them, then stop at a horrifying sight. A sketch of a stitchling. Horribly disgusting as it was in real life, the creature is in a horrifying pose with small, scratched notes all around: '*Unknown origins. No known diets or habits. Known for aggression and desire for carnage. Creature is an amalgam of various dead parts that have been magically stitched together.*'

"Magically?" I read aloud. I remember Doxo saying they possessed or reanimated parts of dead bodies and victims to repurpose them into monsters. What kind of magic would be used in that? Necromancy? Someone involved with the story writing and plot development had to think of some kind of more twisted motives for the villains of this place.

"Bimbik?"

I turn around to Veyanna standing behind me, looking over my shoulder. "Are you well?"

I turn around to look back at the elephuin just before it turns away and waddles quickly back into the trees. "Yeah... just thinking. Sorry."

"Magnificent animals are they not?" she asks with a smile. "Nature simply knows no limits on the beauty it is capable of creating."

"You really like nature," I comment with a small chuckle.

She looks down at me softly, "We varlese are born of nature. The Spirits helped the first of my people to understand its power and desire for balance. We protect that balance, now, and we will protect it for as long as we draw breath. That is why I came to Braveshire. To find the disruption of nature's balance and realign it."

"That's… pretty cool," I reply. *If only it were that easy to put things back to how they were meant to be.*

"Oi!"

We both turn around to see Doxo leaning against one of the trees impatiently. "Are you done sight-seeing?"

With that, we rejoin him and continue our journey past the clearing. Another few minutes go by before we start to see distant flickers of torchlight. The settlement is much bigger than Elmsfield, or at least from what we survived. The hamlet itself looks gorgeous with its tall wood rooftops, darkened wood walls and huge lake off to the east of it. Unfortunately, it is just as Veyanna said. We can see small moving torches venturing away from the town itself; a lot of them.

"Welcome to Spearhead," Doxo mumbles while watching the line of caravans move away from the town. He starts down the hill and towards the town with Veyanna and I close behind. I begin hearing the clamoring of loud voices, clanging metal and disturbed horses. The wall we are approaching has two tall doors with two guards in front of it. The guards, I could only assume as the Crownshields, are wearing armor that has a flat top helm with two oval holes leaving the eyes barely visible. Attached to the top is a bear head shaped ornament piece. The shoulders are oval, wide and huge. They're decorated with metal chains, hanging from the edges of the shoulder plates. The upper arms are protected by squared, fully covering braces sitting loosely under the shoulder plates. The lower arms are covered by vambraces that have several layered metal sheets on the outer sides. The breastplate is made from many layers of smaller metal pieces, mimicking the scales of a fish. It covers everything from the neck down and ending at the groin, but the shoulder area is exposed to allow for more movement space. The upper legs are covered by a chainmail skirt reaching just below the waist. The lower legs are protected by greaves which have curved, pointed edge at the knee point.

They both quickly cross their spears in front of the door as we approach with one yelling, "Halt! Spearhead is not accepting refugees or visitors. Vacate this area immediately."

Doxo approaches them first, putting a fist on his hip and his axe on his shoulder. "Brave Crownshields, I am Doxo the Stonesplitter and I am here to stop the disasters brought on by the Primeval Maze! Allow my companions and I to enter the town so that we may investigate and save these fine people!"

Neither of the Crownshields look impressed with the half-giant in front of them. The second one speaks up, "By order of Her Majesty, Queen Elisabetta, none shall enter these walls as it is being evacuated for the safety of the people. Turn around and go back from where you came."

I can't see his face, but I can feel the irritation radiating from the gnolid. His hand is gripping the haft of his axe like he's ready to use it. I quickly step in front of him and look up at the guards, "Heh… sorry about him. He's a bit cranky. Look, we can't go back to where we came from because it was destroyed. Elmsfield is completely —"

"Wait," the first one interrupts me. "Did you say Elmsfield? You survived the attack?"

I nod, pointing up at Doxo, "With some serious help. He's telling the truth that we are trying to help. We think that the Maze is going to open here next, and we want to stop it if we can."

The guards look at each other with some sort of silent conversation before they look back at us and uncross their spears. "Enter the center of town. Find Shieldmaster Brenn, and report to him of what you have told us."

They step back and push the wooden gates open to let us in. At first glance, the town looks cozy and inviting with its homes and buildings designed like log cabins one would find at a campground. Several of the buildings have a banner waving above their doors, a black flag with a brass spearhead in front of an outline of a kite shield. As the three of us enter, the gates behind us quickly shut and the clamor of voices and rushed footsteps take over the surrounding area. We start walking down a main road towards the noises, periodically seeing people rushing back and forth in our line of sight, big and small, young and old.

"Guess they believe the threat is real," I comment aloud.

"Fear makes one do outlandish things, unfortunately," Veyanna replies.

"Let us find this Shieldmaster and get the hunt underway," Doxo orders as he walks through us and presses on.

The three of us continue into the more populated part of Spearhead where a menagerie of people are moving large boxes, barrels, and sacks out of buildings and homes onto carts or wheelbarrows. It's also the first chance I get to see the different races of people aside from myself, Veyanna and Doxo. There are humans, obviously, mixed in with what I can assume are dwarves, other pucks like me, elves, and various half-breeds like catfolk, lizardfolk, and a few others that are strangely new to me. I start getting rushed and pushed aside by scared people that are shuffling around all over the place, but one thing stands out to me over the rest of this mayhem. A loud, authoritative voice is barking orders and commands loudly and proudly. I scan around to find it and see a human man standing on top of a large wooden stage pointing in various directions as he yells over the crowd. His armor is like what the guards outside of the town were wearing, but he is outfitted with a large billowy cape and a crested badge sitting on his chest.

"I think I found the Shieldmaster," I call out and point. The others look in the direction of where I'm pointing and nod in agreement. We march through the parading crowd until we reach the foot of the stage.

"You two! Keep them from breaking through the guard detail at the front gates! Ceryx, look for looters and bring them to the cells!" he barks out all around before looking down at the three of us. He's an old soldier, dusted with white and gray hair that curls down to his shoulders. His dark-skinned face is wrinkled from frustration or stress. There's a single scar under his left eye, which is clouded white in comparison to the right eye which is dark blue. "Keep moving, citizens! I have no time to escort you!"

"We were told to find you, Shieldmaster Brenn!" Doxo yells back. "We hail from the remains of Elmsfield and were told to speak with you by your men!"

His one good eye looks us over intently with no visible expression on his face. He yells over his shoulder, "Varro! Take my position and keep these people in line!" An elven young man in Crownshield armor hops up onto the stage as Brenn leaves it, continuing his line of command. "Come with me," the Shieldmaster orders before pushing past.

We trail after him, fighting through rushing, panicked people trying to leave this place. Brenn leads us to a large building of refined wooden walls, decorative pillars, and a hanging sign over the door that reads: "Archer's Rest Tavern". He pushes the door open and marches inside, followed by Doxo, Veyanna, then me. It's as nice inside as it is on the outside. Hardwood beams support the upper floor and the huge lamps attached to them. The walls are clear of anything, though signs do show plenty of things used to hang on the walls, though they've probably been knocked off by customers who had too much to drink. What's unfortunate is that it is almost completely empty. Chairs are knocked over, barstools are sitting empty, mugs and glasses are either spilled or busted on the tables and floors. While we make our way in, I notice a few people still inside and away from the mayhem outside; a short, stout woman with bright purple hair braided down her back holding a broomstick and sweeping the floor. Her outfit suggests she works in this tavern as she is wearing an apron with a lot of stains and blotches, a tan blouse with the sleeves rolled up to her elbows, dark brown pants rolled at the cuffs, and big shoes on her feet. Her head turns towards us, revealing a dirty-blotched face and large green eyes with an annoyed expression. There is soft music playing from some sort of string instrument opposite of her next to a stone fireplace. A stalky short man with red, long hair slightly revealing a round, lived-in face. Glittering gray eyes, set well within his sockets, and a goatee to complete his rugged features. His thick hands and fingers are working around a large, intricately designed lute with various shapes carved into the face of it, playing an interesting tune that sounds like it is his first time using it. Sitting at the long empty bar is the back of some sort of adventurer type wearing a pale tan hooded cape with the hood down, revealing a coal-black head with scale patterns. From beneath the end of the tattered cape, a long, black tail swings back and forth gently revealing a pinkish underside. The head turns slightly, revealing a serpentine face with big, yellow eyes with slit pupils that stare at us suspiciously. The rest of the tavern is populated by a few soldiers that stand at attention to Brenn, who salutes them at ease before joining them at the table.

The purple-haired luthien woman approaches the three of us with broom in hand, "Drinks? I could use the coin."

Doxo stares down at her with a smirk, "The strongest ale you can give me, and make it a big one. Perhaps a smaller one for these two as well."

She shifts her attention to me and Veyanna impatiently.

"Um… just a cup of water, please," Veyanna says quietly.

"I'll take something strong," I request.

She doesn't say anything else before she turns on her heels and head behind the bar, completely disappearing. The three of us take one of the tables near the Crownshields. I literally hop up into my seat to get comfy, but my eyes can see over the table. Doxo chuckles and reaches to a small crate knocked over on the ground, turns to me, lifts me up by my shirt collar, places the crate under me, and sets me down on top of it.

"Thanks…" I say feeling completely undermined.

Doxo chuckles, "Anytime, Half-Pint."

The luthien woman comes over to our table with a stepstool, places it in front of the table and climbs up with a tray of three mugs. She places the biggest one on the table first and pushes it at Doxo, who catches it and starts chugging. She then takes the cup of water and nudges it in Veyanna's direction, who gingerly takes it in her hands and sips lightly. The last mug she puts on the table and nudges it to me before stepping down from her stool and walking away. Holding the mug up to my nose, I smell a strong scent of what I think is either whiskey or something else grainy. I take a swig and let it settle, bad decision. It burns in my throat like firewater, sending a mentholated rush of air into my nose. I swallow and feel the trickling burn go straight down to my stomach. I must be making a weird face because both Doxo and Veyanna are snickering at me.

"What?" My voice sounds scratched from the burning alcohol.

Veyanna giggles, "You make funny faces when you drink."

"First time having a real swig of firewater?" Doxo mocks.

Before I can fire back, a gruff throat clears to grab our attention. Our heads turn to the table of Crownshields all looking at us irritably. Brenn stands back up, "So. You were at Elmsfield during the attack?"

"More like… I woke up in the middle of the destruction. Doxo here may know more than I do," I explain.

"Aye," he replies. "I was there as the stitchlings were ravaging survivors of the attack. I, however, did not witness the Maze opening. If I had, I would have entered it to destroy everything inside."

This prompts boisterous laughter from the guards at Brenn's table. Brenn, himself, is unamused in the boasting of Doxo. "You do not bring honor to your kind, gnolid. This 'maze' is an abomination of dark origins. No one in all Preydor can explain its purpose rather than to spit out the foulest of beasts upon the land. Mouths of the Maze open at random throughout all the land, us and Kerogema alike. Reports from all over have claimed that monstrosities are destroying whole villages and settlements."

I pull out my logbook and start flipping through the pages until I come to the stitchling page. "Stitchlings were what we saw in Elmsfield. Magically stitched body parts of victims sewn together to create a mindless and feral beast that destroys everything it sees. Is that like anything your reports have?"

"That and more." We all look to the reptilian humanoid at the bar who spins around revealing their full form. The same black color runs down the whole visible body of this creature, as well as the pink underside color from the tail all the way up its neck. The creature is wearing a leather chest piece with a studded leather extension on its right arm, but nothing on its left. It has three appendages on each hand, clawed and scary looking. On its waist, there's a cloth covering held up by a belt of multiple pouches like a utility belt. Each leg reminds me of the legs of a velociraptor;

angled below the knees and connecting to clawed feet. Each knee has a studded leather brace attached to the front and strapped behind. The creature looks at us with its bright yellow eyes while the slits of its nose flare.

"Eavesdropping, are we exerine?" Brenn challenges. This "exerine" stands up on its thin legs and downs the rest of its mug.

"Khelrah. Its name is Khelrah, and it has been listening intently," she says in a raspy voice. It sounds feminine enough for me to assume it's a woman. "The demons of the Maze are more than just stitched bodies coming back to life. Khelrah has seen barking beasts of smoke, flying daggers with claws and teeth, and putrid giants ravage the countryside from here to Cartarez."

This seems to unsettle quite a few in the tavern. The Crownshields seem to finally show a little bit of fear and unease in them. Khelrah stalks forward and looks at the three of us, "Khelrah believes you wish to find a way to stop the Maze?"

I hesitate for a moment, allowing Veyanna to speak first. "I am here as a representative of Kerogema and the Handler's Guild. The balance of nature has been unset by these strange occurrences and I wish to find out why."

The reptilian woman looks the faun-like one curiously before redirecting her attention to Doxo who is chugging down his drink. "I am here to fight monsters and become legendary. That is all."

Khelrah tilts her head to the side at him before looking down at me. She must see something in my face because her eyes are locked onto me. "I-I'm looking for someone. I think he might have gotten into some trouble involving the Maze. I need to find him. If that means helping to solve this thing, I'll do what it takes."

The musician's music lightly plays in the awkward silence as we all sit there waiting for Khelrah to respond. Shieldmaster Brenn takes a deep breath before placing a map on the table, showing all of Spearhead with a few circled areas. "There have been several areas experiencing trembles and unusual activities that have given the citizens unrest. The Queen's experts in the arcane have tried tracking tremors in the earth that are unusual and without any sort of natural cause. They believe that the tremors are the first signs of an entrance of the Maze breaching the surface."

I look at the map and note all the different spots in Spearhead. "Perhaps we can try to scout out these areas to investigate whether or not there are real signs of danger from the Maze."

"You fancy yourself a tracker, Half-Pint?" Doxo asks with a chuckle.

I shrug and think back to my logbook, "I… I dabble in tracking and trapping. Specifically humane traps and tools, but I think I can help."

Doxo stands and puts a fist on his hip, "Well, you and I shall tear these beasts apart and become legends!"

Veyanna rolls her eyes and stands, "If there is any studying of these creatures to help other regions to survive, I will lend my expertise as well."

I let out a small chuckle and nod. I look back up at Brenn, "We could use some direction. If you have men to spare, we can investigate each of the marks on the map."

The grizzled captain gave a deep sigh and looked at his men, "One of you will accompany each of them and direct them to the quakes. If you find anything, sound your horns. We will do what is necessary to save all Braveshire." He salutes proudly, then receives salutes from his men in response. It's inspiring to see such devotion to a guy like him, even if they are programs created that way. While the plan is being formed, I begin to wonder how Matt and Krissy are doing on the Outside.

Chapter 9

~~~~~ Matt ~~~~~

Vitals are normal. REM is in clear succession. Brainwave activity is stable. Everything seems to be okay so far. Damn the programming that doesn't let me see what's happening to Connor in this damn thing. He's taking a huge risk to go in after that moron friend of his. I look at them both lying down in their stations, making sure there are no physical signs of damage or anything. With so much on my plate after taking over Dominic's position, I hardly have a moment to breathe. My phone is buzzing like crazy in my pocket, probably with notifications, messages, and everything else with the job. Two whole years of keeping up with Dominic's appointments, approving and denying new projects, press conferences, board meetings, and only about four hours of sleep a day are taking their toll on me. The worst thing is that I haven't been able to mourn Robert properly. I went through the phone calls with his family, helping with the funeral, but was not able to attend because of having to get the papers signed for me to take over SnoWire. *Robert… I'm sorry I couldn't help you.*

I get so annoyed with my phone that I take it out and check it. Eighteen missed calls and ten text messages. A couple of them from Krissy asking about Connor. I ignored that one for a moment to see an email notification from the

Board, requesting a meeting with shareholders and discuss the next year's margins. I won't be able to avoid them for long to upkeep appearances and meetings. Hopefully they would both be okay without me for a while so I can head to the office. I do one more scan of the machines to ensure that both are stable enough for me to step away before I head for the door. *Don't worry. I'll be back soon.*

The sun is higher and brighter, causing me to cover my eyes immediately as I leave the labs. The parking lot is filled, people are crowding the sidewalks ahead, and the shadow of the SnoWire building is casting a creepy shadow over the streets ahead. Spending so much time in an enclosed room of blue light and fuzzing static has started to take a toll on me and my brain, but probably not to the extent of Riley and Connor. I walk through the front doors and into the elevator, waiting for the doors to close before shuffling through the messages I received back in the labs. The virtual meeting with the shareholders and board members is starting in a few minutes, allotting me enough time to get there from the elevator. Another message I read over is from Krissy, so I reply: *Connor's fine. Check back in an hour.* The doors open on the executive floor, prompting me to step out and walk down the ominous hallway towards the boardroom. As I get closer, I hear hushed and muffled voices coming from behind the door. Once I open the door, I see them all finish their private conversations and look my way. From left to right, the room is occupied Melanie Fischer, Alan Frost, Board Director Armand Guzman, Kate Flynn, and William Ho. All of them have their eyes on me as I close the door behind me, but it's Guzman that fills the silence with a clearing of his throat, "Mr. Bauer. Nice of you to join us. Please, sit."

I give a single nod before sitting at my place at the table, followed by the rest of the board. Once Mr. Guzman takes his seat, he opens a black folder and clicks his pen. Ms. Flynn takes a remote and clicks towards a screen on the right wall from the table, showing another group of people on camera in attendance; the highest shareholders over SnoWire.

"Ladies and gentlemen," Mr. Guzman begins. "Thank you for meeting with us today as we begin preparation for the future of SnoWire Entertainment and product development. Mr. Ho will be recording the events of this meeting for everyone to receive and review for clarification. Ms. Fischer will preside over our numbers and analytics. The rest of the board will be presenting and reviewing agenda items while Mr. Bauer gives us a report on performance within the company. Mr. Bauer, the floor is yours."

I clear my throat and begin, "Well, ladies and gentlemen, the future of SnoWire is maintaining a good and steady incline of interest, customer base, and innovation. With the new development of special tech to move the gaming industry forward, I truly believe in the future of this industry."

Silence. A couple of the virtual attendees cough before Mr. Frost chimes in on the conversation, "Especially with the inheritance of Dominic's curiously advanced reality systems."

Cough! Whatever schmoozing I had geared up for the board is now choked up in my throat. One of the shareholders filled the silence, "Did you acquire more assets from the late Mr. Dawson's files and software?"

"Not all of them," Mr. Frost admits. "He was very protective of his materials. You know, genius breeds paranoia. But I do believe that one of his most innovative projects can be recovered and converted into a great project." He shifts through his papers in front of him, "One of them is titled *The Mortal Gate*."

Everything in my chest is seized. My blood feels like tiny pricks of cold ice as I attempt to keep my composure. "Y-yes, actually I was a partner on that project. Dominic deemed the project obsolete due to some... major malfunctions of the material and equipment."

The board and virtual attendees all look at me with curiosity before Mr. Guzman chimes in, "I've read some of that report. With the salvaged coding and equipment schematics, I believe we have an employee or two that could help us recreate and improve on the original designs. It certainly seems like it could create a new generation of consumers for us."

"Mr. Guzman, I insist that we −" I don't even get a chance to finish before Ms. Fischer interrupts me.

"According to our surveys and analytics, consumers are looking for a more 'robust and realistic experience' when it comes to games of the future." She displays a chart for the room to view, "Our current stock in nationwide stores is beginning to diminish and we are looking at possible loss of stock and funding. I recommend we move forward with a new project as soon as possible."

"Ms. Fischer," I interject, "with all due respect, we already have a new project in the works."

"Ah, yes. Mr. Wright's *Soulscape* project," Mr. Ho interjects. "Hasn't that posed enough problems for us to consider moving forward with it?"

"Agreed," Ms. Flynn adds. "During his last presentation, there were significant drawbacks he was unable to overcome. I move to proceed with reinstallation, reinitialization, and production of Mr. Dawson's last project. To honor his memory."

"Seconded," Mr. Frost adds.

I can't believe what the fuck is happening right now. How did they recover anything from its deletion? Why wouldn't they run this by me *first*?

"It's decided," Mr. Guzman finalizes. "We shall begin with reinitializing the specs for *The Mortal Gate* and run diagnostics for recovery. We'll have our best people on it."

"Mr. Guzman!" All eyes are on me, making me second guess my outburst. "Pardon me, but I don't think this is smart. As CEO of SnoWire, I move to table this conversation until we have reached further talks regarding the personal effects of… Dominic's belongings. He and his daughter both suffered a great tragedy, and I think it may be disrespectful to move forward with this without knowing why Mr. Dawson slated it."

Guzman squints his eyes at me before one of the virtual shareholders voices their opinion. "I second this motion. As Mr. Bauer holds a higher fraction of the shares and company, his decision takes priority for the time being."

78

There's an uncomfortable silence among us before Guzman takes a deep breath. "Very well. The motion is carried that we will take stock of Mr. Dawson's effects, systems, and all slated projects until reaching agreement on whether to proceed with the discussed project. This meeting is adjourned."

The virtual meeting ends, and the board members all begin to leave the room. I gather myself and head for the same door as quick as I can.

"Mr. Bauer," a disappointed voice calls out. "A moment?"

I gulp as quietly as I can before I turn around. Mr. Guzman is standing at his spot at the table buttoning his blazer, eyeing me down something fierce. "That… was quite a power play on your part. I see you're getting more comfortable in your new position?"

"Yes, sir." I reply honestly. This is *my* company now. I made a promise to Dominic that I would keep his legacy alive. That legacy cannot include any resurgence of that cursed game. "I was on the development team of that game and trust me when I say that the company and the world would be better off if they never knew of its existence. Ever."

He hums to himself, "I see. Well, I distinctly remember that Lorena was also on that development team as team lead. Is that correct?"

That name still makes my skin crawl, "Y-yes sir. However, I don't think she fully understood the extremes that the system puts its players through. The potential damage to the brain, micro emission exposure—"

"I am well aware of all of the damages and exposures that the original system possessed through the initial reports gathered by Lorena's data analysis," Mr. Guzman explains. "But there is potential in its wiring to bring the world a masterful experience of massive multiplayer online environments that everyone can experience in a virtual state. It's what the world wants, and it is what we'll give them." With that, he brushes past me and leaves the room, leaving me alone with my thoughts.

"What in the actual hell is happening?" No one is around to hear my loud thoughts. Perhaps Connor was right, that I can't do this alone. If I'm going to get to the bottom of this, I'll need more eyes and hands to keep Connor and Riley safe while I'm looking into the rediscovery of the game. There's only one way to keep my company from falling under some virtual takeover and keep Dominic's name intact; I need to get the band back together.

Chapter 10

The plan is set for us to break off into teams of two; one Crownshield to go with myself, Doxo, and Veyanna to investigate specific tremor sites. Each Crownshield is given a horn to blow if any trouble is suspected. We make a check for our materials and supplies before we separate from the tavern we convened in, except for Brenn who is going back on his detail to escort civilians out of the city. Doxo and his charge set off to the shanty side of Spearhead, Veyanna and hers are sent to the south gates, and me and the last Crownshield are going towards the town square. The walk is eerie because of the emptiness of what was once such a largely populated city and the disappearing sounds of panic. What makes this more intense is that there's hardly the bustling wildlife or sounds of beautiful nature that was in Albistair. Here, it's bleak and dismal. Not a whole lot of anything. But it also reminds me of the ominous dangers in the air of Albistair, just a little bit more.

"Not much for conversation, are we?" The Crownshield continues looking forward while holding up his torch in his left hand while his right hand rested on the hilt of his blade.

"Huh? Oh, sorry. It's a bit… unnerving around here. Not what I expected it to be like," I admit as I shuffle my little legs to keep up.

"You must have not seen what they did to your people's homeland in Spritewood." He sounded genuinely worried about continuing.

I look up concerned. Obviously, he can't know I'm not really a luthien, but it's still shocking.

"The news spread quickly from Kerogema to all Preydor. The Primeval Maze set loose a swarm of giant flying insects we call xyphelidae. Monstrous wingspan, spanning nearly six feet in length. Carnivorous beasts with venom stingers to immobilize their prey. The beautiful people of Spritewood were not ready for the sudden appearance of the beasts before they were all decimated. It is because of this we Crownshields hope to eliminate the threat to our people, whatever it takes."

That is terrifying. A whole civilization of pucks like me was destroyed by these monsters. "So… you're human. You don't hate or dislike others that are not?"

He genuinely looks confused, "What reason would I have to harbor hatred for non-humans? Everyone has their part to play in the world to prosper and thrive. Whether they are of the earth, water, air, or of mixed blood, we all are part of the same cycle."

That is surprisingly insightful for a program like him. It's also a bit endearing to know that they don't have much prejudice or hatred towards non-humans. But again, why give me another non-human race? Something Lorena said two years ago starts to ring in my ears, *"Everyone wants to escape reality."* So maybe she had a hand in this one too? How many projects did she get involved with that forces people to be stuck in the game?

A small rumble from beneath my feet shakes me out of my trance of thought. The Crownshield and I both look around to find the source of the rumbling, him unsheathing his blade and me taking out my hunting knife. If that Maze opens now, there's no telling what it's gonna spit out at us. The guard looks down at me, "Take my horn, boy. My hands are full."

I nod and grab the intricate horn from his belt and hold onto it, looking around us as we press on. The rumbling isn't consistent, but it is in spurts as we get closer to the town square. From the street we are walking on, the view begins to open a bit revealing a great gazebo in the center of a crossroad path, intricately carved from wood and stone with intertwining vines and symbols I don't recognize. In the center of the platform under the gazebo's roof is a stone statue of a woman in a flowing dress, long curly hair down past the shoulders, her hands crossed over her midsection holding a hammer by its pommel while the head rests at her feet. The face is long and elegant with distinctive eyes that look piercing but comforting at the same time.

"Who is that," I ask.

He looks at the statue, then looks at me. "That is Reylith, the Graceful Judge. She's the patron goddess of Spearhead. One that is respected for her stories of judging the righteous and just from the cruel and sinister."

"Is she worshipped everywhere?" I inquire as I approach the statue.

I hear him click his tongue, "Not everywhere. Most practice of the gods is rare nowadays."

I never once thought of the gods that the people of Albistair worshipped aside from Olagog… or the Archon for that matter.

The rumbling beneath my feet returns. This time, more violently beneath me and the gazebo. The statue is teetering from the vibrations before I start hearing the cracking and crumbling of stone and wood.

"Get away from there!"

I turn around to run, but the floor of the gazebo gives out and pulls me down into a sinkhole. Thinking quickly, I stab my hunting knife into the ground as my little legs kick beneath me. I'm yelling and grunting as I try to keep hold of the knife while my other hand death-grips the horn. I look down into the sinkhole, a dark and earthy hole that looks more like a tunnel that goes at an incline. Through the clattering of wood and stone, I hear a faint fluttering sound deeper inside and what I can only describe as scratching iron nails. I feel a callused hand grip mine as the Crownshield hoists me up from the hole with a loud grunt. As I roll onto my side with heavy breathing, the fluttering and scratching only gets louder before another rumble comes from the mouth of the tunnel along with a black shiny plume of creatures flying out of it like a smoky volcano. The noise coming from this swarm sounds incredibly familiar, like shrill screeching of angry rodents. The plume ends as it begins to swoop and swerve through the air in unison and dive straight down. Straight towards me and the Crownshield.

"Run!" he yells at me before turning away from the oncoming swarm. I stumble back a bit before turning and running as fast as I can. I hear the screeching of the creatures gaining on me as I run. I remember that I have the horn in my hand, so I take a deep breath and blow into it, giving off a resounding call into the open air. The screeching gets more aggressive and louder just before I feel a sharp sting in my left arm, making me yelp out in pain. One black whisp darts past me before turning quickly and comes at me again. I take out my net from my satchel and hold it out in front of me just in time for this thing to slam straight into it. The first thing I focus on is its face; elongated with red eyes and a mouth full of needle-teeth with large, pointed ears. Some sort of bat with dark red and deep blue colors in its body. This thing's wings must be three feet long, leathery and veiny. What is worse is that the edges of its wings have serrated edges that are cutting through the netting. It pushes against the net, cutting through more strands, giving me less and less time to struggle. The creature shrieks out again, but this time in pain as the back of it starts to burn, causing it to retreat and fly up. The Crownshield is holding up his torch with a horrified look on his face.

"These are no normal bats," he utters. "They've never attacked like this before… something is wrong with them."

"Yeah, let's talk about that later when we're not being chased by sharp bats!" I run quickly trying to make it back to the tavern where we all separated. The Crownshield follows me quickly, even with the endless shrieks and flapping behind us both. *Now's a good time,* I tell myself as I put the horn to my lips and blow into it, letting the sonorous bellow yell into the open air. The street ahead starts coming to an end with two different directions to go. I have no idea how winding and confusing this part of Spearhead is, which alarms me when the Crownshield yells for us to split up to confuse them as he darts left, leaving me to run to the right. After splitting up, I turn behind me to see if the plan worked. To my absolute horror, the entire swarm of bats didn't follow me, but went directly after the Crownshield. Everything in my head is screaming for me to keep running and wait for the others to show up and help, but I ignore that voice and run off after him and the swarm of bats. I reach into my satchel and pull out my net as I run in hopes that I will be of some help. By the time I reach the corner where he and the swarm turned, my stomach is in knots as the swarm of bats has begun to circle and surround the Crownshield, who is slashing and swinging to cut them down. But there are just too many. I start hearing him scream and grunt in pain while splatters of blood and gore fly out of the swarm. I can hear constant slices and cuts coming from them like a garbage disposal, and I instantly vomit.

"Step back, luthien!"

I look over and see the reptilian form of Khelrah off to the left with a fused object in her hand that is lit. My eyes bulge out before I jump and roll out of the way as she chucks it into the swarm. The bats are focused on their victim that the explosion went without interruption. A plume of red and black bursts from the swarm, gaining dying screeches and cries from the beasts as about half of them are torn to shreds and the rest are struggling to fly away. I get back up on my feet and turn towards the aftermath, seeing the destroyed remains of both the bats and the Crownshield. His armor had various blade cuts and there were ribbons of his flesh all over. These things cut through their victims to eat the remains. Disgusting.

Khelrah slinks up to me with her tail sashaying behind her, "Khelrah is grateful it was able to make it to you in time. Are you well?"

My stomach is still clenching from spilling out, "Honestly... no. Not at all." I look up at her serpentine face, "But thank you. I'm lucky you got here in time."

She bows her head beneath her hood. "Khelrah has not seen bats look or act this way before. It is concerned they have been corrupted somehow."

Intrigued by her concern, I go to the scene of the explosion and try to look for one that is mostly intact. I find one that is missing a wing, so I pick it up by the one still attached. Khelrah joins me and kneels next to me, observing it and sniffing at it. "It is unnatural... twisted... repurposed."

Something in the back of my head starts to tingle. I stuff the net back into my satchel and pull out the logbook. I flip it open quickly to the next blank page and watch as it starts to scrawl out notes and sketches:

Razorwing bats; nocturnal predators native to the forests throughout all Preydor. Travel in swarms to hunt small and medium animals. Razor sharp barbs atop their wings act in defense and in hunting. Omnivorous in nature, scavenging for food when necessary. NOTE: This species of razorwing is unnatural. Magically converted into a carnivorous brood to hunt and kill. Weak against fire, light, and poisons. Advantages of sight, sound, and smell. Strongest when in a swarm.

I blink. "You're right… something converted these things to be monsters."

"The Primeval Maze," she replies. "It thinks the beasts flew into an open door and were twisted from their natural path."

"So… it doesn't just spit out twisted monsters… it swallows up and twists natural animals and creatures?"

She doesn't give any sign of confirmation as she looks at the bat in my hands, "No one knows what happens when one goes into the Maze, only that they do not come out. Perhaps they do… just not as they went in."

I set the bat down, trying hard not to look at the remains of the Crownshield and observe Khelrah. What is different about her at this moment is the belt of various round objects with fuses sitting atop each one. Some of them are simple black rough iron, but a few of them are dark rough colors of different styles such as cylindrical or boxed.

"You're… a Trapper?"

A small smile creeps on her reptilian face, "Takes one to know one. Khelrah is honored to work with a fellow Trapper."

"Half-Pint!"

We both whip around and see Doxo, Veyanna, Brenn, and one other Crownshield running up to us. They all have some bruises and cuts that become clearer as they come to a stop. Doxo kneels and asks, "You okay, boy?"

I nod, looking at him and the others. "I'm fine. What happened to you?"

"Ravenous bats," Veyanna answers shakily. "I have never seen them attack like that before."

Brenn looks at me and Khelrah, "Where is Orley?"

I look behind me to the pile of gore and bats before looking back at Brenn, "He... he drew the swarm away from me and got shredded... I'm sorry."

Brenn and the other Crownshield look to Orley's remains, approach it and kneel with their swords pointing into the ground. Small mutterings come from both that I can only assume is some kind of prayer or sendoff. I look back at Doxo, "They're called razorwing bats. Regular bats that got into the Maze somehow and came out all fucked up and twisted. Whatever is in there is not good and it doesn't play well with others going inside."

Doxo and Veyanna look at each other before looking back at me, the former with a smirk on his face and the latter with a furrow in her brow.

"...what is it?"

Veyanna speaks first with almost a whisper, "We... we found a door to the Maze..."

"And it is still open," Doxo chuckles through his gritted teeth. "Let us hunt some fucking monsters."

Chapter 11

After Brenn and his other Crownshield finish their prayer, Khelrah and I follow them all back in the direction that they came from. My eyes keep darting into the air expecting more of the razorwings to sneak up and divebomb us.

"Worry not, Bimbik," Veyanna whispers to me with a hand on my shoulder. "We will all be vigilant of the creatures. Hopefully there are fewer than before. Are you well?"

I sigh deeply, not bothering to look up at her. "I... I feel bad. Orley was a good guy, didn't prejudice against anyone or anything. He didn't deserve to die like that."

I hear her click her tongue, "I understand. Many good people have lost their lives to this unnatural thing. That is why I am going to join you and Doxo in the Maze." I gawk up at her in disbelief, but she continues before I can protest. "I believe my real purpose is not just to observe and study the natural order, but to help bring it back to balance. I believe that my skills and knowledge will help in trying to stop this horrendous evil."

"Veyanna... it's going to be dangerous. You shouldn't have to put yourself at risk in an unknown place like the Maze," I try to convince her.

"As sweet as the sentiment is, Bimbik, I am a woman of purpose and mind. I will go as I so wish, and I wish to accompany you and the brute into the unknown. And that is how it shall be," she says with sternness in her voice before walking ahead of me. Her resilience is nothing to scoff at.

Walking ahead, I start hearing some familiar strumming of strings along with a gruff voice coming in the direction we are going. Curving around a building, I see two things that leave me speechless. One, the dwarf-like bard from the tavern we convened at is currently strumming his lyre and singing in some language I can't understand while I lean up against the second thing. There are two raised pillars of stone and earth with a pitch-black interior to it. It has pulled roots sticking out of it from where it sprang up from the earth, and plumes of glowing purple smoke pouring out of it from the floor. There are some eerie sounds coming from the mouth of the door that seem to meld with the dwarf's strumming and singing.

Brenn pulls out his sword and points it in the dwarf's direction, "State your business, dwarrow."

The bearded redhead man smiles as he stops strumming and bows slightly, "Greetings! I am Torbhin Cobblestone, practitioner of the minstrel arts and adventurer novice. I bring good tidings to you all that I would like to accompany you inside of this labyrinth of darkness and dismay!"

I think he's waiting for some kind of applause or other positive response because his arms are out in a magician's "ta-da" pose with a huge smile under his red beard. Brenn tilts his head to the side a bit, Doxo is suppressing a laugh, Veyanna is dumbfounded, and Khelrah is simply just looking at him.

"Dwarrow, you are an unknown and but a minstrel," Doxo says through laughter. "You do not belong in a place such as this. Besides, I am already splitting my glory with these two." Veyanna and I both look at him with a stink eye.

Torbhin chuckles lightly and rests his lyre next to him, "You see where this hellish orifice leads into? Deep below the earth, and gods only know how far down it leads. We dwarrow are people of the stone and iron. Something tells me that my keen senses of the soil will aid in navigation through the labyrinth." He picks his lyre back up and spins it to its backside. Where the face of the instrument was decorated and presentable, the backside has a hard shell of metal studs with a leather wrap on the neck. "As you can see, I am also well prepared for any sort of confrontation that we may meet within it."

Well, I don't plan to look a gift horse in the mouth. "Well, are you sure you wanna do this? It could be a one-way trip…" Not the kind of thought I want to have in this moment, but these guys are throwing themselves at something that is completely unknown and most likely corrupts anything that goes inside of it.

The dwarrow just chuckles and puts his free hand into a fist on his hip, "Adventure is always a one-way trip, my friend! Once you start, you never stop."

We all look to each other to see if anyone else is going to try and talk this guy down from his volunteering. No one objects to it and Veyanna is the one to offer a kind gesture, "Welcome, then, Torbhin. We greatly appreciate your aid in this venture."

"Khelrah is coming as well," the serpentine exerine declares to us all. We whip around at her, unable to read anything on her face. "It is well versed in trapping and tools. It will aid in the attempt to silence this illness."

Brenn is now staring at all of us in bewilderment. "In all my years of service, I have not ever seen such evil... such destruction caused by a single source. Preydor will not know of the ones who are willingly sacrificing themselves to aid in its survival."

"With all due respect, Brenn," I start, "where I came from, the entire land was screwed up, and so were its people, thanks to a single source of power. The ones that stopped it... they didn't seek to be remembered. Just to stop the taint of evil and free the people. I think every one of us here wants to do the same thing. Whatever is causing this to happen, we'll do what we can to stop it."

The Shieldmaster's face goes from unsure and stone-like to one of curiosity and concern. Before he can say anything more, the ground begins to rumble around us. We try to keep ourselves steady as the quaking gets more and more violent. My eyes dart forward and notice that the door to the Primeval Maze is starting to close downward into the ground.

"It's closing! It's now or never!" I yell.

Doxo cackles and immediately runs into the closing door. Torbhin smiles big and shuffles inside, soon followed by Veyanna before it gets too low for her to enter. The door gets lower and lower, but it doesn't stop Khelrah from getting on all fours and slinking into the door like a lizard evading a predator. Taking a deep breath, I say to myself, "I'm coming, Riley." I run as hard as I can and baseball slide into the door as it slams down behind me, causing me to yelp out as I run straight into someone's back. It is pitch-black inside and I had no way of seeing anything.

"Ow! Watch it!" Veyanna's voice reacted to my slamming into her.

"Sorry!" I get up, aching in pain and try to look around. Absolute darkness.

I hear Doxo's booming voice, "Anyone dead? Who has a bloody torch?"

A sound like the striking of a match echoes around us as a small flame creates a slightly bigger one, illuminating Torbhin's face with a big smile under his beard. "Happy I have accompanied you now?"

A groan comes from a very dusty Doxo, followed by groans from Veyanna and Khelrah as they get to their feet. With the small amount of torchlight, I can see the walls around us, the ground beneath us, and the ceiling above us. All of it is dank, dark, and musky. The ground is disheveled dirt and stone that offered no sort of comfort when we all landed. The walls are dark brown and gray of roots and stone, sickly, aged, jagged, and reaching. As if they're trying to extend out and grapple us.

"This place," Khelrah half whispered to us, "is evil… reeks of death."

Doxo lurches forward and hoists his axe onto his shoulder. "Welcome, friends, to the Primeval Maze."

Chapter 12

Sweat is dripping off me as I'm staring down at my opponent. I'm assessing his strategy to try and take me down; ninety-degree squat, both hands propped up, eyes darting to my legs. He's looking to take me down by going for my legs. *Heh, try it amateur.* I give him a gentle gesture to come at me, earning some awe and chuckles from the rest of the class. He grunts as he charges forward, angling downward towards my legs. His eyes dip down. Bad mistake. I slide my lead leg behind my body, allowing him to aim for my other leg. I push him down by the neck, hoist my lead leg around his waist and pull him back onto the mat. I maneuver my arms under his and put him in a full nelson, wrapping my legs around his waist to lock him down. I feel him trying to wriggle out of my grip, but I apply pressure by pulling his arms back. The class is clamoring either for him to get out of the hold or for him to tap out. We're both grunting as we struggle on the floor trying to gain control or keep it. He lets out a huge breath and reaches onto the mat, tapping it three times. I smirk as I gently release him, rolling onto my front and pulling myself up to my feet before offering a hand down to him. With a snarl, he grabs onto my hand for me to lift himself up.

"When facing an opponent head on, don't drop your eyes to your target. Makes it too obvious and you look like a jackass," I instruct, earning some laughs. "Lock eyes the whole way and make them guess."

Everyone starts nodding and agreeing with the instruction. The bells for the door ring with Matt Bauer walking into the studio. His face looks grim, and my heart is now dropping. "Practice your movements and be ready for full-contact next week. Class dismissed." I look at Matt and gesture for him to come to the back while my students are packing up and chatting with each other. I take note that he's not in his usual business suit like the uppity tight ass that he normally is. He's wearing street clothes with a hoodie and glasses like he's hiding from someone. All I can think is that something is wrong with Connor. If he's done anything stupid, I'm gonna kill him.

I take him into the office in the back before closing the door, "What's going on? Is Connor okay?"

"Easy, killer," he comments. "I had no idea you were getting paid to kick people's asses."

"Mixing Muay Thai with Jiu-Jitsu is a good way for me to feel in control after all that shit happened," I explain. "You're not here for small talk. What's happening?"

Matt takes a seat and pulls off his shades, replacing them with his prescription glasses. "Shit has gone south so fast, Kris. The board at SnoWire is trying to reinitiate *The Mortal Gate* for mass production."

I can feel my heart jump into my throat. Images and flashbacks start coming at me like a storm of fear, anger, and trauma. The spiders, terrorghasts, mistwraiths, and that goddamn arena I was thrown into. We had come so close to death so many times in that place and now these psychos are wanting to bring it back. Absolutely not.

"You can't let them do that! You're the CEO now, so tell them no!"

"I've stalled them, but that's all I can do now. Since it was the last thing created by Dominic, the shareholders believe it's the best step to upsell their products," he says through his teeth. "I don't know how they found a copy of the game after I oversaw its decommissioning, but it's in the works. I'm torn between my job, keeping those vultures away from that production, and overseeing Connor and Riley's vitals while they're in *The Primeval Maze*. That's why I'm here."

I tilt my head to the side.

"I need you to help me by coming to the company building. I need to find Dominic and Lorena's materials to find anything on the games while you watch over Connor and Riley."

I'm starting to panic. Connor promised me things would be okay and that he would be safe. But shit just hit the fan and now I need to get involved. "You think we will be enough to stop this? God knows who all has their fingers in this plan."

Riley sighs and pulls out his phone, showing me a text chain with Mark and Danica. "I'm rallying everyone back together. Like it or not, we need all hands-on deck."

My back straightens and my jaw clenches. *Mark and Danica... in the same room again...* I remember how rough the breakup was for those two. It was a few months after the game ended and we got our "royalties" bonus from Matt. They had tried to move past it all after we finished the semester at college. In those months, they couldn't stop fighting. They stopped checking in and hanging out with us until they officially ended it. *I hate to think they can stand to be in the same room in a situation like this.*

"Matt… are you sure about this?"

He stood back up and let out a loud sigh, "There's nothing else we can do but try and stop this on the outside while Connor handles it on the inside. So far, he's remained stable and secure, but needs to have supervision while I try to investigate further."

With that cheery note and idea, I grab my bag and items. *Time to save my boyfriend again.*

~~~~~~

Into the proverbial hornet's nest, Matt drives me to the SnoWire HQ. I remember when Connor started his first day here and how excited he was. He got to work in the industry he loved so much, despite the horror we all lived through, and had the opportunity to use his experiences to create fun games and be paid for it. He would come home every day and talk about the struggles of producing and programming, but it never kept him down. He smiled the entire time he unloaded, and I could see the math hovering in his eyes. He loved what he did, and I loved his passion for it. It was nerdy, annoying, and a lot to digest, but I always found it adorable and hilarious for some reason. Two years of us keeping each other afloat, encouraging each other to seek out therapy and passions to get us out of the nightmares we kept having. Years before I met these nerds, I was simply by myself. My parents dumped me off at some foster system when I was barely able to walk, and I grew up in a constantly moving system of foster homes, public and homeschooling, shitty treatment to sort-of-okay treatment, until I finally stuck out with a family, the Montez's. Amelia and Juan were nice enough to take me in when I was sixteen, the age that most foster kids typically don't even get considered for adoption or fostering. Something about teenage angst and attitude, or some such bullshit. I expected them to throw me out at some point, so my attitude only adjusted to the world they tried to lay out for me. I drank, I smoked, I went to parties, even got arrested a couple of times for some fun times. They hated it but kept me around and kept me in school until I graduated. By the time I was eighteen, I expected to be booted out of the Montez home. Come to find out, they enrolled me into the University of Utah and told me verbatim, "Make something of yourself. It's your turn to take care of you." I haven't heard from them since then. I made a few friends and connections to have places to work and stay, all the way up to the moment I first helped a geeky guy get a soda out of the vending machine.

I step off my train of thought as Matt drives us behind the main building to a shady-looking side building where we are the only car parked. He leads me inside, past a disinterested security guard, and down a series of halls before he opens a door into a lab-looking space. To my knowledge, all of it looks like science-y stuff that I have no idea about and I have no reason to ask questions. Inside this space, I hear monitors beeping, directing my attention to peer through a two-way window where both Riley and Connor are laid out and plugged into that fucking game.

"Is he okay?" I ask as we step inside. I quickly walk over to Connor's side, checking his face for any signs of trouble. I hold his face gently, feeling the warmth of his skin and the slight poking of his stubble.

Matt shuffles over to the computers and makes a few clicks before answering, "Yeah. His vitals are holding steady. There was a spike in REM activity and heart rate earlier while I was getting you, but no lasting damages as I can see."

I take his lifeless hand into mine and brush some hair away from his eyes. "Can we see what he's doing in there? If he's okay?"

"No," he sighs, "there's no screen like other games. *TMG* was purely sensory-visual, and it seems this one is the exact same design."

"So… Dominic designed this one too?"

"That's what I'm going to find out while you watch over these two. Hopefully," he quickly checks his phone, "Danica and Mark will show up and help too."

I clench my jaw, thinking of those two getting back in the same room together around Connor and Riley while they're zoned out in fantasyland. "I still think it's a bad idea."

"I'm inclined to agree with you, Kris, but right now we need all the help we can get to figure this out."

He's right. If we were all back on the same side just to figure this out and stop the game from going viral, we'd have to get over our issues and work. "What's the plan?"

Matt is typing away at one of the computers that has a thumb drive plugged into it. He keeps typing until he clicks his mouse, waits, then pulls out the drive from the computer. "I'm going to investigate Dominic's and Lorena's belongings to see what I can find on either *The Mortal Gate* or *The Primeval Maze*. If they kept any files or hidden drives that have the information, I'll need it to try and piece together a plan against the board. While I'm doing that, you and the others need to maintain contact with me if anything abnormal happens with Tweedle-Dee and Tweedle-Dumbass here. If there's a drop in vital tracking, abnormal brainwave spikes, or equipment malfunctions, call me immediately." He grabs a shoulder bag from under his desk and pulls out three flip phones onto the table. "These are burners that have all our numbers, just to keep any prying ears from screwing with us. I'll try to be back this evening, hopefully with something good."

With that said, he rushes past me in a hurried walk. He opens the door for himself but pauses and looks back at me. "Whatever is happening, we need to stop it. Dominic and Lorena died from this system, and many more will if it goes public. We need to work together on this. Everything else is secondary. Okay?"

My heart sinks a bit, thinking of what could happen if the game is revived and sent out for millions of people to be stuck in. This is some next level evil shit, and it needs to stop. I give him a firm nod, prompting him to leave quickly out of sight. I walk back over between Connor and Riley, silently listening to the eerie beeping of their heart rate monitors.

Chapter 13

~~~~~~ Connor~~~~~

The damp, dark atmosphere of the Maze is unsettling. Even with the small amount of firelight coming from our torches, it's as if the shadows around are swallowing any possible vision ahead of or behind us. I take a closer look at the walls of the maze, feeling my hands along the rigid earth and stone that make up the corridors we're in. It feels cool to the touch with a slight humming through my fingertips as I graze the surface.

"Careful, Bimbik," Veyanna cautions me from behind. "This place is not accommodating to us. It is meant for the beasts that dwell within."

I nod a little as I take my hand away from the wall, the coldness subsiding. "So where do we go from here?"

Torbhin's charismatic self just smiles under his torchlight, "We go forward! Into the winding corridors of this enchanted puzzle and end this unholy blight!" He puts his torch down, picks up his club-like lute strapped to his back and begins strumming small tunes.

Doxo growls at him, "Are you trying to bring all the beasts of this place to our location, you halfwit?!"

"Shh," Torbhin requests. Even in the dim light, I swear I can see a vein popping out from Doxo's head. The dwarrow keeps strumming small tunes until I swear that I see actual waves of sound in the form of silvery arches coming from his weaponized instrument. "We of the dwarrow have certain affinities for the earth we were Forged from. I just simply use a different method." The silver waves of sound are sent straight ahead of us until they bounce off the far wall and rebound to the right and then disappear. "There is our direction forward! Come, Doxo! Lead the way."

Much to his own annoyance, Doxo takes his torch in his left hand, gripping his axe in his right, and presses forward, followed closely by Torbhin. Veyanna follows them with Khelrah next in line, leaving me in the rear. From this angle, I can sort of see Veyanna writing into a notebook she has, probably noting the environment for her studies. This gives me the idea to look into my own Logbook, thinking that I might have some level-up potion or progress bar like in *TMG*. I flip through the pages back and forth and don't see any kind of experience tracker or stat sheets. On the second page that follows the specifics of my character's race, name, and class abilities, there's a description of the game's objective that scares the holy Hell out of me: *Prepare yourself, adventurer, for an experience unlike any other! The tools you gain from the moment the game begins are your only source of protection and discovery. Your goal in this adventure; survive at all costs to discover the dark mysteries of the Primeval Maze. Make use of the environment as much as you can. Craft or scavenge for materials to aid in your quest. Use your wits and skills to overcome fearsome beasts and mind-twisting puzzles in order to reach the center of the Maze and unravel its secrets.*

This isn't some high fantasy adventure RPG. It's a fucking survival game. No leveling, no gear drops, no social reputations to build. Just survive at all costs. *This just got more fucked up than before!*

I almost run straight into the earthen wall until a tail wraps around my arm and pulls me to the right with everyone else. "Khelrah thinks you should watch where you are walking in a place like this."

I take a sharp breath, feeling the scaly skin of her tail brush mine as she lets me go. "Sorry, got distracted."

"It thinks you have something heavy on your mind. Is it wrong?" She looks at me inquisitively.

I sigh heavily, "It's nothing… I think it's just this place. Gives me the creeps."

Khelrah chuckles under her breath, "You are not used to the underground."

"And you are?"

She shrugs at me, "The exerine are a people that build dens in the ground near rivers and swamps. They work above and below the ground, hunting and gathering resources to aid in expansion and discovery. Khelrah learned long ago the plagues that haunt below the surface. The fear, isolation, and emptiness."

I feel cool shivers going down my spine from her tale. It could probably explain how she's so calm and collected being in a place that vomits monsters. "Is that why you became a Trapper?"

She nods, "It learned how to use its surroundings to fend off beasts and dangers that would do it or others harm. Khelrah learned to age faster than most. Taking care of itself above all else."

Torbhin's lute continues playing softly, helping to direct us in the direction his magic tunes seem to help us in. The further we walk down this stretch of corridor; the more things seem to change. The ground is constantly shifting from soft to hard, the atmosphere is swirling with cool air that keeps my hair standing on edge, it smells rank with a little coppery scent mixed with mugginess. What seems to be the strangest thing is that the roof of the maze seems to be getting higher, and the walls seem to be opening wider before us. At the far end of this corridor, it splits into two diagonal directions with no clear indication which direction is the right one. Mazes are such a pain.

"Which way?" Veyanna asks while we all stand looking in both directions ahead of us.

Torbhin strums his instrument again and we watch the silvery wave split in two, one wave going down each tunnel. We wait patiently as Torbhin receives the waves back. He turns to us and says, "The one on the left continues down a straight path. The one on the right angles off a little further. Nothing else can be gleaned."

"I vote for the straight and narrow path," Doxo proclaims. "Often the easiest and truest path."

"And often the one leading straight into danger," Veyanna counters. "These places are like a puzzle. The most complex answer often gets better results. I say the path on the right."

The two of them bicker so much it's almost adorable. Reminds me of Mark and Danica before their split. It was their love language, tearing into each other just to get a rise out of each other. *These two have got to be hot for each other.* Khelrah looks down both paths, her nostrils flare a bit like she's smelling something. She moves in front of Doxo and Veyanna and kneels to the ground, running her fingers along the ground and scanning the surroundings. "Khelrah agrees that the right pathway is the correct way. The ground is stirred with recent movement, suggesting that something moved from there recently."

"You want us to go *towards* the creepy monsters?" I ask dumbfounded.

Khelrah looks back at me, "The monsters come from a place deep within this labyrinth. We follow the trails of the creatures; we find the source. Simple tracking."

"More monsters mean more fun for us," Doxo says through a grin as he tightens his grip on his great axe.

"And further dangers," Veyanna half whispers putting a hand on the whip at her side.

These guys all have useful weapons and tools while I only have a friggin net. I start flipping through my Logbook for anything useful. I find a section of blank pages in it start to fill itself out, titling the section "Trapper's Tools". It goes into detail about Trappers being able to improvise environmental hazards and resources to construct various traps and tools to gain advantage and control the battlefield. As it's a survival RPG, it makes sense that players would need to improvise tools and weapons in the world to survive. One stands out to me and prompts me to look around at the roots, vines, and stones along the walls and ground. I pull at the roots in the walls and break them into small pieces, smelling a strange odor.

"Khelrah, come here."

She takes a knee next to me, "Yes?"

I hold up the roots, "Can you smell this? What is it?"

Her nostrils flare a couple of times. "Sliaire. Parasitic roots that fester with fungal poisons. Interesting that they are growing this deep into the ground. They shouldn't be able to thrive."

"This place seems to attract death and decay," I guess. I take the roots and rummage for a small cloth pouch, put them in it and some kindling before tying the top of it firmly. "The burning of the roots can create a noxious smoke screen."

"Clever," she comments.

I'm surprised I knew that immediately. *Maybe it's like a survival RPG. While TMG is a basic RPG action game with stat mechanics, The Primeval Maze is a survival and crafting game.*

"Oi! You coming?" Torbhin calls out to us from ahead. He and the others are waiting as Khelrah and I jog up ahead. As the corridors open wider, the darkness ahead gets deeper, even with our torches. I glance at Doxo's torch and notice something dark and smokey. Not smoke rising from the torch, but almost wrapping around the flame like dark tendrils. The same is happening with Veyanna's torch, swirling into a slight dimming of the light.

"Uh… guys?"

The torchlight goes out immediately. Complete darkness surrounds us. At first, I am in complete panic, but then get sorely confused because I swear I can make out shapes in this darkness. I can make out tall hulking frame of Doxo a few feet ahead of me with his great axe at the ready. The slightly shorter frame of Veyanna gripping her torch to herself tightly. Khelrah's slender frame is crouched in a wrestling stance with two bulbs in her hands I can't quite make out. Torbhin's short and stocky frame is holding his lute upside down with the club-side facing out. *Is this what Darkvision is like?*

"Keep your wits about you," Doxo growls under his breath. "There's dark magic at play here."

The sound of feet shuffling in the loose soil on the ground and the raspy breathing of a few of us adds to the intensity of the moment. A low grumbling and gurgling sound join in the ensemble.

"Dwarrow, silence your stomach!" Doxo barks.

"That is not me, good sir," Torbhin responds in the dark.

"That's not a good sign," I mumble to myself.

I hear a fearful shuddering sound come from Veyanna's direction. "There… there is a beast among us…"

On cue, the low grumbling morphs into multiple snarls, barks, and howls. Aggressive steps echo around us that sound heavy and close. My attention gets pulled to my right, trying to make out shapes in the dark. Ahead to the right is this large swirling shapeless plume of smokey tendrils, emanating upward like a flame. In the middle of this plume are a set of crimson, menacing eyes. Another set of eyes meets me to my left. And another. All three sets of crimson eyes start to close in on us.

"Incoming!"

In one swift motion, six sets of glowing red eyes set upon us all with loud, aggressive snarls. I get knocked backwards into one of the others standing behind me while nursing a large gash on my arm. All of us land in a dogpile from the onslaught of our unseen enemies. Gasps and curses of pain echo out in the chamber we're in as the snarling, red-eyed smoke figures disappear into the darkness.

"What are they?" Torbhin calls out.

"They're fast and have sharp claws, that's all I know!" I reply from the ground.

"It is too damn dark in here!" Veyanna yells in agony.

I hear some glass rustling against skin and nails before Khelrah yells at us, "Shield your eyes!"

I bury my face in my arm on command as a loud sound of shattering glass erupts into a bright flash of light. The dark smoke plumes let out a chorus of yelps, piquing my curiosity. I peek out of my arm and see a pack of large wolf-like beasts covered in pitch black fur with plumes of shadowy smoke rolling off them. Their paws have large dagger-sized claws, a few of them coated in blood they drew from us. The light begins to dim, and the shadowy smoke begins to cover them again.

"They're weak against light! We need light!"

"That was its only phosphorous bomb!" Khelrah shouts.

Like a mighty lion, Doxo gets on his feet, roars loudly and charges one of the beasts. It is quick because with the first swing of his axe, the beast darts to the side and then pounces. Doxo, to his credit, quickly holds up the haft of his axe for the beast to bite down on. With the two of them locked in a match of strength, Torbhin takes this chance to stand up, rush over and bat at the beast with the metal backside of his lute. It connects with its head, getting another yelp from it as it rolls over onto the ground dazed. Doxo rushes over and lays a mighty downward swing onto the creature, severing its head. Torbhin lets out an approving yell but is quickly overtaken by two of the pack animals, taking him down to the ground.

"Torbhin!" I get my net out of my bag and toss it in their direction. The light has dimmed out and the net falls completely to the ground as if it passes straight through them. Torbhin is yelling out in pain as the sound of rips and tears echo in the chamber.

The darkness has returned and overtaken us. My night vision is only showing large plumes piled on top of Torbhin. A loud cracking *snap* sounds off in the chamber, drawing the creatures' attention towards Veyanna's shape in the dark. A long whip is in her hand as her back is against one of the walls. "I need light! I need to see at least one of them!"

Torbhin's pained noises are the loudest sounds in the chamber, next to the snarling and growling from the creatures. I shuffle my hand around in my satchel trying to find anything useful before I pull out a small piece of flint and steel wool. "Veyanna! Throw me your torch! Follow my voice!" Her silhouette hoists up the doused torch and chucks it in my direction, landing a few feet away from me. I can hear Doxo hastily swinging his axe trying to help Torbhin. I kneel at the torch and start striking to try and get a flame. I hear some of the other beasts' snarl in my direction as if they know what I'm trying to do. I strike faster to try and get a flame until it finally catches. The moment I hoist up the flame, a canine maw is staring me in the face. The torch has pushed back the shroud of smoke and shadows, revealing a gnarled wolf-like face with large canine fangs that look like they can rip me open with one bite. It opens its giant maw before another *snap* echoes in the chamber, forcing the beast to slowly shut its mouth. I look past the beast and see Veyanna holding her whip, which is lightly glowing with some sort of greenish hue, and so are her eyes. She lifts it up and cracks the whip at the beast again, causing it to sit then lay down.

"Help Torbhin! I have this one!" She orders. I nod and rush over to Doxo and Torbhin. The light has illuminated a small part of the chamber, and I see the dwarrow being mauled on the ground by two of those things. With the light directed at them, the same smoking darkness moves away from them, giving the gnolid a clear line of sight as he swings his axe, tossing one of them off of Torbhin and causing the other to recoil and retreat in the dark. I stand over Torbhin, bloodied but breathing, and pull out my hunting knife. "Doxo! They're weak against light! Draw them in!"

"Aye!" He takes his axe head and draws a circle around me and Torbhin. "Do not leave this circle!"

I give him a firm nod and stay ready with my knife. The torchlight is barely enough to light up the chamber in a five-foot radius, which means the beasts will have to get dangerously close for us to hurt or draw away. I scan the lit-up area to try and find Khelrah or Veyanna. More snarling and growling echoes in the chamber joined with Doxo's heavy breathing before one comes into view of the light. I swipe with my hunting knife and miss completely, my elbow disappearing into its jaws. I yell out as a splatter of deep crimson blood smacks the side of my face. Doxo's axe head is buried in the ground beneath the headless corpse of the creature, the head still clamped around my elbow. He rips the jaw open to free my arm, leaving deep incisions from its fangs. Before any banter between us can be had, his eyes dart behind me, prompting me to turn around. One of the beasts is charging directly at us before a rope wraps around its neck. Khelrah is behind the beast holding it back with all her strength. From beneath me, the injured Torbhin kneels on the ground, raises his lute over his head and brings it down on the beast's head with a loud crunch and a yelp. *That's three and one stunned.* When Khelrah releases the lasso she used, her body lurches forward after being pounced on by one of the other beasts. It manages to sink its jaws into her shoulder, causing her to yell out in pain. I run, leaving the circle, and swing the torch into the beast's head. It is stunned and rolls off Khelrah's back, giving her an opportunity to stand up and lunge, sinking two small daggers into its ribs. She stands up and gives me a grateful nod. We return to the circle with Torbhin and Doxo, knowing that two beasts are left.

"Veyanna?!" I move the torch around to try and see her. The snarls and growls are down to a hush. Two of them are attempting to circle, making me scared that Veyanna fell. A set of crimson eyes enveloped in shadowy smoke stares at the four of us bleeding and exhausted. Torbhin has fallen back down on the ground, Khelrah is on one knee nursing her shoulder, and Doxo looks like he's about to pass out. My good arm is stinging from being bitten, resulting in my knife hand being almost useless and my free one holding up the torch. The beast stalks forward, the shadows swirling around it menacingly, as its canine face barely reaches into view of the torch light. It is suddenly thrust into the nearby wall by the last creature, ripping and tearing into its fellow beast. The two of them wrestle, bite, and scratch at each other in a furious fight. I tilt my head to the side confused before Veyanna's hand rests on my shoulder with her free hand. Instead of the glowing green eyes, they are now pale yellow and focused on the fighting monsters. It lasts a couple more minutes before the sounds of fighting end. A set of paw prints start stalking towards us, accompanied by a low growling sound and set of pale-yellow eyes.

"Down," Veyanna commands. The beast slowly starts to lower to the ground into a laying-down position.

Through labored breaths, I ask her one simple question: "How?"

"My training is to understand and influence the behavior of beasts," she explains while holding up her whip. "The magic infused in this allows me to have limited control over simple creatures. These ones are not exactly simple, but when it was separated from the rest, it seemed to be easier to influence."

So as a Handler in this game, players can act as animal tamers to control or command them depending on their level or difficulty.

Kind of how Mark operated as a Totemist in TMG, I think to myself. "Well, that's impressive."

She smiles and nods with approval before Torbhin groans out loudly from the ground. She and I look over to see him in a bloody mess with Khelrah observing and assessing his injuries. He is absolutely mauled from the attack.

"Torbhin, hang in there," I urge him as I shuffle around in my satchel. *No healing potions? This game is a suicide run!*

"We need medicinal ingredients," Doxo commanded. "Search the chamber!"

Everyone splits up after lighting up two extra torches, leaving one of them near Torbhin. My first instinct is to go to one of the downed beasts and pull out my logbook, shuffling through the pages to find information on them. The pages that follow the razorwing bat descriptions begins to fill out:

Smokehound.

Carnivorous, corrupted canine creatures. A pack of infernal creatures that embody darkness and menace. These demonic hounds lurk within an ethereal shroud of jet-black smoke, their forms concealed in an ominous veil. With glowing crimson eyes burning through the darkness, they roam the realms, spreading fear and chaos wherever they tread.

I'm reading over the description and shudder at it. The sketches of how these things look in and out of their shrouds look like demonic coyotes that are larger and smarter. Something further is being inscribed on the page below the sketches:

Crafting Materials:

- *Fur: Using the elusive Smokehound fur, skilled artisans can create a cloak that grants its wearer the ability to blend seamlessly with shadows. When worn, the cloak provides enhanced stealth, allowing the wearer to move undetected through darkness.*
- *Teeth: Smokehound teeth, known for their sharpness and durability, can be fashioned into deadly daggers. These weapons can have a serrated edge, making them particularly effective for tearing through armor or causing grievous wounds.*
- *Claws: By utilizing Smokehound claws, master bowyers can craft a quiver that enhances the potency of arrows fired at night or in shadowy environments. The quiver empowers the arrows with a touch of darkness, making them more accurate and lethal.*
- *Essence: Engineers and inventors can utilize the smoky essence of the Smokehounds to create smokescreen devices. These gadgets can disperse thick smoke, obscuring vision and allowing for strategic escapes or ambushes.*

"Crafting possibilities," I mutter to myself. This is very different from what I'm used to and makes it much more survival-based rather than adventure-based. Crafting materials from downed enemies and surrounding environments to adapt and survive. I reach for my hunting knife and look at the beheaded body of the smokehound in front of me, slightly gagging thinking of what I'm about to do. I carefully attempt to carve the body of its hide starting at its midsection. The smell of death immediately hits me and I wretch out loud. As I'm trying to keep down my virtual lunch, something else occurs to me as I'm cutting; the monsters don't dissolve away after being defeated like in the last one. Maybe this game encourages survival and crafting by leaving the resources available. I hear the others muttering behind me as I continue to harvest what I can from this monster.

I remove the pelt from the carcass before it starts to shimmer dimly, suddenly taking the form of a black fur cloak. I call out, "Khelrah! Come here!"

She jogs over to my side, noticing the corpse before the cloak that I'm holding. I motion for her to take it, "You seem stealthy and quick enough to get some use out of this."

Inquisitively, she takes off her white cloak revealing her full figure of a walking snake with slender arms and legs. Her dark scales decorate all the way back down her head and neck. She takes the cloak and flings it around her shoulders, attaching it by way of a cord across her neck, and flourishes it about to test it out.

"It thanks you, Bimbik, for this gift," she says softly.

I smile and nod before returning to the corpse. I overhear Veyanna and Doxo arguing over their shared collection of herbal components to try and help Torbhin stay stable. I go back to work on the remaining items I think I can take for materials, managing to remove the largest of its teeth cleanly as opposed to the smaller ones being splintered, as well as extracting at least three of its claws keeping them whole. I place them into my satchel and rejoin the others near Torbhin. The once jolly bard with a club is bleeding out of his nose, mouth, and the gashes where he was attacked. Doxo had found some roots and soil to put together a makeshift salve that is mixed with some small bits of herbs that she pulls from a pouch on her belt. They take handfuls of the combined elements and begin rubbing it into his wounds. He hisses air through his teeth as they apply the salve. I take the chance to look at the materials I took off the smokehound and try to think of what to do with them. Looking back at the description of their capabilities, I snatch Veyanna's whip while she's busy and unfurl it, taking the end of it and unthread it. Using the beast's claws, I thread them to the tip of the whip and give her a combative advantage for the future. The teeth I pulled have the makings of daggers if I take some leather to wrap around the base, which any of us can use, but I decide to holster them for later.

"Easy, Torbhin," Doxo says in a gentle voice I've never heard before as he holds him down against the pain. Once they're finished applying the mixture, Doxo and Veyanna rest his back up against the rocky wall for him to rest. Everyone then takes the chance to take a knee, lean against the same surface, or lay flat out on the ground. I think this is the most exhausting that I've felt since being in Albistair. My aching body takes me down to the ground of the maze, and my eyes heavily weigh themselves down until I black out from consciousness.

Chapter 14

This kind of stuff would be more useful if I was still in my Shadowstalker persona, I think to myself as I'm attempting to pick the lock of the corporate storage locker that contains all the Dawsons' personal items. I know that someone on the board is behind it because *I* was the one that locked this place up, but someone changed the lock that I had the key to. Since there are no remaining next-of-kin for either Dominic or Lorena, I decided a year ago that their materials should be stored safely in the company storage in case they can be used or can be kept secure. The amount of irony I'm feeling about that as I'm actively breaking into it to find what I can about Dominic's games or anything secret Lorena may have kept. Out of respect for the dead, I decided it was best not to snoop in either of their materials, but right now I'm regretting it. Especially since I'm trying to break into it in broad-fucking-daylight.

After a few more attempts the lock finally pops. I look around quickly to spot any onlookers before I pull the door open and close it back quickly. It's pitch-black inside, hot, and humid as well. I reach over to my left to find the light switch and flip it on the dim fluorescent lamps inside the compartment. Wall to wall, the Dawsons' filing cabinets, devices, equipment, and collective awards from SnoWire games that made the top lists of RPGs and MMORPGs litter the entire space. My eyes scan the room before my glasses start to fog up from a combination of the humidity and the tears welling up in my eyes. I wipe them clean before I settle on the poster of the first game that I worked on for Dominic; *Buster Charge Online*. I proposed that system eight years ago when I was an up-and-coming developer where players would participate in a PvP/PvE fighting arena environment that operates off skill and item cards. Dominic watched me closely during the initial alpha testing phase where I made all of my dumb rookie mistakes of clipping, data errors, and overall mechanics. I came in to work stupidly early one morning to try and fix all of them myself when I saw him sitting in my cubicle working on exactly what I was going to work on. He smiled at me, waved me over and said, "Let's see what we can do together." He worked with me closely for the rest of the project and gave me credit for its success during release week, then made me part of his personal development team alongside Robert and Lorena. That was also when I decided to come out of the closet because I felt so comfortable with him. I'm sure if he were still alive today, he'd take credit for me and Robert meeting each other.

I wipe my tears away one more time before getting into my investigative mode to find anything that I can. I start with the filing cabinets, knowing it's going to be a long process of trying to find any sort of evidence or helpful material. Shuffling through the first cabinet proved to be fruitless as it was all files on previous budget statements for projects, old personnel files of people that used to be in Dominic's personal team, and some saved interview questionnaires when he was invited onto commercials and shows about his games. The next one suspiciously has nothing in any of the drawers. Like some kind of hopeless act, I reopened them with the thought that something would appear magically. When I reopened the third drawer, something dropped into the bottom making a metallic clinking sound. I reach inside to feel around before my fingers wrap around a small thumb drive with a label strip that reads simply, "*LMD*".

"Lorena Marilyn Dawson," I breathe in surprise. *Why would a drive belonging to her be in one of Dominic's filing cabinets?*

I pocket the drive and start moving away from the filing cabinets and focus on some of the devices collected from their offices and residences. Their office laptops and desktops have no power to them since the storage space provides no outlets, but if they hold any secret items like what the cabinets did, I was willing to sweat bullets to find information.

No floppies in the hard drives.

No external hard drive memory cards.

No hidden thumb drives.

No compact disks labeled some mysterious messages.

Nothing.

"Goddammit," I sigh loudly before taking a seat at Dominic's old office chair. His "throne", he used to call it. The memory curves a smile onto my face as I lean back in the chair. Another loud clacking sound comes from beneath me. I look under the chair to see a dusty tablet with tape on the back of it where it was secured to the underside of it. I peel off the tape carefully and inspect it, revealing nothing but a black screen and silver casing. I look for the charge port to see what kind of charging device it takes. Thankfully it's something I have in my car and can charge it back up on the drive back. I head back for the door of the storage unit, close it behind me and lock it back up. Leisurely, I walk back to my car and open the door before I hear another car coming up in my area, followed by red and blue flashing lights.

"Fuck!"

I try to remain calm as I lean into my driver's side and stash the tablet underneath the seat.

"Sir, please step away from the vehicle and face us," one of the officers demands behind me.

With a deep breath, I step back and close my door, turning to face two police officers approaching me. "Is there a problem, officers?"

The one on the right of me, a short and pudgy man who looks like a turtle stuffed into a shell two sizes too small, puts his thumbs into the loops of his belt. "We received a call about someone fitting your description breaking into one of these here storage units."

His partner, a young woman built like an ox towering over him with tied back blonde hair, steps towards me. "Sir, you know that accessing storage units that don't belong to you is a felony of breaking and entering and criminal trespass?"

"Yes, officer," I reply, "I think I can clear this up. This unit belongs to my stepfather who passed away two years ago. I was hoping to find something in it for a memorial service in a couple of weeks."

They both look at each other and then separate, Shorty circling to my right and observing my car, and the other one stepping closer to me. "Do you have an ID and any proof of relation to the owner of the storage unit?"

Shit. "One moment." I reach into my back pocket and pull out my wallet to retrieve my license. I glance back at the short officer, who is peeking through the windows of my car. "Here's my license. I also have former messages from my stepfather if that is proof enough?"

She takes my license and then looks me up and down, "Unfortunately not, Mr. Bauer. I'll need you to come with us to the precinct until we have this sorted out, you understand."

Shit, shit, shit! "Uh, I guess I do. No need for trouble. Is it possible for me to call someone to come grab my car while I go with you?"

Shorty comes back around and takes me by the arm, "You can make that call when we get there." He pulls me towards their squad car where the other officer opens the back door for me to get into.

Chapter 15

"I don't know how to read these friggin' monitors," I say out loud to the two comatose bodies in front of me. I just keep watching the different colored lines move and beep, which I guess is a good sign for them both. Connor's sandy blonde hair is matted down by the Crest on his head and small beads of sweat fall from his forehead. I take one of the tissues on Matt's desk and dab the sweat off his head. I look back over at Riley's face, seeing he's got the same thing going on, so I walk over and give him the same courtesy. *This is more than you deserve, dumbass.* It's different seeing him without his glasses that he normally wears. Connor was right when he said that Riley has been looking rough. This was only one of about four or five times I've seen him in person in the last two years. Connor tried getting us all together again for a little reunion of sorts several times before, but everyone always had their excuses. Mark and Dani were either fighting too much to go out or claiming they had other things happening. Riley would always say he had work deadlines he needed to meet, which was the same thing Matt would say. I often wonder why Connor tries so hard when everyone else around him barely tries, but then I remember the last time we sat down with his family at Thanksgiving. He invited me excitedly to visit his family in Holladay, Utah. I haven't had a proper family holiday for years, so I was looking forward to this happening. When we got there, it started off rather nicely. His mom, Candice, was over the moon to meet me and she hugged me instantly. His dad, Allan, gave me a smile and a handshake to welcome me. I got to see the house he grew up in, his various yearbooks showing off his nerdy pictures and groups he was in, and everything else his parents could find to embarrass him.

It was the day after, the day of the dinner, that things got rough. I woke up late, but it was due to raised voices outside of the room we shared. I recognized it instantly as Connor and his dad getting into it about something I couldn't make out until I cracked the door open. Apparently, Connor's dad didn't support his interests in game development and design, believing it was some useless skill when he could easily do a trade job that could get him more money. Connor kept firing back that he was doing what he loves and with people he loves, and that the money didn't matter to him. They traded words back and forth until his mom caught me snooping and asked to talk to me. I got dressed decently before joining her in the kitchen, which prompted the boys to stop fighting, and told me about their relationship. It's one where they have butted heads since he was in high school when he was thinking about what he wanted to do after, which had at least something to do with video games or multimedia. Allan didn't agree with it at all and started trying to get him to be interested in something else; auto mechanics, nursing, construction, paralegal, anything that brought in some level of money from physical labor or sitting in a cubical. They had fought about it for years before Allan eventually caved with the help of Candice to send him to The U if he graduated from college with a degree. The dinner was awkward to say the least, but I was there to support him as much as possible. The drive back was a bit tense before he talked to me about it and helped me understand why he buried himself in video games and gaming stores because he didn't feel judged or pressured.

My phone vibrates on the table where the monitors are, pulling me out of my own thoughts. The screen shows a message from Danica:

Outside with Jackass.

"Oof, that's not a good start," I say to myself as I pocket my phone and give one more glance to Connor before leaving the room. Bracing myself for the inevitable, I give a nod to the desk clerk before opening the door. Danica is the first to come inside, wearing a cute white sundress with lily floral patterns and a pair of what I call "Here I Come" heels. *Oh girl, that is the wrong thing to be wearing in this place.* Her dark wavy hair bounces wildly as she tries to put as much distance between herself and Mark as she can, blindly walking through the second door past the clerk. Mark gives an exasperated sigh as he crosses the threshold. He wore smarter clothing, clean-cut jeans, a pair of basketball shoes, and a three-quarter sleeve shirt in a pale green color. I notice he has a new haircut, shaped in a tight fade that angles upward in a fauxhawk, and he's sporting his signature headphones around his neck.

He stops and opens his arms for a hug, "Hey, Kris."

I can't stop myself as I gently squeeze him in a side-hug, "Good to see you, Mark. Sorry about this."

"Don't," he insists. "Those morons did this to themselves. It's up to us to make sure they don't stay that way. Shall we?"

I nod with a small smile as I lead him into the hallway, seeing Dani already next door ahead of us. "How bad is it?"

"About as bad as you'd expect. She's given me the cold shoulder since we got here."

I blink at him, "You didn't come together, did you?"

"Don't be dumb. If we Ubered here, the driver would be a witness to my murder."

Great. "Well, try to keep that shit on a leash while we're here." He nods to me as we finally make it down the hall and meet Danica at the door. She doesn't so much as glance at either of us as I use Matt's keycard to get us inside the lab. They both saunter inside and get their first look at Connor and Riley in their catatonic states.

"Goddammit, why did they do this?" Mark curses as he walks to Connor's side.

"Connor is trying to get Riley out of the game safely," I mutter in response. "I couldn't talk him out of it."

Dani surprises me by putting her hand on my shoulder, "None of us would have been able to, babe. He's the heroic one, remember?"

I give a half-hearted chuckle in response. Mark moves over to Riley's station and inspects him, "Jesus. He looks awful. How long has he been like this?"

I shrug, "Connor and Matt found him like that in his apartment. Those monitors say he's okay, at least for now. We need to keep an eye on them for a while."

Dani takes my face gently in her hand, "When did you sleep last, Krissy?"

"Don't worry about me. I need to keep an eye on my idiot boyfriend," I say as convincingly as I can. I think I've gone about ten hours without sleep worrying about Connor, and I want to be here when he wakes up.

Mark goes back over to the monitors and equipment, "Where's Matt?"

"He went to a storage facility to try and find stuff in the Dawsons' locker," I explain.

By some manifestation, my phone rings in my back pocket. The screen shows Matt's contact, so I answer it. "Hey, did you find what you needed?"

"Kind of. But then I got into some trouble. I'm at a police precinct answering some questions. I don't know how long I'll be here, so I'll need you to pick up my car at the storage facility," he explains all too calmly. "Make sure to take care of it. It's precious cargo."

"Wait, back up," I almost shout. "You got arrested??"

Mark and Danica gawk at me.

"Yes, which means I'll be out of the office today." There's scratching on the receiver. "So, pick up my car and drop it off at the office parking lot. I don't want it towed."

He's trying to cover his tracks. Is the call being bugged? "Uh, sure thing."

"I'll try and update you," he replies calmly. "Oh, and can you get one of the janitors to check my car for bugs? I've been having some issues."

"Y-yeah, you got it." The call ends.

"Matt's in jail?" Mark asks in shock.

I nod, "He has something in his car that he needs us to get. Someone at SnoWire blew the whistle on him, so we need to be discreet."

"Mark can go get it," Danica volunteers for him. "I'll stay to monitor the idiots while *you* try to rest. No one's gonna bother anyone here on my watch."

Mark and I blink to each other but decide that she's right in her plan. I give him the address for the storage facility. "Don't use anything that can be traced. Be careful of anyone around the facility. And for God's sake, be careful."

He nods to me, glances briefly at Danica, then leaves the labs. I take a seat at one of the office chairs and breathe a long sigh, holding my face in my hands. I hear the clicking of Danica's heels approaching me as she sits down. "Girl, you gotta be honest with me. How do you put up with this from Connor? After all that we've been through, he goes and does this shit? Look at what it's doing to you."

I look up at her in disbelief, "Are you kidding me? What kind of fucking question is that?"

"The kind of question you should be asking yourself," she hisses with a bitter tone. "He dragged you back into something you didn't ask for, yet you're here pulling his ass out of the fire he set himself. You've gotta stop this."

I shoot up from my seat, "You shut your fucking mouth. I am here because I trust Connor and what he's doing. If any of us were in Riley's state, he would jump in to drag us out without question. Even you!"

She's gawking at me in disbelief.

"I know shit went sideways for you and Mark, but don't you *dare* try to drag mine and Connor's relationship through the mud to make yourself feel better! If you don't want to be here, then get out." I turn away from her and go back over to the monitors. Connor's heartbeat is spiking a bit. I look over at him and notice that his body is twitching slightly before he stops and relaxes again. My hands curl into fists and I can feel my nails digging into my palms. A soft hand grips one of mine and I turn to see Danica with tears welling in her eyes. My grip loosens in her hand.

"I'm sorry," she half-whispers. "I've… I've been going to therapy ever since the game. I still have nightmares. Bloody, terrifying, dark nightmares where I lose everyone because of that game. Seeing all of this… it's bringing up a lot of things I've pushed down deep to forget. I realize I can't forget it. It'll always be there."

This is probably the most honest I've seen her be in a long time. The fear, the anxiety, everything I've seen in the mirror. Everything I've seen in Connor's face when he wakes up from one of those nightmares. I give her hand a gentle squeeze in return, "Look, I know how stressful and frustrating this is. But Connor would do the same for any of us. Have some kind of faith that he's doing the right thing, and that we are by helping from the outside."

Before she can reply, the monitor starts beeping and blinking red. Connor's pulse is going all over the place. His body begins to twitch and jerk.

"Quick! Help me hold him down!" I race to his side and hold down his arm and leg while Danica takes the other. We struggle against the convulsions of his body. I look at his arm and see long red marks start to form. They're snaking up and down his arm slowly.

"This never happened before!" I am in a deep state of panic. *What's happening to you, Connor?*

Chapter 16

My eyes flutter as they struggle to open against the looming darkness around me. The overwhelming smell of a dead carcass makes me wretch and gag as I roll onto my hands and knees, pushing myself up to my feet. Around me, the others are slowly starting to wake up and assess their injuries. My focus is purely on Torbhin, who is still very much knocked out against the wall.

"Bimbik," Veyanna calls to me from across the chamber. She's lightly limping as she approaches me holding out her whip. "Did you do this?" She gestures to the claws that I attached to the end. I give a simple nod, in too much agony to really speak at the moment.

"Thank you… but I abhor violence," she says quietly. Her eyes fix onto the whip, "I became a Handler to try and tame the beasts of this land, showing them that we coexist as the gods planned for us." She looks at the rotting corpses of the smokehounds and shudders lightly, "But these… things are not of the gods' creations. They are twisted, corrupted. I do not know what to make of this."

"Even the scary predatorial ones?" I ask curiously.

Veyanna's face softens up slightly, "Especially them. All living creatures serve a purpose within our world. Their natural presence helps to create the harmony of the Cycle."

An interesting thought. I wonder who programmed that into her.

A sudden low grumble brings my attention back to the corridor that we all came in from. Veyanna and I recognize the forming plumes of smoke and shadows as the grumbling becomes growling.

"Shit... move!" I turn quickly, grabbing Veyanna's hand, and run towards the others. Doxo catches on quickly and picks Torbhin up from the ground, hoisting him onto his shoulder and running down the opposite corridor, followed closely by Khelrah. I make the mistake of looking behind me and seeing familiar red eyes and snapping jaws shrouded by that smokey essence. More smokehounds were gaining on us and we are still really injured.

"Don't stop! Keep going!" I call ahead as I reach into my satchel and find the makeshift smoke bombs that I made upon entering the Maze. "I need a flame!"

"On the run?" Veyanna blurts out incredulously.

"Just trust me, dammit!"

The snarling and snapping are still hot on our heels. Ahead, the corridor splits into a T-junction. With Doxo in the lead, he banks hard left with Torbhin bouncing up and down on his shoulder. The walls of the Maze start to become mossier and danker the further we go, and the view above us becomes stormy gray with hues of eerie orange flashing in and out. The winding corridor continues to grow longer, making it harder for us to lose the smokehounds.

I yell up ahead, "Someone give me a goddamn flame!"

Doxo skids to a stop at a corner ahead and looks at my small running frame, "My tinderbox is in my satchel! Be quick, Half-Pint!"

I reach up to his satchel and start rummaging around for his tinder box. The eerie howling starts to get closer to us. I pull the box from the satchel, lean down on the ground and strike the box to light the wick on this thing that might not even work against smokey monster dogs, but it's the best I've got. One strike, two strikes, three strikes until a hot enough spark lights on the wick and I throw it in the monsters' direction. The wick catches the flammable cloth on fire, slowly billowing out cloudy white smoke with a hint of green.

"Keep running! I'll catch up," I yell to them. I want to see the results.

"Do not be foolish, Bimbik!" Khelrah urges me. "We must go!"

Before I can retort, the black, shadowy smoke begins to lurk forward into the white and green smokescreen. The two forms intertwine with each other, and a silhouette of a hound emerges, but it doesn't break through. A horrendous hacking sound comes from within it.

"It worked! Let's go!" I turn around victoriously and run alongside the others.

Veyanna calls to me, "How long does the smoke last?"

"No clue! Keep going!"

Without another word, we all continue running through the winding corridors. The hacking and coughing sounds are far enough behind us that I am impressed with myself for that little trick. Before I can celebrate with myself on the run, a loud echoing crash erupts all around us, loud enough to make us stop dead in our tracks. The walls on either side of the group shake and rattle, causing dust and debris to shower down on us. A hoarse groan that reminds me of a trash compactor makes my heart stop, confirming my fear as the walls inch closer. *Fucking run!*

No one has time to argue as the walls start to close in, making the corridor ahead of us get more and more narrow. Doxo has to readjust Torbhin onto his other shoulder while carrying him and running to make it out of the crushing death that is the maze walls. It gets to the point I watch the giant grip onto Torbhin's collar and belt, hoist him back and absolutely chucks his ass forward past the threshold. Doxo then reaches the end and positions himself to try and hold the moving walls long enough for the rest of us to make it. *"Faster, you dolts!"*

Khelrah is the next to make it through as she slides between the giant's legs like a fucking lizard and out of sight. A familiar sound of snarling and snapping jaws has me sliding to a stop and turning around to see the pack of smokehounds starting to gain ground on us again. "Are you fucking serious??" Veyanna yanks on the collar of my jacket and pulls me back into a run. The walls are still crushing inward and Doxo's arms are struggling to keep it open for us. I hop through the gap between his left arm and leg and roll onto the mossy, dank floor of the open room. Veyanna slides through his other side and then tugs on the leather strap across Doxo's chest to try and pull him through, "Doxo, let go!" He begins to slip through the closing walls when he wails out in pain. His left leg is caught in the maw of one of the smokehounds that is trying to drag him back into the corridor. Veyanna helps to pull him back while Doxo's giant fist pounds into the snout of the beast to release its grip. The other smokehounds behind it start climbing above the pack leader trying to get through to the rest of us.

"Cover your ears, lads!"

Too late. A loud, scratching sound explodes behind us, making us cup our ears tightly against the teeth-grinding noise. I open one of my clenched shut eyes to see the smokehounds yowl and whine and cripple down as the walls slowly squeeze them in. Doxo's leg is released just in time before the walls close tightly, spitting black and purple bile from the crack as the monsters are crushed to death. The noise dies down slowly, prompting me to turn towards Torbhin releasing the strings of his instrument, revealing a metal dowel he used to scratch them. "Simple crippling melody," he chuckles in pain.

"Where the fuck was that last time?" I ask blatantly.

He looks at me bashfully with a shrug, "I was… indisposed?"

"*Ow!* Bloody hell!" Doxo screams out as Veyanna pulls his boot off where the creature bit him. A gnarly gash on both sides of his ankle draws attention to the bite marks and his dark red blood from the wound.

"Stop fretting, you oaf," she scolds him as she reaches into her satchel and pulls some cloth out. "This would not have happened if you had not put yourself in the way like some hero. I thought you were in this for the glory."

She begins wrapping the cloth around his wound, making him hiss through his teeth. "I am. But I cannot achieve that glory without... you. Or any of the other puny ones."

Khelrah nearly scares the shit out of me when she leans down and whispers, "It smells arousal coming from both of them."

I snort loud enough for the two of them to come out of their intense gazing and finish bandaging Doxo's ankle. As the two of them have their moment, I turn around to take in a drastic change in scenery: This new area of the Maze is leading downwards into a faintly glowing tunnel with no other paths. Just down. The mouth of this tunnel is covered with moss and some kind of bioluminescent fungi that is slithering inside of the cavernous tunnel.

"Okay... whose turn is it to go into a creepy part of this monster maze first?" I call out with a scratch in my voice.

No one says a thing. We're all looking into the mouth of the tunnel with such intensity that I think someone might suggest we just stay here for the rest of our lives. But I can't do that. So, I clear my throat, pull out the smokehound fangs I had kept from before and take a deep breath, "Onward, I guess."

Chapter 17

Crossing the threshold of the tunnel is like stepping into a swamp-themed haunted house; dark winding shadows only lit up by the glowing fungus all around, sloshing of moss on the ground still wet from some unknown source, and sounds of dripping water and creaking clicks in the far-ahead distance. *Leave it to a survival game to create pathways that seem more riddled with death than the first few.* Each step into this creepy hole gives a resounding squish that is utterly revolting. I am thankful that I'm wearing boots, so I don't have to feel the damp moss squish between my toes. The light provided by the strange glowing fungi has me intrigued.

"Half-Pint," Doxo snaps. "Do not delay us with the flora."

"Just trust me on this and let me see what I can do with it." Using the smokehound fang dagger, I gently cut off a piece of the fungus and then take my logbook out to see if there are any useful properties. The pages of the crafting section begin to fill:

Harvesting Bioluminescent Fungi:

Illuminating Lanterns: The bioluminescent fungi can be carefully harvested and encased in small, transparent globes or lanterns. When properly preserved, these lanterns emit a gentle, eerie glow, making them ideal light sources for the dark passages of the Primeval Maze or other subterranean environments.

Alchemical Potions: Skilled alchemists can extract and distill the bioluminescent compounds from the fungi to create potions that temporarily enhance night vision or reveal hidden magical auras. These potions are highly sought after by adventurers exploring the maze or delving into similar mysterious locales.

"Whoa..." I begin rummaging around my satchel for mixing properties but come up empty. "Anyone have any herbs or components or something?"

Everyone begins sifting through their belongings to find anything I could use. Doxo comes up short-handed only having a few rations and a hunting knife. Veyanna produces a couple of pressed flowers and a couple of unused potion bottles. Khelrah manages to provide some trap items like wire, hemp rope, some springs and slingshot stones. Torbhin pulls out a waterskin he says is filled with some kind of grog he brewed himself, some sheet music, and a pan flute. Thinking quickly, I collect the potion bottles, the grog, and more of the fungi to mix them together. Like a ninth-grade science experiment, the bottle glows that bioluminescent blue brighter than the fungi around us, providing some better light in this dark tunnel.

"Heh, clever," Doxo comments as he takes the bottle and begins moving ahead of the rest of us.

"Uh, you're welcome?"

Torbhin pats me on the shoulder, "Do not take it personally. Most gnolids like Doxo rarely show appreciation outside of combative scenarios. Most stories and songs I have collected of their people involves wars and or bareknuckling their own kin."

I give a soft laugh, "How are you holding up? That was a nasty hit you took."

The corner of his bearded mouth quirks up slightly, "I have taken nastier wounds from nastier brutes. In fact," He grabs his lute from behind his back and tugs on a couple of the strings before playing a soft tune.

"In the realm of stone and fire, I first drew breath,

A dwarrow bard and fighter, never fearing death.

With hammer and with lyre, I'd sing and swing my blade,

Through battles and through fire, my name was widely made.

Oh, I've roamed the land, from mountain to the sea,

A dwarrow so bold and grand, a spirit wild and free.

With axe and shield in hand, and a song upon my tongue,

I faced each challenge, took a stand, and through the battles sung.

I sang in lively taverns, where laughter filled the air,

My tales of grand adventures, a crowd's eager, rapt stare.

From caverns dark and ancient, to the highlands steep and wild,

The Primeval Maze

My songs, both old and recent, echoed like a child.

Oh, I've roamed the land, from mountain to the sea,

A dwarrow so bold and grand, a spirit wild and free.

With axe and shield in hand, and a song upon my tongue,

I faced each challenge, took a stand, and through the battles sung.

I've faced the mightiest dragons, and delved in dungeons deep,

With comrades and with flagons, our treasures we'd keep.

From the depths of haunted crypts, to the peaks where eagles soar,

My axe would never slip, my voice a mighty roar.

Oh, I've roamed the land, from mountain to the sea,

A dwarrow so bold and grand, a spirit wild and free.

With axe and shield in hand, and a song upon my tongue,

I faced each challenge, took a stand, and through the battles sung.

But now I've joined this party, to face the Maze's dread,

A group of hearts so hearty, where heroes bravely tread.

With comrades, true and steadfast, we'll conquer what's unknown,

And through each challenge, unsurpassed, together we'll have grown.

Oh, I've roamed the land, from mountain to the sea,

A dwarrow so bold and grand, a spirit wild and free.

With axe and shield in hand, and a song upon my tongue,

I'll face each challenge, take a stand, and through the battles sung.

His playing comes to a gradual close and he beamed a grin at me. I am amazed by his tale-turned-song and realize this is the most I've learned about him since we began. "That was… that was really good. Did you add in that last part after meeting us all?"

He nods with the same grin, "I see all that occurs in my travels as a grand scheme set by the Iron Shaper himself. Much like the occurrence of those razorwing bats. So, this," he gestures to his wounds, "is but another verse to be added at a later date."

His positivity is infectious, it makes me smile in return. We shuffle a little faster to catch up with the group. The standing water starts to rise a bit more, barely passing Doxo or Veyanna's shins, but starting to come to my knees. The light coming from the makeshift lantern illuminates the tunnel and begins closing in as the cavern gets deeper. "I think the tunnel is getting smaller," I point out.

Doxo turns like he's about to say something before his head hits a low-hanging stone, making him yelp out loud. "Blasted gods!"

We come to a full stop, all of us trying not to laugh while he rubs his head profusely like it'll ease the pain. I take the bottle from his hand, moving forward into the narrowing space of the cavern. "I'll look ahead, you all stay here for a moment."

With that, I proceed through the mouth of the tunnel, seeing that it's getting more and more narrow and short. *Doxo's gonna have to crawl through here,* I think to myself with a snicker. The threshold of the tunnel is getting closer until I can pass into a large alcove that is brightly lit by the bioluminescent fungi crawling all the way up to the domed ceiling. The alcove also has a standing pool of water that is sparkling under the light as if it's made of stars. It almost feels peaceful, but what draws my attention the most is the number of carved holes in the walls, reminding me eerily of a hornet's nest. My mind is a little settled as I see another threshold on the other side of the pool with the fungi snaking into it.

"Okay, there's an exit. Need to be careful about this," I say out loud as I turn back and return to the others, all patiently waiting. Except Doxo, who is still holding his head where he hit it.

"What did you find?" Veyanna asks nervously.

"There's an alcove on the other side. More water than here, a lot of glowing mushrooms, and some weird holes in the walls. We need to be careful to cross the pool and make it to the other side." I point to Veyanna and Doxo, "You two are gonna have to crawl in order to get through. Try not to drink the water in case its contaminated."

Doxo groans loudly, "Fine. Lead the way."

I nod, tightening the straps of my boots. "Stay close, stay alert." I take the lead, followed by Veyanna, then Doxo, Khelrah, and Torbhin. Looking back, I see Veyanna trying her best to shimmy through without getting caught, but Doxo is army-crawling close behind her. I can't see anyone else before we reach the threshold. I hold my hand out for Veyanna so she can stand, which she takes with a smile and nod. Doxo's the next one out, slowly rising to his giant size and cracking his bones from the cramped tunnel. Khelrah creeps me out as she crawls from the tunnel on all fours like a Komodo dragon. Torbhin comes out with a sweet smile and an appreciative pat on my shoulder. The whole group looks around at the pool and cavern walls with multiple little holes in them. The eerie silence of the cavern, aside from the small laps of water against the walls, is enough to make this once boisterous party shut down.

"This cavern," Khelrah sniffs the air, "smells of malevolence… and it hears crawling inside the walls."

"Spiders?" I ask, feeling creeped out.

She shakes her head slightly, "It cannot tell, but arachnids have a distinct sound and smell. This is not that."

"It does not matter, because there is our exit," Doxo points to the threshold on the other side of the pool. He takes a giant step into the pool and waits for something to happen. One, two, three beats later, nothing happens. He fully steps into the pool and begins walking forward, prompting the rest of us to join him. It feels cool to the touch, but also a little tingly for some strange reason. We get further into the pool, which sinks lower at an incline.

"Ow!" I feel a sharp stab puncture through my boot. Torbhin lets me lean on his shoulder so I can pick up my foot and pull out whatever stuck my boot. With a pinch and a tug, it comes free. It's a shard of something that seems discolored and broken, smooth except for some divots and ridges. I show it to Torbhin, who responds with a shrug. Before I can ask anyone else to look at it, a noise draws our attention from the exit ahead. Because of the hollowness of the cavern and the stillness of the pool, a faint hissing sound echoes and bounces off the walls.

"Form up!" Doxo frees his great axe and grips it tightly, scanning the room. To his right, Veyanna mutters something I can't quite hear as she unfurls her whip, the smokehound claws sinking into the water. Torbhin moves to her right side with the neck of his lute gripped in his meaty hand ready to pummel. Khelrah pulls me with her to finish the circle, flashing the clawed fingers of her left hand while the right one grips one of the smoke bombs I made. Not ready to get chowed on, I take both fang daggers into my hands and scan the cavern. The hissing sounds like steam being released from an iron, but it is louder and all around the room. It's almost as if the sound is swirling around us at a slow pace, making pinpointing the source of it difficult.

Khelrah's nose flares and her eyes squint before she points to the left of the cavern, "There!"

The party focuses on where she's pointing with weapons ready. The hissing starts to die down and move in the focused direction. From out of one of the holes in the wall, a small, brightly colored object oozes out and begins moving slowly. It can't be any bigger than an inch, or inch and a half, multicolored with a dark blue head and bright pink stripes. Everyone starts to relax at the sight of this strange thing that is inching closer to the pool of water. Once in it, the creature starts swimming like a coral snake towards us. I gently take a step back with my daggers firmly in my hands, but Veyanna is the one who moves in front of the creature as it approaches.

"Such a tiny thing," she muses. She leans down and dips her hand into the water, letting it swim into her palm. Veyanna brings it closer to herself so she can inspect it. I reach up on my tiptoes to try and get a decent look at it myself. From my view, it's definitely some kind of worm in strange multicolor with a single eye the size of a button. It snakes around her hand in a few circles, leaving a pale-yellow residue in its trail.

Khelrah peers at the slimy worm a little closer before her eyes widen. "Do…not…move," she orders. Veyanna's head tilts to the side, taking her eyes off the worm. What happens next is enough to send me into a state of shock because the worm suddenly swells to a longer and fatter body and opens its mouth, full of spiraling sharp teeth that latch onto Veyanna's left arm. She screams in pain and tries yanking it off, but it is attached like a fully adult leech and won't let go. Khelrah quickly grabs her arm with the worm on it and pierces it on its head with her clawed nails, prompting it to release its hold on her. Khelrah pierces its head in a rough pinch, making it pop like a pimple. Veyanna's arm where she was bitten has a rounded scar that is sizzling. She dips it into the water to make it stop, but it keeps sizzling and spreading on her arm.

"It burns!" She wails.

Khelrah grabs her arm again, opens her lizard maw and clamps down around her wound. At first, I'm horrified, but then she starts spitting out some kind of toxin into the water, making it sizzle. Just like a venomous snake bite, she's trying to suck out whatever that thing put in her. Doxo is holding onto her shoulders to keep her steady while Khelrah works. I move to pick up the dead worm and look at it carefully, noting its slimy exterior.

Then it came again. The hissing. My eyes scan the ceiling of the cavern and watch as a shower of these worms start springing from the holes and splashing into the pool or smacking onto the mossy floor of the threshold ahead. The same sound draws my attention to the threshold we came from and notice the worms have piled on top of each other to block the exit.

"Shit! They're trying to block us in! We've gotta move!" I shuffle through the pool trying to avoid the worms that are swimming towards us. I swipe at the water with my daggers, cutting a few worms down in the process. The violent splashing of water behind me tells me the others are close behind. The shower of worms continues violently with more of them trying to close off the exit. "Doxo! Make a door!"

Doxo is ripping worms off his arms as he bursts past me and starts hacking at the barrier of worms that keeps piling higher and higher. I turn to try and find the others and see them struggling through the pool while it fills with worms. Veyanna is whimpering trying to get away as quickly as possible. I take her uninjured arm and pull her out of the pool. I feel slime fall onto my neck and fumble to wipe it away. Too quick, the worm jumps to my arm, opens its maw and spits out a yellowish stream onto my arm, sending searing pain through me as it burns into my skin. Khelrah is dodging side to side to make it out of danger, the cloak I gave her protecting her rather well against the worms trying to bite and burn her. Torbhin, however, is pushing against a pool filling with those things. I see the strain and struggle in his face before something trips him and he falls into the pool, all the worms in it darting in his direction.

"Torbhin!" I palm both daggers and dive into the water, against the protests of the others behind me. I open my eyes to see a pool of sunken bones, both whole and broken, realizing that it was a bone shard that punctured my boot. It was a feeding pit. Torbhin is flailing in the pool, his tunic caught on some bones, all while worms are starting to dive downward at us. I swim as hard as I can at him, grabbing the sleeve of his tunic and cutting away at the part that's caught. Suddenly, a piercing pain comes from my neck, my elbow, and my lower back. Torbhin is trying to pull away some worms that have latched onto him. With all the strength this body has, I pull him upward with me to breach the surface. We both take in a large breath of air before the swarm of worms surrounds us, circling and closing in.

"Come on! We've gotta get out of this!" I pull on the collar of his tunic, but he pulls my hand from him.

"Bimbik, go! Yer faster than I!" He holds up his satchel from the water, "Take this! Keep it safe! *Go!*"

"Are you out of—" I can't finish my protest before he pushes my head down into the water and away from him. I open my eyes and look up, watching Torbhin's legs flail as the worms swarm him like a school of piranhas. I swim fast toward the rim of the pool where the others are. Two sets of clawed hands reach in and yank my little body out of the water and onto the surface. Veyanna is yelling and crying for Torbhin, Doxo is loudly growling at the wall of worms he's cutting away, and Khelrah is just holding my shoulders. I want to jump in and save him, but Torbhin is now flailing in a corrosive pool of toxin and acid.

"Go now before they try to close it again!" Doxo wraps a giant arm around Veyanna's waist and pulls her away, much to her screaming protests.

Khelrah tugs on me to pull me with her as I'm looking over my shoulder, only witnessing the horrid devouring of the dwarrow Breaker that gave up his life for me to make it out alive. For *us* to make it out alive. My mind is immediately flooding with memories of Askuld the orc scout from *The Mortal Gate*, losing his life by a barrage of arrows.

We make it past the threshold and keep moving as the light from the cavernous pool of carnivorous worms slowly fades away, just like Torbhin's screams of agony.

Chapter 18

Man, what do I know about being stealthy? I live off electronics!

I'm standing up in a transit bus going downtown, crammed with a bunch of other randoms, twiddling my thumbs because Krissy told me to not use anything that can be tracked. I left my phone in my car and it's like I'm missing a limb, given how I run my entire business through it. Since graduating with a degree in music production, I've been trying to solicit different spins and tracks to the clubs and record stores in SLC, with a couple of interested parties while the rest are either no-callbacks or straight up rejecting it. Luckily, I've had luck with my side-hustle as an entertainer for parties and small gigs as "DJ Totym". Goes to show just how much that fucking game impacted me. I might have nearly died there a few times, but I really did appreciate the experiences that it gave me. I grew a deeper appreciation for nature and even took up some martial arts classes to keep fit. I spent some money getting a couple of tattoos to remind me of the shit that went down, like a trident up my forearm and an interpretation of the totem I had just below my neck.

Unfortunately, that's also where Danica and I fell apart. While I feel that I gained something from that experience, she's trying to forget it altogether. Everything she did before we broke up was all about moving out, moving away, and getting as far away from the video game scene as possible. She didn't even want to have game nights with people we invited over, saying she would get triggered and have a meltdown. Since leaving the U, Danica had done her best to forget everything by working as much as she could; from secretary positions to hosting at bars and restaurants, not keeping one for too long and it put a strain on our ability to pay rent. Then there was the constant fighting that would start from the smallest things possible, but they always led back to the game.

"You were the one that roped me into that hell!"

"We could have been better for not being around Connor or Riley!"

"We could've been stuck in there forever!"

Then the last straw, *"Can't you just grow the fuck up and be a man! Your music is worse than the way you dress!"*

She told me up and down that she didn't mean it, but I was done. I packed my shit and left. I don't know how long she was sitting on that one, but I was done being in a relationship where everything I did was not enough for her or wasn't what she wanted. Today is probably the first time I've talked to her or been around her in nearly nine months.

The PA system of the transit bus announces, "Sequoia Street."

I quickly exit the bus onto the street, taking in my surroundings. Looking behind me, it's busy as that part of downtown is mostly business parks and storefronts, but ahead of me it's a little more run down than most other places. Unfortunately, that's also the direction of the storage unit I need to find. I pull up the hood of my sleeveless hoodie and start walking, keeping an eye out for anything shady.

"Okay… gotta find Matt's car, try to get it back to the others, avoid shady corporate types that might be cyberterrorists in disguise. How hard can it be?"

My mind wanders loudly about how I'm feeling some serious Déjà vu when we would plan shit in the Ordowell Bowels or the Crimson Order Watchtower; at first, it would go well, then something would go horribly wrong.

Don't overthink this, Mark. That was a game, this is real life. Stuff like that doesn't work out here. It'll be quick and clean.

With that little mental peptalk, I jog across the street looking around for the storage facility sign. This just proves I know jack shit about directions without my phone, because everything down this part of town looks the fucking same. The street smells terrible, like piss and cigarettes, no doubt due to the homeless population and crummy people around this area. For a day like this, the streets are pretty light and less occupied than what I would've thought. But I guess it makes it easier for me to not be stopped by anyone to look for Matt's car. I don't know how serious it is that the SnoWire dicks ratted on Matt to get him out of the way, but whatever he found must be worth the trouble. *It had better get Connor and Riley out of this safely so I can kick their asses myself for this.*

The more I ponder on this, the more I'm kind of bummed out that Connor didn't call me first to try and help. We haven't talked much for the past couple of years without the occasional text to check up on each other. That's something else he'll have to explain.

I turn on the corner of Sequoia and see a large sign in orange and black that reads "Private Storage" with the SnoWire insignia between the words. *That's gotta be it.* I pick up the pace toward the storage facility, gates open and attendee nowhere in sight.

"Ooookay, that's not a good sign." I scan the opening of the facility for any red flags, minus the missing gate attendant, and walk in.

"All right, Matty, where did you drive your 'Big Boss' car to?" The opening of the facility split into two directions with storage lockers on either side of driveway. Trusting my gut, I head left to investigate further. The place is a damn maze as I'm turning constantly, feeling like a test rat in a lab experiment. It's not until I come up to a roundabout collection of storage lockers and see the black Dodge Charger parked.

"Bingo," I say out loud, thanking God no one was around to hear me say that. "Okay, so Krissy said he stashed something in the car. Wouldn't it be easier for me to just take the car?" Then I remember I'm not supposed to do anything that will get me tracked by the company ass hats. Approaching the car, I try the driver's side door and thankfully it's unlocked. Before I can try to search, I hear an engine coming from down the drive heading in this direction.

"Shit!" I shut the door and run to the back, hiding behind the trunk of the car. Odds are that none of these doors to storage lockers will be unlocked for me to hide in. I kneel as low as I can to avoid being seen as I hear tires approaching, along with some muffled voices. The tires are coming up along the side of Matt's car, which prompts me to crawl underneath the car to stay hidden. The engine dies: from the sounds of it, must be a golf cart used by security in the facility.

"Boss says we're supposed to take the car and stash it at the parking garage across from the main building," a female voice instructs as two pairs of shoes crunch on the pavement.

"I was told that we need to double check the locker and make sure nothing was missing," the male voice includes. "I've got the manifest here. I'll go in and check it out, you get the car ready."

Fuck! I can't be under here when they try to take the car. I've gotta do something. From under the car, I watch one set of boots head to the storage locker, unlocking it and pulling the door open. The other set of boots approaches the car and opens the door, the chassis pushes downward like they are putting their weight inside. I softly shimmy to the passenger side, reach out from under the car and smack the side of the door.

"The hell?" The woman steps away from the driver's side door and walks around to the other side.

I use this chance to shimmy out from under the car and lift up as quietly as possible. The security guard is inspecting the car on the passenger side, so I take the chance to jump into the car. *The keys! They're still in the ignition!*

"Hey! Get out of that car!" I whip my head to the rear passenger window, keeping my hood up before slamming the door shut and locking the doors. She tries opening the door frantically, calling for her partner. I turn the engine over and put it in gear, slamming on the gas and taking off out of the driveway. I hear them screaming out after me, but I haul ass out of there.

"*Whoooooa!*" I yell out loudly as I burn rubber off the street. The adrenaline is hitting me hard, making me pound my fist into the roof of the car and kicking the flooring of the car. Something hits against my heel. I reach down to pick it up, seeing a thumb drive with Lorena's name on it.

"Holy shit... this is what he found!" I quickly pocket it and keep driving until I hit the highway.

I need to ditch the car. They'll be looking for it. I'm on the highway, so I can't ditch it here. If the security guards were smart, they would put out an APB like they do in the shows and movies. If it ends up happening, they'll get me quickly. If they saw my face at all, I'd be in worse shape. I'll need to ditch everything that made me stand out, including my favorite sleeveless hoodie. The drive gives me time to plan any sort of escape to try and keep them from going back to the SnoWire building. *Matt owes me big time for this!*

Chapter 19

Goddammit! I impatiently sit in the holding cell to be processed so I can pay my bail and get the fuck out of here. With any luck, Krissy and the others are getting my car safely back to the workshop. Whoever blew the whistle on me had to be from the company looking to depose me from the company.

"Hello!" No one is giving me any attention and I've been trying to get out of this place for the last hour. I'm sharing the holding cell with three other schmucks who are eyeing me up and down because I'm dressed in my suit, minus my blazer.

One of the officers comes to the bars to investigate, hands on his hips and a scowl on his face. "You Matthew Bauer?"

"Yeah? Why?"

"Your company lawyer is here," he informs me.

I blink. *I didn't call the company lawyer.*

Dramatic steps approach from the hallway until a pinstripe navy blue suit comes into view, worn by a square-jawed Hispanic man with slicked back hair that grays on the sides and square-toe shoes with his hands stuffed in his pockets, smirking smugly.

"Well, isn't this quite the conundrum, Mr. Bauer."

I swallow hard, "Guzman."

The board director keeps smirking and his gaze on me, "Officer, if I might speak to my 'client' alone for a moment?"

The officer gives a slight nod and walks down the hall. I guess Guzman is counting on the others in holding to not get involved.

"So, you were keeping tabs on the storage facility," I guess out loud.

His smirk grows wider, "You should be more aware of what is happening at the company that you oversee. Now tell me what you found in the locker and where you hid it."

"What's the point of this, Armand? Blackmail to get me to give you control of the company?"

He chuckles and buttons his blazer, "I'm not as simple as that, Matthew. I have loftier goals in mind. Dominic did his part of developing the technology that can be used to alter the original programming. All I needed was the right grunt to be willing to test the new product."

No fucking way. "You... you gave Riley the unfinished project to complete and upload. You're behind *The Primeval Maze!*"

"Ah, so he managed to begin his solo alpha testing. Great timing," Guzman sneers. "Now we can start working on plans for beta testing and production."

I grip the bars between us, "Armand... you can't. You have no idea how dangerous this technology is. It has the potential to destroy the human brain. It can sink the company entirely and slap us with charges of manslaughter. Even murder."

He's completely unfazed by my pleas. "Believe it or not, Mr. Bauer, I know more about the potential that the Crest system has than you refuse to believe."

No. No, no, no. "You were behind Dominic's imprisonment in *The Mortal Gate*. And what happened with Lorena!"

Guzman just holds out his arms with a shrug and a smug smile. My blood freezes. *The board directors influenced Lorena to bug Dominic into pushing the production of the game to get him to alpha test it. Which let Lorena trap our team in the game, get inside, and take over the whole damn thing.*

"You son of a bitch!" I lunge through the bars to try and grab him, but he steps backwards quickly. "You killed the Dawsons! *You* killed Robert! And for *what?*"

Guzman straightens his jacket and keeps up his smirk, "Do you know what the greatest weakness is in the world of today, Matthew? Addiction and dependency. Everywhere, our entire population is made up of zombies droning through the streets, faces planted firmly in their phones, opening risky content that makes them vulnerable to data harvesting and identity theft, just waiting for their next big fix. They are compelled by their impulses to receive as much information as they can fathom, therefore they do exactly what their devices demand of them. Now, what can one do with that much information and control over the general population? Harvest data, not just electronically, but physically and mentally. Learn how the human brain can be influenced and controlled through human impulses. Can you imagine how much that research would be worth to the highest bidder? The Pentagon. The United Nations. Foreign dignitaries are looking for a method of population control. Because of Dominic Dawson's genius and Lorena's ambition, we have access to the world's most advanced and powerful tool."

"More like a weapon," I spit back. "A weapon to manipulate the public that is simply trying to find an escape from a shitty world. You goddamn bureaucrats only think about money and position, you worthless fuck!"

The smirk wipes off Guzman's face. For one satisfying moment, I have him rattled. His brows furrow at me, which I have seen on multiple occasions during our board meetings.

"You just fail to see the potential that this product has, Matthew," he says through gritted teeth. "The world is heading for oblivion because of the virus that we call 'free will'. If we can maintain control of the populace that *needs* the restraint, we can lead future generations into a brighter and more fulfilling existence."

"As long as you maximize profit off of enslaving countless people in the process," I argue. "Going as far as imprisoning them in their own minds and sending them to certain death."

Guzman saunters forward, "Only imprisoning those who don't cooperate or serve as nothing more than lab rats. Much like you, your team, and those naïve college students. Thank you for bringing us Mr. Wright and Mr. Woods. You were right, they are invaluable to the company. Mr. Wright gave us the distraction we needed to operate while Mr. Woods gratefully accepted the chance to alpha test *The Primeval Maze*. With the information that is fed directly to us, we'll use his data to perfect the designs and prepare for mass production."

"Armand, listen to me." I grip the bars so hard that my knuckles turn white, "You can't do this. It's unethical and completely insane. You're going to be responsible for the enslavement and death of countless people for fucking *profit*."

"Profit is what makes the world turn, Matthew. Profit, power, and conviction." He straightens his blazer and walks towards the door, "Please do forgive me if I am not ready to have you released yet. Your temperament is unfit for resuming your duties as CEO. I will be fronting operations in your absence. Good day, Mr. Bauer."

No matter how much I yell or swear at him, he just keeps walking. Out of the station, along with the future of the company I promised Dominic I would take care of. I huff back over to the bench, ignoring the stares from the others in holding when something dawns on me; Guzman said Riley's progress was being fed directly to them. They're actively monitoring his state in the game. Does that mean they're also monitoring Connor? *Fuck! I've gotta get out of here!*

Chapter 20

He's gone. Torbhin's gone.

"*Aaargh!*" Doxo is punching the wall of the tunnel repeatedly, screaming in rage. Veyanna is curled up against the other wall nursing her arm and crying quietly to herself. Khelrah is pacing back and forth with her hands on her head.

"Khelrah should have known!" She cries out, "it should have known about the *barramanders*! They are not supposed to be outside of the jungle caverns of Kerogema!"

I shake out of my state of shock, "Wait, what's a barramander?"

"It's exerine for devourworm," Veyanna says through choked up tears. "They are indigenous to Kerogema. Their acidic saliva has been harvested for poisons and their excretion is used for adhesives. They do not congregate in large nests like the one in that cavern and are not known for being carnivorous of large animals... or humanoids."

Doxo growls loudly, "It is this gods damned Maze! It is twisting the wildlife of the surface world and turns them into beasts of nightmares to set upon the people of Preydor! I will find the source of this sorcery and *destroy it!*"

"What if we cannot find it?" Veyanna whimpers. We all look at her on the ground, "What if we are not meant to make it out of this place? Are we destined to be lost and devoured by this malevolent place?"

The group goes silent. Even Doxo doesn't have a retort for the idea that we very well may die down here. Is Riley already dead? Am I too late to save him? I grip onto the satchel that Torbhin insisted I should take for him, wondering why this would be his last request. Opening it, I pull his extra instruments out and a leather tube that is capped. I pull the cap off and slide out a rolled-up parchment. Inspecting it closely I see that it's sheet music, freshly written and titled "Mazebreakers". The lyrics narrate all about how Torbhin joined with us on a whim and didn't regret it for a moment, that we would break the puzzle of this maze and save all of Preydor. I feel a tear roll down my cheek and look at the others.

"Torbhin… believed in us as a group. He knew us only for the past several hours, yet he took the time to write a song about us. He called us 'Mazebreakers', the force that will free Preydor from its fear and torment. It's a big risk, moving further into the maze and facing scary-ass monsters, but this is not the first time I've put my life on the line to save an entire nation against all odds. We have no other way of getting out of this place, other than finding the source of these monsters and shut it the fuck down."

Veyanna is looking up at me with tears streaming down her face, but Khelrah is the one that approaches me and lays a gentle hand on my shoulder.

"It will stand with you, Bimbik," she says softly, kneeling and pressing her forehead to mine before standing back up.

161

Doxo moves away from the wall, knuckles bloodied from punching the wall. "That rotund bard deserves to be avenged, and he will be. Let us break this maze." He shifts his gaze down to Veyanna, which we mimic.

Veyanna sniffs and wipes away her tears, stands up on her hooves and moves close to Doxo, "I am terrified. I want to help save the people and natural world of Preydor, but I am not well in a fight."

"We don't need everyone to be good in a fight," I explain. "You can manipulate creatures with your focus. We need that."

Doxo puts his bear paw of a hand on her shoulder, "I will handle the fights. Your gentle nature brings stability to this group. Keep close and we will survive."

Her eyes shimmer as she looks up at him, feeling some sort of comfort in his words, and nods. "O-okay. I will stand with you all."

I smile softly, thinking that if I was able to rally an entire army against Lorena's knights, I can rally these guys to survive through the rest of this game and save Riley. "Then let's do this, Mazebreakers."

They all solemnly give nods or grunts in agreement as we turn towards the corridor of the maze that lays ahead of us. The bioluminescence of the last level of the maze dwindles out and looks to have an opening back to the top where the ominous orange and red light that illuminates this purgatory. Wherever Riley is, I hope that he's okay. Because I'm gonna kick his ass up and down this world and the one outside.

Chapter 21

Doxo takes up the lead again as we climb upwards and out of the underground caverns, a winding staircase of earth and stone leading up and out of the buried hell where we lost our companion. Everyone's spirits are roughly improved, but not too much. Can't say I blame them. I had a hard enough time getting over Askuld's death in *TMG*, but that wasn't as brutal as what happened below.

Upon reaching the threshold of the stairwell, it doesn't open into another corridor of twisting walls and dead ends, but instead into a vast open courtyard that is probably the most impressive structure we've seen since coming here. A large, octagonal courtyard with great pillars at each corner lifting an ancient looking terrace covered in moss, vines, and strange flowers growing from them. A cobblestone floor forms a sort of swirling pattern into the center, with various forms of overgrowth peeking through the cracks. In the center of the courtyards is a large stone bowl that has pearls of water dropping into it from the ceiling somehow. Instead of the damp, rank smell that has been in the air since the moment we entered, this air smells sweet and different kinds of minerals than what has been around before.

"This is… kind of pretty," I admit. Every step on the cobblestone creates a small echo. I catch glimpses of flittering insects flying in and out of the courtyard.

"Looks are deceiving in this place," Khelrah half-whispers as she inspects the flora and overgrowth.

Veyanna walks ahead of the rest of us towards the receptacle of water in the center of the courtyard. "This... is strange."

Intrigued, I walk over to where she is and get on my tiptoes but can't see well. "What do you see?"

"The water within is rippling... in various colors. Dark colors, like the light that illuminates this maze and the light of the fungi in the cavern."

I bend my head back to see where the water is coming from, only to see the tiniest sliver of light that sparkles with each drop of water that comes down from it. No rain clouds, no signs of any source of water, nothing. I take a closer look at the bowl that the water is in since I can't see what's in it exactly. There's some weird writing underneath the surface of the bowl with some carved images. I take the logbook out of my satchel to see if there's anything that can help me translate it, flipping page to page. I stop at a section that describes various strange runes and Preydorian languages from Braveshire to Kerogema. Veyanna moves out of my way while I run my fingers along the shapes and letters.

"It's some kind of magic lock," I say out loud. The others gaze in my direction, "There's no other way through this section of the Maze without using the bowl's magic to open the way forward."

"Bloody puzzles of the gods," Doxo growls. "Give me something to hit so we can move on!" He moves to a section of the hedged wall, takes a hand axe and buries it in it. The hedge suddenly springs forth to life and swallows the axe. It would've taken his hand too if he kept hold of it. "Gods!"

"The hedges are warded," Khelrah grunts. "It has seen magic of this sort in the jungles of Rus in Kerogema."

"Like all others, it is twisted in this realm into something more sinister," Veyanna guesses in kind.

I look through the inscriptions again and again, trying to understand the puzzle. *I've always hated puzzles in games like this*, I think to myself.

"The colors in the bowl are representative of this realm's energies. It's a trap of some kind," I explain.

"In hues of twilight, find the path,

Beneath the stars, avoid the wrath.

Let colors weave in proper song,

Else the courtyard shall prove you wrong."

Everyone looks at me with expectance. "Dude, all I did was translate. I don't know what the hell it means."

"'In hues of twilight'," Veyanna recites. She looks up into the hole in the ceiling, noticing the light dwindling, "This realm must have a twilight hour. An hour that pierces the veil of magics and reveals them."

"What of the colors?" Doxo asks as he peers into the bowl.

"'Let colors weave in proper song'," I say quietly, thinking of Torbhin. "The colors must follow some kind of pattern, like a song. Like *Simon Says*."

They all look at me confused. "*Simon Says,* a kid's game where I'm from. You press the colors in the order they light up in. It's like a memory game."

"Strange traditions for one said to be from Albistair," Veyanna pries.

"But Bimbik does have good theories," Khelrah defends. She kneels to look at the runes and inscriptions, "Each rune dictates a color that represents the fated elements of this domain. If the sequence of colors can be manipulated to represent the Primeval Twilight, the stars will ignite a path forward."

"So, then we just spill the bowl and refill it with new water!" Doxo sashays to the pillar and attempts to lift it. I've never seen him struggle with something before, but the veins in his arms and neck look like they're about to explode as he huffs and heaves.

"Not all problems can be solved with strength, Doxo," Veyanna says gently as she puts her hands on his shoulder and arm, urging him to stop. With a grunt, he stops and steps aside. Veyanna takes her waterskin and pours out the remaining water before dipping the mouth of it into the bowl.

"What's happen—*whoa!*" I'm cut off as Doxo's large mitt grabs me by the collar and hoists me up on his shoulder.

"So you can stop asking questions."

I give him the bird then focus on the bowl. Veyanna's waterskin dips into the shining green swirl of water and angles it to take in what it can. Magically, the green water

166

goes directly into it and leaves the other colors, purple, blue, and orange, swirling erratically.

"Lend me your waterskins," she urges. The three of us pull them out from our satchels, pour them out onto the ground, and hand them over. "The colors need to 'weave in proper song' for us to move forward. Which means there is a pattern of transition that the water must follow."

"Start with green," Doxo says proudly. "Green is bright, so it goes from day to night."

I give him a gentle pat on the head, "Nice insight, buddy, but I think it's more complicated than that."

"Perhaps the colors must be performed in the pattern of our arrival to this moment," Khelrah suggests. "It thinks you should try the indigo color first, as we plunged into darkness to get here. It is the darkest of the hues."

Veyanna looks at me, to which I shrug and say, "It's a better guess than nothin'. Give it a try, but don't use it all up. Just in case we're wrong."

Hesitantly, she takes up the waterskin she filled with the indigo color and gently pours it in. The moment the water makes contact with the bowl, one of the runes underneath begins to glow with that same color brightly. It seems like it's correct because the air around us tingles gently.

One beat. Two beats. Nothing bad happens.

"Okay... that seems to have worked," Veyanna breathes shakily. "What's next?"

"I am telling you; green is the one to use," Doxo claims as he bends down to grab the waterskin with green water. Bending forward slides me off his shoulder. He doesn't listen to me or Veyanna before he starts pouring the green water into the bowl then stands back proudly. The rune of green glows bright before dimming to an eerie black color, along with the indigo rune. The atmosphere of the courtyard doesn't feel warm and inviting anymore, but instead cold and haunting. Brushing sounds and creaking make up for the silent void around us.

"I think that was the wrong combination," I utter gripping the smokehound daggers. The flowers and plants on the surrounding columns in the courtyard seem to bloom to life in dark, cryptic colors that look nice but creepy all at once. Doxo, Khelrah, and Veyanna all arm up, looking around cautiously.

I have little time to react before my leg is yanked out from under me by something wrapping around my ankle and dragging me away from the bowl. I scramble to try and get a grip on anything I can, but I drop my daggers from the force of the fall. Whatever has me is dragging me to the foliaged walls of the courtyard. Upside down, I'm yanked up along the wall until I'm smack in the middle. My arms, legs, and neck are all Wrapped and leashed to the wall, sharp cuts dig into my skin. I wince and crack my eyes open, watching as four open flowers snake out in front of me: Four purple and black, large petaled flowers with yellowish centers all focused on me.

"Bimbik!" Veyanna runs to help me. The flowers, in response, turn their attention to her. The petals curve inward and pop back out, spitting spores of yellowish gas in her direction. One hit of it and I watch her suddenly go rigid and stumble down to the ground, snaking vines closing in on her quickly.

Doxo roars at the sight of it and charges with his axe held high. Before the vines can attempt to restrain her, he cuts downward and severs them clean. From behind him, Khelrah rushes toward me and tugs at the vines holding me against the wall. The purple flowers start to puff up for another gas cloud. She frees my left arm and I chuck my dagger at the nearest one, the spiked pommel lodges into the center and makes it thrash. Khelrah uses the opportunity to bite down on the vine holding my right wrist, ripping it with her reptilian teeth. I slump forward, grabbing onto her shoulders while she works to free my ankles. Doxo lifts Veyanna into his arms and carries her back to the alter bowl. The vines chasing them stop short of the courtyard gazebo, retreat, and snake their way towards me and Khelrah.

"Get back to the altar!" I yell. We both run and attempt to dodge the vines whipping out at our legs.

"Replace the indigo water!" Khelrah orders Doxo while he cradles Veyanna in his arms. Gently, he sets her down on the ground, grabs the waterskin with indigo water and pours it into the bowl. The gemstones light up again, and the eerie sounds of carnivorous plants stop. The exerine and I stop at the foot of the gazebo and turn around. The plants and vines calmly return to their docile states, the purple flowers receding their blooms and the vines snake back into the hedges around the courtyard.

My attention is pulled to Veyanna's groaning sounds. She's muttering things I can't understand anything she's saying, but it doesn't seem like she's poisoned. "I think she's just disoriented."

"Forgive me, Veyanna," Doxo rasps. "I did not mean for this to occur."

"Incorrect sequences result in mystical safeguards," Khelrah says to no one as she looks back at the swirling bowl of indigo. "We must be cautious, or else invoke the wrath of the Maze."

Yeah, too late for that.

"What is the next sequence color?"

Khelrah and I say at the same time, *"Not green!"*

He rolls his eyes hard but stands near Veyanna, gesturing for us both to take over puzzle duty. I circle the underside of the bowl again looking for signs of the violet and amber colors to determine the right sequence. The indigo gem is still lit up, and around it is lit images of these figures plunging into a hole, moving forward into an unlit path where the next gem sits black and dull. "Try the violet water."

Khelrah doesn't try to argue as she picks up the violet-filled waterskin and gently pours it into the bowl. From my angle, I can see purple and indigo shimmering upward on her scaly face. She looks at me, smiles and nods. *Correct sequence.*

"Okay, two more. Jade and Amber."

Khelrah nods and observes the last two waterskins. Veyanna moans loudly as she sits up and holds her head. "What happened?"

"You got puffed by a pissed off plant," I say flatly.

Doxo winces.

"But" I add, "Doxo was the one that saved you from getting dragged away."

Veyanna bats her eyes upward at the gnolid, who is struck stupid. She gets to her hooves and gently puts a hand on his huge arm, "My thanks, Doxo." She reaches as high as she can and plants a kiss on the lower part of his jaw.

Khelrah and I both exchange glances that say *about damn time.*

I go back to trying to transcribe the images at the base. The violet gem spreads across, showing the figures moving through different paths of monsters and dangers. Something at the end of the path is larger than the other figures; tall, humanoid, crowned. The next jewel lays atop the figure's crown, black and dull.

"Okay… something about this figure is important because the next gem is in its crown," I utter aloud.

"Perhaps the jade jewel is fitting for a crown over the amber?" Khelrah guesses.

"Wait, a crown?"

I nod to Veyanna, who curiously joins me at the bowl and kneels to my level. Running a finger along the figure that I'm looking at and takes in a sharp breath. "It cannot be…"

"You know who that is?"

Her face pales, "Calos."

Everyone around us stills. Even the air seems to freeze in place.

"Who's Calos?"

"The Imprisoned God. Master of tricks and trials," she half-whispers. "Before most of the gods vanished from knowledge and practice, they quarreled among each other sanctimoniously, creating forms of order and chaos that created Preydor and its inhabitants. They finally came to a truce when the first intelligent beings recognized their creators and came together. One god was not in favor of lasting order."

"Calos," I guess. She nods in answer.

"So, he orchestrated the Trial of Trials, a labyrinthine ordeal to test the resilience of the worshippers of his kin. He got so clever with it that he even tricked some of the gods to partake in the trials. Not all of them survived. Those that did went mad and fell from grace. The gods then devised a trick of their own, challenge Calos at his own game on his own territory. He did not see past his own hubris as he began traversing the Trial while the others locked the doors and sunk it beneath the earth. He then became The Imprisoned."

Doxo huffed a laugh, "You are trying to say that this Maze is the prison of a trickster god?"

"And we're the new toys he's playing with," I add.

"Impossible," Doxo spits. "The gods abandoned us long ago. The only thing otherworldly about this labyrinth is the still lingering magics. We control our fates, not the gods."

Khelrah hisses at him, making the hairs on my neck stand straight. "Do not spit in the face of the creators, gnolid. We are far from the security of our home. The gods will prove to us that they are alive and angry."

"Okay, okay, cool it." I may be small, but I'm not about to lose time by letting this go on. "Veyanna, were there any colors or gemstones that were associated with Calos?"

Her nose scrunches in thought and I swear I see the corner of Doxo's mouth perk up at it.

"I… I am not certain."

I run a hand through my hair and try to think, "Well, where I come from, there's a god of mischief that is normally associated with green. A lot of bad guys are green; Scar, Maleficent, Rasputin."

Veyanna takes a deep breath and picks up the waterskin of green. The rest of us step back to wait to see what happens. She pours it in gently, then moves back with a gasp.

Fuck, wrong again!

I'm keeping an eye on the hedges and plants, expecting them to spring to life again. But it's still and quiet, aside from Doxo's throaty growls.

"The water," Veyanna half-whispers. We all turn to see what she is talking about. In the bowl, the water's black hue evokes some kind of mist that is pouring out of it and onto the ground of the gazebo. The mist collects around the base of the altar and then flows directly toward Doxo. He backs away, but it keeps following him and then starts to climb and surround him, no matter how hard or fast he swats at it.

"Doxo!" Veyanna tris to blow the mist away, but the gnolid's giant hand swipes out and backhands her in the face hard enough to send her to the ground.

"What the fuck, Doxo?!"

The mist opens around his face and bald head to reveal blackened, glassy eyes in a rage-fueled stare. With a few heavy breaths, he draws up his axe and swings. Khelrah quickly goes prone like a giant lizard while I fall backwards on top of Veyanna, all of us barely missing his swing.

"The magic must have gripped his mind!" Khelrah shimmies and climbs up one of the gazebo pillars to the roof. "He is not himself!"

Possessed. This place is twisted.

I pick myself up from Veyanna, whose eyes are lined with tears. "What do we do?"

"If the magic water is possessing him, then we need to solve the puzzle." She gets up from the ground as we stare down Doxo. He grunts and takes menacing steps at us, gripping the haft of his axe to the point of breaking. "Solve the puzzle. I will keep his attention focused on me."

I start, "How?? He's huge and you're hurt!"

We have barely any time to react as her hooved foot digs into my chest and pushes me away just before the axe head buries itself into the ground between us. His black eyes dart at me as he pulls the weapon free and raises it over his head for another slice to split me in half. Before it swings down, a length of claw-tipped leather wraps around the haft and pulls. He turns to face the varlese that is pulling on her whip to disarm him.

"Solve the puzzle!"

She keeps up this tug-of-war against her friend and companion to give me time to shuffle for the waterskins. Khelrah drops from the pillar and takes the empty emerald waterskin, dipping it into the bowl to take back the water. I hand her the other empty ones to take the rest of the water out of the bowl, hoping it'll break its hold on Doxo. The test of strength proves to be in Doxo's favor as he pulls against the whip and rips it from Veyanna's hands. He goes into a full sprint at her, but she's pretty fast compared to him as she darts away with a nimble bound, leading him to slam into an adjacent pillar.

"Okay, it's indigo, violet, amber, then jade! Be careful with it!" I yell as I start handing Khelrah the waterskins. She starts with the indigo, igniting the jewel on the bowl. Then violet. The amber liquid ignites the jewel underneath, illuminating the shrouded figure it crowned. She pours in the emerald liquid, and I throw my attention back to Doxo and Veyanna. She's able to dodge him up until she trips on a loose vine and tumbles. The gnolid puts his giant foot on her back to keep her in place and raises his axe.

"NO!"

The courtyard suddenly bursts with a wave of multicolored light and force, knocking everyone down to the ground. The last thing I see before I lose consciousness is one of the far hedges splitting open to a new exit, and I swear I can hear voices.

Chapter 22

~~~~~ Danica ~~~~~

Krissy is finally taking a nap after she and I stabilized Connor from having his seizure with those strange marks that appeared on his body. It wasn't just his arms, but his neck, sides, and legs. *For a nerd, he's pretty fit compared to when I first met him.* When I started my first year at SLCU, I thought I had it all figured out; knock my gen-ed courses out, start my physical therapy courses, get some field study in under my belt, start my own business and be happy. It was all perfect, even when I met Mark for the first time in Intro to Business Management. He was so dorky and adorable in his tie-dyed tank, gym shorts and cross-trainers, those humongous headphones wrapped around his neck. At first, I thought he was trying to impress everyone with his loud music and muscly arms like a lot of the frat-holes that were on campus, but he turned out to be really smart. He aced the tests we had in that course for the first half of the semester, and I was struggling hard. I decided that I'm gonna need some help, and I wanted *his* help. We had study sessions in the library, the café on campus, and then eventually in my dorm. He was sweet, sexy, fun, and hilarious. Everything I wanted in a boyfriend.

Our first year of dating was hot and heavy. It was also the year that I met Connor for the first time. We ran into him on our way to Mark's apartment and, in all honesty, I couldn't see how they were friends. They were so opposite of each other; Mark was outgoing and loud and funny, but Connor was quiet and mostly antisocial. They had nothing in common except for one thing: games. Video games, board games, and those goddamned tabletop games. It was the nerdiest I ever seen Mark when they talked about their games. It took him many attempts and a lot of buttering up to get me to sit in at one of them. It was the longest four hours I'd ever sat through. We had a serious talk about it after and it was the first real fight we had as a couple. Looking back, I'll admit I was harsh about it because I didn't think about what it meant to him. Instead, I thought about what it would look like for me if everyone knew I was dating a geek. *So fucking high school.*

So, when I agreed to help them with *The Mortal Gate*, I did it for him as long as he agreed it would be his last. I only wanted him to get it out of his system so we could focus on our future together. No one, not even Mark, could understand what I experienced in that fucking game. It wasn't just the fact I was turned into a walking cat, but it was what the place was like. We were surrounded by human NPCs that looked at us like we were monsters and freaks, something I've lived through my whole life. The entire game environment just increased the discomfort, discrimination, and sense of hopelessness. I hated it. The strength, agility, and power that came with being Night Silk was great, but I couldn't get over my fear and anxiety of what that place was doing to me. To us.

I think what really made me hate Connor so much was just how calm he was through it all and how he was able to calm everyone else down. He was able to make all these things happen, and I just felt so small. And it's that attitude that almost got Krissy killed.

A loud yawn from behind me pulls my focus as Krissy comes up to the monitors, rubbing her eyes and making her eyeshadow smear.

I reach in my purse and pull out a pack of makeup wipes, "Here. Get cleaned up."

She arches a brow at me then looks at her reflection in a nearby window. "Oh shit... thanks." She takes it, thinking I don't notice the pause, and disappears to the bathroom.

I sigh heavily and take a seat between Tweedle-Dee and Tweedle-Dum, watching their monitors. Riley, to my right, did this to himself. He was so obsessed with staying in the game that he drove us all to this moment. Connor, to my left, is just trying to save his friend. *Why am I acting like a child about this?*

"Connor," I whisper, "I know you probably won't hear any of this, and it's probably better that way. But I want to say that... I'm sorry. I was a real bitch to you for the last few years. I've blamed you and that game for things going so poorly in mine and Mark's lives, but I was just projecting. I let my fear get in the way and I didn't help the way I should have. Mark is lucky to have a friend like you, and Riley doesn't deserve to have you as a friend. You've done so much. I promise we'll get you out of this. I'm taking care of Krissy as best as I can, and Mark is working to make sure those assholes in corporate get caught for this." I gently pat his shoulder, "You don't need to forgive me for what has happened. I definitely wouldn't."

"You probably should, Dani."

Krissy is leaning against the doorframe with her arms crossed watching me. I wipe a tear from my eye gently and take a deep breath in her direction.

"Krissy, I've been terrible. It's why Mark and I are never getting back together," my voice cracking.

"Mark never said anything about what happened. Would you want to talk about it with me?" She sits at one of the office chairs and pats the one next to her.

I hesitate, my hands shaking slightly, but give her a nod. Sitting down, I lean my elbows on my knees and stare at the floor.

"After we had that meeting with Matt where he gave us that money, I thought it would be the answer to our problems. We could pay off debts and graduate and get things back to normal." I laugh dryly, "But there's no going back to normal after something like that. We both had nightmares for weeks. No matter how much therapy we went to, no matter how hard we tried to forget it, it kept coming back. We started to grow apart, do things that had nothing to do with one another. My stepdad started to notice that I was testy, irritable, and very much not myself. He was asking a lot, and I didn't want to talk to him about it because he couldn't have understood what we all went through. He took my deflecting to mean that something was happening between Mark and I, and he started saying all these nasty things about him. And I think because all the things he said just boiled in me, it made me snap. Mark was looking at games online when I got home from a shift at work, and we just got into it. I went off and told him all the things my stepdad told me. I didn't mean any of it. It just came out like a flood."

My eyes are stinging trying to fight back tears. Krissy said nothing, just let me come undone.

"When Mark moved out, I shut down completely. I went to more therapy and tried to untangle everything. I focused less on what had happened and focused more on what I could control in the moment. I was working double-time to keep the apartment while keeping up my internship with a physical therapist. I stretched myself so thin I just stopped doing everything I used to care about. So many unanswered calls and texts from Mark, ignoring all my stepdad's bantering. When I got your message, I felt I needed to present myself better than I actually am. I'm so torn down but I had to look like I was not a mess. My mom always told me to never show weakness no matter what."

"Danica, it's not weak to feel powerless or scared," she half-whispers through her own tears. "Connor was scared shitless for a long time. He still is. But he's trying to do what he can. He's thought about all of you for the last two years, I don't think he's thought about his own health once."

I shake my head, "How? How does he do that? How do you keep it together?"

With a dry laugh, she answers, "It's not as easy as it looks. That first year back was a nightmare. We thought it would've been easier if we moved in together so we could tackle the problem together. All it did was give us loss of sleep and drinking problems. About six months in, we saw what we were doing to ourselves. Matt kicked Connor's ass to work on his project because he believed in him. That kick was transferred from him to me when Connor told me to stop feeling sorry for myself and find an outlet. Turns out I'm really good at being angry, so he got me a trial to a Krav

Maga class. I beat the shit out of so many tough guys that I used it all the time. He dumped his focus into making *Soulscape* and should have been promoted a long ass time ago. Now we know why."

I curled my fingers into a fist, feeling my nails dig into my palm. "They're the ones I should be angry with."

She chuckles through her tears.

"Krissy... I'm sorry for what happened with the river monster. I don't think I ever apologized for that." I don't expect her to forgive me for that. I really did think if she was killed in the game that she would wake up on the Outside and get the rest of us out. I explain that to her here and now, not expecting her to forgive me for it, especially since I hadn't brought it up in two years.

Krissy, for some reason, just gives me a sad smile and takes my hand. "I know you are. I know what you were thinking at that moment. We made it out alive and we relied on each other. You don't have to hold that guilt anymore."

I can't hold back my tears as I lean over and pull her into a hug. We sit there holding each other like two sisters reuniting.

We separate and smile through our tears just in time to hear running footsteps coming from the hallway. Coming to a sliding stop is Mark wearing a dirty flannel unbuttoned, showing his muscle shirt underneath, ratty jeans and crummy shoes, all while hiding his face under a trucker's cap.

"What the fuck happened," Krissy demands.

Mark is trying to catch his breath as he slides down to the floor against the wall, taking the cap off. He's a sweaty mess and completely out of breath. He says nothing as he reaches into his pant pocket and pulls out a small black flash drive. Krissy gasps loudly and rushes over to take it from his hand.

"You found it!"

"Y-yeah," he says between pants, "piece of cake."

"Then why do you look like shit?" I didn't mean to sound so curt, but it's how it came out.

Mark looks up at me with a sneer, "Because I almost got busted by rent-a-cops that were sent to take Matt's car. Had to ditch my stuff and grab this shit from some random laundromat on the way here."

We both gawk at him.

"You said not to get caught, so I improvised!"

"Okay, okay," Krissy says hastily. "We've got the drive, now we need to worry about Matt sitting in a cell while we figure out what's on this thing and keep an eye on the boys."

"I'm done making runs," Mark fires off from the floor.

"Maybe he can post his own bail?"

I shake my head, "He would've done it by now. Something must be keeping him locked up. Maybe corporate?"

"Makes sense," Krissy mutters walking to one of the computer stations. "They're the ones that blew the whistle on him. Probably trying to keep him out of the way. We have to keep things tight here, so he's gonna have to get out on his own."

Mark sucks in a breath through his teeth, "That's pretty shitty."

"We don't have much of a choice. I'm gonna try to get this drive up and running. You two check on the monitors." Krissy pops the drive into the computer for downloading.

Mark and I walk over to the knuckleheads still knocked out when he asks what he missed.

"So, apparently something different is happening this time," I explain. "Connor went into a seizure and started showing signs of pain. Red marks were all over him. We kept him down until he settled enough for him to get back to normal."

"Shit."

"Yeah."

Awkward silence fills the space between us.

"Are you okay?" I ask quietly.

He shoots a surprised look at me before nodding. "Yeah… I just wasn't prepared for all this *Mission Impossible* stuff, y'know?"

I return the nod, "Well you didn't get caught, so that's something."

Another moment of silence falls.

"So, are we talking again?" There's a bit of desperation in my question.

His face goes stone, and he shrugs, "We're here, aren't we? Working together again? More than what we've said to each other in a long time."

"I've texted you," I snap. "Tried calling you."

"There wasn't anything to say. You pretty much said everything you needed."

I deserve that.

"Mark... my stepdad got in my head. He's never been a fan of you, and he saw an opportunity to tell me how he felt," I explain.

He scoffs, "Yeah, Lamar has never been on my list of favorites either. One of the things I enjoyed about dating you was helping you piss him off."

I wince, "Is that the only good thing that came from us being together?"

My question seems to have struck some kind of nerve because he flinches and looks down at the floor. "Of course not, Dani. You were fun, strong, outspoken, and I loved you. But what happened after the game, it's like you became someone else entirely. We both did. There are too many factors in why we fell apart."

My eyes are stinging again as he looks up at me, "Dani, I don't know how or why, but we just stopped connecting. I didn't want it, and I don't think you did either. But I was too quiet, and you were too aggressive, even in our therapy sessions. And I don't think we can go back to what we were before."

He's right. Too much damage has been done to ever go back to what we were. But I don't want to lose Mark. I can't.

"W-what about friends? Starting over? Rebuild trust," I offer.

The longest pause of my entire life. It was like stretching each second into a decade. My heart is in my throat waiting for an answer. He sighs deeply and rubs the back of his neck, flexing his arm in the process. Then, that same arm extends to me with his hand open, "Sure. Let's try that."

Containing my excitement, I shake his hand and smile softly through building tears. With that, I move my attention to Connor and his current status while Mark checks on Riley. I lean over and pull Connor's eyelids open to see if anything has changed when my hand lands on something in the pocket of his jacket. Purely out of curiosity, I reach into his pocket and grab the velvet-covered box. My heart drops.

"Uh… Krissy?"

Chapter 23

Faint, mumbling voices slowly creep into my head as my eyes flutter open. I feel myself leaning against some kind of solid surface, something tightly wrapped around my wrists and ankles. Through the haziness in my vision, I'm now looking at a group of people that look like an indigenous tribe of some kind. They're all wearing these finely woven clothes that look like they're decorated with the same kind of symbols all over. Some have their clothes and headwear decorated with bones while others have feathers or scales. Most of them are wearing masks that look oddly similar to the smokehounds or of the same skin type as those devourworms. On the exposed skin, there are glowing marks like glow-in-the-dark tattoos in weird designs.

"Welcome back to the land of the living, Bimbik," a familiar gruff voice says.

To my right, Doxo is bound by the same restraints as I am while he's glaring up at the weirdos, who all are pointing strange weapons at him. *Probably tried putting up a fight.* To my left, Veyanna and Khelrah are both bound like us; Veyanna looking absolutely fascinated with the people that tied us up while Khelrah's serpentine face is completely unreadable.

One of the tribal folks pushes forward towards me wearing flashier decorations on them; a feathered mask/headdress combo with a black beak pointed downwards, scaled arm braces going all the way up to their elbows, clothes that look like they're woven from vines, thornbushes and some kind of leather hide, boots that look like they're either smoking or giving off some kind of vapor effect, all while carrying a spear of dark wood topped with a sharp point that looks like it's made from...

"Smokehound teeth."

The masked figure tilts their head at me.

"What?" Doxo sneers without dropping any eye contact with our captors.

"That spearhead," I explain, raising my eyebrows at it. "It's made of smokehound teeth like my daggers."

Beak-face kneels down to my level, really having to squat due to my height, and stares at me. Through the eyeholes, I can make out slightly glowing color that looks like the same teal glow coming from their tattoos.

"*Eff ke' secto mah.*" Their speech sounds guttural and scratchy, and admittedly intimidating. "*Su' eff ke'!*"

"I'm sorry, but I can't understand you," I try to explain.

The others behind Beak-face start muttering softly in that same language. I can't understand anything they're saying, but it sounds pretty concerning for us.

"I have never heard this language before," Veyanna says in wonder. She's genuinely intrigued by them.

Khelrah looks around her towards me and Doxo, "It sounds primitive. As if they are of a time or place where the common tongue is not used or familiar."

The murmuring stops as Beak-face stands up and removes the mask. Underneath is the angular face of a striking woman, dark bronzed skin, amber eyes that look as shiny as the gem from the puzzle, glowing teal eyes that really do reflect the color of her tattoos. Her head is bald and decorated with those swirling lines wrapping around it in various swirls and points.

"Who. Are. You." She speaks slowly in English, or Common as the others call it.

Before I can get a word in, Doxo growls, "You are the ones who captured us at our weakest! You owe *us* answers. Who are you, and why are you here in the Primeval Maze?"

More murmuring, this time a bit more curious and cautious. I try to note everyone's reactions on both sides. Beak-face flourishes her spear and points it to Doxo's neck. "Who. Are. You."

Doxo growls in response, the spear barely scratching at his throat.

"We're explorers," I blurt. Their attention turns to me. "We're the Mazebreakers, and we're trying to stop the pouring out of monsters from the Maze from reaching the surface and destroying Preydor."

Beak-face releases her hold on Doxo's neck and steps in front of me, curiosity literally glowing in her eyes. "Mazebreakers. Outlanders. Ones who seek to close the rift to the Primeval Realm."

Everyone gapes in response. I nod quickly, "Yes. And… I'm looking for someone that came here some time ago. Someone from the Out — uh, surface, like us."

The murmuring stops and is replaced by a few choice gasps. Beak-face stares at me blankly before turning to a few of her people. "*Uvenk! Zasar ut' montok vescum* Preydor. *Sha'nat!*"

She puts her mask back on and walks through the crowd. Some of the bigger ones pick us up one at a time to our feet, cut our ankle restraints loose, and push us to follow the rest of them.

Doxo tries to struggle, but Veyanna kicks him in the ass with her hoof and hisses, "Just move, you big brute."

Without any argument, he growls under his breath but starts walking. Even in our current situation, it's funny. We are marching through a new undiscovered corridor of the Maze, but this one is significantly different. The walls are carved and etched stone with various drawn images like hieroglyphics in a cave or a pyramid, ranging from small humanoid images to giant monstrous ones. I can't tell if it's the lighting or from being dazed still, but I swear I can see the images moving. I feel a gentle nudge into the back of my shoulder from Khelrah, encouraging me to not linger too long and keep following. Her demeanor is so calm that it's like she's been in a situation like this before. Our "escorts" keep talking back and forth between each other in that weird language, but it doesn't take a genius to know what they're saying stuff about us with all of those glances and sideways looks. The cobblestone floor vibrates from the sounds of our feet, showing that these people really don't take stealth seriously. *Or maybe they know something we don't about the Maze.*

We come to a sudden stop when Beak-face holds up a hand. Everyone goes silent. I peek my head to the side to try and get a good look at what's happening. There's nothing ahead of us, nor behind us. But that isn't what they're waiting for. The floor beneath us starts to shake, vibrate, in a pattern like footsteps. Giant footsteps.

"Hesha! Foltus esh vah!"

Suddenly we are running forward through the corridor, ducking into different corners and turns *towards* the increased stomping.

"Where the fuck are we going?!" None of them answer me as we're being herded like cattle. A guttural groan like a certain giant mutated zombie I know shatters the air and sends me to my knees. Doxo, Veyanna and Khelrah also cripple to the ground, covering their ears against the sound. None of the indigenous people are brought down by the noise but they all take up their weapons and face behind us. Coming around the corner we ran from is this large, ugly, grotesque motherfucker that stands taller than the fucking walls of the maze. Its skin looks like its melting off of the bones, exposing everything decayed and rotted underneath. Visible veins of green and purple coil up and down its remaining skin that's hanging on for dear life. Its face makes me retch harder than I did with the stitchlings; sunken eyes of pale yellow, broken and rotted teeth with a purple stained

191

tongue barely held inside its mouth. Its enormous footsteps leave these rotting and sizzling footprints that scare me shitless.

"Radhlek!"

We are now in a full sprint running away from that hulking carcass. It gives another loud groan of a roar, followed by large thuds that shake the ground. *It's chasing us!*

I'm suddenly hoisted up by Doxo because my fucking puny legs are slowing me down. The bouncing and rag dolling has me shaken up so much I can't focus on the thing chasing us. It's slow but has a hell of a stride.

Doxo skids to a stop and yells, "What in the hells is this?!"

I twist to try and get a good look at what he's cursing at. Beak-face led us to a fucking *dead end!* "What the fuck?!"

She doesn't reply or comment. She raises her free hand to the dead-end wall and begins muttering words I can't comprehend. The swirling designs on her body match with the now glowing designs on the wall, making it spin and twist into an open passageway. She stands back and barks a command to her people, signaling them to enter the way through. All of them start flooding into it, us included as they push us forward. Doxo sets me back down on the ground after we pass the threshold. Beak-face makes a closing motion with her hands and the wall begins to close again. The large beast roars again and attempts to reach through before the wall shuts.

Everyone is out of breath as they hug each other and speak to one another in their language. What I also notice is that there are more people here than when we were picked up. More men, women, and children all dressed and marked the same as Beak-face and the others. *Is this a whole colony or something?*

"*Junto.*" Beak-face must have given them an order because her people come over and cut our bindings free. Khelrah comes over to me with a reassuring pat on the shoulder, which I give a nod in return. Veyanna and Doxo are going back and forth with a quiet argument.

I break away from the rest of them and approach the leader. "Thank you for helping us. What was that thing?"

"They call it Blightfoot."

From behind the leader, the crowd separates to make way for a tall, orange-red skinned male with fur growing from his hands and all around his face. His nose is sunken in like a lion's snout. He's wearing simple leather on his torso and his legs, but no boots on his clawed feet. He's shouldering a large mace made of what looks like various bones and claws. He stops right next to the tribe leader and stares at me with a sneer of his fanged teeth and emerald, green eyes.

"Sup, Connor?"

I feel the color drain from my face.

"Riley?"

Chapter 24

"Here, I'm called Zasar. I'm an irbulg Breaker," Riley says with a smug look, fist resting on his hip. "This," he gestures to Beak-face, "is Rhyeah, leader of the Yaruk tribe and leader of this settlement within the Maze."

He's here... alive... not a fucking mark on him! Not a hint of worry or fear!

I take a running start, leap up and shove my shoulder into his gut. We both go tumbling down and I am laying haymakers into him. We trade punches back and forth until we get pulled apart by our separate groups.

"You son of a bitch! What the fuck did you do?! Why would you fucking do this?!" I'm struggling against Veyanna's grip, tears of rage dropping down my face.

The one called Rhyeah picks Riley up from the ground and inspects his face. Rather carefully.

Oh, hell no! He didn't!

"It's okay, Rhyeah. He's just letting off steam. Have everyone make a count for resources and get the camp ready to move. We'll need to be ready to relocate away from Blightfoot," he tells her in a soft voice.

Are you fucking serious, Riley?!

Rhyeah nods to him, glares at me, then turns to her people, giving orders and walking away.

Riley looks down at me then to the others with me, "You mind if we talk alone?"

"You are the one that Bimbik has been searching for?" Khelrah asks cautiously.

"Yeah," he says flatly. "And he shouldn't have been. That's what we're gonna talk about. So, if you don't mind?"

I take a deep breath, not taking my eyes off of him, but give the others a nod that it will be okay. Not too convinced, Veyanna led the others aside to try and give us privacy.

Riley takes a deep breath and turns around, "Come this way. Your friends will be okay here, I promise."

Remember when you *were my friend?*

I follow him into a nook within the walls of the Maze where the Yaruk tribe is all convening and packing things up. It's like a small village of people that are all the same skin tone as Rhyeah, all with those strange tattoos that softly glow on their skin. One such Yaruk swirls their hand in the air and makes the ground swallow a small fire to put it out.

"Whoa."

"The Yaruk are very intimate with the Maze and its magic," Riley explains ahead of me. He leads me towards a tent of foliage and shrubbery, pulls the curtain door aside and gestures for me to enter. I sneer at him and walk inside. From the looks of the inside, either he's in charge or he's fucking the person in charge. A mixture of tribal clothes and leather armor is scattered about, some makeshift weapons and tools gathered on a workbench, a single bedroll and a bunch of things that look super official for a scary place.

"Looks like you're living the high life, *Zasar*."

"Better than what I had before," he retorts and closes the curtain door. He sets his weapon aside and walks over to a table with a barrel on it, grabbing two cups along the way. "Want a drink? Dovesh makes a really good drink from the flora in the Maze."

I am stunned. He's carrying on like nothing has been happening. "Dude, are you out of your fucking mind? What happened to you, and why did you agree to work this project?"

I hear him sigh loudly while he's pouring whatever it is into the cups. He walks to a nearby box and sits down, holding out the cup, "You're gonna want this. One of the perks of this programming."

Stomping forward, I yank the cup from his hand and sit on the ground in front of him, "Start talking."

"Okay," he groans and takes a large drink. "It started six months after we accepted the job at SnoWire…"

Chapter 25

Handicap accessible. One of the few perks of having this job at SnoWire Interactive. Head storyline developer and co-designer of Connor's project, *Soulscape*. Six months of base-level production, team building, programming schedules, and nearly fuck-all to show for it. A project that was supposed to be on a two-year budget contract. Connor has a specific vision for this game, and he promised that we would be partners in its development. That it would somehow make up for what happened with *The Mortal Gate*.

Yeah, I'm still pissed about that. I was completely prepared to stay in Albistair as Amocus, to be powerful and strong as a mage, and to *be able to walk*. I didn't care if it was all some elaborate program meant to make players feel the effects of everything they experience. I was strong and free. Then, I get shoved back into reality by my best friend.

Now, I'm back in this shithole world, stuck in a metal prison on wheels, doubling as a storyline developer and a game store owner. I should be happy, right? I should be okay with two jobs that are in my wheelhouse, *pun intended*, and with the massive increase in pay that I'm getting. So many perks and benefits are open to me, yet I could give a shit less. If this had happened before the game, I would have been over the moon. I love games and I love making things like stories for my *D&D* groups. But why pretend to live it if

I could *actually* live it? Matt made sure that would be impossible when he destroyed the data and hard drive for the system.

My train of thought is interrupted by the elevator doors opening on my floor. I politely smile and respond to everyone in the office as I wheel past them to get to my office. Our floor is filled with fun and quirky nerds like me, and I appreciate them busting their asses to try and get things going, but they have no idea how much better things could be if we redevelop Dawson's original Crest program and integrate it with *Soulscape.*

Every time I even suggest that to Connor, he comes back with the same argument.

"It's too dangerous."

"This game has too many possibilities of death."

"It literally puts players through Hell. Do you want to be responsible for what would happen if we Crested the project?"

In all seriousness, yes. I would. Because at least it provides the perfect kind of escape for everyone. The players' options and possibilities would be completely in their control, and they can become who or whatever they want.

"Morning, Ironsides." Connor is standing by my office door with two cups of coffee in hand.

My keys jingle in the lock as I open it, "You're here early. What's the occasion?"

I position myself at my desk setup: Three monitors for three different purposes; animation, storyboard drafts, and a personal gaming monitor. A minifridge stocked with protein shakes and cold brew bottles. An interactive digital pad for on-the-go designs and notes. And a desk filled with figurines, fidget toys and a nameplate with my name on it.

Connor sits across from me and sets the cups down on the desk, one with my name on it and the company logo; a snowflake made of wires and circuits. "I'm here early because I wanted to check in on you. See how you're acclimating to your position. We hardly talk anymore outside of work."

I flip on my monitors and boot up my programs, taking the coffee cup and taking a sip of my usual drink. Hot quad with a shot of milk and a shot of cinnamon. They call it a *Health Point Killer*; I call it the "don't talk to me until I've destroyed this" special.

"Well, the project has been top priority since we're behind schedule."

He sighs, "Touché. I know it's been a headache, but I think we'll be ready for first rounds of alpha testing and bug fixing by the end of the quarter."

I sigh back at him and take another swig. "Connor, cut the shit. You're here to make sure I'm not trying to pitch the Crest tech to Bauer and the board again."

There's defeat and offense in his eyes. *Good. He knows I know when he's about to micromanage me.*

"Riley, why do we keep coming back to this? I mean, did you not think I wouldn't find out that you proposed an altered design of the Crest to board members on their fucking lunch breaks? Trying to go over Matt's head? Over *my* head? I thought we were friends."

"Yeah? Well so did I," I spat back. "I thought you knew me and would respect what I wanted."

"What? A death sentence?" His eyes don't break from me through his seething. "Riley, if you stayed in *The Mortal Gate*, you would be brain dead like Dominic and Lorena. Is that what you wanted? Is that better than what you have now?"

"Yes!" I wheel backwards, "Look at me. I'm useless. I haven't been able to feel my fucking legs for nearly eighteen years! I got my legs back in Albistair and I had purpose. You took that away. Now when we are literally in the fucking workshop where it was made, when we can give everyone a chance to exist how they want to, you pull the plug on it."

He blinks at me in what I can only guess is shock. "Riley... do you know who you sound like?"

"Well, maybe she was right."

Silence falls between us. He slowly gets up from the chair and heads for the door. He pauses after opening it and says over his shoulder, "I didn't want to lose my best friend to a fantasy. It's time for us to face reality. I hope you'll see that soon." He closes it behind him.

Out of rage, I take up a figure on my desk and chuck it at the wall, watching it shatter.

He doesn't get it. He's got everything! A lead position at a gaming company, a girlfriend, working fucking legs, and he was the main-fucking-character in the game. He doesn't know what it's like to live life on the fucking sidelines waiting for your chance at glory and respect. I don't want to be pitied! I want to live, goddammit.

The rest of the workday went by as mundane as it could possibly be, aside from the thick fog of tension between me and Connor during our team meetings. I don't care what he says or how many times he tries to convince me, I know what I want. And if I have to start from scratch to reach Dawson's level, then I will.

Six hours later, I'm on the transit back to my shitty apartment, taking work home with me so I can finalize some last-minute adjustments in the animation styling to fit the dynamic of the game environment. The bus lets me off at my stop and I wheel up the steep walkway that the super refuses to alter or fix. There's no mail today for me, so I'm not gonna be distracted.

A door behind me creaks open and I curse under my breath. "Yes, Miss Wyatt?"

"Can't even have the decency to turn around and greet me?"

This crone has been living here way longer than I have and she thinks she's the fucking queen of the complex. I turn around to see her in her signature pink robe with pajamas underneath, tapping her slipper impatiently, and crossing her arms in offense. Her curled blond hair is frazzled, and her eyes look red from restlessness.

"Taking the day off, I see?"

She scowls, "Yes. I've earned it, and I've earned some rest today. So help me, boy, if you blast that T.V. this evening, I will phone the super and have your ass out of here."

Deep breaths, Riley.

"Well, I'll keep that in mind while I'm working. You know what work is, right? Oh, wait, you just stopped being 'between jobs' recently, haven't you? Or is it 'between woman beaters'?"

I suppress my smirk when her face goes red with rage. I turn my chair back around and open my door, "Don't worry, *Karen*. I'm sure you'll land a good man who's deaf or hard of hearing, so he doesn't have to listen to your constant ragging." I slam the door and lock it before she has the chance to fire off her insults.

Same routine to follow every day; light up my crappy home, lay my work case on the couch I have for guests that never come anymore, go to the kitchen to grab a beer and the leftover Chinese food from yesterday, then land in my sanctuary of a bedroom that is set up with all my tabletop and video gaming supplies. Most of it has been sitting around collecting dust because I've been surfing the web for several months, jumping from one chatroom to the next, one dead-end practice to another trying to find stories and conversations on developing augmented reality systems. If I couldn't get Connor's support on this, I know there's no way in hell the others are gonna help me either. So, I'm finding new contacts. People that have the same dream as me. To develop a world where fantasy can become reality and people can be exactly who they want to be.

~~~~ The Next Morning ~~~~

Knock, knock.

I peel my face away from my desktop, groaning from the pain in my neck and back hunching over until I fell asleep. My screen is still on an off-brand *Reddit* page of a bunch of know-nothings who only talk about how many virtual babes they would fuck if augmented reality would let them. Fucking gross.

Knock, knock, knock.

"Ugh, hold on! I'm coming!" I lazily roll my chair out of my room and head for the door. "I swear to God, Miss Wyatt, if you seriously called the super on me..."

I flip all the locks and open the door. My heart stops. Armand Guzman, Alan Frost, and William Ho are at my door.

"Good morning, Mr. Woods," Guzman says with a smile. "I know it's quite early, but would you mind if we come in?"

"Uh, is everything all right?" I turn to look at the state of my place, "I'm not exactly 'guest ready.'"

"Oh yes, everything is just fine," Frost assures me. "We just have something important we would like to discuss with you. It will only take a short moment of your time."

"S-sure, uh, come on in."

I wheel myself back to give them enough room to enter. I am so embarrassed at the state of my place with my *executive bosses* standing in it. They take up the open space between my couch and my T.V. and wait on me.

"So, how can I help you all? Is this about the project? I know it's been slow, but I promise you —"

Ho puts up a hand to stop me. "This is not the reason for our visit, Mr. Woods."

I keep quiet and let them say their piece.

Guzman clears his throat, "You see, Mr. Woods, Dominic Dawson left behind large shoes to fill in the future of video game development and advancement. Are you familiar with a government mandate to utilize the gaming industry to train soldiers and improve their weapons capabilities?"

"I've heard of it, yes," I answer. "Air Force uses video game analog sticks for drone control, the Marines use virtual tabletop positioning for strategic planning in digitally scanned environments. It has a lot of potential uses."

"Exactly," Frost agrees. "But they are always in need of innovation. We want to give them something that would be able to bring the greatest military in the world to the new age. Through augmented reality technology."

I gape. "You... are you planning to convert SnoWire into a private military contractor?"

All three of them laugh. It's Guzman that shakes his head, "No, of course not. We are just partnering with a sector of the military to help us innovate new technology. It's a partnership more than a conversion. With the technology they recover in their missions combined with our teams and programs, we can generate a new avenue of revenue and an endorsement that will set SnoWire Interactive above all other game developers."

"That is where you come in, Mr. Woods," Ho adds while he reaches into his briefcase holstered on his shoulder. My stomach does backflips as he pulls out a Crest, exactly like what we used in *The Mortal Gate*.

"Dominic had a similar vision of creating augmented reality technology to improve his company, may he rest in peace," Ho laments. The others nod in agreement. "However, the tech he used in this headset he called a Crest is a bit... primitive."

"Are you kidding?" I start. "That is cutting-edge tech that literally dumps the human consciousness directly into the virtual environment, allowing the players to feel, see, hear, smell, and touch everything as if it were real."

Fuck!

Guzman gives a satisfactory smirk as he says, "I do believe we were right, gentlemen."

"I—I'm sorry, I don't—"

"Please, Mr. Woods," Guzman stops me. "We managed to recover surveillance footage of what we suspected. We are aware that Lorena was able to fast-track her father's work and make it viable. We know that you, Mr. Wright, and a few others were given the format and the game to 'test' it. Very unfortunate how it all ended, however."

They know? And they've let us work for them for the past several months?

Frost steps in next, "We hold no grievances, nor do we plan to initiate any lawsuits. What we do plan to do is improve Dawson's work and prepare it for a new adventure."

He hands me a data disk that has cover art on it in a familiar text, swirling in red, black, and green. There's a title on it:

The Primeval Maze.

"We want you to operate on this and help us to conduct its full capabilities," Guzman offers. "Help us design new Crests that require less maintenance and use stronger radio waves. Turn this new landscape into a reality that we can give to our customers and share with our partners to bring in a new era of virtual interaction. It'll be off the books, but you will be well compensated. What do you say?"

I think. I *really* think. It seems off, but even if it is the slightest bit true, they're giving me a way to relive and prosper in my true world. A world where I am strong, capable, and have purpose.

I reach out my hand and take Guzman's, "Let's make some magic."

~~~~ 24 Hours from Now ~~~~

"Riley, you've gotta stop stalling me here. You seriously need to move past what happened."

"I *am* moving past it. There are… bigger things coming. So, let's make it happen." I return to my computer screen as Connor gives me a pitiful look and leaves my office. I couldn't let him see the adjustments I was making to the game mechanics and its compatibility with the new Crests. Guzman promised to have the improvements completed by the end of the workday as long as I finish this part of it. Undoubtedly, he gave Connor a hard time that made him march to my office. He doesn't understand. He *wouldn't* understand that what I'm doing is going to surpass his project. It'll revolutionize everything we know about modern technology and fast forward us to the future. In just a few hours, it'll be greenlit, and I will be back in the system, free to be me.

Something as big as *The Primeval Maze* should've taken five or more years to develop at this scale. But, somehow, Guzman was able to recover the initial designs and blueprints from Dominic and Lorena's software before Matt ordered its purge. *Why would anyone destroy something so beautiful? So perfect.* With initial modifications made to the original Crests to interact with the prefrontal cortex of the brain and react to mental commands in the subconscious, the interface gloves were made unnecessary, just like the playmat. Just a disc in a strong enough system with high RAM and electric output, and it surpasses the original. *I've surpassed both Dominic and Lorena!*

I'm anxiously waiting for the call from upstairs. I've already signed away my ownership of The Cache, no matter how hard J.D. fought me over it. I've put in an advance payment on my apartment, so I don't lose my stuff. Best of all, I secured the same warehouse unit where it all began. It feels right to make the jump there, although I had to use a pseudonym to get it secured since they would remember our last visit there. I don't bother returning any of Connor's calls or texts. Not even Matt's. This time, *I'm* the main character. And I'll get my ultimate journey.

Rrrrrrrrrring. Rrrrrrrrrrring.

My office phone.

"This is Riley."

"It is time, Mr. Woods."

Chapter 26

"And, from there, I booted up at the warehouse, started the game and here we are," Riley says too calmly.

I can feel veins pulsing in my forehead. "I… I want to fucking kill you so badly right now. You selfish, stupid fucking moron."

Riley stands up from his seat and gestures to his body, "Look at me, Connor and tell me what you see."

"A furry, lion-faced jackass living in a fucking fantasy instead of living in reality with people that worry about him constantly?"

He sighs heavily, "I am a strong, walking, respected warrior that has a purpose here. I don't answer to anyone, I don't fear anything, and I never have to worry about anything like bills or pissy neighbors or people walking on fucking eggshells around me."

"Riley, how can you be so dumb?!" I shoot to my feet and throw my arms in the air, "They're using you, you moron! Look at what they gave you! A body that will ensure you never want to leave. Look at what they did to *me* to come in after you! A body that they *know* will either kill me or keep me here, so I don't go after them myself!"

"I never asked you to come after me, Connor," he replies with uneasy calm. "I wanted this for myself. They let me have a world of my own where I can come and go as I please. I have my own method of leaving when I feel like it, rather than being stuck until the game is won. I have no intention of ever winning this game."

There's absolutely no way I'm ever going to change his mind. He's all made up and is willing to rot away Outside to stay here. *I can't believe this. I've lost my best friend.* I try to suppress my anger long enough to ask him, "Fine. I'll leave you alone. Tell me how to log out, and you can fucking rot here alone."

"You're serious?"

I nod with my eyebrows raised in surprise.

"Ugh, fine. But what about your friends out there?"

"Take them to the center of the Maze, let them finish without you and fucking let them live their virtual binary lives," I growl.

He blinks, "Seriously? You, who went out of your way to save Yeskarra, Djaren, Zinis and their people in Albistair, are willing to let these ones just maneuver the Maze on their own without the slightest possibility of surviving?"

"Coming from someone who's playing hero to a tribe of people in a situation *you* helped create? Someone who's playing 'knight in furry armor' to a computer program?"

He shoves a finger into my chest, "Don't talk about Rhyeah like that!"

"Oh my god! This is Nara all over again! You fell for a fucking NPC!"

His cheeks flare up a dark orange color in contrast to the rest of his face, and I know I hit the mark.

"It's more than that, Connor," he says through gritted teeth, a hand rubbing the back of his neck. "Rhyeah and I are bonded. She's Chieftain of the Yaruk and I am its primary guardian… and the Chieftain's consort."

I fall straight down on my ass in a sitting position. "You… you *married* an NPC?! You've only been in here for about two full days!"

"Time works differently here! Remember that it was barely eighteen hours when we were pulled from the game last time? It's been several rift cycles here, plenty of time for Rhyeah to interrogate me, test me, then accept me and fall in love with me," he explains with too much calm. Too much. "I've been able to help protect her people from various monsters that invaded from the Primeval Realm, and it's gained me a lot of respect. I'm helping them to maneuver through the Maze until it is safe for them to return home."

I can't take anymore crazy. I jolt up to my feet and make to leave, but his gorilla hand grabs my shoulder to stop me. "Connor, please don't do anything to ruin this. I'm begging you. Just let me have this."

With a heavy sigh, I grab his hand and take it off my shoulder. "I came here to save you, Riley. Because I can't afford to lose my best friend. My partner. But I can see I've already lost Riley Woods. For good."

I walk out of the tent, leaving him behind. The other Mazebreakers are currently talking with Rhyeah. Doxo and Veyanna are getting their wounds checked while Khelrah looks like she's inspecting the entire camp of its people and supplies. As much as I hate what Riley is trying to defend, he makes a point that I can't argue. I *do* treat these programs like living things and people. There have been many times I've thought about what happened to Yeskarra, Djaren and Zinis after the game was decommissioned and erased. *Were they aware of what was happening to them? Could they feel themselves being erased?*

"Bimbik."

My thoughts clear up when Khelrah draws my attention, waving me over to her. Some of the Yurak cast glances in my direction, others are too busy with packing up the camp.

"What is it, Khelrah?"

She kneels down to get in close, removing her hood and revealing the most serious eye contact I've received. "It does not feel like the Yaruk are being honest or forthcoming."

"What do you mean?" This doesn't sound good at all.

She tugs on my sleeve and pulls me aside where we can get a little more privacy. "It has noticed the marks the Yurak wear on their bodies. Something strange about them has it concerned for the company's safety."

I look over my shoulder to see what she's talking about. The tattoos on the Yaruk are still slightly glowing that bright teal color, the same color as the irises of their eyes. "I mean, they glow, which is freaky. What's the concern?"

212

"Look closer, luthien," she urges.

Humoring her, I look again. One of the Yaruk children suddenly runs towards us trying to catch some kind of ball. I stop it with my foot and pick it up, holding it to the child. They smile big at me with those wondrous eyes, and I think I see what Khelrah is talking about. The marks are moving, shifting, changing patterns constantly. Winding corridors in constant motion on their skin.

The child takes the ball back and says, *"Yu'k'na!"* before scampering away.

"The marks… they're like —"

"The Primeval Maze," she finishes.

It makes sense. Rhyeah was able to open the hedge of the Maze and close it to keep out that decayed giant. They pack up when something dangerous is near like a nomadic tribe.

"It thinks that if the Yaruk hail from the Primeval Realm and their marks reflect the Maze, that they as a people must attract the dangers to them," she guesses.

It must be one of the objectives of the game, to solve the mystery of the Yaruk and their connection to the Maze.

"Okay, let's see what we can find out, then. Keep your eyes open," I say quietly.

Khelrah puts her hood back up in response, gives me a firm nod, then follows me back to Rhyeah. The chieftain is speaking with her people who are continuing to pack up and disassemble the camp.

She notices us approaching and meets halfway, "You spoke to Zasar?"

I nod with a grim look, "I did. Mainly business between us. I was hoping to ask you about the Yurak and the Maze itself."

"We are pressed on time, small one. My people need to be prepared to move on." She gestures to the tribe with slightly sad cadence.

"I understand, but it might help us break this curse and help Preydor be safe."

That statement gets a dry scoff in reply. "Preydor. A surface world of division and chaos long before the Primeval beasts invaded its lands."

"You have grievance with the surface, chieftain," Khelrah asks with a little hiss in her voice.

"Our people were discarded when we first arrived on the surface, just like the Trial Master discarded us."

"Who's the Trial Master?"

"Calos," Khelrah answers with venom. "The one who toys with us mortals. Locked away in his own machination by his fellow gods."

"Of sorts," Rhyeah interjects. "The story of Calos is slightly exaggerated. Calos was not born a god, but a Yaruk. An ancestor of ours. He was clever, cunning, creative, and manipulative. His own genius cost him his eternal rest. Believing himself smarter than the gods, he used Primeval magics to construct the Primeval Maze to test the resolve of the gods. He proposed a challenge; to solve his labyrinth or to surrender their immortality to him."

Oh yeah, the story the others told me was greatly exaggerated. But it also sounds familiar.

"He managed to entice Octos, the Lasting Fury, into accepting the challenge, not willing to allow a mortal to challenge the will of the gods. As God of the hunt, he sought to humiliate Calos by using his own creations to sniff out and direct the correct paths to the center. But the mortal was clever, setting physical and magical traps that ensnared each beast Octos released. They still roam this Maze, only in a different skin."

The smokehounds, devourworms, and that big fucking blight monster.

"Octos became so furious that he attempted to destroy the walls of the Maze to pave his own way through. His rage engulfed him and drove him mad, causing him to lose the wager, his immortality, and even his own freedom." Rhyeah points to the mossy wall that we came through, "You now know the Lasting Fury as the beast named Blightfoot. The god himself decayed and driven ravenously mad."

Even Khelrah gaped and gasped at the revelation before the chieftain continued with her story.

"Calos gained the power of a god and became master of tricks and trials, manipulating men, monsters, and immortals into attempting his creation. But it would not last. Reylith, the Graceful Judge, mourned the unjust loss of sanity and life and wished to do something about it.

Partnering with her mate, Dulesh, they devised a plan to trap Calos within his own folly, challenging him to a race in the center. If Calos were to win, he would take Reylith's place at the head of the Eternal Council. He foolishly offered them anything in return, confident in his own skills and newly taken power to overcome the goddess. Dulesh, a master of silence and secrets, created a silent illusion that was so believable, even Calos couldn't discern its reality. He believed he completed the race in record time and anxiously awaited his opponent to give him what was promised, but she never came. Dulesh secreted her away from the Maze at a weak point in its structure and they both locked Calos in. The Imprisoned One's curse was to forever live in torment of his tricks and trials, never to escape."

What a fucked-up story. Did Riley come up with this? Or was it Dawson before everything happened?

Khelrah spoke up, "How does this explain your people and the Maze releasing hordes of beasts?"

Rhyeah sighs and shows her marks, "Since Calos was of the Yaruk, the gods that remained feared revolt from we who roamed Preydor, even though our ancestors were merely curious of this realm. The Imprisoned One, in his endless madness, found a way to create a tear from this realm to ours, opening it to the beasts that have been plaguing this land. The gods tasked their heralds to herd our people back into the Maze and return home. Calos was not in favor of having us here, forgetting of our kinship, so he has prevented our people from reaching the rift in the realm and return home. One such ancestor decided to make noble sacrifice and give himself to the Maze in return for a way for the Yaruk to stay safe and ahead of the beasts." She gestures to the marks on her skin, "Magic runs deep in our tribe, allowing us to anticipate the Maze's hidden dangers and possible changes in direction."

There is so much to unpack in that shit storm of a story that I think I'm getting dizzy. Banished gods, zombified gods and monsters, banished tribe of people. A dungeon crawl mixed with survival and sprinkled with straight horror. *True SnoWire fashion, no question.*

"How did Riley get mixed in with all of this?" I need to know how he managed to not die in this place for as long as he's been here.

There's a whisper of a smile on Rhyeah's face when she says, "Zasar saved my life. I joined my hunters to look for meat and supplies when we were set upon by a pack of smokehounds. My hunters defended us as best as they could, but there were many of them. Like some feral beast, Zasar rushes in and demolishes them with his club. At first, we were unsure of him due to the rarity of irbulgs outside their mountainous terrain. We took him in for questioning while nursing his wounds. He explained that he found an opening in the Maze somewhere in Kerogema and had been fighting through the corridors for days. He questioned us about our situation and felt some form of sympathy for our people, so he offered to aid us in any way he could. Zasar has been nothing but kind and protective of us and our plight."

Sweet Jesus, she's in love with him!

"What about when you and your people are ready to return to your realm?" Does he plan to go with them? That can't be what happens, because reaching the rift means the game is over.

Rhyeah suddenly seems conflicted, "It is not Zasar's place to suffer in our undeserved punishment. But if he were compelled to, he would be welcomed among our people."

I've had enough. I leave the conversation to find Riley. This isn't how this game is going to end.

But then the screaming starts.

Chapter 27

None of the officers will let me make another phone call. If I can get in touch with my actual lawyer, or maybe the others at the lab, I can get out of this and stop Guzman. If he's as crazy as he sounded when he was here, he's going to create a mess of everything. I can't stop pacing around the cell, still stuck with three other sad sacks, waiting for someone to give me my goddamn lawyer.

"You know, your fancy ass shoes are starting to get really annoying," one prisoner comments. He's a stalky guy with a black fade that frames his square-jawed face. He's wearing common street clothes; dark gray hoodie over a plain white tee-shirt, faded jeans, and a pair of nice Jordans. He's scanning me up and down with light brown eyes and a judgmental smirk.

"I'm not exactly comfortable here. I've got shit I need to do," I say passively.

He leans forward and rests his elbows on his knees, "Couldn't help but overhear. Got some corporate espionage kind of shit going on, don't ya?"

"That's none of your business."

He chuckles and shrugs, "Just makin' conversation. Some big wig like you stuck in the slums with us because your boss is threatened. That's like the start of a movie."

Through my teeth I reply, "Glad my current situation is amusing."

The prisoner chuckles again before I hear footsteps coming in our direction. A couple of uniformed officers approach the door, one grabbing keys. The other one eyes me down and orders me to move away from the door.

"Clayton, your bail is posted. "Come on out," the officer calls.

The prisoner, Clayton, stretches before he gets up and saunters by me. Without a word, he leaves the cell and the door locks behind him. I grab hold of the bars and call out to them, "Please! I need just one more phone call!"

They ignore me completely and I'm left with the remaining two prisoners. I take a seat on the opposite side of the cell from them, cursing under my breath.

How could I be so fucking stupid to let this go on without seeing it? Guzman has been pulling the strings this entire time! Dominic would be so disappointed in me. He trusted me with his company more than his own daughter. I can't let his vision crumble like this.

Two sets of footsteps return about five minutes later, the same officers from before open the door again. "Bauer, your bail's been posted. You're free to go."

I'm frozen in shock. Hesitantly, I stand up and exit the cell, walking through the door to the main hall of the station. Outside waiting for me is a smiling Clayton leaning against the clerk's window.

"You… you paid my bail?"

He shrugs slyly, "What can I say? I've got a soft spot for pissy stiffs like you." He holds out his hand, "Darrel Clayton, at your service."

What the hell is happening? I take the hand and we shake. Firm, callused fingertips, friendly. "Matt. Bauer."

"Wait, not *the* Matt Bauer that's in charge of SnoWire Interactive."

I nod.

He beams, "Holy shit, I was in jail with the head of SnoWire! That's awesome!"

The clerk clears her throat and hands Darrel his personal items; a phone, set of keys, wallet, and a necklace with some rectangular ornament on the end of it. She then gives me my things after him, "Ma'am, what about my car? Is it in impound?"

She flips through her papers with a "could care less" attitude. "Yes, sir. Your car is under investigation and can't be recovered at this time." She passes a clipboard through, "Give us your contact information and we'll notify you when it is possible to get your vehicle."

"Fuck," I whisper. I take the clipboard and sign it, lightly smacking it back down on the counter. Darrel is still here for some reason, just watching. "Look, thank you for busting me out. I can pay you back once I get my affairs in order if you want to trade information."

He smiles and gestures to the door, "Come with me really quick, Stiff." He's out the door before I can even protest, so I groan and follow him. He thumbs a message in his phone quickly and turns around to me. "I heard everything that you and the other suit were talking about. If you wanna pay me back for busting you out, we're gonna talk about it."

I'm dumbstruck. "Wait, so you're *blackmailing* me after bailing me out of jail? What the hell is this about?"

A loud engine revs up, drawing both of our attention towards the parking lot. Cruising in is a sweet looking muscle car; new, Chevrolet Camaro, smooth gloss orange finish with a black racing stripe trailing to the back of it. The rear of the car comes into view with a custom license plate that reads "B15H0P". The driver, a cyberpunk looking woman with a shock of blue hair shaved on one side, leather vest over a tank top, torn jeans and spiked shoes, exits the car and smirks at Darrel.

"They bust you again, Bishop?"

Darrel chuckles in response and shrugs, "Got bored, went petty, got caught."

"'Bishop'?" I ask with an arched eyebrow.

Giving me a wink, he walks down the stairs towards the car and woman. She throws him the keys without taking her eyes off me, "Who's the suit?"

"He's a new friend, Phobia. Set him up in the back," he requests as he hops into the driver's seat.

Phobia? Bishop? What is this, an X-Men reenactment? She waits for me impatiently, tapping her loud thick boot on the pavement.

Whatever might as well get this over with.

Aside from the loud EDM blaring in the car, this isn't a bad ride. The car is smooth and pretty sweet on the inside with the windows tinted and border lights inside. Reminds me of the old college parties I'd go to back in the day. Along the way, Phobia lays it out for me that she and "Bishop" are part of some underground collective trying to stop big corporate leaders from scamming and draining people's money like some resistance. Phobia and Bishop are their web handles, respectively Phoebe and Darrel. When Darrel reveals that I'm the CEO of SnoWire, Phobia is impressed and excited, talking me up and asking questions about what it's like to work at the biggest independent interactive video game developer in the country. For the first time in the last several months, I'm feeling relaxed and am having a human conversation that doesn't involve schedule reports and revenue.

The conversation comes to an end when we pull into a dusty drive that is way off the main road. I'm starting getting concerned again. "Where are we going?"

Neither of them says anything. The car pulls up into the parking lot of what looks like a decommissioned power substation. They get out and move the seat for me to climb out of the back. The whole building is covered with graffiti from multiple artists and delinquents, and I am feeling like this is where I may die.

Darrel opens the door to let Phobia in first, then gestures for me to follow. Inside, it's not decrepit or disgusting, but completely repurposed into a central hub full of computer monitors, screens, loose tech, wiring and a whole vibe that screams *Watchdogs*.

"Welcome to the Gridlock, Stiff."

The setup is a knockout. I've heard of people setting up hacking sites, but I've never seen one. I'm sure I'm committing several felonies just by being here.

At the far side of the building, someone is sitting in a gamer chair typing so fast it's like ASMR level. Phobia skips over to the side of the person's chair and plants a kiss on their cheek before whispering something. The chair turns around and reveals a man about my age in some bright neon colors from his shoulders down. On his head is a helmet that looks like tesla coils prodding out of it and a visor over the eyes.

"That's Cranium," Darrel introduces at my side. "He's our network link while Phobia and I are offsite workers."

"So... you're some sort of hacker group?"

All three of them laugh out loud. Cranium, in a light and cheery voice says, "More like a collective of geniuses protecting the little guys from the big wig snakes."

"We've done a lot of different things with what we have; discreet money transfers, footage leaks, mishandled travel plans and patterns," Phobia lists.

I turn to Darrel, "What does any of this have to do with why you busted me out?"

His face turns serious and calm, "Like I said. I heard what you were arguing about with that other suit. Cranium."

With a crack of his knuckles, Cranium spins around in his chair, faces the monitors and starts typing. A few keystrokes later, Armand Guzman's public records, hidden account information, projects from his office computer, and correspondences with other board members. I'm in shock. These hackers can literally breach the most advanced development company in the nation with a few clicks.

"Wanna take this bastard down?" Darrel asks with a smirk.

My mouth is hanging open like a clown. Then I remember something important. "Let me make a call first."

With some maneuvering and convincing, I anxiously wait for the thumb drive to arrive. Darrel is standing outside next to me tapping his foot. He decides that it's best for him to dawn a bandana mask with a chrome bishop chess piece on it. "This is a hell of a risk you're bringing, Stiff. You sure they won't get pinged?"

"First, it's Matt, not Stiff," I snap. "Second, I followed every instruction that Cranium gave me so that our location wouldn't be compromised. Third, if you didn't trust me, you wouldn't have brought me here."

He scoffs, "Maybe I don't trust you. Maybe I think you're just a looker to have around so I don't have to keep looking at Cranium's ugly face."

I choke. *Is he hitting on me?*

No time to ponder on that while a car is roving towards us. It's a clunker of a minivan, and from the sounds of it, on its last legs with this trip. The engine sputters a bit loudly before parking next to the Camaro. Mark swings the door open and slams it closed, wearing a lot more covering than he usually does.

"Yo, I swear I'm gonna get busted with all these car runs. Krissy was gonna tear my nuts off if I didn't do this," he rants. "Glad to see you're out of the clink though."

"Your concern is very nice to hear, Mark." I gesture over to Darrel, "This is Bishop."

Mark cocks an eyebrow, "Is this a Halloween party?"

"You already brought your mask, didn't you," Darrel fires back.

"Okay, okay, relax." I step in between them and look to Mark, "Did you bring it?"

With a deep sigh, Mark fishes in his pocket and pulls the flash drive out, Lorena's name visible on the white label. My heart drops to my stomach at the sight of it.

"I haven't opened it or anything," Mark assures us. "All this sneaking around makes me paranoid that the feds are waiting for it to be used."

"That paranoia will keep you alive," Darrel replies as he takes it into his own hands. "Damn, this is a top-dollar drive. The Dawson's had access to some good shit. Let's crack this baby open and see what we find."

He makes a quick one-eighty turn and makes for the building. I take this chance to pull Mark aside, "How are Connor and Riley? What about the girls?"

"The girls are fine. The dumbasses, however." He makes a face of worry, "Something happened. They developed some kind of red marks that looked like they were attacked. It's like their bodies are reacting to the injuries in the game."

My throat bobs, "That... that's impossible. We never designed the program to cause bodily harm."

"Well, it fucking happened. We need to get them out."

Stating the obvious, as always. "Let's see what these guys can find and hope that it won't be too late."

Chapter 28

Riley jumps into action quickly, grabbing his club and running towards the screaming. Grumbling to myself, I run after him through the crowd of villagers carrying their children and supplies away from whatever has them freaked. Soon, I'm flanked by the other Mazebreakers while trying not to lose sight of the large orange asshole. People are screaming and yelling things I can't understand, but it's got them in enough panic to run back towards where we came in from.

Riley's large frame skids to a stop, prompting the rest of us to do the same. Taking position near him, I'm looking at a swirling vortex of glowing violet, indigo, jade, and amber, producing strong winds that threaten to blow us all over. The vortex begins to thin and take on a new shape, one that is long and flowing like a cloak in the wind. It slowly opens and reveals a slender body of something humanoid touching down on the ground, standing over seven feet tall, draped in constantly changing colors that look exactly like what we faced with the courtyard puzzle. The feature that draws my attention is what is under the hood of the cloak; a pale gold mask, angular features that highlight a permanent Joker-like smile with narrow slits in the eyes.

"What in the name of the gods is this," Veyanna asks with a shaking voice.

The figure angles its head with an inquisitive gesture and opens its arms wide. "Do you fear that which created you?" The voice is scratchy like they've been laughing themselves hoarse.

'That which created you'?

"Calos," Riley breathes quietly.

The figure, Calos, bows deeply and laughs in a way that sends chills down my spine.

"The Laughing Trickster," Khelrah sneers.

"The Imprisoned," Veyanna trembles.

Calos raises their head and links their long fingers together. "So many monikers for one so misunderstood. Calos, that I am, but *you*," they look directly at me, "you may call me Armand."

Chapter 29

I can't speak. I'm filled with fear and rage that they send all my thoughts into a freefall. Calos, the BBEG of *The Primeval Maze*, is the big bad evil guy of my actual fucking life. The man that has stonewalled my projects since I started at SnoWire; the head of the company's board of directors; the voice of the goddamn investors, and Riley's benefactor for this fucking prison.

"Guzman. How?"

The masked face didn't flinch, "Did you think that Dominic kept the designs of player integration to himself? He had the ability to make himself a god in *The Mortal Gate*, but his daughter lessened him into a lowly hermit. I have no such attachments to challenge me."

"Armand," Riley breathed in confusion, "what are you doing?"

He tilts his attention to Riley, "Merely protecting my investment, Mr. Woods. And ensuring that Mr. Wright here has remained occupied."

"You son of a bitch," I grit my teeth. "You did this. You're responsible for *all of this*."

"Credit where it's due," he admits. "I couldn't have another Dominic or Lorena milling about while I secure the legacy of SnoWire Technologies."

I think my brain is gonna spill out of my ears. "Y-you're liquidating the company. Reformatting."

Guzman snaps his fingers, "You always were so smart, Connor. Honestly, if I had thought you would be more useful to the plan, I would have approached you to partner with us into the future."

"Bimbik, Zasar, what is happening here?" Doxo demands.

"Trust me, gnolid," Guzman quips, "it is beyond your comprehension."

Doxo growls, gripping his axe tighter in his hands. I step in front of Riley and try to cap the rage I'm feeling, "Why, Guzman? You are already a large stockholder on the company. Is this all out of some petty need for profit?"

"You see, Mr. Bauer asked me the same question when I visited him in jail." He sees the gape in my face, but I can't read him through the mask. "Profit is one thing; the material that makes the entire world go round. But control, the ability to usher the world further into a new age, that is true power." He opens his arms wide and looks around the Maze and our surroundings, "Imagine this place being used to challenge and train perfect soldiers in cyber and guerilla warfare. To house the most dangerous of prisoners and keep them contained. To provide new advancements in civilization at the right price. The world is becoming more dependent on progress and advancement, like an addiction. We will provide them their fix."

I look back up at Riley, hoping he sees Guzman for the monster that he is. His face is in shock with no signs of if he understands.

"But why victimize Riley? Why bait me into helping him?"

A long, slender finger taps on the mask's chin as he replies, "As inventive and influential as we are, you are still a threat to our progress. Even one voice opposing the idea will be enough to spark doubt and investigation of our plans. We've watched you closely these past few years, Mr. Wright. You prevailed last time because of your charisma. It rallied everyone to you, gave them hope and courage. It's admirable. This time, however, you are alone. No one will answer your call, nor your plea. Not here."

With that ominous message, Guzman flourishes his cape and disappears into a void. The Yurak start to calm down and check on each other, nothing but true fear on their faces.

The Mazebreakers confront Riley and I, with Riley still completely ghosted.

"Bimbik, what is your connection to the Laughing Trickster," Khelrah demands.

"It… it's complicated."

"So complicated that you cannot explain yourself or Zasar being connected to the prime deity of this place?" Veyanna is hugging herself in discomfort.

With a heavy sigh, I grab Riley's wrist and pull him away, "Excuse us."

He's catatonic, dumbstruck, utterly gone in his own head. I know I've disappointed the others, but this needs to stop.

Now that I know who's responsible for this shitstorm, I need to get out and handle it.

"Riley."

Nothing.

"Riley!"

He blinks those large amber eyes and looks down at me, mouth agape. "I-I thought…"

"You got played, get over it. Now tell me how to log out so I can go handle this."

His eyes are so glassy that he doesn't process what I'm saying at first. "I was supposed to be the only one to access this place… he promised it wasn't for anything other than trial runs on the software… he promised."

I kick him in the shin, earning a yelp. "He lied to you, dumbass! He knew how desperate you were after the game, and he used you! Now, Matt is in jail, I don't know what's happening with Krissy, and I want out!"

He grimaces down at me, and I match his stare. There's no way I'm staying here one moment longer. I have to get out and help the others.

"Fine," he spits. "Say the phrase 'Player Desync'. It's a command code I came up with that should work. And do me a favor: Don't come back for me."

"Don't fucking worry," I respond with a flip of the bird. "Player Desync."

Pause. Nothing.

"*Player Desync,*" I repeat.

Riley blinks in response.

"Nothing's happening." I'm starting to panic. "You try it."

"No! I'm not leaving here!"

"Get the fuck over yourself and try! If it works, you can get me out then come back," I argue.

He's hesitant to the point I'm ready to kick him again. With a deep breath, he says the command code.

Nothing happens. He's still here.

"What?" He's genuinely shocked. "Player Desync." Nothing again.

"Fuck, fuck, *fuck!*" I yell, gripping my hair. "Guzman must have shut the command code down!"

Riley is dumbfounded again.

It's happening again. No logging out. No escaping.

Chapter 30

Riley and I try logging out a few more times. Still nothing. He can't grasp the idea that his promise of a virtual existence has become more permanent and that his trust in Guzman got him stuck here. He's muttering repeatedly that he was promised that the game wasn't gonna be used for anything other than pushing the bar of virtual reality gaming. No matter how many times I tell him that he got fucked over, he doesn't listen.

Not moments later do Rhyeah and the Mazebreakers come to check on us. The Yaruk chieftain carefully inspects Riley, hands on his face and whispering soothing words. I'm getting daggers shot at me with the way my companions are staring at me. *I'm gonna have to spin some shit to make them understand.*

I go on to tell them that Calos is the one that sent me to the village where Doxo and I first met, taking me from my home and smack in the middle of danger to toy with me. When they ask me what his beef is with me, I tell them I found out some secret plans that he had to try and sabotage both Albistair and Preydor, which isn't entirely a lie, and he wants to punish me for it. It doesn't surprise me that they don't believe a word I say. But what does surprise me is how quickly they agree to try and help me take his ass down.

"How does one defeat an imprisoned god within their own domain?" Doxo asks aloud.

No one can think of an answer outside of hunting him down and hacking him to bits. Until Rhyeah chimed in with an idea that sets everyone else on edge.

"There is a possible solution to get you answers. The thornhags."

"What's a thornhag?"

Before she could answer, Riley snaps out of his stupor. "Rhyeah, no. Don't even think of suggesting that."

"If there is any creature that will know how to overcome Calos, it would be them."

"Excuse me!" They both look at me. "What the hell is a thornhag and how can they be of help."

Rhyeah dismisses Riley and explains, "The thornhags are the most sentient and aware creatures to have come from the Primeval Realm. Magical soothsayers that are twisted by the very malevolent nature that combines this realm with ours. They have a symbiotic relationship with the Maze to help them synthesize their power."

"In other words," Riley cuts in, "they're witches that promise things to their victims and destroy them shortly after. They're the worst that the Primeval Maze has to offer, even more than Blightfoot. He's an oozing giant, but not smart and deceptive like the thornhags."

So, either take our chances against a decaying zombie god, or search for thorny witches that might kill us. Goddammit.

I turn to the others, "I'll hold this to a vote. We either press on and try to reach the center, or we seek out these thornhags to learn what weaknesses that Calos has."

There's a lot of doubt on all their faces. Either way spells certain death for us if we're not smart.

Veyanna is the one to break the silence, "I think that we might receive better solutions from the witches. If we are smart and delicate in our questioning, we should be okay. I believe we are all capable of that."

Riley's jaw hangs low at her, "Are you insane? You'll die!"

"No, she will not," Doxo promises as he steps to her side. "I will stand with Veyanna and approach these hags that we may end the danger and protect Preydor."

Khelrah removes her hood and puts a hand over her heart, "The Mazebreakers have entrusted it to aid in the protection of Preydor, and it will not break that trust. Khelrah will join you in meeting the witches."

Something like pride is swelling in me. It's just like the joining of the armies against the Crimson Order and Lorena the Archon. It's no longer about just surviving this game; it's about making a stand against the asshole that started all of this.

"We're gonna need to gear up if we're gonna press on," I propose.

Rhyeah gives a soft smile, "Allow the Yurak to aid in this endeavor. We can provide new materials for you to use."

In a huff, Riley stomps off back to the Yaruk gathered at their loaded camp. Rhyeah looks disheartened but returns her attention to us. "With our resources, we can give you an edge against what is out there. It may not be much but consider it a token of appreciation from my people. We long to be free of Calos and his punishments, to live as a free people once again. Perhaps the Mazebreakers will be that solution."

I truly don't know what happens to these programs when we win these games, but I really hope that they gain that freedom that they're looking for.

Over the next few hours, the Yaruk people treat us to small meals, share knowledge of the Maze that they can provide, and several craftsmen work to make us some items that they think will help us. Riley has been sulking the entire time by himself while Read orders the tools and weapons to be made for us. Khelrah spends some time with the Yaruk healers, gaining knowledge on various herbs for healing and poisoning. As a Trapper, she can utilize those kinds of things like me. They give her a shoulder strap that holds bags and vials of her tools for easy access, along with a set of makeshift masks for the whole group to protect against some of the toxins. Veyanna meets with some of the hunters to gain knowledge of some of the creatures they have seen in the Maze. She's also given a bone whistle said to aid in her Handler abilities with small and medium creatures, along with a new hide and hemp armor set to give her better protection. Doxo follows a different group of hunters that take his axe against his protests and promise him an upgrade. In addition to some wood and vine bracers and spaulders, they outfit the blades of his axe with serrated teeth from smokehounds and reinforce the haft to make it sturdier. They also gift him a pair of gauntlets that have razorwing bat wings on the knuckles that look like a gnarly medieval take on Wolverine. Rhyeah decides to see to my equipment personally from her private stash of materials. Given my frame and stature, she suggests I use some small and quick methods of traps and tricks. She gives me a bolo made of heavy stone directly pulled from the Maze walls, a net made from the vines of the courtyard that is fed by a long line of vines to be thrown and pulled, and a set of smoke bags filled with sleeping herbs. The last thing she gives me is a grappling hook made from beast claws that promises to be sturdy and lightweight.

"I don't think I can thank you enough for helping us," I tell her as I attach all my new tools to me.

Rhyeah shakes her head, "It is my people and I that should be thanking you, Bimbik Steamspanner. I do not know how the spirits and forces led you to us, but it must be ordained that you will end our suffering and the suffering of Preydor."

I smile softly and turn to look at the others. They are all talking among themselves about their new gear and discussing the journey ahead. I then look to Riley, who is just staring at me pissed off.

"Do not mind Zasar. He thinks he is doing what is right for my people. He has a good heart, but it is often misplaced."

"I know," I sigh. "I've known him for a long time. He thinks he's doing what's best for him, but it's gonna get him killed." He's doing this to himself, and he doesn't care about what happens as long as he lives his virtual dreams. "Rhyeah, please just make sure he doesn't do anything stupid to get any of you killed."

She smiles with empathy like she knows what I'm talking about and nods. "Whenever you and the others are ready, we shall prepare your departure."

With a nod, I rejoin the others. Veyanna looks to me softly and says, "This will be quite the dangerous undertaking. Are you ready?"

"Hell, no," I admit with a dry laugh.

"Neither are we," Doxo agrees. That actually surprises me, but he explains, "It is foolish not to be afraid of certain doom, or else doom finds us quicker. We know what is at stake, and we will turn that fear into a strength."

Khelrah nods firmly, "It agrees with the gnolid. If we do not embrace fear, it will poison us all. It awaits the next step of our journey."

With a shaky breath, I nod and lead everyone to the far side of the corridor where Rhyeah is waiting for us. Along the way, the Yaruk are assembled on either side of us, putting their open hands together and reaching their chests in a sort of salute or prayer. It's amazing but also concerning in a way that sets me on edge. Like they believe we're not going to be seen again. Rhyeah holds a stare with me as we approach, then begins muttering some kind of prayer, waving her hands that sparkle with teal colored magic. With a soft and solemn look, she reaches a hand to the closed wall of the Maze, resonates with its energies, and opens a doorway. The way ahead is foggy, radiating this eerie green light and sharp shadows. The ground shifts from cobblestone to damp grass and dirt.

"The way ahead is how you will find the thornhags in their Blighted Grove," Rhyeah explains. "Beware of the fog as well. It is known to drive poor souls into wrong directions or drive them mad."

That's comforting. I take a deep breath and look ahead, "We're off to see the witches. Let's get to it."

Our collective steps squish beneath us with the change of environment. But the sound that makes me wince hard is the sound of the path behind us closing.

Chapter 31

It's beautiful. A silver band with small diamonds embedded in it, a cushion-cut diamond surrounded by smaller ones, and an engraving on the inside that reads: *Let's Make Some Magic.* Connor was going to propose. I feel my eyes stinging with tears welling up in them. I've been staring at this thing for the last hour, ever since Mark got called by Matt to bring the flash-drive he found. Danica threatened to tear his nuts off if he didn't go. Whatever their dynamic is now, it was enough to get him out. I'm sitting in the observation room looking at this gorgeous ring resting in its box.

He was going to propose, and he still went in after Riley. Shouldn't I be angry? I feel… happy looking at this ring. I want to tell him 'Yes'. I need to tell him 'Yes'. I love that stupid nerd. But… what if something happens?

A gentle knock raps on the door frame. Danica is leaning against it with a pitiful look on her face.

"Don't look at me like that."

"Sorry," she whispers. She joins me in another seat, "I don't know what to do or say, Krissy. This… it's great, but it's also—"

"Scary? Trust me, I know." I close the box and set it on the table. She hands me a tissue so I can dab my eyes free of the tears. "I'm not mad at him. I should be, but I'm not."

Danica gives me a soft chuckle in response, "I don't know Connor as well as I probably should, but I do know he does everything for a reason. If he didn't think he'd make it out of this, he wouldn't have gone in. He doesn't plan to stay there. He's coming back so he can propose to you."

Dammit, don't cry.

I reach over and grab her hand, giving it a gentle squeeze. "I'm glad you're here, Dani."

She looks like she's about to cry with me, "I know I've been shitty. I'm trying, I promise. You're my friend and I'm sorry that my issues with Mark got in the way of that."

Without second guessing, I stand and pull her with me into a hug. So much has happened that I'm finally able to take this moment to appreciate what it will be like once this is all over. I'll have a friend back, I'll be engaged, I'll be happy.

My attention is pulled to a noise from the hallway, followed by voices overlapping. We pull apart from each other and peer down the hallway. The security guard is attempting to stop a man and woman in suits from marching our direction, followed by a couple of cops.

"Fuck!" I pull Danica inside and lock the door. "I think they're with the assholes that got Matt arrested."

"What can we do?" Danica is in a panic.

"Lock all the doors, shut the lights off, try to make this place look empty. *Quick.*"

She nods and rushes to the other room to lock the doors. I set to shut off the lights and the monitors, trying to keep the machines quiet. The overlapping voices get louder and closer. Once we finish, Danica and I hide under one of the tables to avoid being seen.

"I was told by Mr. Bauer to keep this wing of the labs off limits."

An aggressive woman's voice replies with, "Mr. Bauer has been overruled in his decisions. The lab is to be closed entirely and all assets shut down."

No fucking way. They're gonna shut down the game and keep the boys trapped!

"Ma'am, I'm sorry, but Mr. Bauer is the head of this building. It was willed to him by Dominic Dawson as it's a separate entity from the rest of SnoWire," the guard explains.

A gruff male voice huffs, "Do you understand who we are? We are the board of directors that Bauer answers to, and you *will* do as we say."

"Okay, calm down," one of the officers says outside the door. "We're here to discuss the legality of these claims. Now do you have documentation that this is private property of someone?"

"It's in my office for reasons like this," the guard says sharply. "Which means if you want to seize this property, you'll need a court issued warrant."

"Bullshit," the woman sneers. "We hold ownership of all of Dominic Dawson's assets, and that includes this lab. Officers, either pull him aside or make yourselves useful."

"Ma'am, watch your tone," another officer says. "I don't care what you do or who you work for, we will do our jobs according to the state laws of Utah."

My heart jumps when one of them tries to open the door, jiggling the handle and nudging into the door to open it.

"The locks were changed?!" They keep trying.

"Sir, please step away from the door. We need to see the documentation on this building to decide how to proceed."

Thank God the cops aren't on a payroll.

"This isn't over," the woman spits, her loud-ass heels stomping away followed by another pair of steps. The guard tells the cops he will show them the contract, and they walk away too.

Danica and I breathe a sigh of relief under the table before she tells me, "Call Matt."

Chapter 32

This is insane! Cranium is literally ripping apart these firewalls that Guzman has set up in his personal files. The problem, however, is that there are a *lot* of them. He's gone to a lot of trouble to make sure that his private files can't be accessed by anyone else but him. Phobia is at her own station providing support with her own skills. Mark is watching all of this completely mesmerized like a child in a toy store. I am behind him watching the chaos unfold when Darrel pats my shoulder, "They'll be at it for a while. Need a drink?"

I'm not one to turn down a drink. Especially in stressful situations. I nod and follow him to a corner of the station set up with a couch, two chairs, a video game setup, and a mini fridge. On top of that mini fridge is a bottle of whiskey and a set of shot glasses, which he goes straight for.

"Oh, I don't know if this calls for—"

"Shut up, you're gonna have a shot with me and wait this out," he almost commands. He puts two glasses down on the piece-of-shit coffee table and pours the liquor. Giving me an expectant look, I sigh and take a seat, accepting the shot.

"To breaking down the suits?" he proposes, holding up his shot glass.

If there's a toast to be made, it needs to be made about the hopes we have for the outcome.

I lift the glass to his and say, "To freedom of choice."

He doesn't object as we drink our shots in unison. It stings on the way down, but something about it gives me a comforting sight of relief.

"And the Stiff becomes the Relaxed," Darrel jokes and leans back into his seat.

I respond with a dry chuckle, "Yeah, I know. Got a stick so far up my ass, I'm a human popsicle. Trust me, I'm aware."

Darrel opens the minifridge and pulls out two sodas, handing me one. "So, what's it like? Running the biggest independent game developer company in the country?"

"When I'm not getting strangled by corporate sabotage?" He nods. "I love it. I've worked there for over ten years, going from a simple retail associate to a beta tester, then becoming part of a developmental team for next-gen content and tech. Now, after… after some crazy shit, I'm head of that which I started so young."

"That's a hell of an origin story," he comments, sipping from his soda.

"What's your origin story, 'Bishop'?" I ask looking at him with intent.

With a shrug, "Oh, you know. The usual 'corporate donkey turned hacktivist' story. I worked obediently for a stock company, trusted the wrong people, got robbed blind, fired under false pretenses, then decided to get back at them." He takes another sip, "I found out some crazy shit my boss was hiding in South America, including millions of embezzled dollars and a mistress. I sent the information to his wife first, watched his shit burn on the front lawn, then sent it to the IRS and cops."

"Jesus Christ." *Impressive.*

He flashed his teeth in a righteous grin, "Turns out I'm really good at stirring the pot of big wigs, so I made it my occupation. Keep off the radar working at a record store and make sure to separate my life carefully."

Hacktivist indeed. I smile with intrigue. I glance back over at Cranium, Phobia and Mark. "How about your partners?"

"Two really smart kids that pissed off the wrong people," his cheeriness disappearing. "When you're young and get bored, you do dumb shit. They happened to hack into a scary dude's mainframe and witnessed some really bad shit. Human trafficking."

My heart skips a beat. "They made a huge mistake in trying to expose it that it exposed *them* instead. I found them through a private server and gave them a place to lay low. Here." He points up at the ceiling, "The powerlines over us provide enough disruption that we can stay concealed as long as we're careful."

"All of this," I say gesturing to the interior, "just to take down the rich?"

"No," he replies simply. "To take down the *worst* that strut about thinking that they're untouchable. Like your boy, Armand Guzman. He's been peacocking around the last two years since Dominic passed away."

The aching in my chest spikes. Two years and it still hurts like hell.

"Well, thank you."

He smiles with a shrug, "No sweat. It helps to be owed a favor by the CEO of SnoWire."

I arch an eyebrow, "A favor?"

"Nothing shady, I promise," he chuckles with a wink.

Before I can argue, Mark paces over to us. "He cracked it. You've gotta see this."

We follow him to the monitors that are littered with Guzman's face and name. It makes me nauseated and angry. "What did you find?"

Phobia pushes her rolling chair away from her station and around to face us, "Guzman is a slimy shit. Not only is he trying to partner with the military on tech produced by SnoWire, but he's also got his fingers in the pie of some private contractors both foreign and domestic."

I feel like I'm gonna be sick. He's trying to turn profit to anyone willing to buy the tech and repurpose it.

Cranium adds, "He's bouncing his finances consistently to keep anyone from pinpointing it. Fucker's cautious, which makes him smart."

My eyes are scanning the monitors to try and piece together my own theories and investigation. One correspondence catches my eye, "That one. It's stamped with the board's email addresses. Pull that up."

One click blows it up on the monitor for everyone in the room to read. It's a seizure order for all of Dominic and Lorena's liquidated assets.

My phone buzzes in my pocket. "Keep looking through that and find everything you can," I say over my shoulder before exiting the building. "Krissy?"

"We're in trouble, Matt. A couple of corporate stooges tried getting into the labs. Your security guard got them away, but I don't think they'll stay away for long."

Shit! They're trying to seize the lab space. If they find Riley and Connor in there, things will get worse.

"We need to find a place to hold them, so they don't get disconnected. If the software is interrupted unsafely, it could fry their brains," I warn her.

"Any fucking ideas?" Danica's panicked voice calls out over the line.

I pace back and forth outside, trying to think of anywhere we can use for a stationary hold. "Listen very carefully, both of you. There's a way to disconnect them from the hardware without disrupting the connection to the system. I'll get something to carry them in. Here's what to do…"

I burst through the door, startling everyone in the process.

"Tell me something good."

Cranium is looking back and forth between monitors, "I'm trying. Two suits are trying to get a warrant to evict the security guard and remove your name from the ownership title."

"He can fucking keep it; I need to get my people out of there first." Mark looks at me alarmed. "The board almost caught them in there. We need to relocate them."

"What about the game? The Crests?"

"I gave Krissy and Danica instructions on how to safely remove them from the hardware without disrupting the system." At a glance, the hackers are all looking at us confused.

"Look, I'll explain everything. For now, I need a vehicle that can carry a lot of people and can hold some decent equipment. I also need to find a place that can be off the radar until we sort this shit out."

Darrel, Phobia, and Cranium all look at each other in some sort of silent conversation. It ends with Phobia and

Cranium going to their respective stations and Darrel gesturing for me and Mark to follow.

"I have a contact that owns a garage downtown," he explains as he marches towards the van Mark drove here in. "We go there, get a ride, get your guys out, and we get back here. The others will make room for everyone."

"Darrel, you don't need to—"

"In the meantime," he interrupts, "You're gonna tell me what the fuck kind of trouble you're in. Don't leave anything out, or the deal's off. Got it, Stiff?" Without another word, he hops into the passenger seat.

Mark looks like he just got kicked in the teeth. "What the fuck just happened?"

"I think our little mission just got hijacked by a group of hacktivists," I reply flatly. I open the back door and hop inside while Mark reluctantly gets into the driver's seat. This whole thing is getting out of hand.

Chapter 33

The air is thick with mist and a dense atmosphere that feels like it's choking me. At the same time, the temperature drops heavily, making my teeth chatter and the hair on my neck stand up. The only source of heat I can muster is my irritation and frustration with Riley. He's so lost in his fantasies of living as a fairy tale warrior that he has thrown caution directly to the wind. He'd rather settle down with a computer-generated tribe of people that are cursed to always remain in this place and he's completely fine with it. I can't let this get in my way. I have to get out and stop Guzman, even if it means getting SnoWire Interactive shut down in the process. Guzman has put every employee's job and future in the meat grinder to play war dog.

I can't help but dwell on what he said before disappearing; *"This time, however, you are alone. No one will answer your call, nor your pleas."* It seems he was right about that. Riley isn't gonna help me. Everyone on the Outside is just waiting for me to finish and leave. I can only rely on myself, even with the Mazebreakers with me.

My mind is too occupied to notice the winding of the corridors being smoother, but also more frequent to throw us off balance. What I notice immediately is that the moss-covered walls are no longer covered and are starting to depict images of scenes that remind me of the puzzle bowl.

These ones, however, are far creepier and look like they were drawn with blood and dirt. People gathered around camps and fires with markings etched into them. *The Yaruk?* The scenes continue to show the figures reaching out towards a dense gathering of branches and brambles surrounding four huts. On the other wall, there are four figures intricately drawn. Hideously intricate. One looks like a haunted tree from a kid's Halloween special, a second looks like a walking snake, a third looks like a larger version of the plants that attacked us in the courtyard, and the last one reminds me of a swarm of razorwing bats. In the middle of the figures, a large, round pot with steam pouring from it. *A cauldron?* In the steam, I can barely make out angry looking eyes.

"So, do any of you have any insight on these thornhags?"

They all shake their heads 'no'. *Great.*

"It has experiences with mistresses of dark magic," Khelrah says. "Many of Kerogema tribes and dens have at least one among their midst. Some use magic to invoke conversations with the dead. Others create tonics of dark purposes. It thinks that if the mistresses were brought to the Maze, they may have been corrupted like the beasts we have encountered."

"Only intelligent and cunning, no doubt." Veyanna sounds very unsure of this encounter. "What could we possibly gain from interacting with such creatures?"

"If the Maze can be solved and stopped, we need to gain the upper hand," I explain.

"One way or another," Doxo adds, "we will be ready to end this affliction. Once and for all."

"I admire your optimism, big guy." He gives me a sharp grin and it goes quiet once again. As the winding and turning hike continues, I can't help but feel like something is just nipping at my heels. Every time I turn back, there's nothing but the shadows cast by some kind of light within the walls. In the back of my head, there's some kind of groaning cackle like the bending of tree branches.

"Not another bloody step without a drink." Doxo's heavy ass plops on the damp ground and makes to grab for his waterskin. Thankfully, the Yaruk refilled our water before we left, but the humidity has us sweating bullets, except for Khelrah.

Lucky reptilian anatomy.

The ground is softened by the presence of grass and soft soil, but ahead of where we stopped is blanketed in heavy fog. Sharp pointed shadows peek through and look like they're moving.

"Something sinister is at work here," Veyanna says through heavy pants. She's gulping down her water and sharing it with Doxo, who drained his own.

Khelrah's nostrils flare open and shut, "It agrees. This fog… seems magical. Something is inside… something predatory."

"Just fucking great," I groan on the ground. Even with our new gear, we're exhausted to the point of weakness against anything. If it's the goddamn Blightfoot, I'm perfectly content staying here.

"Unfortunately, that is our only way to the thornhags," Veyanna breaks it to us.

I let out a loud sigh before sitting up from the ground, "All right. Gear up and let's get ready."

The group nods in unison, holstering our waterskins and getting our new gear prepared. Khelrah generously passes out the masks that help to combat the sleeping powders, thinking it'll help with the density of the fog. Veyanna nervously grips her whip, knowing her whistle won't do any good if she can't see a creature. In a moment of surprisingly logic thought, Doxo keeps his axe on his back and plans to rely on the new gauntlets for protection. My gear is also gonna be useless without precision, so I'm just gonna rely on movement and hope for the best.

Stepping into the heavy fog makes my eyes water, but the mask covers my nose and mouth so I'm hoping that helps with whatever this is. The density of the ground also gets more rugged and easy to trip on. We try to stay close together as the fog gets thicker the further as we go. Everyone is taking their time, gingerly stepping over or around the increasingly difficult floor.

I jerk my head to the right when I hear that groaning cackle again. With a brief pause, my eyes dart around to follow the shadows that are moving like ripples of water.

"Is anyone else hearing—" I cut myself off when I notice I'm on my own.

Fuck! Just like the Ordowell Bowels!

"Doxo? Khelrah! *Veyanna!*"

"Half-Pint!" Doxo yells out. "Where are you?" His voice is bouncing all over. I can't get a good read on where he is.

"Doxo?" Veyanna's voice rings out in a shudder.

"Bimbik!" Khelrah's raspy yell calls out.

"Everyone, stop moving!"

Silence.

"Wherever you're facing, go straight," I yell out. "If you hit a wall, follow it until you find an opening. If it's where we started, stay there. If it's the exit, call out and we'll try to follow!"

There's a long pause, followed by grunts and 'Okay's. This may not be my *best* plan, but it's the best I can muster given the fucking circumstances. With my hands straight out, I walk forward slowly trying not to trip over the ground. It seems like every couple of steps there's either a rut in the ground or some overgrown roots. The fog is starting to sting my eyes and make them water, but squinting isn't doing me any favors either. Those rippling shadows are in constant motion to the point where it reminds me of Medusa's snake hair; always aware, always watching. My hands finally find something to hold onto. A large trunk of a gnarled tree with ashy bark. I use the trunk of the tree to keep balanced while looking through the fog. Something under the bark catches my attention. Something slimy and sticky. I pull my hand away and look at my fingers that are dripping with the stuff. Dark, copper-red, and eerily familiar.

"Blood?"

The groaning cackle returns right as a plume of the fog pulls away, revealing a large, gnarled dead tree with twisted, thorny branches and brambles. Twisted into the branches are bleeding corpses. Desecrated, bleeding corpses. Robbed of life, yet still dripping. Gray, sunken, lifeless skin. All decorated with dim markings of a familiar design; Yaruk.

I yell out and jump away from the tree, only to be met with another solid surface. One that sticks me in various places like a thornbush. I peel away and look up in horror at a large female covered in armor that is made up of brambles and thorns, a helmet of the same material with a facemask that comes out to a point like a beak, large woven arms that look like she can snap my neck with no effort and holding a staff with a large ball of spikes on the top.

Her eerie purple eyes behind her mask stare at me in silent hate and disdain.

"Uh… sorry," I say in a broken voice. "I guess I didn't know this was your… murder tree."

Nothing.

"Yeah… I'm gonna go now."

A soothing voice from behind me beckons, "Nonsense. Allow us to extend our hospitality." The smell of flowers and sweet air gently holds me in place. From behind me comes another woman, this one dressed in green, yellow, purple, and pink petals woven into a dress. Her face is slightly covered from a large hat of vines and blossoms, but her mouth is visible with a sickly green skin tint and rows of sharp tiny teeth in a wicked smile. The staff in her hand is like the large one, but the top of hers has a blooming flower that is the same one from the courtyard that gave off the noxious gas.

"Forgive my sister," the flowery one croons. "She is the strong silent type of the four of us. Isn't that right, Branwen?"

The large one, Branwen, says nothing.

"Where are my manners? I am Isador Thistleheart," the flowery one smiles and curtsies. "Welcome to the Blighted Grove."

Chapter 34

The Blighted Grove. The place Rhyeah and Riley told us about. Home of the Thornhags. Two of them, Branwen and Isador, are currently holding me hostage next to a large, dead sacrificial tree.

Well, this is my fucking luck.

"So... you're the infamous Thornhags?"

Branwen lets out a scratchy growl in response.

"We do not much care for the name that the Yaruk have deemed for us," Isador replies sweetly. "We are simply a sisterhood gifted with the wonders of the Primeval Maze. Our... *appearances*... often earn us less than flattering reputations than what we would like."

You mean people don't like the look of scary death witches?

"So far from home, luthien. What brings you to our midst? You do not seem associated with the Yaruk people," she observes.

With a gulp I reply, "I-I'm here looking for guidance... against Calos."

Both Thornhags seem to shift a little bit at the name. Branwen's clawed fist grips her staff tighter in response.

"Ah," Isador strokes her chin. "The Imprisoned. An interesting plight you find yourself in."

"And not alone," a slithering voice hisses from my left. From the surrounding fog, a humanoid torso covered in a cloak of dead leaves and rotting vines slinks into view, dragging behind them two other silhouettes, one huge and the other horned. Aside from the shock of Doxo and Veyanna being captured, what takes my attention is that the thornhag dragging them in is slithering in on a serpentine tail made of slick, oily vines. Her face is hooded, but it doesn't hide the serpent-like snout carved from an ugly stump. Her yellow eyes dimly glow underneath as she joins the others.

"Ah, Niobe," Isador welcomes sweetly. "How nice of you to bring more guests. Were there not *four*?"

Niobe hisses, "The exerine is as quick as I. She will not get far unless the Matriarch allows it."

Doxo grumbles against his restraints. I look closer and notice the large thorns that are turned inward, making sure they dig into his skin if he struggles. Veyanna is in the same predicament but looks more terrified.

Suddenly, all three sisters turn their attention to the tree I ran into. The trunk begins to slither and warp until it opens from the floor up. Two large hands with clawed fingers reach out and grab onto the threshold. Coming out of the bloody tree is a crone of a woman, hunched over and cloaked in woven thorns. On top of her ghastly pale face is a crown of deadwood brambles. Her dead black eyes hold no light in them whatsoever, but it feels like they're pulling thoughts from my mind like a hook. Her mouth is full of broken teeth under curved lips of blood red. When she fully emerges from the tree, the other three bow their heads in some form of recognition.

"Sisters," she breathes in a raspy voice. "Let us welcome our guests and see to their requests. If it is in our power, we will be of service."

"Yes, Matriarch Briarthorn," they all say in unison.

Her twisted smile returns as she nods to her sisters. Doxo and Veyanna are pushed into the center with me while the four of them raise their hands or staffs in the air and start chanting. Like a collective sound of branches scratching on glass, their chants get louder, their bodies giving off this sickly aura that surrounds us all. The ground rumbles and quakes under our feet before it starts sinking. Like an earthen elevator, a large circle of ground is sinking lower and lower until light is snuffed out. The absence of light is soon replaced by eerie glows of green from beneath us, casting a scary-ass visage over the thornhags. The earthen platform comes to a slow stop and the surroundings are illuminated by torches of green fire, walled with various collected bones, dead plants, collected jars of mystery items, finished with a large firepit of green flames licking the bottom of a dirty cauldron.

Briarthorn steps towards the cauldron first and waves her tree branch fingers through the rising plumes of smoke, "You seek a way to overcome the Laughing Trickster, yes?"

At first, none of us say anything. It's Branwen who uses her gnarly staff to push us forward, closely followed by Isador and Niobe. "The Matriarch asked you a question," the serpentine witch hisses at us.

I clear my throat, "Y-yes. We're trying to stop the blight he's causing on Preydor. We want to close the Primeval Maze off from the surface."

Isador chuckles menacingly behind me. Briarthorn goes to one of the shelves and starts grabbing some things, bringing them over to the cauldron and dropping them into it. The smoke begins to turn different colors of red, black, green and yellow.

"We of the Blighted Grove originally came from the Primeval Realm," Briarthorn explains. "Taking deals with mortals, providing oracle readings, tonics, and fortunes. We aid those who aid us in return."

Niobe slithers around the cauldron, "For a thousand years, we have given and taken as nature demands. The primeval force that orchestrates our very movement and existence."

"Then a voice from beyond the realm beckoned us," Isador intercedes from beside us. "A voice that urged for us to bring order back to a world that had been given a disservice. A voice that promised grand compensation for our aid and power."

The first words that come from Branwen in a low, menacing growl, "And we answered."

It takes me a moment to register what they're revealing to us. "You opened the rift from the Primeval Realm... you bridged the worlds. For Calos."

I can feel the air go cold around me, Doxo and Veyanna. *Where the fuck is Khelrah??*

"We sisters are nothing if not opportunists," Briarthorn replies, subtly putting more things into the cauldron. "Calos wished for balance to be restored, so we provided that balance."

"By infesting the world with monsters and destroying lives?" Veyanna may be scared, but she's got nerve.

"No, my dear," Isador croons with a finger down Veyanna's cheek. "We brought necessary life to influence the natural order of Preydor."

"When you were above," Niobe hisses, "what did you see? What did you experience?"

None of us answer her. Either from confusion or anger, we're dead quiet.

She takes the silence as her cue to continue, "Destruction. Uprooting of natural resources. Mortals unchecked with their disrespect of the earth that gave them life and sustenance. Robbing of mineral deposits and removal of natural homes for wildlife. We saw everything that Calos saw. It was all we needed to strike a bargain."

"The world is in abundance with powerful nature and equally powerful life to coexist," Veyanna argues. With her background, it doesn't surprise me that she's defending surface life.

"Yet you murder, hunt, destroy, and soil the very existence of primeval inheritance," Branwen growls from behind us. The sound of her voice makes my skin crawl, like listening to the scraping of nails on concrete.

"There is a difference between destruction and survival, you filthy hypocrites," Doxo growls in response. The sisters don't show any signs of anger or aggression. If anything, amusement riddles their gnarled faces.

Briarthorn produces a long branch from her own body and starts mixing the materials in the cauldron together. "Enough of this squabbling," she orders. "Our guests, dear sisters, are here for guidance. We shall provide it." She looks down at me with a tilt of her head, "Now. What is it that you desire to learn? If it is within our knowledge and power, we will provide you with what you wish."

"Bimbik, do not do this," Veyanna pleads. "The danger is not worth risking with them."

"The Yaruk told us this is the best option to use. I'm using it."

"Even with the mangled corpses in the tree we witnessed earlier?"

"Ah," Isador quips, "those unfortunate souls were unable to provide the price of what they asked for. That, or they saw fit to try and apprehend us. Every action has a consequence. And a price."

"What price do you demand for our knowledge, witch," Doxo grumbles through his teeth. He groans out when Branwen pricks his neck with her maced staff.

"Our price," Briarthorn states, "depends on the requested knowledge."

Risky, even for a game. But this shit with Guzman needs to end.

"Fine," I concede. "How do we stop Calos and seal the Primeval Maze? For good."

Eerily, all four sisters start to cackle. Briarthorn speaks some kind of chant towards the cauldron before a plume of smoke bubbles over the edge and fills the chamber we're in. I step back and take the hands of Doxo and Veyanna in my own, watching the scene unfold. The thornhags begin a quiet chant together, the smoke climbs the walls and onto the ceiling, and an eerie yellow color cracks through the smoke. The yellow starts taking form of these little images of flying things, imps maybe, that circle the room.

Briarthorn's green-lit eyes settle on me, "The Primeval Maze is a link between two worlds; one of material existence left to its own growth and destruction, the other a realm of raw magic where the strongest survive." The yellow imps swarm together to create illuminated patterns in the air, showing the rift bridging between Preydor and the Primeval Realm. "Calos has found the strength to maintain the connection by feeding the Primeval beasts with mortal matter, giving them strength and becoming indebted to the Laughing Trickster." The image shifts and changes, showing Calos holding his arms open with all the beasts we've encountered surrounding him and obeying him. "But what he has forgotten is that the beasts have a hunger that cannot be sated. And the more he pulls from the Realm, the more their hunger will grow." Calos disappears and the monsters start fighting and eating each other. "To close the rift and seal off the connection forever, you must find the first beast to be brought into this realm. Calos's personal pet and grand guardian of the Primeval Maze." The image shifts into a large, ugly, familiar walking monster with rotting flesh and dripping teeth.

Octos, now Blightfoot. We have to kill a zombie-god.

"Calos spent much of his power and energy to destroy and convert the Lasting Fury into his grand guardian," Isador explains. "By removing the revenant, a grand amount of Calos's power will be extinguished. Then, and only then, will you have the strength to banish him from this realm and seal the rift." The images show Blightfoot's visage being destroyed, releasing this large orb of power and flying to the rift, weakening Calos greatly. "Unifying the power conjured to open the rift with where it originated will be the undoing of that power and all it has produced." The rift sends out tendrils of power, pulling all of the creatures that came from the Primeval Realm back into the rift. It doesn't escape my notice when humanoid figures are also pulled into the rift. The Yaruk.

"Everything?"

"Everything," Briarthorn echoes in answer.

"This would undo everything you had done here as well," Veyanna says shakily. "It would return you to the Primeval Realm. Why tell us any of this?"

"Because of the price to pay," I gasp.

Briarthorn's crooked smile is all the confirmation I need.

"Our freedom is the price. They want to stay here."

I truly fucked us over.

I feel Doxo tense next to me when Niobe sneers, "With your essence, the Maze will be made stronger, and our hold on the Primeval energies made the same. We have watched you from the moment you set foot in this domain."

Isador's whole face comes into view, withered and cracked like a dying flower. "Your strength, knowledge, and conviction will make for tasty morsels. Our Grove will endure and thrive."

The grinding, gravelly voice of Branwen makes my legs weak, "The Maze will open to the world, and we will consume it. One soul at a time." She reaches down and grabs me by the collar of my vest, the restraints on both Doxo and Veyanna tighten against their thrashing. Branwen walks me over to the cauldron, hot and bubbling, with Briarthorn cackling wickedly. My legs are kicking wildly as I'm held over the boiling ooze.

"We give thanks to the Primal Powers that bring us this bounty and deliver its essence to the living force within and around us," Briarthorn recites. Before she gives any signal for Branwen to drop me in, the chamber fills with a different kind of smoke. Purple smoke.

A loud familiar voice echoes inside, "*Masks!*"

Chapter 35

The earth above us crumbles lightly, showering some debris into the chamber. Niobe hisses loudly, *"The exerine!"*

Doxo uses the distraction to elbow her in the gut, reach to his belt and put on the mask. Veyanna whips her head to the side, connecting her horn directly into Isador's nose so she can do the same. Growling loudly, Branwen uses her free hand to stab the top of her staff into the earthen roof above us, sending sharp brambles directly into it. The purple smoke continues pouring in, now snaking upward into Briarthorn's face. If the sleeping concoction didn't knock her out, it did make her confused and distracted. My whole body is shaking as I'm held in Branwen's fist while she's stabbing the roof, creating more and more giant thorns to try and catch Khelrah. If I try to get out of this, I might drop into the cauldron. I reach toward my satchel and take out the grappling hook Rhyeah gave me and hoist it in a random direction, hoping it catches. The hook attaches to a nearby shelf in the wall, and with the way she's quickly whipping around, she loses her grip on me, and I hold on tight, trying to swing around the cauldron. Two large hands shove me midair away from it, throwing me to the ground. The sleeping smoke starts to make me drowsy when another pair of hands, softer and more delicate, push the mask onto my face. Above me, Veyanna and Doxo rush to my aid and pull me from the ground while the thornhags struggle to find Khelrah with their magic. Thorns and decayed vines snake through the whole chamber, threatening to bring it all down.

A clawed hand brushes my shoulder, followed by a quiet and familiar voice. "It has come to aid you. Back towards the east wall slowly."

Thank fucking God! She must be utilizing the cloak I made her!

I give a gentle nod, take Doxo and Veyanna by the wrists and gently walk backwards while the thornhags struggle to flush Khelrah out from the walls. The moment my back hits the wall, Khelrah's voice is there again. "When the door opens, run. Do not hesitate."

I don't get a chance to ask for clarity when a pressurized hiss comes from behind me, revealing a hidden doorway. That same sound grabs the attention of the thornhags, staring angrily and hungry.

"Run!"

Loud angry screeches follow us through the hidden doorway as we haul ass out of the chamber. The earthen path out is dark ahead, but it beats sticking around to be eaten by crazy tree witches. The tunnel eventually breaks through the surface of the ground, and we are back in the Grove. The heavy fog of the Grove has started to thin, and across the distance, there are more and more trees with dead Yaruk decorating it like a bloody Halloween sacrificial field. Aside from the horror show, a dim gap in the far maze wall catches my eye. An exit.

"Book it!"

We all move as one towards the exit of the Grove, praying to whoever the hell is listening that the witches keep docile until we reach it.

Like a fucking slap to the face, a large hedge of living brambles shoots up from the ground and blocks our path, along with familiar cackling. We skid to a stop and watch as the brambles surround us.

"They're trapping us in," I say in panic.

"No, they are not!" Doxo roars and takes his axe to the brambles in our way, chopping and hacking at them. Sickly vines and branches weave together after each hack against them. I'm getting flashbacks to the underground cavern where we lost Torbhin, and it sends me into a state of shock. Doxo's growls of frustration turn into a high-pitched ringing in my ears. The ringing is replaced by the cackling of the thornhags. I turn around and watch them as they materialize through the brambles and out of the ground. Their hungry eyes fixate on us, mixed with some otherworldly rage.

"Knowledge has been granted," Briarthorn growls, her thorned arms glowing with otherworldly power.

"The bargain was struck," Isador purrs, her blossoming staff puffing with the noxious toxin.

"Now the price must be paid," Niobe hisses, her sickly pronged tongue slipping out menacingly.

"And you will pay what we are owed," Branwen growls with a grip of her staff, ready to swing. Before the staff comes down in a mighty swing, a loud, bellowing roar rattles the Grove from above. An orange lion-ape with a club raised overhead comes down with a heavy swing and breaks through the barrier behind the Thornhags. From the debris, Riley stands there huffing and snarling, his bone club gripped tightly in his hands.

"You'll pay for the Yaruk lives you stole!" he growls loudly. With a rushing charge, Riley takes a large swing on Branwen, throwing her into the opposite wall. Whipping his head to us, he yells *"Fuck shit up!"*

Like we're the friggin' Avengers, we roar out and charge forward. Veyanna unfurls her whip and lashes it out, grabbing onto Isador's staff and yanking it free from the witch's grip. She yelps out in surprise, even more so when Veyanna takes her hoof and power stomps on the staff, snapping it in two. It takes me by surprise long enough for Briarthorn to extend her thorn-vine arms and wrap around and constrict me, pushing the bladed needles into my skin. I yell out in pain, feeling the air being squeezed out of me. Over my outburst, I hear Briarthorn scream in her own pain and the squeezing of the vines decomposing and flaking away. Doxo's axe is dug in the ground after chopping her arms off. He grins with pride, turns back towards the thornhag, and charges at her with a loud battle cry. Khelrah is in melee with Niobe, two reptiles fighting for dominance. The serpentine witch darts side to side to meet the exerine Trapper blow for blow, swipe for swipe. Niobe is aggressive and quick, having the advantage of a snake tail to maneuver expertly. What Khelrah had to her advantage was agility and a tail of her own to make quick strikes. One wrong move allows Niobe to thrust Khelrah's feet from under her and force her to the ground. Before the thornhag has a chance to strike, I take the leashed net from the Yaruk and toss it at her. The net wraps around Niobe's head and I use the length of the leash to pull as hard as I can, giving Khelrah a chance to regain her footing. The thornhag thrashes and hisses loudly in anger trying to pry herself free from the snare. Khelrah rushes to my aid and pulls with me, forcing the witch onto the ground with a heavy thud. The net comes free, and we both run from the scene.

"Get to the exit," I yell out.

Without waiting for agreement, I run as hard as I can around the barrier that's holding us in. The corner of my eye catches Veyanna sprinting past me around the same barrier. When Khelrah and I bank around the side, Doxo and Riley are already there, waving for us to hurry. We're so close to the exit when Riley points behind me and yells something I can't understand. Before I can turn to look, I feel Khelrah's foot push into my back and thrust me forward and into Doxo's grip. A rumbling sound erupts from behind me, along with a pained cry. I turn in Doxo's arms, and my breath catches in my chest. Khelrah is impaled on a magically formed deadwood tree, just like all the Yaruk bodies in the Grove.

"*No! Khelrah!*" Doxo holds me firm, keeping me from leaping out to help her.

The exerine that took a chance on us so we could make a difference and save the world above, the one that helped train me in natural resources and learning to trust my own instincts, is now magically trapped in a tree that is bleeding her dry. The thornhags focus all their attention on Khelrah, chanting as they approach her. There's a sickly green aura erupting from the tree and covering her body, pulling something from her and being devoured by the witches.

My eyes are stinging with tears, but hers are locked onto me. No sounds of pain, no crying, just an empathetic look.

"It… I thank you, Bimbik," she says weakly. "Do not let this world fade into darkness." Her black-tinted scaled skin starts to fade and gray, and the light in her eyes becomes dimmer.

I'm screaming and thrashing in Doxo's grip on me. Riley yells for us to follow him through the corridor, but all I can do is watch as Khelrah's life is drained from her and devoured by the thornhags. Her face doesn't twist into horror or pain, just the smallest hint of a smile before we disappear into the Maze and away from our friend.

Chapter 36

"And that's about the extent of it."

I scan Darrel's face for confusion, apprehension, or disbelief. Instead, he takes a short pause before whistling loudly.

"Y'all are into some heavy shit, but I'm here for it," he admits with amusement.

Mark looks back at him through the rearview mirror, mouth agape and eyebrows raised. "Dude… you're serious?"

"Dude," he responds, "I'm a hacktivist with a history of seeing the weirdest shit in people's search histories and taking down sickos with deep pockets. If you think that a company using video game technology to fuck with people's minds and freedoms is gonna surprise me, you'll have to try harder than that."

I guess that's that, then. Honestly, I didn't think he'd tell us to turn around and forget we ever saw him at this point. I've never given much thought to the kind of impact that hackers have on what we do. Then again, I've never given anything much thought outside my career with SnoWire. But the brief time spent with the Gridlock has shown me some different sides to what is outside the workplace. I met Robert *in* the workplace, and we connected mostly through our love of the work. But this is something entirely different. After telling Darrel the whole crazy story that makes even *me* question my sanity, he's still all the way in and has no pressing questions about it. *Would I be stupid to trust this? Or is it something I can put a little faith in to overtake Guzman's megalomania?*

"Lost in thought, Stiff?"

He pulls me out of my own head with a cocked eyebrow like he's studying me.

"Yeah… but I thought we were past the 'Stiff' thing."

He chuckles, "Hey, we all have handles, maybe that's yours? Or is it your character name from that game you got stuck in?"

"Heh, yeah. *Ryrzakh* would be a popular name in the hacktivist world." We both laugh.

"I don't know, Matt. I think 'Stiff' fits pretty well in our world because you plan to stiff the big boys upstairs with your own sense of payback." He smirks at me, and I swear I can feel my stomach knot up. "Nothing like a good feeling of payback, amiright?"

I turn back around and face forward, trying to keep my nerves in check. I can't tell if it's just the adrenaline of everything happening all at once or this new feeling of… attention? But Darrel is working me over, and I can't decide if this is good or bad. I'm supposed to be focusing on getting the others away from the labs and trying to expose Guzman for the snake he is, but I can't stop thinking about the willingness of Darrel and the Gridlock in helping us.

Mark keeps driving according to Darrel's navigation to his contacted garage in Glendale. I rarely visit this part of SLC, but I doubt that Guzman and the others do the same.

Darrel leans forward between Mark and me, pointing ahead, "Yeah right up ahead. Look for 'Miller's'."

Sure enough, there's a corner body shop named "Miller's". Small, unnoteworthy, plain to the eye kind of vibes to it.

"Park on the other side of the street," he instructs.

Mark finds a parking spot near a vacant lot across from the shop's garage. "What now?"

"Leave the junker here and let's go in." Darrel hops out from the back and puts a pair of sunglasses on before walking across the street. Quickly, Mark and I hop out and follow. Thankfully no one is taking a second glance as we walk inside the shop. It's one large garage with a few junkers lifted, some completely stripped, and a couple of them being rebuilt. The mechanics inside all take a moment to look at us before going back to their business.

"Bishop, you sonuvabitch!"

We all look past one of the cars being rebuilt and see a young woman marching towards us. Tanned Latin skin, curly dark hair tied back into a loose ponytail and under a bandanna, oil-smudged worker's tank top, garage jacket tied around her waist, stained jeans and heavy boots that slam the concrete with each step.

"Rita, sweetie, how's bis?"

Rita? Sweetie?

"Don't 'how's bis' me, *pendejo*!" she yells, smacking him with a towel. "You almost got my hustle busted with that last stunt you pulled!"

He flinches with each swat but laughs through it. "Easy! Easy! Your shop wasn't even in any of the transcripts. If any fuzz came sniffing, it was probably one of your boys."

She stops hitting Darrel, tilts her head to the side, then looks back at the others working on cars. "Which of you chicken shits narc'd?!"

"Rita, focus."

She whips her head back on Darrel as he gets down to business, "My guys and I need a ride. One that's unmarked, big transport space, and decent condition but nothing that draws attention."

Rita scans us up and down, taking a longer look at me. "They look like narcs."

"Yo, we're not narcs," Mark snaps, looking down at himself.

She squints at him a little closer, "Whoa, no shit! You're that disc jockey! DJ Totym or something?"

His face lights up, "You know me?"

"Yeah," she nods, walking away back to the car she's working on. "Kind of a weird-ass name, but I've been to a couple places you performed. Not bad mixes."

Great, on top of the shitstorm, now I've gotta deal with his ego on top of all this.

"And who's the suit?"

I blink.

Darrel suppresses his laugh, "New guy. Bit of a stiff but smart as hell. We're doing a job, and we need a ride."

Rita leans into the hood of the muscle car she's working on, "Still haven't said what the job is and how I'm gaining from it."

He groans and leans against the car lift, "What do you want? Make it small, I just got out of holding."

With a pause, she emerges from the hood and has a creepy smirk on her face. "Apologize to Ricky, and you'll get your wheels."

"Ah, shit. Not this again."

"You apologize, and we'll call it good."

"No."

"Yes."

I clear my throat, getting their attention. "Look, we're in a hurry. Darrel, apologize and get us a ride."

They both blink at me, but it's Rita who cackles, "*Darrel?* I see you let someone else rut around with ya, you sly dog."

I blink this time, only for Darrel to sigh loudly and drag his hand down his face. "Fine! I'll call him, apologize, then we're done. Now get me a decent van."

"Call him right now, and I'll get you the keys."

It's the first time I've seen him irritated and I can only guess that this Ricky guy is important. Darrel takes his phone out and dials a number, all while Rita is watching and smirking with her arms crossed.

"Ricky? Yeah, shut up and listen. No, I'm the one that called you, so shut up. Look… I'm… I'm sorry. I didn't mean to hurt your feelings and lead you on. Yeah, she's right here. Yeah, she did. Well, quit airing out your dirty laundry to everyone and it wouldn't be a problem. Fuck you, too. Bye." He hangs up the phone and pockets it, "Happy now?"

"So happy," she smirks and kisses his cheek. "Stay here." She saunters away to some kind of office on the other side of the garage.

Darrel turns to me and Mark, both of us awkwardly standing by.

"What?"

"Nothing," Mark says quickly.

I'm too curious. "Old flame or something?"

"Or something," he repeats. "Drop it and let's go."

The van is definitely conspicuous enough to go by unnoticed. Black matte paint, lightly tinted windows, decent tires and engine to get across town, all while sporting brightly colored 80's hairband-style font that reads "DOWN WITH THE SYSTEM" on both sides.

"How badly did you piss your friend off to get us lugged in this piece of shit," Mark groans behind the wheel.

Darrel says nothing while he clicks away on his phone.

The inside is spacious in the back, which is exactly what we need. Open flooring, bench seating on both sides, front driver and passenger seats, no windows except for the front and back. I text Krissy and tell her to be ready. I also give her the instructions needed to purge all the rudimentary systems that can be used to trace our IP.

"Okay, once we get close, we'll need to go around the back and act quickly before anyone has the chance to notice what we're doing," I instruct.

"What if they have cameras and shit to clip our faces and the ride?"

Darrel intervenes, "Cranium's on it. He's working on cycling the camera feeds while Phobia sets up a workstation to keep your boys from going comatose."

I can hear his irritation from the front, so I turn around to face him. "Darrel, I know that you're taking huge steps and risks helping us. I want to thank you. You didn't need to do any of this for us. Whatever we can do to pay this back, you just say the word."

He looks up at me from his phone and just stares. We just look at each other with a mix of understanding and mutual exhaustion. None of this is what we could have anticipated ever happening, yet here we are.

"If you mean that, Matt," he says with the most intensity I've heard from him, "then make sure we don't go down in flames for all of this."

I give a firm nod and hold out my hand for him to take. After a brief pause, he takes it, shakes it once, and holds it for a bit longer before letting go.

Ten minutes later, Mark pulls around the street behind the SnoWire building. He hits the breaks and says through his teeth, "*Shit.*"

Sure enough, there's a security cart in the alleyway that leads directly to the damn labs.

"Son of a bitch!" It has to be Guzman or the other board members. "Keep driving and try not to be shady."

"Oh sure, don't be shady in a fucking creeper van," he spits. The van moves leisurely down the road and parks along the corner.

"Let me think," I grumble to myself, trying to think of any way to get us into the labs and get the others out. "If the cameras are on a loop, then it should just be about getting security out of the way."

"It'll take a long ass time to get those bodies in the van, so they'll need a big distraction," Darrel adds.

"How much time do you think?"

We both look at Mark.

"I recognized those two guards from the storage facility," he explains. "If I can piss them off enough to go after me, you get the van loaded up and I'll hop in after. You leave me, I narc on you both." Without another word, Mark throws his hat in the back and hops out of the driver's seat, running back towards the alleyway.

"Is he always this stupid?"

I just nod before shifting over to the driver's seat, "Just trust that these idiots actually get things done."

I pay close attention to the rearview mirror, watching Mark jog to the alley, turn, throw up both middle fingers, then book it away down the street. One beat, two beats later, the security cart is zooming out after him. I wait until the cart banks around a corner to put the van in reverse, moving down until the alley is in view and turn.

"Cameras?"

Darrel gives a thumbs up.

I send a pre-made text to Krissy saying "*Now!*"

We both hop out of the van, open the back doors, and wait. Barely a minute passes before the lab doors burst open with two bodies in office chairs flying out, pushed by two frantic girls and a very confused security guard.

"Mr. Bauer? What the hell —"

"Not now, Charlie!" I help Krissy and Danica load the guys into the van comfortably and safely. I whip back around to him, pull out my wallet and empty it into his hand. "Do yourself a favor, Charlie, and get another job." Before I can give him a chance to respond, Darrel slams both doors closed after the girls get in and pats me on the shoulder. I take that as my cue to jump back into the driver's seat and pull away from the building, back out the way we came in.

I look both ways before Danica asks, "Where's Mark?"

Like a manifestation, I hear him yelling from the left of the street, *"Fucking go! Open the door!"* The security cart rips around the corner after him.

"Hit the fucking gas!" Krissy yells from behind me.

Quickly, I turn away from Mark and the oncoming cart. In the rearview, Krissy is opening the back doors for him to leap into mid-sprint. He faceplants right on top of Riley's limp torso, the girls slam the doors closed, and we haul ass out of downtown.

Darrel pounds on the roof of the car with his fist and laughs out loud, *"Fuck,* this is fun!"

"Yeah, that's one way of putting it," I say with pounding in my chest. I look in the rearview at Krissy, "Status update?"

Krissy won't take her attention off of Connor's body, tears welling up in her eyes.

"We got them out like you instructed," Danica fills in. "But some weird shit is happening to their bodies again. Like they're being burned or something."

"Okay, that's pretty fucked," Mark says looking down at them both. "Let's get to the Gridlock first before we freak out."

Danica and Krissy give us confused looks. "Ladies, this is Bishop, and he's gonna be helping to take down Guzman while we keep those idiots alive."

Darrel gives them a huge grin and a wave, but Krissy is still in a state of disbelief. I can't tell if it's at what we just pulled off or if it's about what we're doing, but she is refusing to let Connor's arm go. There's a lot that needs to be done with so little time to do and discuss it.

Please don't die in there, you morons.

Chapter 37

Everything in my head is screaming for me to wiggle out of Doxo's grasp and go back for Khelrah. To break free from them all and risk facing the thornhags again to save a computer program that gave everything for us to have time to run. It must have worked because those witches aren't chasing us, meaning they got exactly what they wanted, the price of knowledge. I don't know how long we've been running from the Blighted Grove, but the scenery is drastically changing again from that damp, dank, mossy environment filled with thorns, vines and humidity to a new one of smooth-carved sandstone and sculpted pillars scattered everywhere into another open courtyard. This one reminds me of images I've seen of Egyptian pyramid interiors and temples built of sandstone.

The group finally comes to a stop near a set of carved pillars. Doxo sets me down gently, looking over me to make sure I don't do anything stupid. I'm just leaning against a pillar in complete shock, trying to drown out Veyanna's sobbing and Riley's labored breathing.

We lost another party member. No revivals, no restarts, no forgetting the horror. Torbhin. Khelrah. Would they all *die before the end? Is that the point of this fucked up game?*

I stare up at a pillar I'm resting against. The sculpted pillars have murals carved into them of a familiar smiling maniac with their arms spread open over a sea of snarling beasts and screaming humanoids.

Calos. Guzman. A fucking monster.

I take my grappling hook firmly in my hand and start hacking at the pillar, chipping away at the murals of Calos, angrily growling with each swing. Every angry thought is poured into each swing until a hand grips my wrist. Riley holds me steady and looks at me with some kind of worry that I don't want or need.

"Don't pretend you give a shit about what I'm doing," I growl and rip my hand away from him.

"I do," he urges me. "You know I do. You finally get why I'm here and what it means to connect with these people."

"This isn't the same, Riley! You're living some fucked up fantasy life here and I'm trying to survive! Everything about this game is designed to *kill us!* You're not gonna get your happy ending, you fucking idiot! Guzman is going to make sure *neither* of us leaves!"

He blinks like he's offended.

"Don't fucking look at me like that. You thought you were gonna have a fairy tale ending with your tribal wife and never have to worry about living like a grown-ass adult, and Guzman knew it! He fucking used you and then got exactly what he wanted from us. Dawson's entire algorithm and technology to make into a utopia-for-profit!"

Without another word, I storm off and away from the others. I just can't do it. I can't take all of the reminders of trauma, fear, and possible death. It's the exact same thing I've told myself for the last two goddamn years, yet here I am. Repeating history because I think I can save everyone. *What the fuck is wrong with me? I'm doing this to myself because I have a damn savior complex. It's like Guzman knows that and that's why he's killing off my companions. He doesn't want me dead, just out of the way. Even suffering.*

A soft wind blows through the corridor I stormed off to, raising some bits of sand into the air. I follow the sounds of trickling dust around a nearby corner and stop. It's a smaller collection of sandstone pillars circling a giant ornamental stone that heavily resembles the Rosetta Stone, only with hieroglyphic pictures all around it. They're more detailed than the ones where we stopped. The shapes all depict five different scenes. Three of them look vaguely familiar with winding and sharp corridors, four-legged dog beasts, an underground cavern of water and many worm-like creatures. The next side makes my heart stop: A wooded grove with four hag-like creatures with bodies stuck in trees.

"A map... it's a map," I breathe out.

I move to the next one. A clear sign of pillars and columns are littered everywhere. Towards the top of the carvings, a large, patchy, two-legged beast with a maw of jagged teeth, stuff oozing down its body, and a foot planted firmly on a skeletal body.

"Fuck... Blightfoot." *We're in an arena with a giant zombie-god.*

Looking to the last side of the stone, it shows a large open area with a giant structure in the center like a colosseum of jagged rock. Inside of the structure, a diamond-like symbol that seems to shimmer in the sandstone.

"The rift... that's where the Primeval Maze ends."

There's hope to end this once and for all. We're so close.

"Connor?"

I don't give Riley the satisfaction of turning around. I'm staring up at the mural, at the end of the line.

"I'm sorry."

I scoff.

"I'm serious," he insists. I catch a glimpse of his large frame to my right as we both stare up at the stone. "I didn't want to think you were right about all of this because of everything I'm capable of while I'm in here. I wanted to believe that I could actually walk, be strong, and be everything I've been missing out on since the accident. I was so desperate to feel like I could be somebody that I got taken advantage of and got people hurt. I'm sorry."

I turn to look up at him, "Wow. That almost sounds genuine."

"Come on, Connor, I'm really trying here."

"I know, and that's the problem." I turn back to the map and point, "That is our way out." Then I point at Blightfoot, "And *that* is the key to getting out. The moment we take that thing down, the whole maze becomes weaker and unstable. Guzman becomes weaker. The moment I pass through that rift, the game is over. You're trying so hard to apologize when I know that when the moment comes, you're gonna back out just like last time. You'll be stuck here, and possibly end up just like Dominic. Worst case scenario, you end up like Lorena and go full supervillain to rule your own world. The only way that won't happen is if you leave with me, and we both know that's not how this will end."

The heaviest silence falls. He knows he has a choice to make, and I'm beyond thinking he's gonna do the right thing.

As if he's reading my mind, Riley kneels down to my level and looks me in the eyes. "I don't blame you for thinking that Connor. I didn't give you any other reason to think otherwise. But let this be it: I'll leave with you. I'll help you get to the end of the Maze, we'll stop Guzman, and we'll leave the game together. After that, you can cut me out or whatever you want. Let this be my last chance to gain your trust back."

Honestly, I'm blown away. I thought he was going to fight me tooth and nail over this mayhem. *Do I believe this?*

He stands back up and takes a deep breath, "I'll go get the others. You see if you can make anything of what we're seeing on this stone, and we'll make our next move. Just… think about what I said, okay?" Then he leaves.

Maybe this is exactly what needed to happen for Riley to see what he's been doing, not only to himself but to everyone else. I want my best friend back, and I want to believe that he finally sees how batshit crazy this is. I study the stone a little more, focusing on the murals that reflect this area and the final area of the game. According to the thornhags, we have no choice but to face down Octos and destroy him. Only then will Calos be weak enough to face and the rift be ready to close and defeat the Maze. The makeup of the area we're in is like hundreds of large pillars both standing and fallen. Looking closer, there are divots in the stone that I don't quite understand if they're part of the area or if it's chipped away from aging or something. Following the pattern of pillars throughout the map, I spot a central clearing that seems to be free of all those obstructions, but it also holds the carved visage of Blightfoot in front of the only opening out.

The sound of footsteps draws my attention. Riley is leading Doxo and Veyanna to the stone. Doxo's large arm is draped over Veyanna in a nurturing and empathetic way, the latter's eyes still red from crying.

"Veyanna…"

She shakes her head, "Do not worry. Have you found a way out?"

With a reserved sigh, I nod and look back at the stone. "There's a lot of shit in the way, but that's not the biggest issue. Literally." I point to the large image in the clearing of the mural.

"Blightfoot," Riley groans.

"What do you know about it, aside from its history?"

"Think of a zombie that oozes corrosive acid from all of its wounds," he explains. "I watched some of the hunters try and take him down. Every time they strike, it would bleed acid that ate through the floor. I've even seen him take handfuls of his own blood and lob it at prey. They disintegrated slowly and painfully."

That's horrifying.

"And without its destruction, we cannot stop the Maze?"

No use in sugarcoating it, so I just nod to Veyanna. The fear in her eyes speaks volumes.

"We will prevail," Doxo assures her. This is probably the first time I don't believe the bravado or confidence coming from him. He actually sounds... scared.

"A massive thing like this must have some kind of weakness, right?"

Riley strokes his chin, "The fact that he's large gives us advantage of speed, but to get close means that we are in splash distance of his acid."

"So, we attack from a distance," Doxo suggests. "Utilize the surroundings and improvise ranged attacks."

"Maybe," I mutter. "Our weapons and tools are meant to trap and break beasts, so maybe we can make some traps to slow it down and cripple it before destroying it."

A slow-rising collection of hissing sounds interrupts the planning process. All around, the sounds gradually get louder, like a combination of skittering and hisses. The atmosphere is warm, but not hot enough I think for the air to be rippling with heat. But the pillars, broken sandstone slabs, and the walls around are rippling and moving.

"No one move," Veyanna whispers with a sudden sharpness in her voice.

Her cautious tone makes more sense when the rippling slows down and reveals the source of the hissing and skittering sounds. Hefty lizard-like beasts the size of Gila monsters blending in with the sandstone colors, piercing green eyes, claws like large fishing hooks, barbed spines all the way down to the tail, and blue forked tongues. Dozens of them surround us with hungry looks in their eyes.

Doxo and Riley both grip their weapons aggressively, despite Veyanna's warning. We're too exhausted and not recovered enough for a fight against a bunch of monster lizards, but I don't want to go down like this.

The beasts slink towards us closer to the point I can see saliva dripping from a couple of their mouths. Then, a low-pitched whistling sound makes the monsters stop and tilt their heads in confusion. Behind me, Veyanna is rhythmically blowing into the bone whistle she was given by the Yaruk. Like a scene from *Jurassic Park*, she's using the whistle to influence the monster lizards and make them pause in their advances. From the group in front of us, one larger beast with a black colored spine moves through them like it's an alpha of some kind. Veyanna inches slowly ahead of us, despite Doxo's warning growl. The alpha lizard and Veyanna meet in a tense middle ground where she kneels to the ground in front of it, still rhythmically playing the whistle. It tilts its head from side to side, listening to the notes she's playing. It's the craziest thing I've seen her do. She slowly stops blowing the whistle and just simply stares into the beast's eyes and it mirrors the action. Seconds go by before she stands up again, steps back, and waits. The alpha lizard skitters back through the group of others, who all in turn follow it away. All of them skitter away and back to where they came from.

"What... the hell was that?"

With an innocent smile on her face, Veyanna holds up the whistle, "Seems like it helps me master my understanding of creatures here in the Maze. Those were sandstalkers, but of a different subspecies than the ones of Preydor. The alpha was ready to have its brood feed until we came to an understanding."

"Wait," Riley gapes, "you can *speak* to them?"

She nods, "They are the first intelligent creatures I've been able to comprehend. Aside from the..." She didn't need to finish that sentence. "With an understanding that they will soon return to their true home, they are allowing us safe passage."

Doxo and Riley relax their weapons and do a once-over of the area, confirming that the lizards are all gone.

"Okay, then," I sigh. "Well, that's one less thing to worry about. Hopefully."

Looking back at the stone one more time, I tense my shoulders and point to the east, "That's where we need to go. Let's go hunt a zombie god."

Chapter 38

On this tourist trek through the new landscape, I can honestly say that I prefer this type of desert setting to the Great Expanse from *The Mortal Gate*. The ground is slightly softer and less cracked like the ground of the Expanse, the heat is less intense but still warm, and the only thing that is the same as the Expanse is just that; the massive amount of space and walking with the intermittent littering of sandstone pillars. As we are walking, the silence outside of our footsteps is haunting. We know exactly what waits for us before we leave this part of the Maze, and we are dreading it. We've lost two people already, and it's very likely that we'll lose more before we make it to the end. In all this, I'm still brewing over what went down between me and Riley, how easily we were at each other's throats and then quickly changed it to him agreeing to leave with me. I'm still trying to wrap my head around it all.

"Was there any rhyme or reason to the layout of this place?" Veyanna is scanning the surrounding area very carefully, either trying to look out for Blightfoot or the sandstalkers she made friends with.

"Didn't seem to be, honestly. It just showed a field of pillars and then a large space of nothing. That's where tall and ugly will be."

"And we are certain that destroying the beast will weaken the Maze and its presence?" Doxo doesn't seem too convinced of the idea that killing an undead giant is enough to stop all this from happening.

"I don't trust anything that those murder witches say, but it's all we've got," I say with a hard swallow. *Khelrah's sacrifice won't be in vain.*

There's something satisfying about stepping on this terrain that's less disgusting or foreboding than the others we've been through since the start. It's almost like walking on a firm beach, minus the water and salty air. But there's something else in the air, something that is just getting worse the further we walk in the arena. Strong, dingey, like a thicker taste of iron.

Along with the strong smell, a faint whistling from far ahead of us fills the silence between us all. We stop in our tracks and look around for the source of the sound. At first, it sounds like the buzzing and humming of bugs mixed with slowly increasing wind. That idea quickly changes when I look ahead and see a subtle shadow moving towards us, followed by billowing clouds of sand.

"Shit... *sandstorm!*"

"Find cover!" Riley yells out, running towards a sandstone column.

I watch Doxo pull Veyanna to a toppled pillar and get her under him, covering her with his massive frame. I shuffle to a nearby destroyed slab and crouch down as low as I can. The force of the wind nearly knocks me over as the sharp, shredding winds of glass and stone envelops us in a giant cloud. The wind is so loud I have to hold my ears tightly against my head. Barely squinting, I can't see shit through this storm. I think someone is trying to yell out against the winds, but it's too loud and the debris is relentless.

Wait, the masks!

I reach into my satchel, exposing my ear to the roaring around us, and pull out the mask Khelrah gave me. I put it on, take off my vest and wrap it around my head to cover my ears and eyes as best as I can. *Time to* Dune *this bitch.* Standing from the ground, I push against the storm to try and find the others. The storm is so thick with sand that I can barely see my own hand that's trying to cover my eyes. I feel pins and needles pelting against me with every step forward. I can't even tell if I'm walking in the right direction from where I last saw the others.

"Doxo! Riley! Veyanna!"

Nothing.

"Anybody?!"

More nothing.

Dammit!

I keep moving. That's all I can do is keep moving. Eventually, this storm has to let up and we can reconvene. My small frame does nothing to help me against the wind and sand as I push against it, trying to either find the others or another form of cover.

The ground under my feet vibrates. One thump. Another thump. Spaced out about ten seconds apart.

"Blightfoot..."

Another thump, this time closer. I have *nothing* that can defend against that thing if it's coming after us in the storm. *Is it even affected by the storm?*

The next thump is so close that it makes me lose my footing and I fall backwards, but I don't hit the ground immediately. Instead, I fall back into a sloped pit that rolls me down until I land in some kind of pool. A pool that smells like what I was getting earlier before the storm. A pool that is starting to burn me on contact.

I scream in pain. It feels like my skin is being eaten away. The cloth of my clothes is being dissolved away and my skin feels like it's on fire. I dig my hands into the surface of the ground where I fell to try and get out, but another thump in the earth sends me right back into the pit and pool. I scream again.

"Connor!"

I look up from the pit and see a familiar bone-club in my face. *"Grab on!"*

I reach up and grab onto a spike of bone. The club tugs upward and pulls me out of the smoldering pool, thrusting me up onto solid ground. The pain is unbelievable.

"Get his clothes off!" Veyanna orders. "The acid will keep eating away and get onto his skin!"

Two pairs of hands are tearing away my clothes, but I'm in too much pain to be bothered. I feel the heat of the floor against my back, which is nothing compared to the acid eating away at me.

"Keep him still," she demands. Doxo's hands grip my wrists and Riley holds my ankles down. I hear some rustling and mumbling, but I can't bring myself to focus on anything else other than the burning. A cool sensation replaces the burning, along with soft hands over my arms and legs. The combination of sensations sends me into a shaking fit I can only think that a seizure feels like.

"Keep him still! Doxo, put a leather strap between his teeth!"

A firm strip of leather gets shoved in my face just as I almost bite my own tongue. The cooling sensation spreads over onto the most painful parts of me. My body convulses more and more until I fall limp, and everything goes blank.

"Connor! Come on, man, wake up!"

I let out a loud, hoarse groan. My eyes flutter open to three figures standing over me. The menacing cloud of sand is gone, my body is aching, and everything is fuzzy as my eyes try to adjust to everything. It's noticeably breezier; my clothes are gone. I'm covered in what looks like Veyanna's half-cape that she's been wearing since the beginning.

"Thank the gods, you are awake," she sighs heavily, putting a gentle hand on my shoulder.

"Ugh… what happened?"

Her hand keeps me from sitting up, "You were gravely injured. An acid pool threatened to melt your body away."

"An acid pool?"

Riley, to my left, points over and shows me a crater that dips down. I creep over and see that this crater is filled with steaming green and yellow acid. The pool is in an odd shape with specific curves and dips. Like a large footprint.

"Jesus Christ..."

"Yeah," Riley sighs. "Octos is one *big* mother."

Blightfoot's footprints leave pools of acid that come from its own body. That's what that smell was, and the quakes. There were more steps moving towards the dimming light ahead of us. A trail to follow.

"Get your rest, Half-Pint," Doxo urges. "We will be no good against the beast if we are not at full strength."

"What about the sandstorm?" I groan, clinging the cloak closer to me. "We can't take another hit from that thing."

"Veyanna's lizard friends can help with that," Riley explains. He points to the far side of the arena where a wall of the Maze is, showing a small dark spot at the base of it.

Without warning, Doxo picks me up in his arms with the cloak draping over me. We make our way to the far wall and see a cavern big enough for us to fit in, so we maneuver inside and settle in. Veyanna gives me permission to cut up her cloak so I can stay covered up, so I turn it into a tunic of sorts to be able to wear it properly. The dimming light outside is enough for us to be able to see outside and keep an eye out for danger, so we all hunker to the back of the cavern as far as we can. Riley takes up position at the mouth of the cavern, offering to take the first watch. Doxo and Veyanna take a section of the cavern and rest together, the latter resting her head on the gnolid's chest with his arm around her shoulder. The pain and exhaustion are too much for me to make any mental note as I flatten out on the floor of the cavern and pass out again.

Chapter 39

I explain to Matt and Mark the entire thing of what happened since we last saw them. The marks on the boys, the attempt to break into the labs, even the ring in Connor's pocket. Mark swears up and down he didn't know about it, and I don't even bother to ask Matt if he knew. He and Riley are still very much unconscious with those damn Crests around their heads, and there's no telling when this will all be over. I keep thinking that I'll finally do what Danica did and demand Connor give all this up. The gaming, SnoWire, all of it. *But what if he resents me? What if he changes his mind about proposing?*

That train of thought is interrupted when Matt explains who his new friends are, how they've been helping, and what they're planning to do when we get where we're going. *This is fucking nuts! First, we become a bunch of virtual adventurers, now we're fucking around with hackers and corporate takeovers.* I'm not against extra help, but none of this is what I was expecting. I don't think any of us did, honestly. In a strange moment of quiet understanding, I feel like we all understand that we wouldn't have been able to do this without each other.

The van turns off onto a dirty road leading away from the burbs, which Darrel promises is where we're supposed to be going. Even Danica is looking at him with RBF about it.

"Just trust him like I do," Matt asks. I swear that I see a small smirk coming from both him and Darrel. I don't have enough time to remark on it before we come to a stop. Everyone gets out; Mark, Matt and Darrel team up to get Connor and Riley out from the back. The small spraypainted building doesn't really make me feel comfortable, but the boys are going straight in without any hesitation. The door opens quickly, a girl with some sick gear on in the open doorway.

"Phobia, strip and ditch the van," Darrel says firmly as they push past her. She just gives a nod and runs for the van, jumping into the driver's seat and tearing out.

Inside, it's like something out of a movie with all the neon and hardware. In a far corner, there are two chairs set up in a lounging position. Following Darrel's lead, we take the boys over to the chairs and lay them down softly, making sure everything with the Crests is still functional and safe.

A weirdo with some decked out helmet comes over and starts looking over the Crests. "Yo… this is sick! Full cerebellum and frontal cortex integration, reactionary sensers for occipital readings and brainwave regulating. Is it pinned into their heads for full synaptic immersion?"

"Cranium, take a breath," Darrel nudges with authority. "They need to be acclimated before we start Jacking in."

"Wait, what do you mean 'Jacking in'?"

He looks at me with a bit of reserve, but then looks at Matt. "We stole some material to help build an interactive firewall breaker to get us access into some hardcore systems. We call them 'Jacks', because we jack in and jack them up."

Matt blinks rapidly, "S-so what you're saying is you have a way to interact with software systems by dumping your conscious brains into a binary network?"

Cranium hops into his chair, "Precisely. It's like VR gaming to hack into specific systems. I've been working to see if I can alter it in order to sync up with the Crests and get some eyes on your friends there."

I can't believe what I'm hearing. They can actually go in and watch what's happening with Connor and Riley. "Do you think we can speak to them when you're Jacked in?"

"That, we haven't tested," Darrel explains. "Every time we use it, it's for covert jobs. We try to be as discreet as we can."

This is huge!

"When can we start?"

Cranium skips over with a couple of cords in each hand and starts hooking up some wires to Riley's Crest. With a little bit of time, he claps his hands together before moving over to Connor, doing the same thing to him. They look like something out of *The Matrix*, but if it's the thing that helps them get out, I don't care.

Rubbing his hands together, Cranium smirks under his headset and says, "Let's Jack in."

Chapter 40

This time when I wake up, nothing stirs me or scares the shit out of me. I wake up on my own, feeling the aching in my bones from countless miles walked, endless beatings, and overall exhaustion and heartache. Through a squint, I see that Veyanna is awake, but Doxo is knocked out, and she's staying in his embrace. She's smiling. Against all of this, she's smiling within the arms of a big brute with a big heart and ego. Riley is sitting down at the mouth of the cavern looking outward. I get to my feet and join him, silently watching as another sandstorm is blasting through the arena.

"It's nasty out there."

I nod, "In more ways than one."

He sighs deeply, "This isn't gonna end well for them. You know that, right?"

I look back at Doxo and Veyanna with a heavy heart. "I wish I didn't care about how it's gonna end for them."

Riley turns to me, "I get it. I treated everything and everyone here as real living people. Look where it got me."

"It's programming. Dawson was good at making realism work in a fantasy land. You remember *Buster Charge*?"

He chuckles, "How could I forget? Hottest MMORPG Battle Royale game of the century. The NPCs were almost as smart as the ones you see in *Tron*."

"Whole digital playground of cyberpunk gamers buying upgrade and gear cards right out the ass just to beat the shit out of each other in a digital arena."

"We saved up a whole month to get the Buster Arc and team up against the Breaker Tower," he reminisces with a smile.

"Those kids were *pissed* when we left them for the Seeker Swarm to get to the next floor," I laugh with him.

We both give a soft chuckle to the memory of what it was like to just be two young idiots enjoying a game just for the sake of having fun. My laughing slows down and I give a soft sight, leaning my head against the threshold.

"This might be the last one for me."

I see his head tilting out of the corner of my eye. "What do you mean?"

Closing my eyes and taking a deep sigh, I keep looking out to the sandstorm. "I'm leaving SnoWire after we get out of this. I'm leaving the gaming world behind. At least for a while."

He gets up to his feet, but I don't look at him. I can't. I know already what to expect.

"Connor, that's your entire life," he says softly. I hear the shock in his voice. "You studied it for years and are part of the biggest gaming company in the country. You're just gonna leave that behind?"

He's not wrong, I think to myself. *My whole life has been about games and fantasy. Playing it, writing it, making it. But this... this isn't what I wanted from it.*

"I'm asking Krissy to marry me," I say outright. I hadn't said that to anyone else other than Krissy's case manager from the foster care system. Something about it just felt meaningful to me. "I can't keep putting myself in positions that keeps me from doing that. I've been afraid of so much. Adulthood, the real world, fully committing to my relationship with Krissy. I need to wake up."

I finally look at him, and there is devastation in his eyes. Like I just stuck a knife in his gut and twisted it in a complete circle.

"Then what is the point of pulling me out of this if you're just gonna leave me behind?"

I knew this would happen. "I'm not leaving you behind, Riley. If you want to take my job at the company, then it's yours. I just want to take myself out of the equation of all this corporate sabotage and virtual imprisonment. I'll still be around, and you can finally take creative lead on the projects."

He's dumbfounded. Saved by the throat clearing, Doxo pulls our attention away from each other.

"We are in need of a plan to take down and eliminate the beast before moving on," he states.

Veyanna comes to his side and looks at me, "Perhaps our resident Trapper can develop some form of a trap or diversion to best handle Blightfoot?"

I guess now of all times is to remember that I *am*, in fact, a Trapper. I take out my logbook and attempt to find anything on traps. With us running and dodging everything, there's been little-to-no reason to use traps to keep something still. This time, it's our only chance of trying to end all of this. With as much stress and tension we're currently under, it's gonna take a miracle to muster something up to take down a zombie god. As I'm flipping through my book, a few pages catch my eye, and a smirk begins to form.

"We'll need to deconstruct some stuff." I look at Veyanna, "And we'll need help from your lizard friends."

She nods firmly, Doxo mimics my smirk, and Riley just stares and waits.

"Right... Let's set a trap."

I don't usually brag about myself, especially when it comes to planning, but I honestly am impressed by this. Thanks to deconstructing some of the bones and bladed attachments from both Doxo and Riley's weapons, the unraveling of my lasso net, and the fast work from Veyanna's army of lizards, the trap is about complete. Using the remaining resources that we've gathered from the smokehounds, razorwing bats, and some of the devourworms, it's looking professional. The last touch to the plan is the remaining sleep powder bombs that Khelrah had made. It's tearing me apart to waste her tools on this, but it'll be useful.

The final part of this whole thing might not be as smart, however: luring Blightfoot in.

"Absolutely out of the question!"

"Doxo, it's the only real option we have," I explain. "If we go hunting for Blightfoot, we're dead before we even get a shot. This is what we need to do."

He's so heated, I swear I can see steam puffing from his nose like a cartoon bull. Veyanna is the one to calm him as she comes to his side, putting a hand on his face to turn his focus on her.

"It is going to be okay, Doxo. I will be okay." Reaching from the tips of her hooves, she kisses him gently. He returns it with a scrunch of his brow, as if he's trying not to break. When they separate, she gives him a soft smile before turning attention to me.

We nod to each other as I hand her Torbhin's lute-club. I honestly don't like how this diversion plan was calculated either, but it's just the only viable plan we have to lure Big-N-Ugly to us.

With a deep breath, I exhale loudly. "Okay, everyone to your posts. And pray to whoever it is that's listening that this works."

Doxo grunts, keeping his eyes on Veyanna as she takes her post out in the open. After a couple of moments of silence, he finally splits from the group and heads to his position. Riley and I share a tense stare before we split and head to our respective positions, waiting for this shit to go down. I take count of us in our positions and whistle the signal to Veyanna. I take notice of the way she tenses before positioning the lute in her hands, giving a couple of plucks of the strings, and then begins playing. While she's no Torbhin, it's still a good attempt. She's playing and singing the Song of the Mazebreakers that he wrote, softly at first before she raises her voice. It's burning my chest with pain. If we had everyone together, this might be possible. If I had *my* friends and team together, this might be possible. But with just the four of us, minimal resources, and only a shred of hope piled under uncertainty? I have no idea how this is gonna play out.

Whether by good or bad luck, that answer is now coming towards us. Long, quaking steps start shaking the ground, getting bigger and sounding closer. Veyanna doesn't stop playing or singing. Not even when the large-framed shadow of Octos, the Lasting Fury, the dreaded Blightfoot, comes into view.

Chapter 41

I want to vomit, but I can't. It'll blow our cover. But it looks like more of its skin and muscle has started to decay and fall off. Like a skeleton with a loose, patchy sheet of skin hanging off of it, its grayed flesh is missing more than before, its bones are yellowed with strings of its green acidic blood, turning purple under the skin. Its gangly fingers sport jagged, broken nails that look like they can cleave us apart without effort. The face is the worst part, because it's moving slow enough now and we're not actively running away from it. The one remaining eye is sunken in its skull with some kind of yellowish glow coming from the empty socket. A large, open mouth of gross, yellowish-green, broken teeth with strings of green oozing from between them. If this is the aftermath of the god's corruption from Calos, I can't begin to think what it looked like before.

Veyanna's voice is starting to shake, but she keeps singing and playing. I can't see him, but I can *feel* Doxo's fury just building and building the longer we sit here.

Don't. Not yet.

Two more giant steps lumber towards the varlese Handler. Her voice not softening as she looks up at its towering frame.

Not yet!

The sound that comes out of this thing's throat curdles my stomach. A wail that scratches the whole way out but thrums so loudly I feel like I'm in *Jurassic Park*.

Not yet!

Peering back over my cover, I watch as Blightfoot begins to move like it's going to lean down and snatch her up from the ground. One more step forward and its foot sinks suddenly into the pit that was dug up especially for this outcome. Makeshift pikes and stakes puncture right through its foot, one of them made from my grappling hook to keep it stuck and locked in like a fishing hook.

"NOW!"

Doxo leaps from his cover and runs for the giant beast. Riley starts swinging a long vine-leash made from my net and bolos, hurling it up at the lurching thing. One precise throw and it rests onto the back of its neck. With a running start on the slanted sandstone pillar, I dart upwards and jump to catch the weighted end and grip it in my hands. I'm swinging and hanging from it like George of the Jungle, waiting for the next part.

"Hurry the fuck up, Doxo!"

With a guttural roar as a response, Doxo takes his axe and cleaves into the beast's ankle, severing the tendon with a mighty strike. Blightfoot lets out another blood-curdling wail and starts leaning forward.

Veyanna reaches up and grabs me by the ankles, pulling me down to the ground.

"Pull with everything you've got!"

Riley grunts and roars loudly from the other side while Veyanna and I combine our might to pull. Before this moment, she and I strategically laced smokehound claws and razorwing bat wings into the vine rope. I can see them piercing into the giant's neck as we're pulling. This can end in a number of ways, but we just need it to end one, with the beast dead.

Across the way, I notice Doxo joining Riley in this tug-of-war, pulling the beast down inch by inch. It's so distracted by the cleaving of its ankle and still-trapped foot that its focus loosens from straining against us.

"Keep pulling!"

Blightfoot growls and snarls, holding its weight up by its mangled hands. It's starting to push.

"Veyanna! Keep pulling!"

I let go and run in the direction of its sickly head, skidding to a stop directly underneath it. Flint, granite, and two wicks attached to bags of sleep powder. I'm striking the stones together to get a spark. Just one goddamn spark is all I need. I barely miss being drooled on by Blightfoot's disgusting acid that the ground is sizzling. *Sizzling!*

The strike of the stones finally catches, and the wicks burn. I take one pouch in each hand and stare up at the zombified mouth directly above me.

"Bon Appetit, you ugly motherfucker!"

With as much strength as I have, I hurl them upward one after the other. The first one misses entirely, getting under the chin and hurtling down to the ground. The second one, by some stupid luck, manages to get caught between two jagged teeth. The smoke begins to burn and cloud. I run back to Veyanna, her hooves digging into the ground as she pulls, and take up the remaining slack.

"How long will it take?!" Riley yells at me.

"I don't know but keep fucking pulling!"

The smoke is billowing into its open mouth. In truth, I hatched this plan without thinking if it needs to breathe, but it has to do something. Blightfoot starts hacking and grunting as the smoke rolls into its mouth, slightly pouring from the open eye socket. The taught line starts to pull more in our direction.

"It's working! Give it all you got!"

With a unified roar, we all pull as hard as we can. With the bladed spikes digging into its neck, Blightfoot suddenly lurches forward and its head hurdles to the ground. I chose this exact spot because of the number of fallen sandstone pillars and how high up they are. The one that the zombified head is falling towards is about a foot taller than Doxo. My eyes are closed, but I hear the spine-chilling snap and crunch of bone against rock, followed by a giant thud that shudders the ground. Veyanna and I fall back to the ground, losing our grip on the vine rope. I lean up on my elbows and look over. Blightfoot's neck had snapped and folded up, forcing its eyes and still-open jaw to point up at the sky above us. No breathing, no twitching, no groans.

Veyanna is huffing next to me, leaning up on one side. "Is... is it dead?"

Before I get a chance to answer, a squelching sound with splattering acid blood comes from the other side of the snapped neck. We quickly run around the pillar to the other side, watching Doxo furiously chop at Blightfoot's neck with Riley standing back and watching.

"Doxo!"

His enraged face twists back to us, his teeth are clenched so hard I think they might shatter.

"It's dead, Doxo. You can stop."

His huffing gradually starts to slow, bringing him back to the large, slightly-less scary barbarian we know. Veyanna gently takes his wrist in her hand and pulls him away from the body.

"It is okay, Doxo. We have accomplished our task. Let us reach the end of this nightmare and return home," she says in a soothing tone. "Together."

Taking deep breaths, he just simply nods and relaxes in her grasp. The four of us move away from the giant carcass all the way down to its feet, noticing a large path of acidic footprints coming from the northwest direction. Maybe if we follow the prints, we can find the final spot of the Maze and beat this thing once and for all.

But, not before a familiar groaning sound grabs our attention from behind. We turn in unison and watch as the body of Blightfoot starts getting up from the ground where it fell. Its head is still snapped backwards but the whole body turns around to face us. Its hands reach back and yank up on the head, snapping it back into place. I swear on the Outside, I probably pissed myself.

There's only one option right now.

Run.

Chapter 42

Without a second thought, we're running. Blightfoot wails loudly and takes a gigantic step forward. It shakes the ground so hard it throws me off balance to the point I run into Riley's side. I'm certain we'll be dead with the next big step from the monster. I hear a familiar growl of pain and look back, watching as Blightfoot's severed tendon sends him hobbling back down, but this time he's reaching out with both hands.

"Incoming!"

Riley and I leap away from each other to avoid the giant hand that is barreling down on us. It smacks so hard that it leaves an indentation in the ground. I roll far until I'm flat on the ground. Blightfoot's face is visible, but it's not looking in my direction.

"Doxo!"

Veyanna's cry springs me to action as I bolt back up to my feet and run around the hand. It starts lifting from the ground and I see Doxo howling in pain as a large gash in his back is bleeding uncontrollably and afflicted with Blightfoot's acid.

"Fuck!"

"He is wounded! Help me!" She's tugging on his arm, keeping his back out of the sand. I rush over to grab his other arm and pull. Blightfoot is still trying to recover from the spill as it gets to its hands and knees. Something must've torn into its chest because there's a sickly green and purple glow coming from it that I didn't see before.

Maybe some kind of weak point?!

"It... it is... weak," Doxo says through labored breaths. Riley finally rushes over to us and helps by grabbing his legs. "We... we must—"

"You are doing nothing!" Veyanna is choking back tears. "We will find another way!"

The ground shakes again, making us drop Doxo face first on the ground. I look back and Blightfoot is clawing at the ground, pulling itself towards us like a true undead monster, drooling and groaning.

"I don't think we're gonna make it out of this," Riley says with the most fear I've heard from him. "It's just too big."

"S-so am I," Doxo growls as he slowly gets back to his feet. The wound on his back is still sizzling from the acid. He huffs and grabs his axe, cracking his knuckles with gritted teeth. "I came here to become a legend. To earn glory. But the greatest glory is ensuring that my companions live to tell the tale. Zasar, I would be grateful if you would allow me to use your weapon."

"Doxo, no!"

Veyanna is in front of him, his face in her hands. "Do not do this. You will die!"

318

"I am already dead, Veyanna. I can feel the acid taking hold in my veins. Even if we escape, my life is now forfeit."

She begins sobbing. *I* begin sobbing. He pulls her face to his own and kisses her deeply. Once they separate, minus their foreheads resting against each other, he whispers to her, "Live, my fawn. Live."

He pulls from her and looks to Riley, holding out his hand. With pain in his eyes, he hands over the bone-club. Doxo's eyes then fall on me, with so much humanity in them it hurts.

"You are brave, Half-Pint. Truly. Lead them home and end this nightmare." I don't know where he learned this from, but he lowers his fist to me. I bump his knuckles with my own, tears streaming down my face.

With no more words to have, Doxo limps away from us. Veyanna refuses to let go of his arm as he is holding both his axe and Riley's club. Riley gently pulls her away from him and holds her in place. Every step he takes away from us is a stab of burning pain in the chest. Blightfoot crawls forward again, groaning and snarling, that spot in its chest still radiating the glow.

"I am Doxo the Stonesplitter of Braveshire! In the name of the Stone Father! Preydor! The Mazebreakers! *I! Will! Not! Fear! DEATH!*"

He charges directly at Blightfoot. Riley and I hold the crying and screaming Veyanna back as we watch. With a few long strides, even with the gaping wound in his back, Doxo plants his feet and leaps up with a mighty roar and sinks the blade of his axe into the beast's chest. It lurches

319

forward in pain, but Doxo is using Riley's club to hammer at the weak point with savage swings. The glowing in the chest starts to burst forth from the wounds in rhythmed glowing.

"Oh no! Get back!"

I push Veyanna as best as I can with Riley's help away from what I think is about to happen. Even over her crying, I can hear Doxo's boisterous laugh0-9ing behind me. Blightfoot's roaring grows incrementally louder until a thunderous boom sounds off in the entire arena. A wave of purple and green thrusts us all onto the ground. Looking up to the sky, that beating purple and green source that kept the dead god walking spins rapidly and then shoots off to the northwest like a comet.

And then, there was silence.

No more giant, roaring monster.

No more loud, psychotic laughter of a gnolid Breaker.

Nothing.

Chapter 43

With this experimental technology, there is no way in hell I'm letting Krissy go in first. Of course, she fought me tooth and burning insults about it, but ultimately, I trusted her to manage the guys and keep an eye on the Gridlock.

Now, here I am, sitting in a gaming chair with Darrel plugging me into their little "Jack" network.

"You sure about this, Stiff?"

"Hell no," I admit. He cracks a smile for a brief moment. "But if this is what it takes to get them out and get dirt on Guzman all at once, I'm in."

He stops for a moment and looks me solidly in the eye. "Impressive, the amount of shit you're going through for those two. From what you've told me, they're idiots."

I glance over to their unconscious bodies. "One of them is an idiot," I say pointedly at Riley. At Connor with Krissy by his side, I say, "The other one is just a bleeding heart trying to save people. Hell, he saved my life. I owe this to them."

I glance back at Darrel, and there's a genuine smile on his face that makes my face flush. He finishes hooking in the wires to this headset and says, just before pushing the visor over my eyes, "Let's have a real talk after this, 'kay Matt?"

I don't even get a chance to respond before the visor starts flooding my vision with binary codes streamlining in front of me. Faster and faster, they race across my field of vision until a single figure forms; a hashtag with a padlock linked in the center.

"Gridlock. Clever."

I hear a snort in response before Cranium's voice invades my head.

"Okay, boss-man. Here's the deal: You're gonna literally lose your mind to the system. When you're in there, you won't be able to hear what's happening out here, but your brain will pick up activity inside. If you can, try to describe as much as possible vocally and we'll hope that you tell us rather than go mute. Again, experimental."

That's fucking reassuring.

Darrel's voice butts in, "The main thing to focus on is finding your guys and seeing if any of Guzman's dirty laundry can be picked up in the process. You ready?"

I exhale loudly and give two thumbs up, "Beam me up, Cranium."

"See ya on the other side."

One keystroke later, I don't feel my body anymore. Just a loud buzzing in my head. Then, my vision is watching copious amounts of data stream by me like a river rock.

Fully *Matrix'd* in, it feels like swimming in open air. My ears are starting to pick up some other sounds that sound like jumbled voices being mixed in a blender. There's so much information that it's almost too much.

Breathe... Focus... Find Connor...

I repeat that same mantra a few times before homing in my focus. As if by some grand manifestation, I see a bright white dot slowly start to grow.

There's my exit.

Focusing on that growing spot, the data streams start to slowly disappear and is replaced with blinding white surroundings. I raise my hands to rub my eyes.

Wait... my hands?

I look down and see my body. I'm wearing exactly what I was wearing when I Jacked in.

This... is this real?

"It's real, numb nuts."

I know that voice. That mocking, haunting, condescending tone. I slowly turn around and feel my heart lurch up into my throat.

Two figures are in front of me. One is tall with slicked back blond hair, wearing a navy-blue blazer with no tie, black slacks with matching shoes, and inviting green eyes. The other one is slightly shorter with similar blond hair tied back in a loose ponytail, less formal clothing that fits a least-interested attitude, and greenish-brown eyes. The most notable feature of her is that she's missing an arm.

"Dominic? Lorena?"

Chapter 44

"Well, good to know your memory still works and you're a friggin' Einstein."

"Now, now, Lorena," Dominic scolds. "We've talked about your curt attitude."

I'm very much convinced that I'm dead. Because they're *supposed to be dead*.

"My boy," Dominic says with a soft voice. "I understand that you must be quite confused. Please, take what time you need in order to come to terms with this."

Still frozen in place, my eyes scan the white void around us. The way it feels, how my brain is fuzzy with everything around me. Connor said something about a place where he and Dominic convened before coming to our rescue at Sacredcrest.

"Is… Is this the Hollow?"

"Another point to dick-for-brains," Lorena drawls.

Her father sighs before acknowledging the question, "Indeed, it is. Quite a spacious void, I know. Not quite what you were expecting."

"N-no… You're… you're alive?"

A loud groan from Lorena. "No, dipshit. But not quite dead either. It's fucking confusing."

"What Lorena is trying to say," he interjects, "is that this is a bit of Purgatory. While our bodies are decayed, our conscious minds have found a way to compatibly integrate with the system. However, it seems that the system is specifically designed for SnoWire programming like a bridged link."

My head is fucking spinning. This level of technology shouldn't even be possible. Yet, here they are talking to me as if they haven't been dead for the last two years!

"It would be nice to *not* stare at blank white all the fucking time," Lorena groans. "But the jackass that made this place didn't make an *escape route*."

"Glitches in the SnoWire software are spontaneous and often immediately patched. This one is just simply… smaller and easy to miss," Dominic explains. "It was quite lucky for us to slip into after the decommissioning of *The Mortal Gate*."

"S-so, hold on!" I try to bring attention back to the insanity at hand. "You slipped through an unpatched glitch in the game's software, managed to not be completely erased, and your conscious minds are now just coded to exist here?"

Dominic smiles, "That's why you were my best and brightest, Matthew."

"Just blow him already and be done with it, Dad."

Crass insult aside, I can't seem to comprehend it even if I actually get what happened.

"The question is, though," Lorena states pointedly at me, "why the fuck are you here?"

"I-I didn't mean for this to happen. I thought I was being pulled somewhere else."

"Don't tell me you were trying to enter the mainframe of *The Primeval Maze*," Dominic asks.

"H-how do you know about that?!"

Dominic turns to his daughter, who rolls her eyes and snaps her fingers. Strips of data streams around us, forming visual screens of various places I don't recognize. A burning village, a walled settlement with soldiers, a swarm of bats, a gaping hole in the ground.

"You've been watching it…"

"Like a horror comedy," Lorena scoffs.

The images then start following a group of characters adventuring together; a tall muscular, gray-skinned warrior, a fawn with a whip at her side, a reptilian humanoid wearing a hooded vest, a stout dwarf with a huge instrument on their back, and a small blue-haired guy.

"If you're wondering which one he is, he's the half-squat," Lorena points.

Connor. A gnomish looking thing instead of a muscle-bound orc.

"He is resourceful, I'll give him that," Dominic comments. "But this is taking a much larger toll on him."

"Good," she spits and gestures to her missing arm.

"How come you haven't left here to go there?"

"We can't," Dominic says with a tone of disappointment. "Whatever glitch that existed in *The Mortal Gate* doesn't exist in *The Primeval Maze*. We can only sit, watch, and hope."

"Hope?"

"That he doesn't die and kicks Armand Guzman to the curb," she hisses in answer.

I'm dumbstruck.

But, before I can demand answers, Dominic shushes us both.

"Look."

The screen is now focusing on Connor. He's laid out on the ground of some area with the fawn and some large, orange-furred humanoid.

"Riley?"

They both nod.

I can't get to them. I can't help them. Not from here. All I can do is watch. And, as Dominic said, hope.

Chapter 45

The ringing in my ears dies down. My body is aching like I just fell from a two-story drop. But none of that matters in comparison to the frantic sobs coming from Veyanna.

"D-Doxo…"

My heart is shattered. I lean up to see Veyanna limping back to where the explosion came from.

"Vey…" My throat is scratchy. "Veyanna…"

A set of large hands scoops me up under my arms, helping me to my feet. I look up at Riley, who's staring at me with a look I can't quite read. His focus moves to the direction of Veyanna, and I follow suit. Her cries get louder when she disappears.

Either she found him, or he's not there. Either way…

Slowly, Riley and I walk back to the scene of the tragedy that was Doxo's final heroic moment. She's kneeling on the ground, heavy breaths mixed with broken sobs. In her hands, she's holding Doxo's axe.

I feel like I'm gonna puke. It's too much. Especially when we get close enough to see that the axe and the club are all that remain of the gnolid Breaker and the beast he conquered.

I slowly approach and put a hand on her shoulder. At first, she flinches at the touch. But then she relaxes knowing that it's mine.

"Veyanna… I'm so sorry."

"Why did he have to do this?" Her large watery eyes look up at me. "Why did he have to die? We… we did not have enough time… I —"

The only thing I think to do is to pull her into a hug, as tight of one as I can muster. She hugs me back and cries harder, making tears flood down my face.

"The big…stupid…selfish brute!" She says in between sobs.

I clench my eyes tight. Is *this* the legacy of the name I promised to keep alive? Would Dominic be ashamed that I let this happen?

"Veyanna… he was big, stupid, and selfish," I crack through my voice. "But he was strong, protective, and loyal. To us. To you."

Her grip on me somehow tightens more.

"He saved my life without knowing who I was and trusted me to help him bring this place down. I think he realized the same thing about you the first time we met. You stood up to him, didn't let him belittle you. I think that's when he knew."

Krissy…

She nods into my neck. "I-I believe it… I do."

I nod back, gently drawing her away from me so we can lock eyes. "He said for you to live, Veyanna. And if it's my last act, I will make sure you live. For him and for you."

Her face drops. "Bimbik… I cannot lose any more friends… do not let yourself be a martyr. You must have someone to live for."

Krissy…

"I do. And that's why we're going to finish this. Finish what we started. We're gonna break this Maze, and we're gonna go home."

She wipes away her tears and looks at Riley. "You wish to return to Rhyeah?"

I look at him like it's a test for his resolve.

Riley takes a deep breath and says, "If I don't make it back, she'll know what it was all for. If I return to her, we'll make sure that Doxo's name lives on."

I'm stunned, but she's smiling and nodding. She stands up and keeps Doxo's axe firmly in her grasp. "Where do we go next?"

I hum to myself for a moment, "The thornhags said that defeating Blightfoot would inflict significant damage to the stability of the rift at the center of the Maze, while also weakening Calos."

"That blast of energy did collect and move in that direction," Riley states pointing to the northwest.

We all look in that direction, the same direction that Blightfoot's left footprints, and see a strange sight. Like a lightshow, there is a faint swirling of colors; purple, yellow, red, and green. In a sequential pattern.

"That looks like some freaky magic shit."

"It must be the rift of the Primeval Realm."

A deep, thoughtful sigh comes from Riley. "So, we're following the acidic footprints of a now-dead undead god to find and face a living god to save the realm. Fan-fucking-tastic."

"It has to end, Riley." I hold his gaze firmly. "One way, or another."

His brows furrow at me, but he nods in agreement. "Okay. Let's do this, then."

"For Doxo," Veyanna whispers.

"For Khelrah and Torbhin," I respond.

And so, the walk begins.

Chapter 46

"Ugh, does he always have to pull that motivational speaker bullshit?"

Lorena knows how to hold a grudge. Then again, he kind of cut her arm off.

"Have you always suspected Guzman might try to take over the company?"

Dominic shook his head, "I hadn't the slightest idea. I knew from the start that my ideas and motivations wouldn't be seen as profitable to some, but never did I think it was possible for me to be blindsided like that. Then again, I thought I knew my daughter better."

I angrily look at Lorena, who just shrugs. "Hey, he gave me the idea, and I rolled with it. Gave me what I wanted, and everything was almost as I planned until your jolly band of misfits stepped in."

"And at what point was killing Robert part of your plan?" The question that's been burning in my chest for the last two years, and I can finally get an answer.

It makes me see red when she replies with, "He didn't know how to survive. If he'd just quit panicking every five fucking minutes, he might still be around."

"How dare you!" I launch myself at her. With the advantage in my favor, we hit the floor, and I put my hands around her neck.

She did this! She *is why Robert's dead! She needs to pay for what she did!*

Some unseen force separates us. I'm ripped away from Lorena, and she's planted firmly to the floor. Dominic is in between us holding out his arms like he's telekinetically holding us down.

"Enough, both of you. There are deeper matters to handle than your grievances." He looks at me, "Matthew, I'm sorry about Robert. But he's gone and you're still here. You can make sure what happened to him doesn't happen to anyone else. You're the one here with the express ticket in and out. You *need* to stop Armand."

I get up on my feet, not taking my eyes off Lorena. "And how do you suggest I do that. He took control of the company in my absence and probably has me on some watch list."

"By outsmarting him," Lorena says through gritted teeth. "He's gotten cocky and doesn't expect to be taken out at the knees. He's about to have a cage match with your friend," points to the screen of Connor and Riley, "and is vulnerable. Find his weakness and use it."

I look at the screen and watch Connor, Riley and the one called Veyanna traverse the sandy arena towards their final goal. To Guzman. *If he's using the same tech as we are, maybe I can infiltrate it. It'll take time and maybe Darrel will know how.*

"Oh, and, cut ties with Woods."

I blink. "What?"

"Guzman has his hooks in him. Just like he did with me," she warns. "If that hairbrain doesn't do it in there, he'll sure as hell do it out there. We've watched him. He's not giving up on that place. Not even for Connor."

I look back at the screen worriedly.

Dominic must sense it because he comes to my side and puts his hand on my shoulder. It feels so real.

"I left you my legacy because I trust you, Matt. Do not hang onto what I would do. Focus on what you know you must do."

Taking a deep breath, I nod. "Okay. I know that I can observe what is happening, but there must be a way to get a warning to Connor. Didn't you have that ability with *The Mortal Gate*?"

"I did, but this is different," he explains. "Without a direct line of contact, we can merely observe. But, if you were to create a line, a glitch if you will, then perhaps there's a way to slip in."

"Which means messing with the coding directly," Lorena hypothesizes. "The main system hard drive is at the company building."

"Which I'm currently banned from," I remind them.

"Then you better figure out something, Bauer. Otherwise, your friend, Connor?" She gestures to his gnome-like form, "He's dead already and doesn't know it."

Chapter 47

"This is taking too long."

I haven't been able to stop pacing back and forth for the last fifteen minutes since Matt was Jacked in. There's sweat pooling in my balled-up fists.

"Krissy, pacing around won't speed it up," Danica says from a nearby couch. Darrel has been monitoring Matt the whole time, that chick Phobia came back and is in her own pink and black chair crunching a keyboard, and Cranium is doing that two-times over. This merry band of nerds is quite literally doing all it can, but it's not enough.

"Girl, come sit."

"No."

"Kris." I turn to Mark, who is now taking an uncomfortable seat next to Danica. He gestures to the open spot between them, "Please."

Damn them. I take a deep breath and join them on the couch. I think the intensity of the situation is taking away the awkwardness I'm currently sitting in.

I feel Danica's hand on my back, "It's gonna be okay. There's nothing we can do right now."

"I can't accept that, Dani. I have to be doing something, there's gotta be something."

Mark nudges me, "Kris you're gonna drive yourself crazy and that won't help Connor. You need to stop for a moment. When we get a better idea of how to deal with this, then we'll jump into action."

"This isn't a game, Mark. We're not magic warriors anymore, we're just us."

"What does Connor need more?" I raise a brow at Danica's question, "His girlfriend stuck in a game alongside him and equally in danger? Or a future wife who is keeping him safe on the Outside?"

The words pelt me like rocks. *His wife. He's gonna ask me to marry him. That means he* will *come back.*

Another deep breath and I'm leaning back against the couch. Dani lays her head on my shoulder and Mark puts a hand on my other one. We're all here, and we'll make it. Just like last time.

"Matt?"

Darrel notices movement and goes to take the helmet off. "Easy, don't yank on anything."

I'm instantly on my feet. Matt's face is free of the helmet, but he looks pale. My heart drops.

"Matt?"

He looks at Riley's unconscious body, then locks eyes with me, "We have a problem."

The next twenty minutes are a flood of confusion, anger, frustration, and pure shock. One, Dominic and Lorena are computer ghosts stuck in a void. Two, Guzman is directly involved in what is happening right now in the game. Three, Riley's a backstabbing bastard. Four, if we don't find a way to shut this down, Connor could die.

"Why the fuck are we just sitting here?"

"Because we need a plan," Matt repeats. I must've blacked that out because everything else is just batshit crazy. "Guzman is smart, resourceful, and has the company backing him up. But I think we can use that."

"What'd you have in mind, Stiff?" Darrel is fully locked in. *How the fuck are they so calm about what all is happening?*

"We divide and conquer." He points to Cranium, "You'll need to maintain your station and monitor everything that happens in their brainwaves. We need to make sure their vitals stay stable." Then to Phobia, "I need you to try and collect all the data you can find on the other board members at SnoWire. Squeaky clean or dirty, I want it all." Then to

Darrel, "You're gonna help me get into the building so I can find the interface Guzman is using."

"What about us?" Mark stands from the couch with a fire in his eyes I haven't seen since his days as Konvos the Triton Totemist.

Matt takes a breath, "You'll help Phobia gather the intel. Do whatever she tells you to." He looks at me and Danica, "I need one of you to come with me and the other to stay here in case anything goes wrong."

I hesitate. Do I stay and twiddle my thumbs? Or do I go and not know what will happen to Connor?

Cranium pipes in, "Have the girlfriend stay. I may have a job for her." All without looking away from his monitors.

Danica pats me on the shoulder before nodding to Matt. He looks at all of us cautiously, "This is not what any of us were expecting. So, expect anything to go down. We don't know quite how stacked on tech that the board has, but we know they control what we need. If it gets too nasty, run. Don't be heroes, don't be stupid. Run. Okay?"

Everyone nods. Not together, and with hesitation, but we all nod.

"Okay. Darrel and Danica let's go. Everyone else, keep us posted." The three of them leave without another word.

"You, DJ," Phobia points at Mark. "I need you to take my ride and plant a slicer." She throws him a set of car keys and a small device, "I'll text you the location. You scratch my baby, I scratch you."

I can't tell if Mark is insulted or impressed, but he gives me a look that says *Take care. Both of you.*

I give him an answering nod back, and he leaves. I walk over to Cranium's station, "What do you need from me?"

Without looking away, he gestures with his thumb, "Sit down and Jack in. You're gonna be our eyes and ears in the system."

I freeze. *Put that on? Go into the Hollow? With the Dawsons?*

"I-I don't think—"

He spins in his chair and stares at me through his digital goggles. "I hear everything that goes on in this place. I know you're worried about him. You might not be able to go Tiefling warrior mode there, but you'll know if he's safe. Do it or don't, it's up to you." He turns around and faces his monitors again.

I stare at the Jack that Matt was just in. My heart is racing. Too many things can happen. I'm becoming that scared girl again. I can't do that to myself. I love Connor, but I need to do this for myself. All that training, all those years being bounced around in the system, and everything from *The Mortal Gate.* I can't let it break me.

I walk over to the station, pick up the helmet, sit and fix it to my head. The visor comes down, and I Jack in.

Chapter 48

I use what leather bindings I have left in my satchel to help fashion a strap for Veyanna to carry Doxo's axe on her back. It's been a quiet walk so far, and it doesn't surprise me. Three members of the party are dead, we have one final area to cover, and we have no clue what to expect. The only thing that's certain is that Calos, Guzman, will be there. Waiting for us. Riley, having his club back, makes some last-minute inspections of it to make sure it can withstand another fight if it comes to it. There's no telling what killing Blightfoot did to those weapons, but it is most definitely something since they survived and Doxo didn't.

Is there something behind that? What happened? And how do we know if his sacrifice wasn't for nothing?

Veyanna is clinging tightly to the strap, making sure that the axe doesn't fall, as we follow the giant footprints filled with acid. Luckily no sandstorms have swept through. One thing that I can't look away from is that pulsing light of colors. Like the Keystones and the enchanted water puzzle, those colors must have some kind of significance. There was fear, rage, envy, sanity, and power. What about this realm? Are they the same?

"Riley."

"Hmm?"

"Given your time with the Yaruk, did you get any ideas about what's in the center of the Maze besides the rift?"

His feline face scrunches in thought, "Not a lot. It was like not talking about the boogeyman or he shows up. The most I know is that the Yaruk believe Calos made his home there. I don't know if that means figuratively or literally, but that's what they believed."

Great.

"So, this whole time, you've been playing hero and getting laid rather than actually inspect what's happening here." The bite in my words is intentionally there.

He must've felt them because a growl escapes his throat. "I didn't think it would come to this. I'm done apologizing for it because I'm trying to fix it now."

"Right, fix it," I repeat. "You changed your mind really fast to suddenly up and leave your virtual paradise."

"And what are you doing? Pissing and moaning about me living *my* fantasy when you're here feeling for what isn't real." He holds his arms out, "All of this is real to them, and that makes them real to you. Otherwise, you wouldn't have cried for them. Any of them, here or there."

"Both of you, enough."

The heat in Veyanna's voice burns right through our argument. "I know not what this quarrel is with you, but this is not the time to fight each other over it. We have an objective and the people of Preydor are counting on us to rid them of the Maze's threat. Now shut your mouths and keep moving."

I guess that's all we need to hear, because we shut up and follow her obediently.

The awkward silence lets me sort through the mess that Riley told me. Who hasn't felt like the video game characters they invest so much time into don't feel real? Roleplaying games are specifically for creating bonds and connections with NPCs for loyalty or social-emotional learning. The developers create such deep and meaningful characters to develop friendships, rivalries, and relationships with. Sure, there have been cases where people got really crazy with them, sexualizing characters and obsessing over voice actors. But the important thing is knowing the difference between fantasy and reality. I am heartbroken over the loss of the others, and I wish there was a way to revive them. But that's just how this game works. The least I can do is make sure one of them survives and hope that their virtual existence gets better.

Something coming over the horizon draws my attention: A large, rust-colored gate in the wall of sandstone. It has jagged points on top of the doors and almost looks like a jagged crown. The Blightfoot footprints are heading directly towards it.

"I think we found our exit," Riley half-whispers.

Veyanna points above the doors at the swirling colors we've been following. "We are nearing the rift."

"We should do an equipment check before trying to get through."

With silent agreement, we unload our equipment and make an inventory. Veyanna has the bone whistle, her modified whip, the small healing ointments from the Yaruk, and her bestiary. She looks longingly at Doxo's axe and takes up a chunk of sandstone, attempting to sharpen the bladed heads. Riley is carrying the same healing ointments from the Yaruk, a set of bone-knuckle bracers, a smaller club like a truncheon, and his bone-spiked club. I have the remaining untwined vine rope from my net, the spiked caltrops I saved, one of the healing ointments, and nothing else. My modified armor was burned away, and my grappling hook is still stuck in the trap for the Blightfoot. I flip through the logbook looking for anything useful and stop on the ugliest page I've seen so far; a section on Blightfoot. Aside from the obvious bullshit that killed Doxo, it highlights a lot of details about the acid it bleeds. In a controlled combination, the acid could be used as a noxious gas grenade of sorts. Using the loose sandstone around, I cobble together some pieces and take them to the nearest acid pool. As carefully as I can, I lean down with a hollowed-out stone and scoop up some of the acid. Luckily it doesn't burn through it. I take some of the properties of the healing application and sprinkle them into the stone, quickly covering the open top and pushing firmly. I hear the sizzling of the acid and components, some steam rolling through the crack until it seals. One good throw against something solid, and *boom*.

I'll be throwing this right in Guzman's smug fucking face.

"Bimbik."

I turn around. Veyanna and Riley are waiting for me. I join them and we walk towards the giant doors of the gate. It gets taller and taller the closer we get until we're close enough to see that the door is inscribed with weird etchings and symbols I can't comprehend. They're twisting and intertwining with each other in a hypnotic pattern.

"Anyone know the secret password?"

No one laughs. Instead, Veyanna approaches the door and brushes her fingers lightly against it. With the touch of her fingertips, she leaves a streak of twisting colors like running her hand through water.

"Powerful magic is housed behind these doors," she breathes.

"Powerful monsters could also be behind them waiting for us," Riley replies.

I approach it and put my hand against it, watching the rust color smooth away in a wave of colors. I feel some of the etchings under my hand, so I peek under and see a word in a weird language.

"Veyanna? Can you read this?"

She kneels and squints at the inscription. "I… I can't quite—Wait." She blinks a little more and looks at it again. "It says 'close'."

"Well, we need it to open," I groan. I swipe my hand at the door's surface again, revealing more of the inscriptions in that same language. "There's more to it. Maybe we can translate the whole thing." I start running my hands back

346

and forth, rippling away the rust color and revealing more of the inscriptions. Riley runs his hands along the ones I can't reach, and Veyanna begins mumbling different words from it all. When we can't reach any more or any higher, Veyanna recites what she read:

"Through shadows deep and mysteries veiled,

To the Door of Sanctum, the truth unveiled.

Speak the answer to the riddle's call,

Or be forever barred from the chamber's thrall.

In the realm where dreams and shadows dance,

Where echoes of laughter in darkness prance,

What is the key to Calos's lair?

Speak the answer, if you dare."

"It's a riddle," Riley guesses. "A spoken password to open the door."

"He's the God of tricks and traps. Makes sense," I mumble begrudgingly.

We start muttering to ourselves about what the answer could possibly be. Wanting to avoid more monsters sprung from wrong answers, we want to try and get this one right.

"I'm stumped."

"English courses never were your strong suit," Riley quips with a snort.

Before I can jab back at him, there's a glimmer in the door that passes as quickly as it came.

"Whoa, did you see that?"

Veyanna nods, "Something answered the magic's enchantment."

"What did we do?" Riley pushes at the door, but it doesn't come open. He pounds on it in frustration. "Just open the fuck up."

"It's gotta be something that we did to make it react…"

Guzman's whole thing is to keep us in here. If he's watching, he's probably laughing at us right now being stuck.

Wait.

Calos, the Imprisoned One.

Before that, he was the Laughing Trickster.

'Where echoes of laughter in darkness prance, what is the key to Calos's lair?'

"Laughter…?"

The rusted door melts away the color and the inscriptions illuminate all the way to the top. A central line of light splits the door, and it creaks open, slowly and ominously.

"You did it, Bimbik!"

I smile, but only for a moment until I see what is past the doors. It is dark, but slightly illuminated by flowing streams of magical color like an aurora borealis. The structure of the walls inside reflects the structure of the door, rusty with slight coloring of inscriptions and murals.

Slowly, we each step through the threshold of the gate and are met with stone floors like a castle or fortress. As if the atmosphere and environment from outside the gate can't touch it at all. The creaking of the gate sounds again, and the doors slowly close behind us. As soon as that magical lock clicks, a haunting laughter echoes all around us.

Chapter 49

Okay, this is gonna go one of two ways:

One, we get in, I find the software connection that Guzman is using and find a way to shut it down, possibly even shutting down the game altogether and getting Connor and Riley out.

Or two, we fail, get caught, get arrested, fry the system with their brains still intact and possibly kill them.

"What's going on in your head, Stiff?"

I look over at Darrel in the driver's seat of his not-so-conspicuous car, then back at Danica in the back seat.

"I'm thinking so much shit can go wrong and we're going off of a bunch of theories," I admit. "The company going under is one thing, but possibly endangering the guys more?"

"You're not gonna let that happen," he assures me. "We're gonna bite these suits in the ass and take them down. It's what the Gridlock does, and that's what you'll do."

I snort, "What? So, I'm part of your hacktivist movement now?"

He smiles, keeping his eyes on the road. "We don't have coats or badges or anything, but why the hell not? You've shown us more fun these last eighteen hours than we've ever had. I'd be interested to see what else you're capable of."

I have to look away and out the window to keep him from seeing the heat rising in my face. It doesn't help that Danica pokes me playfully in the side.

"So, what's our plan? I assume you can't just walk in as the CEO," he asks.

I clear my throat and swat Danica's hand away. "We need to get to the upper levels. The hardest part is getting past the front reception area and the security post. The only one that was willing to help me isn't here anymore."

"A distraction should help, right?" I'm surprised by Danica's offer. I look back at her with raised brows, but she shrugs. "If there's a big enough issue up front, you should be able to slip past?"

"I mean, I guess so. But are you willing to do that? You won't be able to get up there with us."

She furrows her brows and crosses her arms, "I'm here to help. I can do this. Let me pull out some Night Silk moves to get this done."

"Whoa. That's the first time I think I've heard you reference the game at all."

She takes a deep breath, "My therapist says there's a time to reflect, and a time to accept. I'm accepting that being in that game actually showed me some stuff that I think I can use. Just trust me on this."

I look at Darrel, he gives an approving gesture, and I nod back at Danica. "Okay, you give them something to focus on. Darrel and I will take care of the rest. Once we're in, get away and out of attention. The biggest issue aside from that is that the elevator will log my ID scan, making us have little time to act before we get caught."

"You leave that to me, Stiff." He pulls up and wiggles his phone in his hand, "Bishop's got the goods to trick that shit."

I smirk at his confidence and nod. The plan is made.

We're outside of the SnoWire building, disguised to the best of our ability with hats, glasses, inconspicuous jackets, and the crowd around us. Darrel waits for me to go inside first, and Danica is out of view waiting for whatever signal she deems right. Inside, things have barely changed, except for the increase in security. All faces I don't recognize, which means security's been restaffed for the purpose of keeping me out. People and employees are flooding the reception floor.

Whatever Danica's scheming, it better be fucking good.

I might have manifested a little too much for it, because a loud set of footprints stomps inside, and a voice yells *"Give me your fucking supervisor!"*

Oh. My. Fuck! She's pulling a 'Karen' routine!

A security guard stops her with a hand in her face, "Ma'am you need to calm down."

"Calm down? Calm down!?" She swipes his hand away from her face. "Your goddamn company ruined my goddamn relationship, and I want to fucking talk to your fucking supervisor!"

Oh… she's taking out two years of pent-up rage on the whole company.

Another guard comes in for backup, "Miss, if you have a complaint, call the number on the—"

"I'm not gonna complain to a machine!"

Every head in the area is now fixed on her and the guards. *Well, it worked.* I take the chance to slip past people getting their phones out to record the argument.

"Someone in this goddamn building better get me someone in charge, or I'm gonna start breaking shit!"

I don't want to be around long because I know she's not lying about that. I slip past the detector and go straight for the elevator. With my ID ready, I wait for Darrel while listening to people talking about what's happening.

Therapy does wonders, but this is karma at its finest.

Darrel gives a soft whistle and takes his phone out, tapping on a couple of apps. "Scan it."

I nod and scan the card. At first, it starts to read my name and badge number, but Darrel hovers his phone over the scanner and it glitches, showing *his* face and a security guard number.

"That's awesome," I say with a chuckle.

"Thank your raging friend out there," he says. "Wouldn't have been able to swipe the guard's card without her."

I chuckle again as Danica's loud voice gets cut off by the closing of the elevator doors.

Chapter 50

"Are we sure that putting her in that thing is a good idea?" I'm watching Krissy with the helmet on her, not moving or anything.

"She's fine, disc jockey," Phobia says as she combs through digital files in her station. "Focus on your task."

I groan and continue my cyberstalking task. Each of the board members are good at staying off the more popular platforms like Facebook, TikTok, and Instagram. But their Indeed profiles and business pages are not as hidden as they'd like. Fancy college education from the Stone Age, a few failed business ventures, and a history of stock market investments.

"Anything for you?"

"Still swiping through data streams," she says, clicking away. "They definitely like to keep things as clean as possible."

I scoff, "Which means they've got something big to hide. We'll find it."

"That's what I'm talking about," she agrees, holding a fist out. I hesitate, but I bump fists with her and we're back to the grind.

"So, you always wanted to be a hacker?"

"You always wanted to be a spinner?"

"Yes."

"Yes."

I turn to her, "What started it?"

She cocks an eyebrow at me, "You really wanna play 20 Questions right now?"

"Well, we'll be here for a while until we find something that sticks."

Her head leans back against her chair, and she laughs dryly. "Trust me, Romeo, you don't wanna mess with this. I dug up my fair share of stuff on you. You and Danica have your baggage and I don't think that shit is resolved."

Well, there's that.

"Touché." I return to the screen and try looking for anything.

"Hey, did you come across anything about a company called 'Apexi'?"

I scroll back through what I've dug up and stop on the stock market records. Right there in all of their histories;

Apexi. I start researching the company and notice how complete shit the website is and how funky the links are.

"Oh shit… it's a shell corp!" I roll over and show her the laptop. "No visible assets or productivity. Not since 2015."

Her fingers fly across the keyboards, pulling up tab after tab of stuff on Apexi. She pulls up one large tab and displays plans for specific funds to be used in the development of a familiar-looking piece of technology.

"Oh my god… those are Crests."

"Militarized Crests," she clarifies.

"Militarized Crests for both foreign and domestic buyers," I point out.

"How the fuck are they gonna militarize video game headsets?"

I think back to all the things we went through in the game. "Prisoner interrogation, warfare experience, mental imprisonment, any sick fucked up thing they can think of."

One moment we're gawking at what we found, the next there are red bars reading "RESTRICTED" covering it.

"Shit!" She clicks away again, "Someone saw us snooping! Download everything you can before they're swept!"

We've been made. Someone knows what we're doing.

Chapter 51

The Hollow is exactly like what Connor and Matt said it would be. A large white void of absolutely nothing. It feels like I'm standing on solid ground, but there's no sound, no breeze, nothing else around.

"Hello?" I don't wanna do this, but I've got no other choice.

"Lorena? Dominic! Anyone?"

"Well, well, well. If it isn't the badass Tiefling girl."

I turn around and see her. My blood boils. The same bitch that trapped us, tortured us, and almost killed us, is now staring at me with such a smug look on her face.

"Lorena," I sneer.

The smirk just pisses me off and she knows it. "Look who came begging for help with her lover boy."

"Coming from a computer ghost with one arm," I fire back.

"So clever," she groans. "You're wasting your time. You can't help him. His outcome in the game determines his fate."

I curl my hands into fists, "I'm not gonna sit on my ass and do nothing while he's in danger. Matt said you need some kind of glitch or slip in the system to be able to help or talk to them."

"Which doesn't exist, dumbass."

"But what if it did?" Her head tilts to the side, but I continue. "What if a glitch could be made for someone to interact with the game like last time?"

She's actually thinking about it like she hadn't thought about it before.

"It's possible, but it is a risk."

Dominic's voice throws me off guard as he pops up on my opposite side. "You must be Krissy. I've heard good things about you."

"Dominic Dawson," I acknowledge. He nods his head. "What do you mean it's risky?"

He hums and starts walking about in the empty space. "To create a glitch rather than one spontaneously appearing in a code takes a very dangerous grid outage to disrupt the flow of the program. If that happens, there's a possibility that the system will have a total reset and wipe."

"In other words, cause a single surge, and we can all be digital dust. Your boyfriend included," Lorena simplifies.

My heart stops.

"Ladies?"

We both look in Dominic's direction. He's brought up a screen of a weirdly lit chamber following three people.

"Connor?"

"The half-squat," Lorena points.

"Riley is the larger one, which puts Connor at quite the disadvantage," Dominic admits.

Riley do not stab him in the back, or I'll kill you myself.

"They're in the epicenter of the Maze. Guzman will be there in his avatar state," Dominic observes. "This will determine what happens after."

"After what?"

He looks at me with empathy, "Game over."

Chapter 52

This place is massive. Far more detailed than anywhere else we've been. Those carvings are glowing in those same ominous colors that led us here. Our reflections can almost be seen like smudges in the walls while we cautiously walk further inside. Every so often, we'll encounter statues meant to depict Calos and murals of his beasts. Ugly, twisted, horrific like they all belong in a haunted house. With how this place looks, it might as well be. The same haunting laughter is just echoing and ricocheting off the walls.

"Calos's domain is… unpleasant. Unsettling." Veyanna's eyes dart from mural to statue in a constant pattern.

"This is what happens when you mess with forces you think you can beat easily," Riley mutters.

I swat his thigh, "Shut up. You're not making it any better."

He gives me the *I'm just saying* look. I return his look with my own that says *Shut up and keep moving.*

The hair on my neck and arms stands as if something creepy is sending shivers down my spine. A feeling of unease and eyes following me mixes with hot breath to something that's not here.

"Bimbik? Are you well?" She puts a gentle hand on my shoulder.

"Huh? Yeah," I assure her. "Just... something off here. Besides the creepy statues and stuff."

She nods in agreement, noting all the creepy decorations of this place. "He is a creature of malice and trickery. It is important for us not to fall victim to his machinations."

"We're three prisoners of a magical maze now standing in the domain of a fallen god that wants to see us squirm. Probably has an army of beasts waiting for us, and you come up with that little pep talk?" Riley stares straight ahead. He means every word of what he said.

This isn't right. Something's going on with him.

Before I can ask what crawled up his ass, the laughter suddenly stops. The eeriness of the quiet is off-putting and brings us all to a dead stop. It feels like the floor is shifting under our feet and the walls are rippling in a weird, hypnotic way.

"Everyone, stay close."

We hunker together as the large, empty space of the interior shifts and spins, the colorful magic twisting with it.

A haunting voice lingers into this swirling vortex.

"So, you live, and you have made it to my Sanctum. Most impressive. The final trial is at hand, and I await your presence. Step lightly now, Mazebreakers, else you should join in my eternal madness."

The twisting magic gets more intense until the floor feels like it is no longer spinning under us. I pull myself away from Riley and Veyanna just enough to see that the scenery itself has changed. We're in this open courtyard made of the same stone material as inside the main hall. This "Sanctum" has a large spiraling tower shooting straight up towards the sky with various bridges all the way up. Decorating the tower are these swirling mirror-like objects, each with different colors of energy radiating from them. Each of them is tethered with glowing strands leading from one to the next all the way up. At the very top of this tower, that large surge of swirling energy that erupted from Blightfoot is pulsing like a heartbeat. It doesn't escape our notice that there's a winding staircase around the entire structure with no protective railings. It's a tall climb and a very long drop.

"This is dangerous," Veyanna says lightly.

"I'll guess that the source of the rift is somewhere up top," I say with a finger pointing up.

Riley's eyes scan around the open courtyard and at the surrounding ring of arches. It's like standing in a Roman Colosseum, but darker and more menacing. "Odds are, we're being watched right now. No way that Calos would leave this place unguarded."

"Then we work fast." Veyanna tightens the strap holding Doxo's axe and grips onto her whip, "Upward." She leads the climb.

I give a long, exhausted breath before I climb up the first step. They're not spaced out far apart to cause a problem for me, but it still is a long way up. Like doing upward lunges on the bleachers in high school.

"Want me to carry you?" I can tell he's just fucking with me, so I flip him off without looking back at him. He passes me on the walk up, gaining distance to Veyanna. I look up, noticing that the first bridge level is still about a dozen feet up.

"Fuck me."

Up and up, I go, needing to hoist myself up a couple of steps. I'm already getting exhausted, which doesn't bode well for the rest of the trip up. I don't know how I managed to get this far with how fucking weak I am like this.

"Connor! You need to see this!"

"Give me a fucking *minute!*"

I climb about twelve more steps and, thankfully, am on the first level platform. On my hands and knees, I take deep inhales to catch my breath before hearing the clopping of Veyanna's hooves.

"Bimbik," with a worried tone in her voice, "Zasar seems to be very concerned with what we've just found."

I hold up a finger, asking for her to give me a moment, then I creak all the way back up to my feet. Following her, we turn the corner to a cool and scary sight. The mirror-like object that we saw from below is swirling a faint purple around the ring, and the center is rippling with an icy blue color. Riley is staring at it in shock and waving me over to him. Stepping next to him, I peer into the image. Inside, like looking through a window, is a landscape that is scary familiar. Great green plains with mountains off in the distance. Below the mountains is a fortress-like castle with a path leading up along the face of the mountain. Everything in my chest caves in with recognition.

"It's Albistair…"

Chapter 53

"Albistair? Did you not say you were from there?"

I'm too stunned to answer her. Matt told me that he decommissioned the game entirely. But there's Albistair, with its lush green lands, the same craggy mountains, the barely visible river that pours into the ocean and home of the Tritons, the forests that belong to the Centaurs. It's all here.

"It can't be," I whisper. I can't think something like this is possible. "Riley, do you know anything about this?"

He shakes his head, "I... I have no clue." His fingers brush the rippling image. Like a twisted stroke of fate, his fingers push through the image.

"Powerful interdimensional magic," Veyanna gasps at the sight.

"The rift into the Primeval Realm was opened here, according to Rhyeah," Riley says as he pulls his hand away from the portal.

"So, somehow, Guzman was able to link the data from *The Mortal Gate* here. But how?" I glare at Riley. "You've been working on this for over a year and you have *no idea* what the fuck is going on?"

"I'm telling you; I have no idea!" He's getting angry and defensive.

"Enough!" Veyanna again stops us from pursuing it further. "There are various rifts open on the way up. We must find the first one. It is the catalyst of the magic here. We close that, we close them all."

Like we've ever been that fucking lucky.

Veyanna leads the way up to the next level, the great axe bobbing up and down with every step she takes. I walk after her, not saying another word to Riley. I don't believe he doesn't have an idea of what Guzman and the others did with this game over the last couple of years. I hear his aggressive footsteps behind me like he's annoyed I'm being so slow. Turning around to tell him to fuck off, the words get caught in my throat. Behind him, something is pushing through the rift to Albistair. Something with long, clawed fingers, grayish skin, and an angular head with a maw full of jagged teeth. Three eyes, barbed spine, finned tail, and a wailing screech of a voice.

A terrorghast?!

"RUN!"

Riley looks back, then forward, grabs my arm and pulls me with him up the stairs. The nightmarish screech quickly follows after us, sending me mentally back to the first game and putting me in a state of fear I haven't felt in a long time.

We don't make it far because the damn thing scales the wall and leaps out in our way. All three of its eyes narrow down at us, saliva dripping from its teeth.

"What in the blazes is *that*?"

I pull on her sleeve to back her up slowly, "Something not from around here. Back it up easily."

"Nope! Fuck that!" Riley launches out with his club and smacks the terrorghast in the head, dazing it and almost launching it off the stairs. Its large claws manage to cling to the stairs before it can fall completely.

"Climb!"

I push Veyanna up the stairs and we all take off as fast as we can. The beast screeches as it struggles to get back up the stairs, giving us time to climb. The next platform is just within reach, this one with an orange ringed rift and that familiar silver rippling. I can't keep myself from looking into it, curious of what is on the other side. Inside, the landscape is not a fantasy one, low or high. It's not even modern like the Outside. This one is high tech, glowing blues and whites everywhere, overlooking a large dome arena. Over the wind and the terrorghast screams, I can faintly hear sounds of blasting and cheering.

"Oh, my god… That's *Buster Charge!*"

I'm too distracted that I miss the fanned tail sweeping my legs from under me, sending me flat on my back with my head dangling over the ledge. In an all-too-familiar situation, the monster's jaws are open over my head with my arms pinned. The smell of its breath is just as horrible as before. I kick up into its midsection, but it's not doing anything but pissing it off. The jaws almost close around my head when it gets jerked back and away from me. Around its neck is a leather cord with clawed tips dug into its neck.

"Get up!" Veyanna is pulling with all her strength, keeping it reined in. I shuffle to stand back up, reach into my satchel and take out my remaining smokehound dagger.

"Connor!" Riley yells from up the stairs. "*Push it in!*"

It takes me a moment to register his plan before I take a running start and stab my dagger into its midsection. It staggers the terrorghast just enough to get it off balance. Veyanna uses the chance to pull it back with one good yank, sending its upper body directly into the rift. It's flailing on its back, the tail still pretty dangerous, even when she unfurls her whip from its neck.

"Help me push it!"

I wrestle one of the legs to try and push. It's heavier than what I can lift, but I'm too full of adrenaline to back down. One of its claws manages to cut my cheek when I look to see Veyanna doing the same thing. Finally, Riley comes back down the stairs and grabs the tail, digging his foot into its backside. One good push from all of us is what it takes to send the beast straight into the cyberpunk MMORPG world of *Buster Charge.*

We stand back, waiting to see if it works. The terrorghast manages to get back on its feet, snarling at us through the rift. It lurches back ready to lunge, but a blue and white beam of energy ricochets from a nearby surface and pierces it through the head, leaving a smoking hole where its ears should be.

Through my heavy breathing, I point at the rift shakily. "Th-that can't be possible! What the fuck is going on?!"

"I'd be delighted to explain that to you, Mr. Wright."

That creepy voice with a wicked smile sends shivers right down my spine. I turn around to see Calos, a.k.a. Armand Guzman, floating mid-air off the platform away from us.

"Guzman… you did this?"

The wicked-grinning mask nods, "My greatest project that even the great Dominic Dawson failed to notice. Now, if you would be so kind, Mr. Woods, to escort our guests?"

I blink and turn to Riley. Sure enough, he's holding onto Veyanna's arm tightly and pointing his club at me. "Don't fight this, Connor. Just do as he says."

Chapter 54

"That son of a bitch!"

I can't even punch the video feed to smash something as I'm watching Riley, Connor's best friend, turn on him and help Guzman.

"That bastard." It's the first time I've heard Dominic even remotely sound surprised.

Lorena smacks his arm, "Dad, what the fuck is going on?"

His eyes are glued to the feed, watching Riley push Connor and Veyanna up the stairs of the tower.

"Armand has created a nexus of all the game worlds I've created…" He points at the next rift they pass, one that is golden ringed with the image of a pseudoscience take on the Greco-Roman era. "*Demigod Exodus*. One of my first creations with the new software upgrades."

"*How?*" Lorena demands.

He tears his eyes away from the feed and looks at her with a fury that even makes me nervous.

"*I don't know!*" He starts pacing, "Everything I had built... *everything* I had accomplished was for my passion and the passion of the world's gaming community! Every time I made a technological advancement with the company, someone from the board would try and push private contracting in my face, and I'd push it away!"

I watch the realization hit Lorena like a freight train. "He told me that *you* were the one who opted for privatizing the company. That you didn't trust me with the plans and changes that would be made, which is why you chose Matt." Her hand reaches up and grips her scalp, "He fucking played me... he knew I wanted to take over and he gave me the fucking bait!"

"How long was Guzman employed at SnoWire?" They both look at me confused. "How long? Where did he come from?"

Lorena looks at her father, waiting for answers with me.

"Armand came to me as an investor when I was first building the company nearly thirty years ago. I had the ideas and the ambition, but none of the funds needed for a start-up. He was a young business assistant to one of the investors that turned me down. He told me my vision was wild and near impossible, but in the best way. We spoke, got loans and funds, and began a start-up. I was to run the business and creative teams; he would head the directory and shareholders." He gives Lorena a sympathetic look of guilt, "A few years later, I met your mother, we married, then a year later you were conceived. Armand told me to take a sabbatical to see to her health during the pregnancy. I accepted immediately."

Her eyes are lined with tears, but she says nothing.

"When I returned, he had hired two more trustees that he highly regarded for the company's interest. They spearheaded expansion and growth, getting us the building we have today. I thought that it was everything I had envisioned and moreover. But Armand thought we could go even further. He was the first one to suggest that we branch out into private contracting, using our advancements to provide services to the military or highest bidders. I refused."

"Why?" Not that I blame him for turning it down, but he doesn't strike me as someone who turns down opportunity.

"Because I grew up in an absent home where video games were my caretakers and best friends. I would always get the best, beat the best, and befriend the best. I wanted to keep that feeling alive with everyone who took a chance on my games and designs. Not for money or journalism, but for the passion of the community." He scoffs at the video feed, "Armand thought me a dreaming idiot, and we fought over it for months. That's when Ellen and I began to drift apart. I would come home so exhausted and still fighting with Armand that it invaded my home and personal life."

Lorena fights back tears of anger or shame, struggling to speak.

Dominic clocks this and his face drops, "I wanted your mother to have some semblance of the joy that she and I held. That was you. I wanted to keep you terribly. But with how things were escalating, I didn't want to take my frustrations out on you, too."

This is why she hated him. For so long, she thought it was because he loved his company more than her. She imprisoned him in his own creation to get back at him.

Lorena clears her throat, "So when I asked you to hire me at your company, you didn't think that would affect us?"

He shook his head, "Of course not. By that time, Armand finally went back to his duties with the trustees and shareholders so that I could have some peace and create one last great design. One I could make with you, and then be done."

"Why didn't you ever say anything?" Her words are broken in her throat. Even I'm starting to tear up.

"Because you were already against me, Lorena," he says with slow steps toward her. "You were already convinced I had abandoned you. Even having you in my place of work, top of the chain, smart as a whip, I never fully held your trust."

Silence. The kind that shatters whole worlds.

I would've given anything to have a conversation like this with my birth parents. If they gave a shit.

I hate myself for doing this next part. "Look, we need to figure out how to help Connor and take Guzman down before he either gets permanently stuck or worse."

Lorena wipes her tears away, "If… If Guzman has a nexus of all your creations, there's gotta be a kill switch, right? Something that permanently disrupts the encrypted access from one platform to the next?"

Dominic clears his throat and starts thinking again, "In case of a large-scale viral attack or error code overload, yes. Like the one that was used to permanently delete *The Mortal Gate*."

"Guzman must've made a copy under the radar," I guess. "So how do we use the original kill switch on his remake?"

"It would have to be manually plugged into his hardware and activated through a security code," Lorena explains.

Dominic strokes his chin, "Which is in the main offices where base-level employees are not permitted."

"Which is where Matt and Darrel are currently going."

They both look at me surprised.

I shrug, "What? We made a plan."

"Then you must go back and inform Matt what he needs to do," Dominic urges.

I look back at the feed, Connor still being held prisoner.

"We'll keep an eye on Lover Boy for you," Lorena groans. "In the meantime, we'll see if there's any kind of weak point or shitty-patched glitches we can use."

I nod hesitantly and try to unlink from the Jack.

"Krissy?"

Dominic locks eyes with me, "When this is over… go be happy."

I blink a couple of times in confusion, but just give him a firm nod and disconnect.

I push the visor up from my eyes and awaken to Cranium, Phobia, and Mark all shuffling to pack stuff up and click things on their computers.

"What the hell is happening?"

Mark pulls me out of the chair, "We got caught! They had a backwards tracer in their search!"

"The Substation's compromised," Cranium barks. Every scan of the screen reads *FILES DELETED*. "This is not a drill! Go, go, go!"

Phobia is lugging boxes and cases out the door with Mark's help. I look over to Connor's body frantically and run to get him ready for moving.

Phobia shouts from outside, "Shit! They're here!"

Cranium panics and grabs my arm, "We've gotta move!"

I yank away, "I'm not leaving him!"

"Krissy, they're not gonna hurt 'em! They need them! We'll get them back!"

"*No!*" I'm fighting back tears, "Leave Riley for them, but don't you fucking dare leave Connor here."

With a loud groan from under his mask, he yells for Mark to help. We lift him up from the chair and walk out the door, leaving Riley's unconscious body behind. *Fucking traitor deserves worse.*

Outside, Phobia's pulled the van around with the back doors open. We haul Connor inside, slam the doors, and she hits the gas. The last thing I see from the back window before we kick up dust is a fleet of black cars with blue flashing lights on them gaining on us fast.

Chapter 55

The elevator opens to the executive floor, thankfully empty in the hallway. Slowly, we walk out and survey the adjacent halls. A few suits walking in and out of rooms, but not noticing us. With a silent gesture, I have him follow me down the hall and to the right. There are muffled conversations happing in some of the rooms we pass by, meaning that this floor could fill up at any moment if we get this wrong.

"Where're we headin'?" he asks quietly.

I gesture ahead, "The presentation room is ahead. That's where most new projects are presented in their final display. If he's using the program actively, he needs a large enough bandwidth to support it."

"Shh!" He yanks me away into an open broom closet and shuts it. Before I can ask, I hear radio static and muttering from the other side of the door. We're holding our breath until the voices and static gradually goes away.

"Good eye," I compliment.

"In more ways than one," he quips.

I roll my eyes, "Now's not the time for 'Seven Minutes in Heaven', Darrel." I open the door and look both ways for onlookers.

"Does that mean there'll be time later?"

"What? I—uh—shut up! Come on!"

We quietly exit the closet and close it. As inconspicuously as possible, I walk straight up to the door while Darrel keeps an eye out. With my ear pressed to the door, I can hear faint muttering sounds.

"Okay, I think he's in there. Whatever happens, just be ready to get out."

Darrel turns to me and smirks, "I go if you go. I stay and kick some corporate ass if you do."

I want to thank him for everything he's done so far, but again, no time. The doorknob rattles, but it doesn't turn. *Shit, locked.*

"I don't suppose you – "

"Step aside, Stiff." He nudges me aside and swipes my keycard. A few clicks and nudges later, the door clicks open. He waggles his eyebrows at me and opens the door, letting me go in first. I expect to see Guzman sitting catatonically with a Crest fixed to his head, but instead the room is empty. All but empty chairs, three monitors fixed on the far wall, the conference phone, and a small note attached to the phone.

I walk carefully towards the phone, Darrel approaching from the other side of the conference table. I reach forward and grab the note.

Enjoy the show, Mr. Bauer.

-A.G.

"Fuck."

Darrel raises his eyebrows when the screens flicker on, showing a large landscape with a spire in the center of it. And around it, a floating robed figure ascending up the stairs, followed by a faun, a gnome, and a furred warrior behind them.

"Fuck! He played us right to this moment! He's not here!"

Darrel watches the screen while I have my crisis moment. "Where else would he be, Matt? Think!"

Where would he go? He's playing games, literally. *He wants an audience.* I look around the room and notice the cameras in the far back corner.

"I have an idea. Stay quiet and follow me."

He doesn't say anything, but the look on his face says it all. Coming out of the room, a couple of employees spot us and start murmuring. I avert my gaze and lead the way to the only place I think we can gain some semblance of control over the situation.

"Keep your face from the cameras as best as you can," I utter back to him. "We're taking the stairs this time."

He gives a grunt in response. I hear radio static again, so I grab his arm and rush us to the stairwell door.

"Gogogogogo! Down three floors!"

We shuffle down the stairwell as fast as we can. Two floors pass and the door upstairs swings open with two voices using a rushed tone. One more level and Darrel swings the door open, which we both go through and close as softly as we can. With a pat on his shoulder, I lead him down the left hallway. A sharp turn of the corner, we press against the wall, waiting to see if any of the guards following know where we are. Several moments pass and nothing, so we relax a bit.

"Where are we?"

I point down the hallway, showing him a massive room of servers and monitors all alight with power and juice. "The heart of the beast. The central servers."

His eyes sparkle with amazement. Something in his head must have figured out what I'm planning to do, because he turns his gaze to me and asks, "You sure about this?"

Grimly, I give a nod. "If there's any hope for Connor, we need to do this. Find Guzman's direct link, send a surge, and disrupt his connection."

Darrel takes a deep breath, exhales, and smirks. "Let's do it."

Chapter 56

This is what death row must feel like. The warden leading the condemned with a crony behind them to keep them in check. The walk up is like a museum tour of all of SnoWire's greatest accomplishments. *Buster Charge, Demigod Exodus, Arcane Academy Online,* and a few others I don't immediately recognize. Guzman is leading us to the top, probably for one final villainous monologue before he does whatever he's planned to do with us. I got enough leeway with Riley to have him let Veyanna's arm go so she can walk comfortably. She gives me several glances of empathy and anger; whether they're for me or Riley is hard to read. The sky is eerily red with shades of black when we get high enough to look over the walls that surround this place. It's from here that I can see everything; the entire Primeval Maze in all its winding corners and corridors with areas cut off by different veils of magic.

"Beautiful, is it not?" Guzman's smug voice carries a grin that I can see even through his laughing mask.

"I bet it was definitely better before you fucked it all up," I mutter. I hear Riley clear his throat as if to say *Don't be stupid.*

The laughing mask turns to face us halfway up the second to last flight of stairs, making the three of us stop in place.

"You make me seem like such a villain," he drawls. "Can't you see this is what we do? Our profession is to create new, wonderous, dangerous landscapes for people to explore, experience, and enjoy. *We* at SnoWire are gods, and we can be more if you would just simply let things run their course." He turns again and continues the climb, "By now, your partner Matthew is watching all of this happen while he blunders in an attempt to shut this down. All while your little girlfriend and two other nobodies are being arrested for cybercrimes, breaking into company grounds without express permission, and a few other things that I decided to slap on. It is quite inevitable that this is where the games end, so to speak."

I feel burning heat rising in my chest and face. Is it rage? Or is it guilt? Everyone I care about on the Outside is being targeted while I'm in here being held captive by my prick of a boss and my supposed best friend. Riley's done well keeping his mouth shut the whole way.

We reach the pinnacle of the tower to a flat, open surface with only a few key things of interest: The first is a large, stone, pointed throne with a maze-shaped spiral adorning the center and a red cushion draped in the seat with a smokehound chained to either side of it. The second is a pyramid that is intricately carved and glowing from the center, shooting a thin green beam straight up to the sky. The last is a single stone ledge that leads out to nothing, but a long ass drop down to the base that would kill someone on impact. It's a goddamn stone gangplank and he plans to make us walk it.

The smokehounds flanking the throne are barking and snapping their jaws, held tight by some kind of leash tied to both arms of the throne. With a snap of his fingers, they stop barking and sit obediently while he takes a seat.

"Okay, so you brought us to your fancy throne at the tallest point in this place. Whoopdy-fucking-do," I drawl at him. "Save whatever fucking egotistical speech you have prepared and just get on with it."

I expect him to get pissy and maybe even lash out, but all he does is sit back behind that mask. "Connor, my boy, you watch too much television. I didn't bring you here to give some epic monologue. I brought you here to offer you a choice. The same choice I offered Riley."

He gives Riley a nod, to which the big idiot goes to the pyramid in the center of the platform, grabs the top and turns it. The cap of the pyramid easily turns clockwise, and the line of green light opens what I can only guess is a rift like the ones we walked past. Through said rift, I see Krissy's frantic face while she's looking down at me while clamoring voices overlap.

"Door one," Guzman proposes, "you go back to your life on the Outside, resign your post from the company, and refrain from interfering with our work. In exchange, we will give you a severance pay, and you will not have to worry about us anymore."

The rift changes again, this time showing Albistair. Exactly as I remember it.

"Door two; I send you and Riley to Albistair, where you can live out your fantasy heroics in a land you already know. The company will take care of your bodies and make sure you are sufficiently aided to keep your brain functions

384

normal. Your own world to roam or rule, whichever you prefer."

I glance at Riley, who is giving me eyes that seem to plead for one of these "doors" Guzman is offering. He twists the pyramid cap three times counterclockwise so the rift closes.

"Door three," Guzman says grimly, "I kill you, here and now, and leave your rotting, brain-dead corpse for your friends and family to deal with. Your official obituary will read that you had a stroke from the exposure of old equipment, and no one will think twice about it."

I'm frozen in place. Two options leave SnoWire to the dogs and God only knows what they plan to do with it all. The other option takes away both other options at once. I knew there was a reason I was thrust into this gnome-sized body. He doesn't want me to be a threat or a challenge against him.

"You're a fucking psychopath," I manage to get out. "You are really willing to murder someone, so your fucking company becomes some technological Sith Empire to satisfy your ego?"

He stands from that ugly-ass chair and steps forward, "The future is digital, Connor. Soon, the entire world will want an escape from the travesties they know and live in, and I intend to give them that escape. For a price." His fingers graze the pyramid, "I will build as many worlds as possible to gain as many interested parties as I desire. Military factions will use it to train their soldiers, children will beg and scream to be part of this universe, men and women of all psychological deficiencies will pay any amount to live out their fantasies. SnoWire is the future. You will need to decide if you are part of that future."

My eyes shift over to Riley who is nonverbally begging me to make a choice that is impossible for me to make. I then look at Veyanna, confused and heartbroken.

"What about Preydor?" I look back to Guzman, "What about all they suffered? Are you going to keep terrorizing them like puppets for your amusement?"

I can tell he's rolling his eyes behind the mask, but he snaps his fingers again. Three bright lights flash near him, and transparent images of Torbhin, Khelrah, and Doxo appear in their place. They're motionless, their eyes closed, as they hover off the ground. Veyanna gasps loud enough to grab everyone's attention as her eyes fix on Doxo's lifeless form.

"I can reset the entire thing," he offers. "But know, that the system works according to the programming. They will still be recruited by other adventurers; they will still die in the Maze. Maybe in different ways, but that is their fate." He stares at Veyanna, "That is *your* fate. The Maze will not be broken."

Her eyes shine at the brim with tears and her hands cover her mouth in pain and fear. She is programmed to suffer. To watch everyone she cares for suffering.

I've had enough. Of all of this. Of Guzman's fucked up games. Of Riley's backstabbing. All of it.

"Fuck. You."

Riley's eyes widen and Guzman's head tilts to the side.

"What did you say to me?" His hounds start growling.

"I said, 'fuck you', you psychotic, egotistical, walking fucking cliché." I ball my hands into fists at my side, "You, a fucking money-grubbing, bloodsucking corporate vampire, are *not* the savior or schemer that you think you are. You are nothing but a goddamn parasite that feeds off people's insecurities, hyper fixations, hobbies and passions. In here, you may claim to be a god, but you are nothing but a coward in a mask, in here and out there."

I turn my attention to Riley, "And *you!* You insecure, victimized, scared pansy. You're so fucking upset with your life that you're willing to become a fucking vegetable so you can live a fake existence. You think your life is nothing Outside because of your wheelchair and unhappiness, but you had *everything*. A job, friends, a future, and a best friend that would've seen everything with you to the end. Wake the fuck up and live."

He's speechless. His hands are shaking, and his eyes are staring at the floor.

Guzman breaks the tension with a slow, mocking clap. "Very touching, Mr. Wright. It seems you've made your choice." With a snap, he releases the smokehounds and they pounce with ravenous intent.

Chapter 57

"Fucking drive!" Mark yells from the back of the van.

We've been chased by these black cars for the last ten miles like something out of a movie. No matter what roads we take, they find us and keep up the chase. I keep my grip on Connor's body to keep him from being whipped back and forth on the floor of the van.

Phobia smacks Mark's arm in the front, "Shut the hell up and let me drive, jackass!"

"We need to fall back to the safehouse," Cranium shouts from the back.

"Not with the fucking Men in Black on our asses!"

"Then *lose them!*"

"Do you wanna drive? Why don't we pull over, I'm sure they'll let us pull a Chinese fire drill before chasing us again!"

I shut my eyes tightly, "Shut the fuck up and just drive! We don't have time for this!"

Everyone shuts up and focuses on themselves.

"Cranium, keep him steady," I growl. "I need to call Matt."

Hesitantly, he nods and grabs onto Connor's body while I get my phone out. One of only a few numbers in the burner, I dial Matt's number and wait for him to pick up. Three rings and nothing.

Come on, Matt! Pick up!

"Krissy?"

"Matt, you need to listen closely."

"What the hell is happening?"

"Shut up and listen! Dawson had a kill switch for the original game to wipe it clean and erase it. Do you know it?"

"Yes. I was there when it happened. Why?"

"You need to use that same one on the hardwire connection that Guzman's using to interact with the game. It'll disrupt the game and cause a force shutdown."

"Right… right! I can do that, but we need Connor's conscious mind out of it first. Darrel and I have an idea. Keep the phone ready and we'll unplug him."

"Okay." The line goes dead.

"If that kill switch works, it could fry the brains of everyone that's in there," Cranium warns.

"We know," I snap. "We're gonna unplug him first when Matt and Darrel are done doing their part. Until then, we stay moving and lose these assholes."

Phobia is driving so badly it's a wonder we haven't been pulled over by the *actual* police.

Mark points ahead, "Take 49th, then a tight turn on Hulgan!"

"What?"

"Trust me!"

She groans and hits the gas. "Hang on, morons!" She whips the van into a sharp left turn, getting honked at by other cars, then takes a hard right. The street Mark led her to is a large parking garage with company vans and cars. All black.

"Park it in the basement level and shut it off," he instructs.

Not questioning, Phobia eases the van to the basement level, finds an open spot against one of the far walls and pulls in. The engine dies and both Phobia and Mark join us in the back lying low.

"What now?"

Mark lets out a deep breath, "Pray."

Chapter 58

Snapping the phone closed, I keep an eye out for guards outside the door while Darrel gets his portable device out. I can't help but watch as he plugs in a USB antenna and starts tapping various buttons on the device. It's like watching a magician at work.

"Okay, I'm starting an uplink to prep a bug surge," he says out loud. "When I'm through the security and firewalls, we'll have a small window to find Guzman's connection and upload a surge before we get spotted."

I nod, "I'm glad you're here. Thank you."

He looks up with a small smile, "It's been fun. I just hope we don't end up in prison for this. They won't let us be cellmates in there, which would be a shame."

Joke or not, it makes me huff a laugh. His screen blows up with popups and links, and his fingers fly across the screen through various files and codes.

"You ever imagine a day that you would break into your own company's servers to upload a virus?"

I huff another laugh, "Not at all. But it never felt like it was my company anyway. I wasn't ready to take the helm and I think all this shit happening under my nose just proves that point."

"The way I see it, they've been planning this shit for a long time. Don't blame yourself. If it were any other way, I bet you'd make some fun stuff with this place," he assures me while typing on his device.

Maybe. But then, this wouldn't have happened.

"All right!" He slaps his hip, "I'm in! So, we need the source code to find him."

"Guzman would've password protected his source code, if he was smart," I ponder. "Someone like him would use the same password for everything."

Darrel types quickly on his device, "Okay, I'm running an algorithm of common corporate passwords. Unless you can think of what it'd be, we'll be playing the waiting game."

Before I can start guessing, the doorknob starts rattling.

"Hey! Who's in there? This is a restricted area!"

Fuck my luck!

"Shit!" Darrel is typing again, trying to break through. "We're out of time!"

"Just keep it up," I tell him. With a deep breath, I walk towards the door. I can hear him hissing at me to stop, but I open the door and step outside, facing two security guards. "Gentlemen. Is there a problem?"

"Mr. Bauer?" One asks in surprise. "What are you doing here?"

"Well, it *is* my company, isn't it?"

The other one crosses his arms, "You've been put on our no-fly list until further notice."

I wave my hand at him, "I wasn't doing well. Stress of the job and all. The paperwork is still being sorted through for me to be checked off that list."

They look at each other, then back to me. The first one steps away to speak into his radio. The other keeps his glare on me, making me uncomfortable.

"So, what exactly is the issue?"

He tightens the grip of his crossed arms, "Until you're cleared, you're not permitted in the building, sir."

Fucking Guzman.

"Look," I say reaching for my wallet, "I'm not gonna lie. I'm a workaholic and can't stand to think anything is compromised with my work." I take out all my cash, five hundred dollars, and hold it up. "Let's chalk this up to a misunderstanding, let me finish my inspections, and then I'm out."

I see his gaze go back and forth between me and the cash in my hand. He looks around and takes the money from me. "Does this include an extra vacation day, sir?"

With an irritated sigh, I reply with, "Take the whole damn week off. Clock in remotely to collect, and you're solid. Deal?"

He smirks and tips his hat at me before walking away. With a sigh of relief, I step back inside and lock the door. Darrel raises his eyebrows in expectation.

"We're definitely gonna go to prison after this."

Darrel nodded and continued his work.

Chapter 59

~~~~~ Connor ~~~~~

It all happens so fast. The snapping jaws of the smokehounds dart directly at me and I have no time to react. I'm immediately pinned to the ground with my hands pushing up against its chest to keep it from biting my head off. Its claws are digging into my shoulders, making me yell out in pain. The other one I can hear barking and snarling, but I can't tell if Veyanna is okay or not. The only thing I can think to do is take one of the daggers I have, giving the beast a better chance of ripping out my throat, and try to stick it into the beast. Its canines graze my neck when I stick it in the ribs, causing it to yelp out and retract from me. My shoulders are stinging with pain, and I feel blood running from them. Everything burns as I push to get up from the ground, gripping the dagger firmly in my hand while holding my shoulder with my free hand.

Veyanna is bouncing around with her whip snapping back and forth against the smokehound hunting her. These ones seem more resilient than what we've faced before because she's not gaining any control over the beast. She can't get still enough to try and use her bone whistle.

I glance over at Guzman and Riley, just watching the chaos unfold. Guzman is leaning back in his throne and watching while Riley is standing off to the side with a sad look on his face. Not an ounce of him seems like he even wants to stop this.

I let my shoulder go and reach into my satchel, take the grappling hook out and grip it tightly in my free hand. The smokehound locks eyes with me, both of us trying to anticipate the next move. It is antsy and hungry; its red eyes fix on me and the glint of its silver fangs shine against its black visage. With a loud bark, it pounces towards me. Using my size to my advantage, I run at it and then fall straight on my back, the grappling hook raised above me. The way it jumps gives me enough space to hook one of the points into its gut, causing it to roll over to its side and take me with it. I'm now straddling its chest with the hook still lodged in its gut. I take the dagger and shove it into the beast's neck, causing it to gargle in pain as it chokes on the blade in its throat.

Veyanna is struggling with her beast as I see a gash in her shoulder. In a desperate attempt to overcome it, she reaches behind her, grabs Doxo's axe, and makes a heavy swing. It's bigger than she is, and her form is off, but the wild swing launched the axe out of her hands and indirectly cutting into the beast's hindleg. The smokehound yelps loudly and struggles to recover, giving her time to take out her bone whistle and blow it. Its ears perk up and it becomes dazed, even confused by the sound. Slowly, she walks towards it with the whistle at the ready.

"As entertaining as this is," Guzman's voice rings out, "I'm ready to end this all now."

"Couldn't have said it better myself," I spit. Removing my dagger and grappling hook from the animal, I lock eyes with Guzman.

He stands from his throne and reaches for his mask, pulling it away from his face. Behind the mask is a twisted face in a crazy, Joker-like smile, eyes so big and prominent that they look like they're about to fall out of his skull, and skin as warped and discolored as the Maze itself.

"I am a god here, boy," he sneers. When he talks, his lips don't even touch because of the crazy smile permanently fixed to his face. "You think you can beat me in *my* world?"

I smirk at him, which I don't think he was expecting. "I don't need to beat you, Guzman. I just need to win the game."

Quickly running to the pyramid, I reach up and pull the capstone off. The rift light disappears and the magical presence of the tower with it. Both Guzman and Riley yell "No!" as I hold it in my hands and back up towards Veyanna.

"Connor, don't do this!" Riley begs, "That's the only way into the other worlds!"

"Good to know," I mutter. I look at Veyanna, who reclaimed Doxo's axe, and smile at her proudly. "Go back home and tell everyone the Maze is defeated."

Her eyes sadden, "Bimbik?"

Thrusting the capstone towards the open air, I mentally command it to open a rift back to Braveshire on the surface, then push her through. She stumbles but lands on soft grass, letting out one last cry before I shut it again.

Once the rift is shut, I turn around to face the villains of this world and the one Outside. With the capstone in my hand, I hold it over the edge of the tower.

"You lose." I drop it over the edge.

Riley and Guzman both run at me, the former dropping to the ledge like he's going to catch it. The latter reaching back and sporting long twisted nails that might as well be claws. He uses them to stab me in the chest and hoist me in the air, glaring into my eyes with pure hate and rage.

"You stupid bastard!" He growls and holds me up higher in the air with his claws in my chest. I wince and grunt at the pain. My eyes refocus on Riley off to the side, who looks horrified. In a moment of hesitation, he turns and runs for the stairs, leaving me behind to die at Guzman's hands.

"You have no idea what you've done. Now I must fix what you have destroyed," he growls up at me. "You will not live to see your failure, nor will you be able to return to help your miserable band of outcasts. I promise you this."

Grunting through the pain, I start chuckling. He's taken aback by it. I spit some blood that's pooling in my mouth to the ground and glare at him with a smirk. "If... if I'm going down... you're going down with me." I reach into my pocket and pull out the sandstone acid grenade I made before we entered this place.

"See you in hell, Guzman."

I smash the bulb against his face, watching as the acid splashes all over it. He howls in pain, gripping his head with his free hand. I grab his wrist and lean away, pulling the clawed fingers out of my chest. Putting all my weight into it, I lean back far enough for him to lose his balance from the pain, and we both tumble from the top of the tower into a freefall.

The last thing I see is a bright light that is coming at me fast, or that I'm falling towards, before I enter oblivion.

Chapter 60

"Something's wrong!"

Connor's body is shaking and he's grunting in pain. Cranium and I are holding him down as best as we can.

"It's some kind of seizure," he says in a panic. "Grab something for him to bite on and roll him over on his side!"

I take my leather bracelet off while he turns Connor on his side, then I shove it between his teeth.

Mark looks at me worried, "He could be hurt in the game. Check his body."

I nod and start looking at his arms and legs for marks. Nothing. Mark pulls up his shirt and then gasps with, "Oh, fuck."

There are four bruised spots across his chest like he got jabbed with a pitchfork. He keeps grunting and coughing against our hold on him.

"What is that?" I'm choking back tears. "*What the fuck is that?!*"

"Phobia, get us to the safehouse STAT!"

Without any objection, she pulls out of our hiding spot in the parking garage and burns rubber to wherever their safehouse is.

"Don't die in there, you idiot," I whisper into his ear, kissing his cheek. "Don't you dare fucking leave me."

Chapter 61

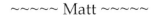

If my heart could throw up, it would be right now. Waiting for Darrel to break through Guzman's heavily secured system is killing me. God only knows what's happened with Danica downstairs.

"Darrel?"

"Almost. Two minutes."

That's when the doorknob starts jiggling again, followed by unfortunate and familiar voices.

"Bauer, open this door immediately!"

That's Frost from the board!

"Break the fucking thing down!"

Fischer!

"We don't have two minutes," I hiss at Darrel.

He waves me off and keeps clicking away. The door handle shakes more violently. Suddenly, Darrel plugs the thumb drive from his device into the main server and hits the *Enter* button on his screen. The servers flash and blink uncontrollably, their fans fail to stay on. This happens for about thirty seconds before they get back to normal.

"Let's hope that was enough," he says through gritted teeth. He grips the device in his hands and smashes it against the corner of one of the servers. The thumb drive in his hand finds its way into my pocket. He's so close to me I can feel the heat coming off him. "In case you manage to not get locked up, keep this safe at all costs."

I nod. In this moment, it's just the two of us. The door rattling and banging is white noise in my ears as I look at Darrel with gratitude and admiration. He's given up so much and will probably suffer bigger consequences for this.

Fuck it. I close the distance and press my lips against his. It's short-lived when the door flies open with four security guards filing in, Madeline Fletcher and Alan Frost standing outside of the door with Danica between them being restrained by one of the guards.

Darrel and I are pulled away from each other and are forced to have our hands behind our backs. Fletcher marches in first, her face twisted in anger.

"What the hell did you do, Bauer!"

I don't give her the satisfaction of an answer, not even when she smacks me across the face.

"You crazy bitch!" Danica yells from outside the server room. "Keep your fucking hands off him!"

"Shut your mouth," Frost hisses at her from the side. "Boys, take these people out of here and to the basement level."

Fletcher grabs the destroyed device Darrel was using and holds it in front of his face, "What did you do to our system, you little shit!"

To his credit, Darrel gives that playful smirk and says, "Just taking care of a really nasty bug in your servers. You're welcome."

Frost has to physically hold her back while the security guards of my company that was stolen from me take us to the elevators. Danica looks at me with sorry eyes, but I give an empathetic smile meant to say *It's okay.*

The doors of the elevator open ahead of us when Fischer sneers from behind us, "You're going to regret this, Matthew."

We turn around after loading inside, and I just give her the most annoying smile I can muster. "Either way, you lose." The doors shut, and down we go.

Chapter 62

I can't believe we were so careless in snooping on the board members. Maybe if we were more careful, we wouldn't be here right now. The only thing I can do is keep my friend still during his seizure and hope that it'll stop. Krissy is holding him tightly and I don't blame her for a second. This is the scariest thing I've ever been through, even compared to the game. The van begins to slow down and the sunlight is blocked out by some kind of roof or enclosure. When I poke my head up, I see we're in some kind of large garage, but everything is too dark to make it out clearly.

Phobia puts it in park and looks in the back, "You two stay here and keep an eye on him. Cranium and I are gonna get something to move him in."

I nod in understanding before they both hop out of the van and walk away.

"I need the Jack." Krissy says it so quietly I almost didn't catch it.

"What do you mean?"

"Something's wrong," her voice cracks. "I need to know what's going on. I need to get back to the Hollow."

Did she really see the Dawsons in there? How can they help if they're cyber ghosts? "Kris, we can't do anything but keep him safe."

"I don't want to just sit here on my ass!" Her outburst sends a jolt through me. "I *can't!* Could you do this if it was Danica? Just sit by and watch her try to bite her tongue off in a seizure?"

"Of course I couldn't!" It's probably the first time I've defended her in the last year. "I'd be angry and scared, but that wouldn't do her any good. It won't do Conner any good either. We are being chased down by money-grubbing thugs and suits, the others have been radio-silent for too long, and we're probably never gonna have normal lives again. If Connor was out of the game, he'd want us to try and think rather than do anything stupid."

Tears roll down her face and her lips are quaking. She wipes them away and nods, taking a deep breath to calm down. That's when the back doors open with Cranium and Phobia pulling up an office chair. We all lift Connor out of the van, notice that the shaking stopped, and put him into the chair. They lead us out of the garage and into a dimly lit hallway. It's decorated with posters of people and display cases of records and tapes.

"What is this place?"

Phobia looks around while wheeling Connor ahead, "A decommissioned radio station. We have the electricity turned on under another name that pays it out of their credit card. Some snobby rich dick that won't notice a few hundred a month missing."

406

I'm drawn to the various posters of radio artists and musicians featured on the walls, but I refocus on the task at hand. Phobia wheels Connor into a station booth and flips on the lights. Just a bit smaller than the substation we came from, this place is decked out with a bunch of hacker stuff; repurposed equipment and screens, monitors and keyboards set up, wires everywhere like motionless snakes. Cranium flips a few switches and all the electronics and gadgets spring to life.

"Put him in the sound booth," he instructs. "I'll get some stuff prepped up."

In the adjacent room, Krissy and I roll him inside and set him up in the center. All around are different pieces of repurposed equipment like a friggin' futuristic command center. Phobia nudges me aside and puts some wires onto Connor's Crest.

"What are you doing?" Krissy asks with clenched fists.

"We use this place to beta test new equipment for us to play around with," she explains, wiring up the headset that leads back to the control room of the booth. "We were working on a way to get visual reads from the Jack system for everyone not using the headset. If I can rewire and refocus the Crest's output, we should be able to see what he's seeing and figure out what the hell is happening."

There's hope that we can see what Connor's going through. I put an assuring hand on Krissy's shoulder, to which she lays her hand on in response. We watch and wait until Phobia and Cranium give each other a thumbs up. He starts typing and flipping switches. There are small sparks coming from the wires, but nothing seems to affect Connor's state.

"Okay, should start broadcasting…. *Now!*"

The screens flip on and show a throne sitting at the top of a tower with a pyramid in the center of the platform. What makes us all catch our breath is seeing a tall, cloaked figure with its claws lodged in the chest of a small, blue-haired character.

"Connor!" Krissy holds her mouth and holds back sobs.

The marks on Connor's chest are the same as what we're seeing on screen. My friend is dying in the game… and he may die for real.

Chapter 63

No... no he can't be dying. Not like this!

I feel my heart ache and my throat close at the sight of his game character being impaled. The room is dead quiet, waiting to see what happens.

Maybe it's game over and dying means he can safely come out! It has to be different from before, right?!

I don't expect any audio to come up, but we start hearing a conversation between the two figures.

A creepy, hoarse voice says, *"You will not live to see your failure, nor will you be able to return to help your miserable band of outcasts. I promise you this."*

"Is that the board guy?" That son of a bitch!

The room goes quiet again as Connor's character reaches into his pocket and pulls out a round object.

"See you in hell, Guzman."

He smashes the object against the tall guy's face, causing him to scream and get off balance. I hold my breath and watch as the little hero pulls off of the claws and yanks them both over the edge of this tower. Guzman is screaming and flailing the whole way down, but Connor is calm and quiet in the fall. Right when I think I'm going to see my boyfriend's character die from the fall, the screens go fuzzy, and the feed is lost.

"What happened?!"

Cranium is clicking buttons loudly, "The feed was cut off! Some kind of glitch!"

The glitch? Oh, my God.

A few seconds later, the feed returns, and it shows the base of the tower, but no bodies. Not Connor's. Not Guzman's. They're gone. I look at Connor in the room carefully and check his pulse. It's so faint and slow it's almost not there. I pull open his eyelid to see if he's reacting to anything. His pupils are huge and unresponsive. A truly catatonic state.

Mark asks from behind me, "Is he gone?"

"I… I don't know." I can't stop the flow of tears that drop on his blank face that I'm holding in my hands. "I don't know."

Chapter 64

A cool breeze brushes my face, the vein in my temple is pulsing loudly, and everything just hurts. My eyes flutter open to a dimly lit scene; I'm surrounded by crumbling stones with wind whistling through the cracks. The dim light is coming from sconces with the smallest flicker of greenish blue light. My hands graze the ground, feeling the dusty floor I'm laying back on. No cushions, carpet, blankets, not even a layer of hay or concrete. The floor is hard stone and grains of dust and rubble. Leaning up from the ground, I notice that I'm covered in a ratty, tattered cloak and robes, covered in dust and soot. Wiping off the dust, my hands are bluish gray, slightly bony and frail.

"Ugh."

Everything aches when I push off the ground and get up on my feet. I take in the room and look around at the faded murals of people and buildings I don't recognize. In the far corner, a couple of items are sitting there. A rusted, chipped, weathered sword, a splintered bow with a frayed bowstring, and a gnarled branch with a carved handle.

"Wait a second…"

Scanning the room again, there is a set of double doors of aged wood barely hanging on by the hinges. With a gentle push, the doors creak open to a bleak, bone-littered landscape. The sky is swirling with gray and black clouds, mists of silver and blue, and things flying across it. What I thought was the wind now sounds creepy, echoing wails and cries of things I can't begin to believe. Far below the mound of land that this building is set upon are wandering shadows wandering decrepit paths decorated with bone altars, gravestones, and torches of the same bluish-green light. What freaks me out the most is what is visible from afar; a large, accentuated bridge that winds above a chasm of swirling mist. Coming from the chasm are large, twisted spires reaching upward to the sky like decayed fingers of a dead god.

"No… that's impossible."

From the misty chasm, an enormous worm-like silhouette bursts from under the bridge, letting out a roar so loud it echoes across the entire landscape. It shoots upward and begins winding around the bridge like a coiled snake before diving back down into the chasm.

"Its… It's *Soulscape*."

My game. My creation. And now my prison.

AFTERWORD

Thank you for reading *The Primeval Maze*!

I want to also thank my beta readers, without whom I wouldn't have been able to make this story possible.

Please leave a review!

This story is available on Amazon, where you can leave a review and tell me what you think!

Follow my links below to stay up to date on any and all of my current and future projects. Thank you for your support, and I'll see you on the next adventure!

Facebook Page:
https://www.facebook.com/overtonbooks

My Official Website: www.overtonbooks.com

Instagram: https://www.instagram.com/overtonbooks/

ABOUT THE AUTHOR

Seth Overton is the author of *The Mortal Gate*, his debut novel that explores the idea of escaping reality versus escaping from yourself.

Born and raised in Missouri, he has found enjoyment losing himself in a good fantasy or science fiction book to feed his love and appreciation for imagination and creativity. Taking his love for books and writing, Seth became an English Language Arts teacher graduating from the University of Central Missouri to teach and inspire the next generation of writers.

Seth currently lives in Texas with his wife teaching high school and works to write enjoyable, relatable, and compelling stories for his readers.

Made in United States
North Haven, CT
04 December 2024

61446784R00259